# The Sz`a`Th Chronicles
# Book 1
# SCRIBE, SPELLCASTER AND MHYST

**Jinnie MacCallum**

---

# The Sz`a`Th Chronicles
## Book 1
## SCRIBE, SPELLCASTER AND MHYST

DOUBLE DRAGON

**A DOUBE DRAGON PAPERBACK**



**ISBN: 987 1 78695 811 2**

*This Edition Published 2022 by*
*Double Dragon an imprint of*
*Fiction4All*
*https://fiction4all.com*

# Prelude

Squatting down on his haunches, the creek swollen with the rain pelting down on him, the matt black sword blurred beneath the waters removing the dark crimson blood of the Warrior who the Dark Mhyst poisoned. He stared at the current, snaking the red hue further down the creek, eventually blurring from view.

He turned to the forest; the heavy rain made the dark green seem impenetrable. Blinking to see through his eyelashes was just as useless; the Elf slowly made his way and stood hidden in the forest trees' undergrowth. His hearing acute, he listened in the teaming rain.

His green eyes watched the pale, weather-bleached oak sign swing from the Taverns brass hooks. The gable roof overhang screeched painfully with metal on metal in the wind gusts. He had taken the markings of the Warrior; protocols were done when a Warrior died, especially one of the Sz`a`Th. Regardless of whispers, he knew they were poisoned.

He looked at the Regimental insignia he had taken from the Warrior's uniform, recalling her earth-brown eyes, startling with gold diagonally slash in the Wolf Nation's genetic trait. Staring at him, pleading with him, and her voice exhausted as she fell to her knees. 'In my kit…is what you need…Ranger, I am a Sz`a`Th Warrior and Wolf Nation– I was wounded by a crossbow bolt poisoned, kill me, end it….' Her Malak and S`ahrn head wrap, similar to a flat turban headdress, had fallen off in their fight. Honey, brown wavy hair fell from its intricate Wolf braid from her shoulders to her waist. 'I ask to die by honour…the poison will not let me take my own life….'

'Name, Warrior, what is your name, and I will give you honour.'

'Silver Crescent…Sergeant Ry`arma, Sahn`Frwh, taken from the Lake City of Cran`dk, one winter past when Mah`sden's poison infiltrated our food and water…' tilting her head upwards to stare at him gave her a hard core stance. Something endemic in seasoned Warriors, she looked at him. Those brown eyes haunted him. 'My Sahn`Frwh sword, blades and belongings go to my brother, and his name is Ji`rah of the Sqn`xn Nation of Wolves, he was informed…I was dead, missing in action against Mah`sden.'

The Warrior, standing before her, was something of Myth; if her brother did not hear the howl of her death, he would never know. Looking back up at the tall Warrior, she exhaled her fogged breath. 'Kill me; I ask you that much of you, Elf Ranger.'

In one movement, he picked her up firmly against the large tree's trunk and pierced her shoulder to the tree with his blade.

Ry`arma's eyes rolled with the pain 'don't torture what you can't comprehend, Ranger. I've been fighting Mah`sden's poison for days; nothing you can do to me can do any more harm. I die free.'

He smiled, raising eyebrows 'Ji`rah would have my balls if I tortured you, Sergeant; breath deep, Ry`arma.' He paused, wiping another tear from her cheek. She smiled weakly. 'To win this war, you have no idea how important your life is! I will not kill you, your brother I know, and he does not need your death, howled across the regions, the Green will heal you…hate me if you wish. Still, there will be a time when you will rescue Ji`rah and even I Sergeant'.

Tears fell not for the pain, but she knew being healed by the Green meant time for her would be longer.

She took a deep, sharp breath, and the Wolf Nations blaze flashed fiercely at him. This Warrior feared no one, which was a strong ally if you could reason with them. NK`las breathed slowly; his hand gently wiped a tear, and she did not flinch.

'Tell Ra-ra…his scar has my name. Tell the hot head…' tears fell slowly. She fought the poison and the pain...' I own his sorry bloody arse….' Blood dark black slid worm-like from her lips 'tell that bastard I love him, always pack!'

'Tell me, does Ji`rah know your Sahn`Frwh swords name?'

'Yes'

He removed the blade as she slumped to the muddy earth; green mist covered the Warrior, and she was taken to the Green Realm. He would keep her safe and hidden. He had a suspicion that the Greenman knew how to heal the poison. Finding the elusive bastard would be another thing. It would have to wait. He had another appointment, and his heart was not in that meeting.

Rain pelted down as he stared blankly at the sign swinging hypnotically through the storm; the screech of rusted metal on metal seemed an excellent match to the name in the local language and the Runic text of the Sz`a`Th. Only two people sat inside 'The Screaming Crow Tavern', but they expected the third person soon.

Inside, the black stone fireplace was massive; the wood-burning from hot magenta to rich, thick yellows, warmth pulsed from the stone.

"So… do you think the 'Heart Guards' chosen will succeed?" asked the Lord of W`tr, musing at the froth foaming from his tankard.

The E`rth Lord glanced at his friend across the bar of the Screaming Crow Tavern as he poured his friend and colleague another lager.

Lord M`orus rubbed his hands not from the cold but more from the deluge pouring out of the skies, rubbing slightly arthritic knuckles; rain excited the E`rth`n Lord. The rain beat a primeval tune to his soul, and his bones ached painfully.

In one thought, logs were lifted onto the two open large fireplaces, sparks danced up the chimney, and flames oozed over the timber heating the Tavern.

"Lazy even for you, M`orus, but better than me getting up and doing it."

M`orus smiled slightly. "We are both getting too ancient, Lod`n."

His friend scratched his beard, frowning and scratching his ear simultaneously.

"Some are of Royal lineage Princess's and Prince's some know this, and some do not, and they will be balanced with specialised 'others'. When he said 'others', he referred to those of Myth hidden from Man. There are no upstarts in this chosen group. For they were chosen at the beginning of magic itself."

"That amount of pure blood is all we have against him." He said, enjoying the rain twistedly; it was love, hate, love, and sensation that prickled at his senses...storms created from magic always affected him this way. He knew the process, Petrichor, but it still excited him every time he sighed the scent of rain on the earth.

Above and if the old story was true, Eight Heart Guards below, of all the royal bloodlines of Myth and Man and Woman, all trained as the elite Sahn`Frwh Knights of the Death Watch, all able to walk between the Veils that protected one reality from the other. Guilds that some had trained all their life would be necessary, eight above as below. All from the sixteen guilds, all Warriors of different and mixed heritage of Myth and

Man and Woman. None knew of this storm coming into their lives, and no one knew who would survive.

While Lord Mah`sden was ruler only in the name of the Sz`a`Th regions, his power lay in his ability to poison those of the Sz`a`Th, turning them into his Warriors.

He also had the Necromancer Sorcerer Nah`leq Dral`north, who had renamed Mah`sden Warriors the Dark Sz`a`Th, a basic term but one that halved the vast armies of those of the Imperial House of the Sz`a`Th. Dral`north had his agenda. At the same time, he manipulated Lord Mah`sden and divided the legions of the Sz`a`Th Army. Yet even he had a cold feeling in the depths of what once was his heart, he knew those of the Elements of H`dn E`rth, and those above he could not manoeuvre in any form, be it his dark elements, magic or persuasion.

The Necromancer watched the dark mirror, a voyeur to the 'Screaming Crow' and wished he had been privy to the words spoken. Being Necromancer did have some drawbacks, and eve's dropping was one and also reading minds...he stood in his labyrinth of stone watching the images play out before him.

"Aye…but, do you think these 'Heart Guards' chosen to protect the Dominion Lord will succeed? They are all nearing their sixteenth winter, some not much older than the Scribe while others are younger; it is a heavy burden for young men and women to carry."

He again asked as he sipped the foam from the top of his lager.

"Was it wise in asking those of H`dn E`rth to help - I mean, do you think we can get a Dark Elf to side with us of O`pn E`rth? M`orus that is one hell of a stretch to ask. Even I would have trouble trusting those of H`dn E`rth; they would always have a hidden agenda," stated

Lod`n, licking foam around his mouth.

"I haven't asked," he sighed; he just wished what had begun four hundred winters ago had stayed four hundred winters ago and not reared its skeletal hand in warning to them. "Anyway, there are already laid paths that will direct the 'Heart Guards' to their destiny; I hope by the time of his twenty-fourth winter, the Scribe will accept the mantle given to him. That is my concern, Lod`n; this will not happen with magic, though it will sometimes be necessary.

The large man who served as the Tavern Keeper smiled and shrugged.

"If he lives that long, you're a sneaky bastard M`orus; I hope you realise that we can ask no more of these 'Heart Guard Warrior of the blood. Will it cost them their lives? " He replied, eyeing the storm. As Lord of W`tr, Lod`n enjoyed the weather blast he had created, watching through the open door of the Tavern. This storm was ethereal opaques of darkest greys to black, to deep purple, blue hews. He smiled, and he loved a bloody good rain. He could conjure up a storm, flood or sun shower if he wished, for his element was water, just as M`orus's element was earth.

The other two Elemental Lord and Lady were preoccupied with other business and had declined to meet at the 'Screaming Crow' Tavern. He did not answer, for he knew they would all become the living dead just to live; he sighed at the irony of the oxymoron that they had to die first to live.

'Not a bad storm, Lod`n", praised the Lord of E`rth, smiling as Lod`n scratched his beard. He would not answer his friend. He knew the answer already.

'Not bad?' Lod`n looked at him' bloody brilliant, I reckon…wait until I need to roll one in.'

M`orus thought he would need to find a waterproof

dwelling, if not high set, should Lod`n ‘roll one in’ as the Lord of W`tr wiped the bar again.

Standing hidden from their view and senses, most essential their elemental magic, a young man, his cloak with its cowled hood, throwing shadows with the ease that it took an Elf to run a hundred leagues. His green eyes slanted towards his temples slightly as rain streamed off the material, not cotton nor wool, but something more potent and woven with ancient spells in time.

Those green eyes studied the night sky heavily overcast with the storm, yet two moons – outlined silver rings smoked out by rain clouds eerily formed the figure eight. He noted the date-time and location but would not mention this ‘sign’ for a better word escaped him. The twin moons of this world were called many names by the many nations of man, and Myth existed. This eclipse happened every four hundred winters, and like the seasons, it brought forth change, more, an ingress to war and ultimate sacrifices.

He sighed; this would be a bloodbath, and between the Nations of Man and Mythhe silently said a prayer in Elf as leaves above him danced, sprinkling the words in rain script only he could read.

Blinking slowly, he wondered what these two fools had done this time. Out of respect, he was related to one, probably both, when he thought of the tangled genetic lineage of the Nations of Myth, and who was he fooling? They were all tangled with the Nations of Man.

There was nothing else to do but enter the Tavern and listen to his Uncle and Lod`n. And see how many lies, where truths and how many truths were lies.

He stepped out of the forest and the comforting closeness.

His steps were lighter than a finch in spring.

Leaving a little or known trace through the muddy road, yellow pools of light from the Taverns leadlight windows. Dipped onto the muddied ground, patchworking the brown earth and water haphazardly in some strange watercolour painting, he stepped into the Tavern.

Both looked back at the door as it closed, and a young Warrior entered. Tall at 6’4,” his eyes were the deepest forest green and tilted slightly to his temples.

The top of his ears wore the filigree ear clasps common to his people. As a Warrior, his ear clasps were matt black, not the intricate silver design worn by others of his race.

This Warrior had ethereal grace and stealth. He was removing his cloak of green and black. The cloth rippled the air in waves showing that it also coveted this Warrior by cloaking him when necessary with invisibility.

Once removed, the cloak revealed his appearance.

NK`Las’s dark hair was trimmed short; beneath the hair, a white tattoo of runes in a horizontal line behind his ear, denoting his Op`n E`rth Elf. His beard was dark. He’d kept a bit longer than the close trim.

He glanced quickly around the Tavern, which was empty except for the two middle-aged men at the bar.

“Uncle M`orus, Lod`n, I received your request; one question. You haven’t told me who I am to be Heart Guard too?”

The young Elf Warrior wondered why something had not been used for 800 winters. Now been brought back from a time only those of memory remembered. ‘Heart Guard’ meant to die protecting those you had been assigned as ‘Heart Guard’. He assumed there would be others assigned in time, depending on how extreme it was to keep this person alive at all costs. He doubted significantly, they had been told, and no one would know outside those assigned. Dying was one thing; being undead was the other element in this. He blinked slowly; a lot of blood would spill; he was confident of that.

"NK`las, lad, prompt as always, glad you could find us."

NK`las raised his eyebrow at his Uncle, considering his Uncles instructions were extremely vague. He wondered if they were testing him.

"A map would have helped you know!" replied the Lieutenant leaning on the bar. He drank the lager poured by Lod`n.

"Now, why would an Imperial Ranger Warrior and an Elf at that need a map to find us through the forests, mountains, and rivers that were his childhood playground?" Lord M`orus asked with a questioning smile at his nephew.

The Lieutenant glanced sideways at his Uncle, placing the empty tankard on a well-worn dark oak timber bar.

"I wonder…" he replied, then drinking more slowly from the second tankard, leaning on the bar, he added. "So who is this Dominion Lord?"

With Four Hundred winters of peace behind them, the Sz`a`Th was a nation of Warriors whose inner light and strength came from the Mhyst. Their seven senses with a power appearing over the left chest just above their heart in a sprinkled spiral of blue dots crowned an internal force that crowned. Once this coming of age came at sixteen winters some earlier, their chosen guilds were chosen by the design of the Mhyst, it was neither tattoo nor birthmark, though it resembled them, and all wore tattoos showing which guild. The desired level of that guild, and their home region of birth, had now somehow become tainted, twisted and murderous.

Peace was now a memory, lost in the screams and blood of innocents and Warriors. Causing a fracture in the Mhyst, and the chasm was widening.

Keeping peace through the many regions on the mainland and archipelagos that surrounded all that existed was proving difficult; in fact, it was now entirely out of hand. They were losing well-trained Sz`a `Th Warriors not through a change of allegiance and birth but through the black sorcery that had begun the Four Hundred Winter war – eight hundred winters past. They were now, in a word, bloody desperate.

Dark shadows of deceit caused death and repression of their beliefs of the Mhyst and its teaching, which permeated all aspects of their lore.

Add to that, Spellcasters were eliminated too swiftly. Now under the protection of the Sz`a`Th – a turnaround for the Sz`a`Th. No one wished to return to those centuries as an enemy in the Four Hundred Winters War.

Too much was lost, faith, skills, knowledge, trust, and allegiances were destroyed, and those of H`dn E`rth vowed never to align themselves with the Nations of Man again.

Getting Lieutenant NK`Las to attend their meeting had more to do with Lord M`orus's sister. The Lieutenant's mother and father, the Royal King of the Elves of O`pn E`rth.

The ruling Monarch of O`pn E`rth Elves already made his point that he would not be sacrificing his people for the Nations of Man under any circumstances.

NK`Las told his father little of his comings and goings. NK`Las mother was someone who understood being empathic was better than criticising, unlike those of his father. This is due to different mindsets regarding the Nations of Man and Elves" politics, which bored the

Prince to avoid them at all costs and stay an Imperial Elf Archer and Ranger. This kept him incognito to his father and away from his father's world.

Spellcasters were still under a cloud of cynicism as far as the Sz`a`Th was concerned. Could you trust Spellcasters when, even they were slowly eliminated?

The Dominion Lord's prophecy was nearing its truth, but the Sz`a`Th had a more impending problem to deal with than a tortured Sz`a`Th Warrior screaming out a blood-soaked oath over his Sahn`Frwh Sword four hundred winters ago.

NK`Las was an unknown, a Warrior, a Warrior of the Swords, Battle Axes, and Crossbows – all Archery – he had been the last Warrior standing at the great battle that ended the 400-winter war. His name is unknown. Had he been Spellcaster, they would have taken more notice and lay their greatest mistake therein.

To leave a Warrior in battle was against all Lore, whether Man, Woman or Myth, Warrior or Spellcaster was ever left behind. This Warrior of the Sz`a`Th, the act, hung like a cloak of evil, cowardice, and conceit for all that meant to the Sz`a`Th. Finding who purposely left his body behind was something even magic could not locate. Someone was hiding a heinous crime. But who? Which Nation.

The journey that Lieutenant NK`las of the Imperial Elf Nation of O`pn E`rth was determined to correct, one wrong even if it cost his birthright, you just do not leave anyone behind in War or Peace. He would find this Warrior and bring his remains home – to whichever Nation he was born.

He was determined to do this, but now he needed to work out the cat’s cradle of interference, his uncle and, no doubt, others that had been injected deliberately from lies to truth. And that unravelling would cause, he sensed more harm than anyone knew.

No one of the Nations of Man had encountered those of Myth, Elves, Dwarves, Trolls and others more hidden, had not been seen anywhere during the Four Hundred winter peace. Few had mentioned it for fear of alienation and ridicule if they had. All presumed the Four Hundred Winter War, which preceded the order, had wiped out all traces; some hoped the centuries had diluted such Myth's genes from the Nations of Man.

Those in the 'Screaming Crow' Tavern knew otherwise, merely because they were of the Nations of Myth. Whether the Nations of Man were ready or not, now was the time for the Nations of Elves, Dwarves and Trolls to save the Nations of Man.

Pouring them all a third lager, Lod`n stirred the frothy white head of his beer with his finger, then sucked the foam off loudly and burped.

"M`orus, do you think they will accept us? Will we fit in?" Asked Lod`n as the Lieutenant and M`orus grimaced at the loud belch across the bar.

The Elf Lieutenant sipped his lager thoughtfully, picking at the cashew nuts Lod`n offered him.

"Sure Lod`n, if we can expel air like you, we should find this the most straightforward task yet, that the Spellcasters have asked us to do."

"Fix - is the word NK`Las; this is their damn mess, not ours." Grumbled M`orus loudly as lightning snapped sharply overhead.

"And the name of this Dominion Lord I am supposed to track down is?"

Lord M`orus glanced at his nephew, then stared at his tankard, answering slowly.

"Taelen is his name; he's an Imperial Sz`a`Th Scribe, last known place of residence, the Taayra`Ge Keep."

"I'm to track and protect a Scribe. Can he fight?"

"Oh aye, lad, he's Sahn`Frwh Warrior as well. He can fight."

"Death Watch Warrior…" he frowned at both of them. "Just what have you two done?" NK`Las green eyes narrowed; he had an ill feeling crawling up his spine.

Lod`n belched loudly again; he grinned broadly at both M`orus and NK`Las. All three hoped they would succeed; the price was already too high. What payment all knew would be a high body count, and history would point its skeletal finger, blaming them if this all went horribly wrong.

All three sensed the voyeurism of Lord Nul`YK, the sudden chill ignored by the Elemental Lords, except NK`Las, who stared past the windows to a face he held with dread. The Prince of O`pn E`rth Elves could see this Necromancer because the Necromancer was a Dark Elf. His lineage snaked down to H`dn E`rth. NK`Las shivered as he drank the dregs of his lager as Lord M`orus asked.

"Someone walk over your grave, lad? That was some shiver."

NK`Las glanced at his Uncle as he pushed the tankard away from him.

"Something like that, Uncle, something like that." NK`las could not cast off the eyes of Lord Nul`YK. The Necromancer had stared directly at him.

All the Necromancer sensed was three men drinking in the Tavern.

Lod`n's storm was also a protective manifestation. The Necromancer could detect no words or thoughts; it was not in his skill set. Still, Lieutenant NK`las was wary and wired as only seasoned Warriors could be.

All he heard was the cyclonic storm outside. Only

Lod`n knew who had intensified its power.

Lod`n looked at NK`Las to M`orus, ‘seems someone is viewing us, but nothing will or can be detected by him. NK`Las, you are a rather sorry liar lad; he may be old in your eyes, but we know absolute bastards of the realms beyond this’ he winked and downed his lager, burping loudly.

# CHAPTER 1

The youth, a Sz`a`Th Imperial Scribe of sixteen winters, felt drained from his before dawn translations. His back ached from hunching over the ledger, scribing ancient runic text to the universal language. He stood; the wood and leather chair creaked with relief from the movement.  Stretching up with his shoulders, he arched his back and relaxed with the ease it brought to his tall frame.

The Scribe closed his eyes for but a moment, resting. Breathing in the icy salt air of early winter on the Tali`z coast. Under his amethyst, blue eyes, a lack of sleep-circled dark was evident. He rubbed his face slowly, feeling the new growth of dark beard on his skin-the—the sounds of the Keeps occupants filtered through the open window. The wet courtyard below was awake.

Sharp piercing sounds of steel and broadswords clashed as Warriors played out imaginary staged conflicts that came from the courtyard below his window. Rapid, sharp thuds muted softly as arrowheads and crossbow bolts pushed by straight shafts embedded themselves into the thickly bound hay targets.

Taelen's blue eyes opened, pale, dark grey winter light of early dawn; it reflected what the day might bring. The youth's eyes wavered between an amethyst blue and a strange purple tint caught in the prism light from the window. Dark eyelashes as black as the hair cut short and in the Keeps Warrior style hid his eyes for a second as he blinked. His neat, close-cut beard had him look a little older than his fifteen winters.

The dark blue metal of the quill he was using had

blocked yet again with the black ink. Inferior ink was bought from the north, where the word of strange unrest came. He hated the cheap ink with its incompetence.

The youth dabbed the quill on the damp cloth he lent on the thick limestone windowsill. The cold sharpness of the black rock that was the Taayra`Ge Keep cooled his agitation. Uneasiness had been scratching at the perimeter of his thoughts well before dawn.

The ledger Taelen was deciphering had been written in ancient runic script, challenging to read and even more complicated when spoken. The old language was a series of lilts and clicks.

Though an Imperial Scribe, he was also a Warrior and would have been happier practising his sword in the courtyard than deciphering the ancient text. He shook his head; it did not matter to him; he was an Imperial Scribe of the Sz`a`Th, nothing more to the Lord of the Taayra`Ge Keep than that.

Master Melicq, had been the Senior Scribe, a man ancient in winters and in his ways when Taelen had arrived at the Keep. One of a hand full of survivors of a vicious attack of Lord Mah`sden's murdering Dark Warriors. He was thrown into the dark winter ocean while his mother was butchered and drowned.

The Sergeant of the Blade had saved Taelen. Sergeant Anston now sparred in the courtyard below in a well-choreographed training drill.

Master Melicq's concern for the ledger had been consuming, even when he had passed away shortly after Taelen had taken mastery of the problematic dialect at age thirteen winters.

The Master had died strangely, an older man in his shadow winters. He had taken the ledger from a dying Warrior. The Warrior, the lone survivor of a shipwreck, had asked for the Master Scribe specifically by name.

The Warrior had the marking of the Ogdoadic Knight, a silent and specialist arm of the Sz`a`Th. No one of the Keep had seen an Ogdoadic Knight, and his death left more questions than Taelen had liked. When he gave the ledger, the Knight lay moments from death bound in thick sail canvas and had handed it to Master Melicq. The Knights' ocean green eyes stared at Taelen as he said to the boy.

"One of the eight-pointed stars will seek you out, be not afraid boy, he seeks you, be not afraid of destiny's needs, or the deeds he will demand of you…you must promise this to me…they are wrong…there is the eighth book…you are that book – tell none…or those who have died in heinous deaths will be for naught." His words had scrawled against Taelen's mind, etching images that Taelen could never erase. He had the same ill feeling that morning.

The Master Scribes' features had withered at his first touch of the book. An unknown Spellcasters ward had been placed on the ledger. His fate had been sealed immediately with no resident Spellcasters at the Keep.

A myth surrounded the Eight Books: each breath was another volume of the Seven Books of the Sz`a`Th, Simply called the Seven Books, not Eight was the Eight Book was unknown. He could never let the knowledge of the eighth book have time to breathe. His agonising screams echoed within the halls of Taayra`Ge Keep as his body decayed more with each torturous breath he took. He had died seven pain-filled moons later.

The rune design on the ledger that burned into his hand was the sign of 'P`rth'. In the language of Scribes and the lands' language, it meant 'rune of mystery'. Its meaning was open to others' initiation to a hidden message

Yet, all this meant nothing to the young Scribe of

thirteen winters. He had ledgers to decipher, with Apprentices still too young to be trusted with quills and the inferior ink. Instead, he nurtured and taught them like a big brother and insisted they instinctively knew the blade's swing and the arrow's aim. Taught the use of each blade of the Sahn`Frwh Sword, it was not thought but instinctive, as inconspicuous as taking a breath.

The only man who could assist was his Master Scribe, who was dead. He now had to occupy that grey space in between where Master Melicq had been for so long.

The Commander of the Keep Captain T`nyson, a Sz`a`Th Warrior, Sahn`Frwh trained and a veteran of the E`boda Plains Six Winters War, where there had been the word, of those of Myth appearing, where arrows with mystic marking always killed never maimed. Large double-sided broad axes spun cartwheeling into Dark Warriors, eliminating them.

Most Sz`a`Th Warriors who had survived killed themselves in strange, unorthodox ways - for suicide was not the Sz`a`Th way. Yet many had just done that. When the darkness of war casts a blackness across the minds of those who had witnessed the unspoken horrors of war, sometimes, living is too complicated, and there are ways a Warrior will leave, and there are worse things than dying for Warriors. Peace was one of them.

Captain T'nyson had strangely agreed with the Cook, Veh`nese, regarding Taelen's position at the Keep. Taelen could not shrug the feeling that he sensed that Veh`nese the Cook, Sergeant Anston and Captain T`nyson knew who he was but would always steer his questions of origin away from him.

Taelen stood as tall and powerfully built as the Warriors fighting mock battles in the courtyard below. Most afternoons, he spared with them, much to their discomfort. Naturally, he was identical in skills. He was uncanny in his step and strike and deadly with the Sahn`Frwh sword and blades. He smiled, remembering one old Warrior watching him sparing saying, 'Lethal as an Elf…deadly as a Dwarf…cunning as a man – wary as a Wolf, wise as a Raven, you will be right lad…you react…a Warrior who thinks, dies quick…a Warrior who reacts lives.' Those who exercised daily with Taelen were relieved his duties as Keeps Imperial Scribe, and not a Warrior made him absent from their drills.

Though Taelen had been apprenticed as one of the Taayra`Ge Keep's Scribes since six winters old, the youth had also been taught the defence tactics of the Sz`a` Th Warriors. The Cook, Veh`nese, had made that point to the Commander so many winters before.

Taelen watched one particular Warrior. The Warrior called Brae was a winter younger and only slightly shorter than Taelen.

At nearly sixteen winters old, the youth below was skilled. However, Brae's internal anger and arrogance were and would be his end.

A warrior who bears a grudge is as dangerous as the enemy who follows blindly.

Had the Sergeant at Arms not been as active and no doubt wiser, and a seasoned Warrior, the younger Warrior, would have felled him by the series of furious blows that were being levelled at the Sergeant.

The Sergeant's fast footwork saved him from a lethal blow from the youth.

The frustration and anger that drove Brae ferociously on became short-lived as the Sergeant at Arms cracked the flat of his broadsword across his shoulders of Brae. And shoved the youth to his knees, then pushed his boot down onto the back of the youth's neck with a swift kick, driving his sword close to the lad's crotch enough that he felt the blade's vibration against his balls. He did not move.

Anston was not the Sergeant of Arms due to his war history; no Anston, even with one hand, could disarm a skilled Warrior, and an angry one was easy.

"Fight like that in battle, and you will die." He snapped, his voice cold as the wind that blew off the grey Taayra`Ge Ocean below the Keeps walls. The Sergeant's large chest rose and fell with frustration.

"Would be easier to tame a Tah`n Wolf than placing some intelligence between your ears. I train you, Corporal so that you will survive a battle. Not so you lose your bloody temper and not see the next blow that will remove your head from those shoulders, too swiftly for you to take your last breath."

Brae angrily shoved the Sergeant's boot from his neck, leapt to his feet, and swung around, his fist in full flight for the Sergeant, who brought up his blade again. Brae twisted, narrowly missing the centre of Anston's edge.

Anston grabbed the young Warrior's fist in his pincer grip. The metal of the Sergeant's prosthetic hand bit hard into skin and bone.

Holding Brae's hand high, his dark forest green eyes bored into the young Warriors with contempt for the stupidity that could kill the youth in combat.

"Do not threaten me…ever, do you understand?" His voice cut through the background noise of Drill in the courtyard, which ceased.

"It just might be my blade that removes your stupid, bloody head, Corporal." The Sergeant's voice conveyed truth to those in the Courtyard.

Broadswords stopped mid-defensive as Warriors stood still, hot breath fogging before their faces, chests heaving to fill with air from a fast-paced drill session, as their Sergeant held his own blade against the youth's heart.

The sweat shining on their bodies suddenly felt icy in its covering.

"Do that asinine action again, and I will not kill you, Brae," he shook his head furiously with the youth, slowly moving his face centimetres closer. "No! I will transfer you to the Northern borders where your bloody stupidity can be used against Lord Mah'sden's men. It will not be mud on their boots but your blood soaking their leather." Anston's tone heated with frustration burned in his throat. His eyes narrowed as his lips drew back over his teeth clenched tightly.

Taelen watched as the Sergeant slowly released Brae's hand. Brae's eyes glanced up at the window where Taelen stood. Taelen ignored Brae's glare as his own eyes and intuition stared intently at a dark shape, a ship not more than two hours from the Keep.

"Well! What are you staring at, Corporal?" The Sergeant roared as he acknowledged the look in the Scribe's eyes metres above in the tower.

Taelen tore his eyes from the ship, obeying the Sergeant's demand.

"Sergeant, a black-sailed Galleon is but two hours off the coast heading our way."

"What flag do you sense, Corporal - QUICKLY?" His voice did not give away his cold gut concern.

"Lord Mah'sden's ship sails toward us." He shouted, staring down at the Sergeant in the courtyard below.

The Sergeant gave two short, loud whistles through his teeth, which stopped everyone from their duties.

"EVACUATE THE KEEP" He yelled with all his strength, "THIS IS NOT A DRILL…THIS IS NOT A DRILL", and silently spoke in Sz`a`Th to all to make their escape immediately. If not, hide or death would be theirs.

Beyond all the adrenaline, hours before and kilometres from the Keep, someone rappelled down the cliff face in the inverted position known to only be used by one region. She was now standing horizontal on the vertical cliff wall with her long black and white hair tied tightly; she did not need a distraction.

Two arrows had to be sent simultaneously. The Warrior stood with rigging supporting her firmly. She dressed in the black uniform of the Raven Nation. She knew it would be two winters before meeting anyone receiving these two arrows, but it was imperative. She nocked the first and let it fly the kilometres to the Keep. Then she flipped on her back, still in the rigging; she knew the next one was as important as the first arrow.

She focused on a Warrior in her mind; she breathed slowly, had the terrain in her mind mapped, closed her eyes, pulled back, stared for a second at the storm clouds and released the second arrow.

Kilometres south, Sasson, a Karranja Warrior patrolling the forest outside the Castle and docks, looked north up the coast. He breathed out as he stood on the coastal beach bereft of anyone.

The arrow thumped centimetres to the left of his left boot. He looked warily, pulling it out and studied the feathers, then the tip, frowning. He wiped the sand off the shaft and sighed his breath on the stem of the arrow, a blue script illuminated with his name, date, region, and place. His arm burned and tingled, where the scar ran from inside wrist to elbow crease. He had no time to contemplate the meaning as an urgent shrill whistle coded came to him on the wind.

Taelen reached out to pull the wooden shutter; when an arrow hit the wood centimetres from his left hand, he felt the message's energy had not had the time but shoved the arrow into his kit.

The Raven Archer sent one more arrow, from the top of the cliff crag. Far from her, a R`atogh Warrior, crouching low, his reflexes fast, was a Tracker. His hand shot out in a blur and caught the arrow before hitting the tree. He glanced at the fletching black with slight white feathers. A small smile appeared as he then read the message.

T`tamu sighed profoundly and asked the forest to protect this young Raven Archer. He frowned, for he knew her and knew she was four winters younger than he, and he was eighteen winters, this lass fourteen winters. She must be bloody brilliant at her quild, he thought as he put the arrow in his kit and left just as quietly as the arrow had arrived.

She sent off five more arrows, all to different nations of man, woman and myth, and shivered not for the cold blast off the ocean onto the cliff face but from a 'knowing deep in her soul that many would die.

The young Warrior rappelled, inverted down to the rocks below, and retrieved her rigging. The sky above igniting cracking thunder and lightning statically, the gale hitting the coast was coming fast, and she needed to finish what had begun too long ago.

She released her hair as the wind took hold of her hair Ar`qi shook her long hair, folded down into a Raven, and flew into the storm's air currents. It would be many winters before she would see the three who received the arrows; if any of them survived, it was in the hands of the Elements. Ar`qi black eyes rimmed with delicate white and even finer black blinked as she flew.

Again she nocked her arrows and let fly to Ji`rah, a Warrior of the Sxq`rn Warrior of the Wolf Nation. The young Corporal stood on the battlements of his Uncle's Fortress Castle and watched the arrow hit the wood door he had just closed from a long shift on the Battlements. His heart was saddened as he read the runes. He swore under his breath, 'that's all I need is some bloody prophecy.

Her last was to a Silver Crescent, hidden in the forest on her horse. As the arrow hit the giant oak, she pulled it out, immediately healing the tree with her hand; frowning, KH`Dn stared at the runes glowing. A tear slipped down her cheek, and her shoulders shuddered as she. Two winters into the future was a long way off. She slid the arrow into her kit on her back and sat on her horse in the pouring rain, her heart heavy, Ravens rarely ever made contact, and one had from far away. Only a Ravens arrow flew so hard long, and fast.

Anston cursed under his breath. His anger was for the timing of the attack. Above he watched the gulls screech their warning about the Keep for a second. The adrenalin hit, and his temples pounded with the urge to live. Two hours was not long enough to remove the entire staff and the Garrison attached to the Keep.

His black booted feet began running into the Keep; if anything, he would be the last man out of the Keep, as the Lord and his family were away with the Captain and half the Garrisons' strength, attending a conference in the North.

Taelen's eyes moved to the black grey winter sky. The words of the man he knew as Anston and his Guardian spoke as cold as the wind that blew off the Great Grey Taayra`Ge Ocean.

"The wind changes its direction for a reason of nature. The man or woman turns their path to the goal of survival. When both Mhyst and wind change together, there will be much death on the wind; remember, Taelen, we are Warriors of the Sz`a`Th, 'Winds of Mhyst'. He smiled at the thought.

D`hôte ducked his head into the room where Taelen stood, gathering up quills and ink and wrapping them firmly. He also burned parchments in the large fireplace as quickly as he could break their seals.

He had been quick to understand that anything that was Sz`a`Th could and would be used by Lord Mah`sden to destroy them.

Taelen looked at D`hôte; his youngest apprentice ran in, helping him burn all they could find.

"Are you scared, Corporal?" asked the young Scribe as he stared out the window. Taelen threw in the precious parchments to the flames of the fire.

"This is no Drill", his voice was low. "If anything, D`Hôte, we must remember who we are and our training," Taelen said, pushing the ledger he had been deciphering into his backpack.

He shoved it at his Apprentice and grabbed the boy by the shoulders. Bending down to D`Hôte, Taelen held the boy's green eyes with his intently.

"D`Hôte, listen to me and listen good; take this to Veh`nese the Cook. She will take you to a safe place."

"But you, you must come, you have too, Taelen", the boy pleaded as his eyes darted to the window, hearing the pounding rhythm of the drums of the ship."

"GO! D`Hôte, we have done this drill before. I am a Corporal of the Sz`a`Th. My duty is here. Now go, I will find you." He stared intently at the boy of ten winters; he could feel the boy shaking beneath his winter clothes. "Go, this is not a drill, and I am ordering you, lad, not telling you."

D`Hôte looked out the window and over the din outside as he heard the ship's order to lower the longboats for the attack. Tearing his eyes from the scene now unfolding on the shore, he nodded and ran from the room, down the back stone stairs to the kitchen and searched for Veh`nese.

Taelen's mind swung to the dark shadows of Warriors on a Ship. He saw himself swimming, clinging to the debris around him. Warrior's laughter and the bubbling sound of air and blood mixed as throats gashed, yawning with blades; he heard the splashes that bodies make as they dumped into a black sea haunting him, shaking the images from his mind, he took the Sahn`Frwh sword in his hands and uttered the oath of the Red Crescent.

As the gates were being attacked, he heard Cook's voice; arrows hit the defences as the sound of metal on metal clashed outside the Keeps oak gates. He listened to her order staff and Warriors alike to safety. Screams and cries ensured the bloody battle was escalating

Taelen joined others; the assault on the Keep began, and the gates gave way to the pounding of the Dark Sz`a`Th, the name Lord Mah`sden's followers were known. He stood as the Warriors were left prepared to defend the Keep.

Corporal Tad`c and Corporal A`Dn, both Sz`a`Th Warriors, fired cross bolts in rapid succession, killing six Dark Sz`a` Th Warriors as they came in through the gate. Tad`c was hit with an arrow through his thigh. A'Dn immediately handed his crossbow to Tad`c while he broke the bolt and pushed it through, healing as he went. Both worked in unison, turning and pivoting to kill as many a Dark Sz`a`Th Warrior as possible.

The Sahn`Frwh move, with their backs at each, they each turn used another blade, for the Sahn`Frwh was a multiple-bladed sword; there was nothing like it anywhere. Seen for the first time was as if each Warrior partnered with the other in a dance, each step choreographed as if one Warrior was moving instead of two. This drill could be used with up two six Warriors, their backs to the other, swinging their Sahn`Fwrh Swords without a connection. If you listened to their heartbeats, they beat as one, which was what rhythm they fought—called the dance of the chosen, some just named dance of extinction.

Taelen's vision burned with white Mhyst, blurring his vision. Slowly it faded as he shook his head, and the Warriors breached the defence; bracing himself, he focused on the enemy advancing towards him. Shaking his head as Warriors of both sides yelled battle cries entering the Keep

Screams came from behind him as those who had not fled were cut down where they stood. He felt for the women of the Keep who had not yet escaped. He caught Tad`c with a blade in his back, being carried by A`Dn and D` Ron grabbing two young grooms half their ages on their way. All wounded, A`dn yelled to Taelen, 'We go north I have ordered from Captain Yassarn –' an arrow hit him in his chest as they managed to get through secret doors and tunnels. Others wounded left. 'Taelen…we have orders to leave. You must leave now' No more words did Taelen hear as A`Dn's mind became unconscious. Stone walls slid shut Taelen knew A`Dn had received the orders just as he did in his mind.

There was no time to think but only to act. Corporal Taelen spun his Sahn`Frwh sword around, decapitating three Warriors simultaneously. Absently he heard curses that they had not been told Sahn`Frwh manned the Keep. Taelen smiled as he continued his defence. He watched as Warrior after Warrior collided with the energy that was the Sz`a`Th, one of his Sergeants missed his footing on the entrails of a fallen dead Warrior.

Taelen used his Sahn`Frwh sword pivoting through the air to the Sergeant, disembowelling an Archer; with one hand, he assisted the Sergeant to his feet, and then both worked as one. He spun the two-meter swords in opposite directions, decapitating and severing what limb or torso came within reach of the deadly blades.

Both ducked as choreographed moves were shown to them and drilled into them until the training became just part of them. Intuitively they breathed as one made them lethal. One Sahn`Frwh Warrior was a force. Two of them, back to back, trained in the way of that sword was deadly poetry - beautiful execution of death, swift, instant, painless.

Blood and gore replaced mud and slush; iced winds cut deep into those still fighting for survival as rain lashed the coast in winter storms.

Taelen heard his name scream into his mind with such intensity that he stumbled. He stared at the arrow protruding from his right shoulder, his mind not acknowledging the shaft for a second, and then the pain burned deep.

The Sergeant he had been fighting side by side with him bent to his aide, but Taelen screamed at him to run, leave him, as another arrow split the arrow already embedded into his shoulder.

Handing Taelen two blades from the Sahn`Frwh Sword, he stared at the Corporal Scribe as Taelen stood in deep pain.

"Go, get help, send the alarm, go by the tunnel in the Stables, go to the E`nihs Garrison to the north at the T`hzic Straights…." He staggered and smiled slightly as his friend held him up. "Go, you can do no more here, Dek`hlan." The Sergeant nodded and left swiftly, as Taelen turned to see one of the Keeps staff fighting off two Warriors as they tortured her.

His Mhyst birthright burned deep purple on his chest as he swayed at the debauchery. Staggering slightly, he threw both daggers into the Warriors' backs, assaulting the young woman; they crumpled to the rain and mud of the flagstone courtyard, dying instantly. She took their two swords and began fighting alongside the others, her anger taking out more than one Warrior.

He stood with the support of his sword, making his way to her. He could not understand her words in his mind, then turned to see a Dark Sz`a`Th Warrior screaming towards him. Taelen spun the Sahn`Frwh sword slowly, then threw the sword impaling the Warrior to the Keep's open gate. He also felt the deep cut to his thigh as a sword sliced into him, and the warm liquid of his blood ran down his leg.

He felt the hands of someone pulling him into an alcove then, screams, screams and the smell of burning flesh.

Taelen crawled to the open courtyard to see the young woman tied to the horse tether. Her gown burning, and her flesh's smell fuelled what adrenalin he had left in him.

"Ki`arya!" His voice called to her. Stumbling to her, his Mhyst confused, caused the icy wind to extinguish the flames that had burned her legs, one a blackened stump with no foot.

Taelen fell to the mud and blood beneath Ki`arya and the Warrior.

He heard the Warrior ask the young woman a question with his name at the end.

"No…!" he gasped, sobbing his emotions "he is just is a Corporal, not a Lord, he is Sahn`Frwh… not the Dominion Lord…your spies have lied to you, Sergeant", she sobbed, groaning in pain from horrendous deep burns.

"Touch her again, and she will kill you, won't be me,' shaking his head 'won't be me." Taelen snarled through his teeth, ignoring his pain.

"He seems to like you, lass!" Taelen stared at the Lieutenant, whose sword was pointing at his thigh.

"Leave her alone…she is telling you truths…would she lie to you as she cooks slowly? She can tell you anything more." His voice groaned back at the Lieutenant. Mud splashed the Warrior's boots as he gave in to his injuries, falling back in the dirt and gore.

'Ki`arya sleep', he said to her mind in the silent speech of the Sz`a`Th. He watched her eyes roll white, and her head lolled forward, supported only by the bindings of leather tied tightly around her to the post supporting an awning off the kitchen door.

"Your turn, lad. Our Archers have had a bit of target practice with you." Taelen lay motionless

; to his left against the Keeps inner courtyard wall lay Brae, one of the Corporals he knew more by reputation. He leant where he fell with three arrows lodging from his shoulder. His eyes open, staring at him and the Warrior whose blade rested in the air at Taelen's throat. Taelen knew the Corporal was not dead. His eyes blinked very slowly.

Rain began to fall down, and Taelen willed the Elemental Lords to help them and aid in their rescue. If anything, cut this attack short.

"Lieutenant, the weather is against us if we stay; we have enough slaves for Lord Mah`sden and the mines."

Taelen followed the voice to see fifteen Keeps staff and Warriors beaten and wounded to his left. One was his female apprentice Scribes, Yhy`h. She was supporting two Warriors with wounds, and her eyes did not leave him as the Warriors yelled over the torrential rain.

"Do you want this one?" the Lieutenant asked as he held the sword at Taelen's throat?"

The other Warrior, a Captain, just stared at Taelen

with disinterest. Rain fell more substantially as the Warrior weighed the weather and carried a Corporal wounded down to the longboats and then onto the ship.

Shudders rippled through Taelen's chest, coughing violently, bloody spittle sprayed his chest, laying slack-jawed in his blood, turning the mud around in him in rust-streaked tentacles from his wounds. It took all his will just to stay conscious.

"Nah", he drawled with the northern ice islands accent ", kill him; he will be more hindrance than a help. His lungs fill with blood as we speak. He can neither swing a sword nor pick in the mines." He stared around the courtyard and stopped at Brae's lifeless form. "That one still has life. I will take him. Instead, his body is built for the mines, and this one is not as thickly set."

"Easy, the choice is death!" the Lieutenant raised the sword as Taelen stared at Yhy`h, supporting the Keeps two Warriors; she closed her eyes, saying silently in mind speak.

'I cannot save you, my Master Scribe, but I can make the pig miss your throat.'

Taelen stared glassy-eyed, watching the sword dripping with rain and blood come down suddenly with all the force the Captain could use.

Metal sliced through his skin, scraping past his collarbone, pinning the flesh on his shoulder to the bloody mud of the courtyard. Anchored to the earth, he could not move.

Waves of pain from his shoulders and thigh eased him in and out of conciseness. All he heard was the aftermath of battle as teaming rain fell. He, at times, caught Dark Warriors looting those dead and wounded. Eyes half-closed with the pain, he helplessly watched those of the Keep he had lived with for ten winters and staggered now as prisoners from the ruined courtyard and down to the beach's black sand.

Rain fell steadily as D`Hôte's voice filtered through his thoughts, making him open his eyes filled with rain. He blinked the water away as D`Hôte sheltered his face with his body. He suddenly felt very, very cold.

"Corporal Taelen, wake up." Taelen felt the hands of his Apprentice resting on his Mhyst marking above his heart. The lad's hand still that of a boy tingled in humming vibrations that were the Mhyst waking him.

D`Hôte's eyes, full and green, stared down into the amethyst, blue eyes of the Sz`a` Th Warriors.

"Where are the other Scribes?" he asked, his voice scratched in pain as the boy's fear levelled.

"Gone into the mountains and beyond, or taken. Corporal, except Yhy`h, I can't locate her…." He said, his eyes catching the ship that now sailed out of view. "We have to go, Corporal; you need to stand." The boy turned and cursed as he looked around the courtyard.

Sergeant Anston's concerned face focused as the Sz`a`Th Warrior assessed Taelen's wounds.

"Lad, this will hurt, but I need you at least semi-conscious to help me heal Ki`arya," said the Sergeant glancing now as stretcher-bearers carried her to the caves along the cliffs.

"It is your decision Anston; my Mhyst is burning. I can't control it."

"I need to remove the arrows, but first, this sword that has you pinned like a duck is ready for slaughter."

He touched Taelen's third eye with the palm of his hand and reefed the sword with his metal pincer that served just as good as a hand would. He felt the dawn; Taelen sucked in air through his teeth, exhaling with a groan. His vision went white from the pain, nausea rose, and Taelen fought control not to faint.

"Told you it would hurt a bit," Sergeant added

grimly.

Taelen just closed his eyes tightly shut, as Anston, with his healing, held the shafts firmly, the wood close to the skin, then pushed the arrowheads through to the other side of his shoulder and out the back.

He did not move as the Sergeant began healing through the Mhyst, placing his hand on Corporal Mhyst's birthright above his left chest. Particles of light appeared, changing from blue to mauve to white, sprinkling and sinking beneath his skin, tingling as the Mhyst healed him.

The Sergeant then healed both sword wounds; skin once again was new, leaving thick scars on his shoulder and thigh. He was unusual and thought wounds healed this way and never left raised red keloid scars. This worried the Sergeant more for the future healing of the Corporal before him. He could think of only one reason: the Dark Sz'a'Th's swords and arrows had been poisoned, or magic was there. The healing left Taelen light-headed and weak.

“Lad, I need your help to heal Ki`arya now; the leg is beyond saving and needs to be amputated at the thigh.”

He heard Sergeant Anston giving orders to those left wounded and walking and watching as they laid her on one of the beds in the caves used in emergencies.

Everyone who survived the attack now lived in the caves that hugged the brutal Taayra`Ge coastline. Those who had not would now occupy graves outside the Keep's walls. He quickly glanced at Taelen and D`hôte as they stood on the sandy track that led back to the Keep.

“You both do not have to come; burying friends is the hardest task. We will never forget them; we will tell their stories.”

D`Hôte helped Taelen to his feet; the older leaned on him for support.

Both stared at the Sergeant who had saved their lives with his own discipline and courage.

"No, we will come," said D`hôte, his mind reeling at what he would see within the Keep's black limestone walls. He helped Taelen to his feet. The pain had gone just as the Sergeant had said it would.

A miserable small group of survivors dug graves and medically healed those whose wounds could be seen. Not a pleasant one as the first bodies were that of fleeing kitchen staff; their throats split open from the 'Mah`s', a vicious hooked blade that caught hold of whatever organ or bone it picked and dragged the piece out of the wound. Windpipes, tongues and spines, all organs lay as bloody as the corpses.

A flat-bladed sword had impaled one of the young Stable Wards, his face unseen, as the blade drove through the base of his skull, pinning him onto the door they had escaped hours before.

His feet hung motionless centimetres from the stone floor, not touching the now tacky stones that his blood dripped down, patch-walking the flagstones large and dark as the coast slowly; Taelen held the body of the young boy as Anston pulled the blade from the door and his skull.

"Who would lift a child… then impale him on the door like a trophy?" asked Taelen as he gently carried the boy's body outside to bury.

"The same person who would throw a young boy into the ocean to drown…" answered Anston, quietly recalling how he had saved Taelen from death as the crew and passengers were slaughtered ten winters past when they had arrived on the coast by Mah`sden's Dark Sz`a`Th. Sergeant Anston removed corpse after corpse.

He had been a Sz`a`Th Warrior all his life, yet burying those he knew was something that training could never prepare a Warrior. They were taught to survive battles and wars. They were never taught how to die, never showed how to kill, and he suddenly felt tired beyond his soul, tired beyond life. Yet he knew this was just the beginning of a slaughter that would stain lands ancient and new. Sometimes, being a Warrior who survived was the most onerous and saddest burden.

His steps felt heavier than his heart as he carried the last body from the Keeps grounds.

Twenty-six of the Keeps staff were buried outside the gates. Six of the dead were Sz`a`Th Warriors. The others were kitchen staff, stable hands, the blacksmith and his apprentices. Each grave had a flat black stone that the Sergeant had placed where their heads lay beneath the black soil. Each had their names, region, guild, in rune with the date that caused their death – on all one word, 'Mah`sden'.

Their combined healing within the Mhyst restored the others to their health before the murdering attack. Now it was the young girl they would care for. Veh`nese tended to her, changing her bloodied and burnt clothes to a soft woollen grey tunic.

While Taelen and Anston together healed as much as they could with the Mhyst as their only healing tool. The caves already held food and equipment to last a lengthy siege if necessary. The caves were near labyrinths, their size and carved deeply. Had they been more prepared and aware of Mah`sden's approach, the death toll would have been less.

Taelen scribed a eulogy in ancient Sz`a`Th rune. It would survive time, it would glow like a light in the dark, and they would be remembered. The Sigal representing 'courage is never forgotten' was carved into the stone rampant. The Sahn`Frwh Sword also had abilities others rarely knew.

The Sergeant left orders to the ten Warriors due back in three days. Instructions; only they knew where to find the brass cylinder he would secure for them.

Ki`arya lay deathly still; his Mhyst had contained her life, cocooning her life energies in a pale mauve light that hovered over her skin like fog. Now he had to remove her leg and heal the other as best he could.

Her foot had burned to a charred black stump in the intense fire. He had somehow extinguished before death could consume her life. He wondered if she would ever thank him for that and what he was about to do.

The others had narrow escapes also.

Veh`nese had hidden in the caves with D`Hôte and the others, Anston had been knocked unconscious at the back of the Keep and left for dead, his only wound a nasty gash at the lower part of his skull, blood caked to his head, and uniform ran a red line thick and across his throat.

"There is no way I can do this, Anston…." The Sergeant gripped him by the shoulders firmly.

"I can order you lad, or I can ask you, your Mhyst is different, and I shall explain that later. Now, only you can save her."

He studied the youth before him, adding, "For some unknown reason, you both seem to have something in common that I am unaware of."

He bowed his head slightly and then looked up into Taelen's eyes. He wanted to tell this Master Scribe of sixteen winters the truth of his identity - but he could not. It would wait. Other things weighed just as heavily on the Sergeants' heart at that moment.

"This girl saved your life, you don't know that, but I do. They tortured her to try and locate you. Now it is your turn to save her life."

"I don't understand, Anston, they were looking for the Dominion Lord, and we all know he is just a myth, told to children at night."

"Save her, and I will discuss at length that Myth. You have to hurry."

"Why…are they coming back to finish off the living?"

"They are coming back to find you; it seems young Brae has a loose tongue!"

"Why do they want me? I'm just an Imperial Sz`a`Th Scribe and a Sahn`Frwh Warrior; I am nothing."

The weathered Sergeant sought to tell the Corporal before him so much, but now was not the time; he wondered, would there ever be a right time to tell Taelen of his heritage. Taelen took a deep breath and nodded to the Sergeant that he would heal the young woman, who was only fourteen winters old; she too had been on that ill-fated ship Taelen had been on as a child.

Washed clean with healing scents, she laid beneath the fresh white sheet. Taelen gently folded back the sheet to reveal her legs were deeply burned; he knew he would need to use his healing Mhyst. She would die.

The Corporal Scribe touched her upper thigh, where the skin was pale calico. Here he traced a line invisible to others but not to his eyes. The deeply burnt leg was amputated above the knee, and the wound healed immediately at his touch.

The burns on her other leg were healed but left scaring; the reason evaded him to the point that he turned to Anston.

"I don't understand why it works and doesn't." Speaking of his Mhyst energies, he used to heal.

"You are on the cusp of your 'Mhysting' Taelen, "something's work now; others do not. Once you have

Sung the Mhyst, you may be able to heal," answered the Sergeant explaining that when the Mhyst delivered its full energy at seventeen winters, the Sz`a`Th came of age.

Fragmented images splinted her screams into his mind torturing him many nights after as he fought with the demons of that battle at the Taayra`Ge Keep.

Sergeant Anston secured the cave Ki`arya was in with others from the Keep as they left for the cave he was in with Veh`nese and D`Hôte.

As the ship returned to the Tali`z Coast and the Taayra`Ge Keep, Anston pulled the thorny 'Kalu' shrubs as tall as a man across the mouth of the cave. Faces and hands stung as if the 'Kalu' blades struck them blindly. Dry cold air soothed them as they entered the cave.

"Sit right up to the back of the cave, get as low as you can to the ground, don't even breathe. The Keep is empty, all are in the caves and tunnels, and those who left by horseback, all horses had rested so by the Elemental Lords, let's hope they find nothing to satisfy their lust for slaughter."

Anston laid them against the wall and then himself. They lay like corpses for what seemed hours. No movement came from within the cave.

The wild shouts of Warriors and Mariners came from outside. Taelen held D`Hôte's hand, squeezing it to reassure the boy. Thunder cracked as lightning made a strangely twisted silhouette of the Kalu's that hid them.

Anston laid still, his mind chanting silently an ancient runic ward of protection over the four that lay upon the cold, dry sand. Lightning sharply lit up the outside world as Warriors pushed around the Kalu`s bushes at the cave entrance.

"I lay a curse for these bushes, the Goddess of Creation. They serve no importance than to slice the skin from our arms."

"You whine too much, J`het, but you are right if our Lord wants to search every cave for some 'whore's bastard'. Then let him get sliced up like a lamb roast."

The Warriors voice shouted orders into the storm for them to return to the Keep.

Anston lay still, controlling each shallow breath so that none could see his chest rise and fall. Lord Mah`sden knew of the boy's existence. His heartbeat was as cold as his hatred for the Lord of the Sz`a`Th.

The Sergeant's mind poured across the maps he had memorised for such an escape; the most significant challenge was now the weather and the food they had. What niggled at the Sergeant's mind were what gains Corporal Brae would have now that the youth's existence was known.

Somehow he would make sure the lad he knew as Taelen and the prophecy would be kept separate. He made an oath to the boy's mother as she died in the ocean with him holding her.

Anston crawled on his stomach to the cave entrance. There the Sergeant sent out his mind shrouded from discovery. The ship had left the small cove near the Taayra`Ge Keep and was now within the storm's fury. The Keep was empty as all now hidden in the cliffs' caves; they would stay there until their own Warriors came to retrieve them in a few days.

The Sergeant at Arms turned to the others; even in the darkness, he could feel their eyes upon him.

"They're gone; Mah'sden Warriors have left with the ship. There are many things right now we must do. The first is to come out of the cave and breathe. Leave your belongings inside." Anston said, then he stood and spoke in the ancient dialect of the Sz`a`Th. The shrub cursed by Warriors bent and let them pass untouched.

"Why didn't you do that to start with?" asked D`hôte, his face bloodied like the others from the sharp-bladed thorns.

"Because you only crave silence and pray not to be found if you feel your blood trickle upon your skin. The blood slides like a cold earthworm down your warm skin, did it not? Fear is a wonderful friend some days, D`Hôte."

D`hôte agreed with the Sergeant; his green eyes looked even more significant in the evening sky, and rain fell upon his face-melting his blood into the water.

Taelen and Veh`nese stood silently beside them.

"The smell of freedom and your taste makes your silence and discomfort seem worth it."

"Aye, but will they come back?" asked Taelen, his blue eyes staring after the ship.

Taelen began shaking and grabbed the cloth of his jacket, twisting it into his fist tightly around his chest as he doubled over, gasping.

"What's wrong with him?" Asked D`hôte, going to Taelen's side as the youth fell to the black sandy soil wet with rain. Taelen gasped and breathed hard but could not ease the pain screeching through his body.

"It is the first chanting," said the Sergeant "it will pass in moments, but the second is the most painful."

Anston made his way up the winding path to the Keep. The painted runic sign of a massacre upon the Keeps large oaken doors as a warning to those who came and, more importantly, an obscure runic design that told those of the Death Watch, the Sahn`Frwh Warriors, that survivors were within the Taayra`Ge Keeps dark limestone caves.

The Runic sign of death chilled their skin as the rain ran off everything, blurring and rinsing the blood back into the earth.

"Where do we sleep tonight?" Veh`nese they walked back upon the hard black sand of the southern coastline. The ocean waves crashed down relentlessly as the rain fell. There were no gulls in the sky at that moment.

He replied with profound exhaustion by reading her thoughts and those of D`hôte and Taelen.

"No, Mistress, I will not make you sleep with tortured souls; we sleep within the cave, as I have ordered the others," his eyes scanned the black, green ocean. "It is still not a safe place to be, but the cave is out of harm's way for us."

"Where are the other Anston?" Taelen asked, staring at the darkness that rose and fell in the land's last fading light.

"If they escaped to the mountains then, they live to travel south and north to the Garrisons. If they are unlucky, then they are on that ship. They all have their orders, even the Keeps staff. May the Elemental Lords keep them safe" The word hung grimly upon the air. As if crucified by their thoughts, Taelen spoke.

"Mistress, if you felt my 'Mhysting', would not others have felt it also?" Taelen looked from Veh`nese to Anston; they did not have to answer.

"Then this attack was to find me", his voice low, did not show anger.

"I have never lied to you, Taelen," he said as they walked back along the beach, the rain giving them some respite from burying the dead.

"You are seventeen winters today if I'm right. Eleven winters ago, I sailed with you, your mother, and 'him'." He said, not mentioning Taelen's father.

"When that bastard murdered your mother, and I won't mince my words, he's evil. I failed those I had given the oath to keep her alive." Veh`nese touched the

Sergeant's arm thoughtfully." I vowed as your mother's eyes died, and her body sank beneath the waves to save you."

He paused again, and when Taelen looked at the Sergeant, tears fell down Anston's tanned, weathered cheeks.

"I tore you from his arms as he held the Mah`s against your throat." He looked where his hand had been and flexed the metal claw." I figured you were worth saving, lad," and smiled.

"I grabbed you and leapt off the bow into a storm; somehow, I tied the stump and tied you to it." He looked at Taelen "The shock of what had happened and no doubt watching what you were strapped to." He shrugged. "You wiped it all from your mind. Then he fell silent until a couple of moons ago when you started getting the nightmares".

"Why did you always say, Cook, chopped your hand off?" asked D`hôte walking slightly to the Sergeant's left.

D`Hôte had come to the Keep as a boy of five winters rescued from the beach after a ship had broken up in a fierce winter gale that had pounded the Tali`z coastal region for three moon cycles.

"That's easy to stop young boys eating what the Cook carves." He said, ruffling the young boy's honey brown hair. " Veh`nese was her Ladies maid, she had come earlier to prepare the Keep, but her husband and children were on the same ship as us. They died with Taelen's mother." Again, the burly Sergeant let the tears fall.

"The Sergeant also lost his wife and son on the ship," added Veh`nese, "Life is not easy, D`hôte, but you know that because you have lost your own parents," Veh`nese replied, grasping the boy's hand in hers tightly.

"Aye, but I never knew them. I can't remember them." He said as the wind tufted at his honey brown hair cut short in the Keeps style. "That is the hardest thing," he looked at the Sergeant and changed the subject. His frown moved the blue shell slightly away from his third eye. The blue ocean Dur`n sea shell, always sliced to show the spiral denoting life's flow, fell flat on his forehead.

"Can you teach me that chant? So those bushes won't slice and dice us" Anston's laugh was sincere in its sound, and the others joined in.

"Aye," he sighed, "It's about time the Sz`a`Th language was spoken again. And I will tell you of those who will help us; they have not been seen except by few who believe and have faith that when blood flows heavier than a slaughterhouse, the old myths are not myths but just need to be freed when all is lost, sometimes D`Hôte, faith and hope is all we have in the darkest of times. They are like twin flames to show us there is a path ahead if we look and believe."

With Lord Mah`sden's bloody rise to power came laws forbidding free speech of regional dialects, Guilds and poisoning of the Mhyst, especially the ancient tongue of the runic script of the Sz`a`Th. Such suffocating ruling breeds contempt. Below the surface, the lives of many were living secret lives.

They climbed the black limestone cliffs that led to the caves. Outside, Anston recited the chant to have the bush move so they could safely enter.

Anston then pulled a dark cloth across the opening of the cave.

"Now you can light the lamp, D`hôte; it's to your left" the boy did as he was asked. Both Taelen and D`hôte were amazed at the cave. There were four stretches to sleep upon and food.

"Before you deluge me with questions, this is one of many 'safe' caves, but this cave is of a few that are only known to me, and if you'd been paying attention. It is not the same cave we hid in." Anston removed his tunic and coat, "We eat now, and tomorrow we leave here to go north." He said simply.

Anston sat at the cave yawning mouth; the ocean below crashed white foam against the black knuckles of the cliffs. The slight tremor felt with each wave kept the Sergeant awake.

His green eyes scanned within the darkness, a gift they said of night sight for blood given in battle. Sz`a`Th Warriors only received the night sight when they were wounded, which stayed with them till their last breath.

The wind ruffled Anston's black hair, and an agonising groan from behind startled him, but as he turned, he realised Taelen had started his journey within the Mhyst.

The youth had flung off his shirt, his body twisted as he lay whimpering. He held his fisted hands tightly to his temples. Anston crouched low and crawled on all fours to be beside the youth. His hands did not touch him. Contact even mentally would cause the young Scribe intense pain.

"Anston, I'm burning…I can't breathe. Am I going mad?" asked Taelen, his voice tensed with agony as each spasm tore air from his lungs.

"The first chanting is the most painful, but relieving and controlling is harder. That is the challenge. You must master the 'singing of the Mhyst.' And be, as one." Said Anston, his heart going out to the Scribe. "Sit here on the dry sand, and place your hand on my Mhyst birthright", Taelen did but recoiled. The pain tore deep inside him, flashing white light blinding only a moment.

“Taelen, the pain you felt then, is not my pain; it is yours. You must remove your mind to a place cold, beautiful, blue and white, nothing but ice; remove yourself to that level. Touch my Mhyst, and I will touch yours. Close your eyes but see the place where you must rest.”

Taelen’s hand trembled as he touched the warmth of Anston’s skin. The dark purple of Anston’s Mhyst birthright glowed softly. With the warmth of their skin, Taelen's psyche was removed to an isolated mountain plateau.

The Scribe blinked as freezing winds swirled around him. Silence enveloped him. White snow, blue sky with soft clouds carpeting whatever lay below the white cliffs he stood on surged slowly beneath the plateau.

The crisp crunch of snow underfoot made him turn sharply; Anston smiled.

“I like your safe place, lad. It is soothing even to me” Anston looked out over the cliffs.

“Where is this place?” The Scribe asked as his amethyst, blue eyes seemed more intense than ever before. Anston’s own eyes watered as he looked at the Scribe’s eyes.

“The plateau is different to all of us. Mine is a worn wooden wharf, bleached by harsh cold winds, battered by relentless storms of the most southern region of the coast. It is there that I am at peace. When the Sz`a`Th was nearly annihilated in the Mage Wars. A ‘Pal`thic’ passed Lore within the Mhyst; she gave us this called ‘Singing the Mhyst’. She gave us her last heart's breath to provide us with refuge. In extreme cases, we use such sanctuaries. It is not a place to hide in games. It is a place to learn, reflect, and heal if necessary.”

Taelen listened to the words of the Sergeant. For the first time, Taelen reflected on the man beside him. He had been a father to him and friend when he had, had no reason to. Who had made many sacrifices to his time to teach and mould Taelen into a Sahn`Frwh Warrior?

"You should be remarried, Anston. Why have you not."

"No, she died on the ship as Veh`nese told you; Cook has made me whole again in her own way. I am a Warrior, Taelen. I need space to breathe and be myself," he paused. "I am too set in my ways. Who would want to spend what's left of a Sergeant's life anyway." He shrugged indifferently. "Maybe I'm too selfish. I like to be me and do what interests me."

He squinted as he watched the clouds, more from the exposure of his soul to the young Scribe than to the brilliance of the snow below.

"I do not think of you as selfish. You are one of the most giving people I know. It may sound like youth words, but there is someone for each of us. You just have to know when the right person enters your life."

"Ah! The wisdom of youth is not the lack of romance in my life. I should tell you more about the Mhyst. I shall be at the cave entrance." Anston turned as Taelen went to watch him; Anston had seemingly vanished. Only the icy wind touching his face was all the feeling he had.

Taelen felt detached; at times, he weakened only to feel the fire in his blood; that edge of insanity that beckoned his weakness. He stayed, and his strength built his determination to succeed in meeting the Mhyst.

"Sergeant", Taelen's voice came from his back. The icy southern ocean winds were squalling, blasting gusts with the black sand of the coast. The Scribe bowed, stepping past the bushes, intent on cutting anything and anyone. He noticed Anston standing at the cliff edge.

"What are you looking at?" Taelen could only see

the boiling black ocean with a sky with a strange grey, purple and orange glow. He shivered in the cold touch of the wind.

"Your first skill is to 'sense' the ship that has taken our people as slaves; it is done the same way a seer uses their skill to see."

Taelen replied, "I can see within the ship." The surprise in Taelen's voice made Anston smile; the boy's gifts were emerging. The Scribe let his thoughts fly against the coming storm as black as night they stood in. He startled slightly as he watched the siege, something he never saw, but now he observed in his mind's eye.

A young Warrior of the Sz`a`Th was bloodied from head to toe. Three crossbow bolts protruded from his body. They sensed the life force in the youth ebbing and his shade waiting.

Taelen saw the Seafarer's black blade towards the already wounded youth's bare throat. Without thinking, Taelens Mhyst healed Brae

Anston watched, amazed as Brae's wounds healed and the thud of the Crossbow bolts sounded muffled as they fell to the ship's decking, making only one look back.

Energy surged deep within Braes's body as he lifted the blade from his boots; the arc of the black edge smeared lightly with the red blood of the Seafarer's hand as it hit the decking with a sick mute thud. The scream of disbelief brought more attention than Taelen had anticipated.

"The prophecy lives." The cry of recognition chilled Anston as blood sprouted onto the walls in the abstract script of anger unseen. The Seafarer slumped to the floor as a young woman ran to his aide and held his arm tightly, bandaging the stump heavily. Anston watched as she began sedating the Seafarer with the only healing she had, words.

The Sergeant grabbed Taelen's arm firmly. Concern held the Sergeant's face for the Scribe before him on the black cliffs of the Taayra`Ge Ocean.

Iced wind and sea spray for a moment blinded them.

"You must stop now, Taelen; before you are detected, the Warrior has already called to you being alive." Taelen could not hear his words.

"You are mistaken. He can only sense the Mhyst; he cannot see me, and I am no prophecy. I think you got hit harder on the head than you thought, Anston."

The cargo hold before them was a dark pit of agony. Taelen and Anston saw mainly Warriors of their Keep.

Taelen noticed the same young woman who had aided the Warrior Brae and had helped the wounded Warrior after losing his hand.

She moved between the Warriors, tending them with grace and tenderness beyond her fifteen winters.

Her grey gown of an Apprentice Scribe was beyond recognition. Blood darkened the cuffs and hem in a tragic lace unevenly woven in pain and grief.

Where she had wiped her bloody hands on the gown were violent scrunch marks of now deep black-red blood.

The young woman had been splinting a Warrior's forearm; her fingers stopped frozen in their movement. Then she began rebinding the forearm. Her fair skin was smeared with crimson blood, not her blood. The dark earth brown hair was back in place by the blood of those she had healed. Oyster grey eyes swept sideways and looked directly at Taelen and Anston.

"My Master, Sergeant Anston, I would welcome you." Her speech was silent to their minds. Both Warriors felt the calming mental powers crisp on the perimeter of their thoughts. Not forced upon them, but there, all the same, telling them only part of her capabilities.

"As you can see, we are those who did not leave the Taayra`Ge Keep in time".

Her large oyster grey eyes stared at them, tears dropped from exhaustion, and unspoken fear welled as she soothed a Warrior of the Keep.

Anston wished he could just pick her up and take away from all that had happened to her.

"Please, you must not come like this, not now. The Seafarer, who cursed, does he curse you? You are the only one I know who can 'heal'." Her delicately arched eyebrow rose slightly as if answering her question.

Sudden angry footsteps came quickly to her from behind the Warriors.

"YOU" her eyes rose as tears fell to meet a fist that struck her face, knocking her back across the Warrior she had just tendered.

"Some Seafarers and Warriors need your healing; our healer just died. Get up there", he ordered arrogantly.

The girl pulled herself to her knees; her lip and the left eye began swelling. She blinked back tears slowly and spoke to the Warriors she was healing. Reassuring them silently, she would return and, for the least injured, heal and stitch those less able.

Her large grey eyes watered slightly. Two Warriors lifted her to her feet.

Smoothing down the grey gown of her Scribe Guild, smeared with the gore of wounded Warriors, she turned to face the Seafarer who had just backhanded her across the face.

"I am not one of the Sz`a`Th, Sergeant of the Marines" he turned swiftly to her as she continued, "I do not know why you need a Scribe to heal your men". the intake of breath beneath decks held, as the Sergeant of the Marines swung around at her, pacing slowly down on her slight stature.

The sweat and filth of battles hung over him and seemed ready to explode into another form of violence that was merely his training. Eyes bloodshot from stress and fatigue widened, their colour of blue black seethed as intense as the storm that tossed the ship violently across the enormous dark waves.

The Mariner's large hand held her chin firmly as he steadied his legs on the lurching of the deck.

"I do not question orders." He barked, but tensed broad shoulders slumped as if calm suddenly held his heart. His thumb gently wiped the blood from her lip that he had caused with his backhand earlier.

The Sergeant of the Marines turned to the two Mariners still holding her. His voice had lost its aggressive edge. Instead, he said, "Release her."

The two Mariners also seemed to be overcome with either fatigue or a change of heart. The Mariners let their arms fall to their sides, releasing their hold on her.

She looked back at Taelen and Anston, 'I will be safe,' she said silently in mind speech.

"Our people need to be healed, Mistress. Our healer has just died." The Sergeant said quietly. The young girl looked up at the Sergeant and nodded in the semi-darkness of the hold.

"Show me where they are".

They watched in silence as the slight figure of the young woman followed the Sergeant up the narrow ladder to the upper deck.

"What is she?" asked Taelen looking back at Anston.

"You're Apprentice Scribe, it seems, is a Pal`thic. I can't understand why I never noticed her before," Anston considered.

"I never paid her attention; she was just another Apprentice." He frowned and asked, "I thought Pal`thic's were E`rth'n creatures, more fable than fact?"

Anston still watched the vision before him of the ship and the girl. Anston wondered who had sent such a girl with such powers. A Pal`thic could sway the mind, convince one of many things, and even persuade someone to do something entirely out of character. They were also talented Spellcasters and linked some said by blood to the great Elf clans of old.

"Seems others must have sent her to you, Taelen. Their Lore is complex and simplistic; keeping to any Lore is challenging. Let's say they just keep to themselves." He pondered the girl again, "If the Elements have sent her, someone somewhere knows a lot more than we do and has the information we need. I fear the future will be a bloody path for us all."

Taelen searched around the hold of the ship and found Brae. The Warrior sat passively with an air of contempt dramatically fired within his deep leaf green eyes. His hair, an earthy brown, was short at the back with the top length braided into a design that fell defiantly to his shoulder at the end. It was the blue Dur`n quill shell from the Taayra`Ge Ocean they sailed upon.

The Dur`n blue quill shell was the emblem of the Keep, a rare and valued find on the dark sandy beach below the walls of the black lime-stymied fortress. All Warriors of the Keep wore the same single braid, but all wore the blue shell differently. Taelen wore his on a silver chain, Anston wore his at the centre of his braid, and young D`hôte wore it on his forehead over his 'third eye'.

Brae was a winter younger than Taelen, trained as a Warrior of the Tali`z people. The young Warrior was over six feet tall and slightly broader of the shoulder but equal in strength and more substantial in weight.

Brae and Taelen had fought against each other within the courtyard of the Taayra`Ge Keep under the watchful eye of Anston.

The muscles within the young Warrior's jaw flexed angrily as he watched the young Apprentice Scribe depart to the upper deck.

“Why does Brae not move and fight?” asked Taelen.

“The Mhyst is his gaoler, Taelen. No chains or ropes would hold him. You know that from the training you have had with Brae. Where most Mhyst’s guide and unite us, some confine and unravel those who are, the grey of the soul.”

“Aye, that is the truth,” he said quietly and released the Mhyst. The visions dispersed slowly like the ocean waves crashing against the cliff beneath them.

Taelen had watched, sometimes with envy, at Braes training with the Sergeant beside him. The Warrior trained as a Sahn`Frwh, who goes out alone and kills silently as a shade or assassin. Taelen had completed his training as a Sahn`Frwh Knight, where Brae, a winter younger, still had to finalise.

“Do you know where they will be taken to?” Taelen’s intuition told him it would not be to freedom.

“The ship's name is the ‘Iferous’, he said, raising his eyebrow,” It means ‘Carrier of Freedom’ a sick optimist must have named her.”

His voice held a rare hint of sarcasm that the Sergeant hardly expressed.

“But in all reckoning, I’d say their off to the coastal port of K`hir and then upriver to the Lake Garrison of Cran`dk”.

Anston was not happy for such a place meant a conflict of interest regarding the Sz`a`Th. Thankfully Taelen’s mind was elsewhere.

"Do you know the girl's name? You were the Master Scribe of the Keep"

"Yhy`h is her name when she came about three winters ago. However, she never showed signs of any 'Pal`thic' tendencies. She never really spoke, and I assigned her to decipher the texts of the Tali`z, mainly the Runic writing of the Priests."

Taelen returned to the cave with Anston standing and watching the weather beyond the cave entrance. His green eyes seemed preoccupied with what was on his mind. It was not the change of colour of the clouds. He wondered what other storms were on the horizon boiling.

"She is a strong young woman Taelen, but it will take all the will she has to stay alive on that ship. Not many women I know could survive. Many would go insane. Once she is at Cran`dk, she will be used as a Scribe within the Guilds and have the protection of the Captain there, who is a good and sincere man. He will not like Brae, though." A slight smile touched his lips as he thought of the blonde-haired Captain. No, he would not like Brae one bit.

Veh`nese met them with hot drinks; she observed both of them. "And who have you two been spying on may I ask?" she laughed as both looked at each other, slightly reminding her that even as men, these two could still have the hint of guilty boys caught doing something they shouldn't have been doing.

Taelen accepted the pottery mug of steaming hot sweet-spiced tea, it was too hot to drink, and he blew on the surface to cool the liquid.

"Veh`nese, what do you know of 'Yhy`h?" he asks, sitting down on the ground within the cave, his back against the rough stone of the walls. Here coldness and the harsh touch of limestone could be felt through the thick winter cloth shirt he wore.

"Yhy`h is the girl, with the rune tear shape in the deepest purple tattoo of her right cheek, is she not?" she gave the D`hôte his meal and Anston his, then sat herself down.

"I wouldn't know," Taelen replied, raising his eyebrows and shaking his head as he looked at her over the food he was eating, "I really can't tell you."

Veh`nese sighed and smiled. "You tell me then what you have noticed about her."

"Her script is precise and well-measured, and the use of ink was..." Veh'nese cut off his answer. The humour in her voice slightly annoyed him.

"If I wanted to know how well the girl could scribe, I would have asked that," replied Veh`nese. "But since you have a view that does not enter into her personality," she smiled ", Yhy`h is caring, strong-willed, and I might add she thinks highly of you, Taelen. Why is beyond me since I now know you had no idea the girl existed till now."

"Yhy`h can calm the horses at night, and she speaks to them silently," said D`hôte. "I've seen her even convince Brae he wasn't interested in her. But he was and is."

"She's different. I like Yhy`h." The young boy replied.

Taelen frowned and thought of the young Apprentice Scribe. He had never noticed, only in passing the workload to her that the other Scribes were too young to undertake. Feeling awkward, he changed the subject of Yhy`h away from him and asked about the Lake City of Cran`dk.

"This place Cran`dk, you mentioned. Are we going there?" Taelen asked, staring at the arch of pale light that filtered into the cave entrance. Feeling uncomfortable with the discussion of his lack of attention to Yhy`h, he changed the subject.

"Aye, we have to. I would rather avoid the place if there were a choice." The edge of reluctance in Anston's voice gave a hint of foreboding. "I have heard of unsavoury happenings there recently."

Taelen went to ask but caught the shake of Veh`nese head, bidding him not to ask the obvious.

'Shadows of the Mhyst', thought Taelen. The title drew him tightly, and tingling in his eyes brought them to water. The book's title carried an urgency within him, hunger deep down inside that purred impatiently to be fed.

That night Taelen dreamed of the Mhyst; its deep blue-purple hue danced in swirls through his subconscious. Runes glowed opaque white, forming words, sentences, and warnings. He dreamed the dreams of those poisoned trapped in their bodies, but like child puppets unable to move, they needed and wanted to, especially the Sz`a` Th Mhyst Warriors now within the poison. They wept inwardly for the atrocities that they had done by Mah`sden's Warriors. They cried for the person they were and wept. Would once the poison was gone from them, male and female Warriors, would they be understood – would mateships survive this war on the Mhyst? He wondered this too.

# CHAPTER 2

Veh`nese woke him gently as she had for the past ten winters.

"Taelen, it's time."

His amethyst blue eyes were startling as always first thing upon awakening. Veh`nese thought absently that they would break many a young women's hearts. She knew those young women in the Keep had spoken to her about the Master Scribe and his elusive nature. Now she thought he was no longer a child; he was a man, a Shadow of the Mhyst.

"Veh`nese is it late?" he inquired, stretching his body, interrupting her thoughts.

"No," she replied, smiling ", it is too early; the moon still lingers within the pale morn. Anston wishes us far from here, so we must pack and be gone."

Taelen glanced around the cave.

"Speaking of the Sergeant, where is he?"

"Waiting, Taelen, for us. He has a small skip down in the next cove."

Veh`nese gathered her pack and the backpack belonging to D`hôte.

Taelen rose, grabbed his backpack, and followed her petit shadow into the early dawn.

The skip could staff six; if the winds prevailed, they would make the port of K`hir within twelve hours. He hoped the ship with the Sz`a` Th Warriors would already be entering the mouth of the L`Hariz River at the T`hzic Straights. Taelen had heard that the Straights were deadly even when the were still.

Anston was a skilled mariner; at times, Taelen wondered what had possessed the Sergeant to take a career upon the land. His love for the sea was only one a mariner would understand.

The seas were ominous, and the rough weather concerned the Sergeant as it did Taelen.

"There is a small cove to the northeast and a Garrison small but..." his eyes stared at the dark sky above them; he never ended the sentence because he then realised he did not know if the Sz`a`Th still held that position. He said a silent prayer to the Goddess for their safety. The storm was what he had tried to steer around; luck was not to be their friend that day.

Anston with D`hôte and Taelen steered with all their strength to hold tiller and sail on the course, hands and fingers blistered, then bled upon the wood. The sails creaked and strained with the wind that filled the canvas to the breaking point.

They fought for control of the skip; currents and swells tossed them dangerously. Hours passed until they were close to the cove that Anston had spoken. An enormous wave suddenly overshadowed the skip.

No one was prepared as the freak wall of water rose and smashed the skip into the ocean's deep green depths, where the currents' strength pulled them back and forth like flotsam.

Taelen felt an arm brush his face. His hand gripped the limb tightly, kicking with what strength he could find and with his lungs on fire, ready to explode, he breached the water, coughing and dragging D`Hôte's still a boy to the surface. The last wave rose high, flinging both Scribes into the air. D`hôte landed heavily upon the beach. His lungs spewed up the saltwater with the heavy contact with the sand, wet and hard.

White lacing water tugged angrily at Taelen's hair and skin; ice-cold water currents clawed in skeletal fingers along his back as he came crashing down upon the black beach with a thud.

Taelen could hear the sound of coughing and retching. He felt the warm saltwater and bile retch from his throat as he, too, began breathing and retching in coughing spasms that left him exhausted. The waves push him further onto the sand, repeatedly rolling him back down into the cold, wet grave he had just escaped.

He cried out croakily, his voice nothing but a rasp, his throat on fire as someone moved him. They lifted him from the cold hard sand and the ocean-pounding waves until he could hear them no more.

Taelen felt hands remove and cut wet sandy clothes away. He was immersed in warm water; his skin burned hot with the contact. He attempted to push their hands from his skin. The water terrified him. He opened his eyes; grit and saltwater only made them water and burn. Hushed voices inaudible in their cloaking accents murmured around him in the grey space he had found himself in.

He was dressed in winter clothes but soft and dry; he groaned as someone bound his arm and ribs and another bound his eyes. The ointment stopped the burning; the cold, thick film slid over his eyes and formed a veil between his visual perceptions.

Their voices spoke in a dialect he had not heard, yet vaguely once before he could remember from somewhere in memories where childhoods collide with reality.

Nevertheless, the moment slipped from his thoughts as stabbing pain from his arm had Taelen breathe in sharply as he gasped. He still could not see those who had strapped his shoulder.

Every day the bandages were changed, and they fed him. For the first time in his seventeen winters, he cried, heart-wrenching sobs that tore from his soul, the pain with each sob wrenching at his ribs, and the tears scorched his eyes. Taelen's grief overwhelmed him totally.

On the tenth day, strong hands removed the bandages slowly from his eyes, his own hands touched them, and the picture in his mind was of a Sz`a`Th Warrior. The man sent memories spiralling through Taelen's mind unnerving him.

"Se` Han also se ah laman?" asked the Warrior; his eyes held patience, Taelen vaguely recalled but could not catch.

Taelen gingerly pulled himself into a sitting position on the bed and slowly went to touch his eyes, the strong hands that earlier had removed his bandages now held his hands.

"Yen ET she ta Laman." Taelen could feel the despair well up from within him.

'I DON'T UNDERSTAND." He cried in the dialect of the Taayra`Ge Keep. He did not wish to answer, for he did not know if this person was the enemy or not. Then sensing what the man was trying to say, he opened his eyes slowly.

The man before him seemed relieved when he blinked slowly and focused his vision upon a pair of eyes mirrored his colour and vibrancy. He stared at the man, whose eyes were identical, even down to the mauve light, flickered ethereally.

"Oh… I knew you were of the Sz`a`Th. Your family is alive; you are fortunate to have survived the T`hzic Straights."

"You're mistaken; I have friends on the skip, but …no, I have no family living."

The Warrior said nothing as Taelen looked at his hands. The healing skin was soft and pink compared to his olive skin; he slowly flexed his fingers, hearing the crackle of knuckles.

“All your fingers are attached, lad.” The Captain said with no ill intention, smiling slightly as if he had viewed the scene before with other Warriors.

“I know,” he said quietly, glancing back at the Warrior standing. The man was tall and broad-shouldered as Taelen; the only difference between them was the fair hair of the Captain. Taelen felt he was looking at himself as only older. He looked out the window and smiled.

“If that is not your family, you have some very good friends. Where were you going?”

“Where did Anston say we were going,” asked Taelen but was surprised at the Warrior's response.

The Warrior turned suddenly, his face with a more hopeful and surprised reaction than the anger Taelen had expected.

“You did say Anston? Did you not Anston Th`riou?” asked the Warrior, bending down close to his face, “and the woman who is she is not his wife.”

Taelen moved back into the pillows, his hands tremble, for he could feel the power of the Mhyst in this Warrior; its essence was strong. He had never sensed such a pull from any Mhyst before. He watched the interaction of his friends’ names with this man erupted expressions Taelen could not fathom.

“Veh`nese, they have been my guardians for as long as I can remember,” he answered.

Again, the Sz`a`Th Captain called to one of his men standing guard at the door in their language. The ‘common language’ spoken across the regions had not yet been expressed in front of Taelen.

“You will not harm them?” Asked, Taelen pulled himself up slowly.

“What!” the Warrior smiled broadly and laughed,

"Hell no, lad, they are old friends. I would give my life for these two, but age has changed us. That even old friends have failed to recognise each other."

The voices fell to a murmur, and the sound of footsteps came back into the room to Taelen.

Anston stood at the door to Taelen's room and walked in with D`hôte and Veh`nese. All had abrasions that were healing; they rushed to Taelen's bedside.

"You like giving us a scare?" said Veh`nese kissing him tenderly on the forehead" he wiped a tear from her cheek.

"No, I don't, but I think I've gotten us into trouble; the Warrior here says he knows you two."

Anston and Veh`nese looked at one another and then turned as the Warrior entered.

He stood leaning within the architrave, a matt black blade in his hand, the handle and pommel of the dagger etched with a runic design.

"Ten winters ago, I gave a Warrior of Sz`a`Th a blade," Veh`nese hand cupped her mouth as a sob escaped.

Anston reached down to his black boots and pulled out an identical blade to the one the Captain held.

She shook her head, "No, please," D`hôte pushed in front of them. His green eyes held a deep unseen strength that Taelen was not surprised at seeing. D`hôte was one who would persevere until he achieved his goal.

"I don't know who you are, Captain, but you will not harm them; we are Tali`z of the Ocean Keep of Taayra`Ge, survivors of a massacre two weeks ago."

Anston placed his metal claw on D'hôte's shoulders which the boy held tightly.

"D`hôte, it's all right. We are not about to be slaughtered by the Sz`a`Th," Anston said with a slight smile.

Anston bowed low, as did Veh`nese; D'hôte shrugged and bowed quickly. His eyes did not leave the face of the Warrior before him.

"Anston, Veh`nese, please, a lot has changed in ten winters; one thing that has not is old friends." His arms opened as Anston hugged him warmly, and Veh`nese cried against him as she told him of the deaths of their spouses and children, and then more quietly, the attack on the Taayra`Ge Keep that brought a tear to the Warrior's face.

Taelen watched in silence, not entirely understanding what had happened. He had never seen the Warriors that had saved them; though the Red Crescent tattoo at the left temple told him they were Sahn`Frwh, he felt he knew absolutely nothing of the world outside the Keep.

"Could someone enlighten me?" he asked, his voice a hoarse whisper.

Anston moved to the side of the bed. He pulled a small wooden box from his tunic tied with a blood-red cord; he studied the box's lid engraved with the rune of the Sz`a`Th as Veh`nese and D`hôte left the room in hurried and excited whispers.

"The story that Veh`nese and I told you before we left the Keep was true to a point. This box is your heritage and legacy. But because of Lord Mah`sden and his followers, I'd concealed the box." He handed the small box to Taelen, who slowly opened the lid's softwood made from the Rowan tree. Within this protected wood sat a medallion of silver. Etched into the metal was the design of the Sz`a`Th in the ancient runic flourish. Taelen touched the carved raised silver of the rune, shifting, seemingly becoming fluid, then again became the solid silver metal of before, yet now along with the words of the Sz`a`Th, was his name and date of birth.

This medallion was like nothing he had ever seen; the three runes were unique and surrounded the medallion's edge. They were written in the formation of a bindrune. Yassarn had seen the same fluidity in the air; he shivered not from the cold but from a premonition he had had as a young boy. He shook his head as if to rid himself of the vision that had haunted him…his father had shown him the same medallion, but when he had touched it, instead of his birth, it had shown the date of his death.

"Was the Keep attacked because of me?" He asked, looking at Anston.

"I've never lied to you, have I?" Anston's dark forehead wrinkled in concern for the Master Scribe.

"No.". Taelen answered quietly, his eyes brilliant in their blue studied the Sergeant.

"Then, I will tell you this Mah`sden is not your father." He bowed his head," I know your actual father; He is a good man Taelen. Promise me you will not judge him on what you think you know or hear. To understand what happened seventeen nearly eighteen winters ago, you must get to know the man and not the myth." He frowned and looked up. "Promise an old Sergeant that, will you."

Taelen sighed, "I promise," then he added, already knowing the answer," We can't travel together anymore, can we?" Blue eyes rose to meet green.

"No, lad, we can't. The Captain here has asked me to stay at this outpost," he smiled. "Veh`nese and D`hôte are staying with me. It seems D'Hôte has told me he wishes to be Sahn`Frwh, and that family you mentioned… " he said with a slight smile and wink…" they might have been there right in front; of me."

"Me?" he asked, his eyes stinging slightly.

"Destiny is an unwanted bed partner sometimes", Anston paused. His eyes rested on the youth he had loved as a son. "I have guided your destiny to this point, Taelen. Within your life, we pray for freedom." Taelen threw his uninjured arm around the Warrior, which taught him all the skills he would need to succeed.

"I forgot one thing", he dug into his pocket and opened his fist, "these are for you."

The two double silver clasps of Lieutenant of the Sz`a`Th were placed in his hand. The engraved swirl of the Mhyst stared back at him, pulling at his soul.

"You are a Knight of the Mhyst, Lieutenant, you are also Sahn`Frwh, you are of the Death Watch", he smiled, "don't forget to visit."

The Sergeant walked to the door, took one last look at Taelen, and left.

Taelen took a deep breath, his eyes resting on the Sz`a`Th medallion.

"Maybe he's finally found that family you said he would have one day." The Captain said from the doorway.

Taelen glanced slowly up at the Captain, "So, will you tell me who you are?" His eyes went to the window. All he could see was the grey sky and misting rain.

"My name is Yassarn, I'm a Captain, and I do surveillance along this coast. At its most desolate part of the coastline is its most vulnerable at the peninsula."

He watched Taelen closely and continued.

"I served with Anston before you were born." Taelen narrowed his eyes.

"Is there a direction you're taking me to?" he said, "because if there isn't, I need to find a way to get to the Lake City of Cran`dk."

"We leave tomorrow for Cran`dk. I will get the release of the Taayra`Ge Keep Warriors." He turned to close the door; he bowed his head slightly in thought and turned to face Taelen.

"Captain, eleven winters ago, my mother took me in the middle of the night. The last thing she told me before the Lord slit her throat with a Mah`s blade was that a man with my eyes would tell me the truth. Tou`hia was the last word she spoke." his eyes stayed upon the Captains. The silence between them was a challenge; neither wished.

"Don't you think you've been silent long enough, Captain?" Taelen's voice held no hint of his emotions.

The door closed in a whispered sigh behind the Captain; his steps were slow and cumbersome. The Sz`a`Th Warrior sat like a man whose most intimate past was about to be revealed.

"Have you ever loved Lieutenant, that intense love that comes from someone who inexplicably feels like you? Sometimes, you're lucky." He smiled more to the past than to Taelen, his blue eyes smarted with emotion, and he looked away. "I am descended from the Imperial House of the Sz`a`Th, the older brother of two. Heritage is a destiny one can never escape from." He shrugged

"Mah`sden is my brother, an arranged marriage by Lore of Sz`a`Th, a woman I had been betrothed to since my Mhysting at sixteen winters."

Yassarn smiled, raising his eyebrows in the irony of life.

"But destiny became twisted instead of the woman of my soul." Deep sadness pulled his shoulders down, and it was a struggle to drag air to his lungs.

"My brother wed her as she carried my child. I have been told that my own 'wife' died in childbirth in the east when visiting her family a winter after our marriage. K`iaz was the perfect wife; she was a beautiful, talented, intelligent, shy creature," Yassarn bowed his head, "and

I should have loved her wholly instead of dutifully." He inhaled deeply and sighed.

"In one moment, I lost all that was cherished and given. Mah`sden murdered our father, something I am yet to prove to my people. Mah`sden removed me to the rank of Lieutenant of the Foot and sent me here to E`nihs Garrison, at the mouth of the T`hzic Straights."

Yassarn fell silent; he slid his hands into his uniform trousers pockets

Taelen was as silent as he waited for the Captain to continue.

"You see, my brother wanted me as far away as possible. I cannot complain that the 'Third Crescent Foot' has been a good mistress. However, as a 'Red Crescent,' we are as invisible as the caress of a summer breeze. I could tell you many things. But as far as the rest of the Sz`a`Th are concerned, we belong with the Death Watch."

"Interesting, but what happened to the child your brother's wife was carrying."

Yassarn looked at Taelen, "Any son of my blood was said in Sz`a`Th to be the child that would have the blue to white Mhyst. His Mhyst would burn white within him." His eyes held Taelen with such concern that the Captain stood and walked to the window, afraid of the emotions now rising like floodwaters through him.

"Did she have a son?" Taelen watched the Warriors' shoulders braced as his head rose to look outside at the clouds.

"Aye, she did" his voice was low. "I only found out my son was alive yesterday," Yassarn turned slowly.

"My birth name is Tou`hia; it is yours, Taelen. You are my son." Yassarn walked to the door; his hand rested on the brass handle, turning the lever down. He did not look back but walked out slowly and closed the door. He leant against the dense dark oak wood.

The Corporal glanced at his Captain. Teh`c's green eyes reflected the same green as the leaves of the Tisro trees that grew far along the dark grey coast of the Taayra`Ge Ocean, narrowed in concern.

Teh`c had been the only one who knew who the youth was inside the room. Anston had told the Captain when he had been standing guard as he was now beside the closed door. He looked directly at his Captain, who stood opposite him in the corridor.

"Captain, to be a father doesn't mean he will hate you." the Captain glanced sideways at the Corporal.

"I heard last night; Sergeant Anston has a voice that carries. I will not tell anyone, Captain."

"Anston does have a loud voice. I'll grant you that. But right now, I don't know I have gained a son who does not need fathering."

"Ah, you're wrong there, begging my youth. I don't think to father is what the Corporal Scribe needs."

"Oh, Aye, and you're an expert on this, Teh`c; you haven't spoken to your father for four winters. So what does Taelen need, Corporal?"

"Could be understanding or maybe just a good friend, Captain; the father thing will come when you both least expect it." Teh`c glanced back with a smile that lit up his olive skin. Two dimples appeared in each cheek, dissolving whatever reservations the Captain had stored away in his thoughts. "Taelen needs to see not just who you are in here," he said, tapping at his own heart. "He needs to see what we – those who know you, those who have served you. One day Captain needs to see the King just saying"

"Aye, Teh`c, you are right, of course." He walked a few steps away, "If anyone wants me, I'll be down on the beach." Teh`c nodded silently, chewing his lip.

"Aye, Captain," he said, softer than he would typically have addressed his superior.

Teh`c's green eyes followed the shoulders that seem not so broad now, and he sensed it was a confused man that left the room. The Corporal could only guess at the cyclonic myriad of thoughts that now had caused those shoulders to stoop.

He chewed his bottom lip again with the idleness of long hours on guard duty when thoughts wandered, and eyes slipped to a third eye. His thoughts saw the Warrior Scribe staring out the window behind the door that flanked his back. The youth sat in the bed, his hand resting on the box of Rowan wood.

Teh`c turned, his hand resting on the brass lever of the door handle. He inhaled the fertile earth of the origin of the wood and opened the door.

"You're Taelen, aren't you?" He smiled at the youth's reserve. "Feel like escaping this room for a while?' His dark eyebrows rose in a silent answer.

"The rain is only mist outside; it'll not harm." He watched Taelen's eyes as brilliant as his father's blue amethyst in colour. Taelen glanced around the room, then looked at him like the Captain had done only moments before.

"Aye, it will not harm." The Imperial Scribe replied as he tentatively swung his legs out of bed as the Corporal handed him some clothes.

"Here these are mine," Teh`c gave him his uniform," I have others, and you have none, and we are similar in size and height."

The Corporal helped Taelen dress. Teh`c stuffed the empty sleeve into itself and said, "I'll carry the tunic. The weather is mild, but you may find it cold down on the beach, but we will see."

Teh`c guided Taelen out of the dark stoned

Garrison. Taelen realised the building was a small coastal Garrison but as large as a Tavern with provisions for horses and forge; in all essence, they were self-sufficient. The Garrison was fortified strongly, and the magic wards of Spellcasters' wards prickled his senses.

The black limestone was constructed into a two-story Garrison fortified for the heavy winter storms of the southern ocean. The Garrison could house Warriors that it would need if attacked. However, he wondered why these Warriors of the Sz`a`Th were here; to him, it seemed a waste of workforce; why place the elite Sahn`Frwh this far from their duties?

Teh`c took them down a well-worn path to the beach where the ocean boiled and chopped with white cresting waves. The black sand of the coast seemed at one with the black-green of the Taayra`Ge Ocean. Taelen shivered from the coolness and the beauty of the area. Their boots crunched upon the freezing black sand.

"Here, take the tunic. You will freeze." He smiled as he helped the youth with the tunic. "It fits you well."

"Where are you from, Corporal?" asked Taelen as the Corporal eased him down on the rocks to rest.

"Far from here, I'm afraid." He said smiling, the two dimples bringing out a roguish larrikin quality in him that was difficult not to like. His black trimmed short. "The islands I come from are north, south-east, " he said, pointing across the crests of waves and the horizon. "Their name is the Archipelago of the Thes`q. The word means were the sunsets, and the moon rises." He smiled, dimples deep, causing Taelen to smile in response. "The sands are so white; that it blinds you on a summer day." He laughed. "You know, it squeaks under your feet when you walk upon it and is soft and dry like the talc mined by the Dwarf miners of H`rdn. The Ocean is magical, a turquoise mauve that seems to be an impossible colour, and…you have to like fish…fish…fish…" he laughed smiling broadly, "and vegetables, I prefer and miss crisp fried seaweed actually."

"Do you miss it compared to this?" asked Taelen, who then asked, "You believe in the Dwarfs?"

Teh`c eyes narrowed as he breathed in deeply; the icy cold fingers of the wind ruffled his fine black hair playfully.

"No different to the Sqh`xn Nation; some of our best Scouts are of the Wolf Nation." He watched Taelen as the lad stared out to the ocean and wondered what thoughts were there; for some reason, he liked the lad no older than himself.

"You'd be surprised, Taelen, what I have seen, they believe in the Nations of Man, and yet we don't believe in ourselves." He shrugged. "I believe in myself, do you?"

Taelen could not answer; the Corporal seemed to know more than he did, making him awkward.

Grey dull light of the washed clouded sky made his skin seem darker and his eyes more intense. He shrugged at his answer as he followed the movements of white and grey gulls overhead that looked motionless in the winds.

"No, I don't; my home is with the Sz`a`Th and the Death Watch." His eyes pained shortly at a memory. Taelen sensed the Corporal's discomfort and said nothing.

The Red Crescent moon that was the sign of the Sahn`Frwh creased in his dark olive skin as the Corporal squinted into the dim light of dusk. He looked along the coastline to their left. His green eyes watered in the cold wind.

Taelen watched the ocean's turbulence as breaker

after breaker crashed and foamed in madness with each beach strike.

"Corporal, why are the T`hzic Straights of all places along this coast now patrolled by the Red Crescents?"

"Good question…" Teh`c said with no smile upon his face, "I would put it down to popularity," Taelen smiled at his sarcasm ", you might say out of sight, out of mind. Besides, you never know when someone will wash up on the shore." He replied with a grin that confused Taelen more, but before he could think of another question, Teh`c had added.

"I will walk up there a bit; I'll not be more than ten minutes. I'll be in sight, so I'm not deserting you." He smiled slightly. "You will be alright?"

"Aye, I'm sorry if my questions…." Taelen looked down at his hand as he did when awkwardness overcame his confidence.

"You didn't; it's just my Father is an Elder, and I come from a large family even by my islands standards; nine children is enough. He had ideas he wished me to follow, which I did for a time. My father is good at what he does; being an Elder, he is just not good at being the father I needed. Sometimes I wish our relationship had been more of a friend than an acquaintance." He paused and looked intently at Taelen.

"I needed my father to understand and show that he cared for me more than he did for the affairs of the Archipelago's Council and of a tradition of the family's line in cartography." His green eyes glanced back at Taelen. "Sometimes, it is hard to forgive parents' inadequacies and harder for them to realise that sometimes children have their ideas to follow."

"Nine kids?" Taelen said incredulously.

"Mum wore the boots at home," he said, tapping his black matt boots—two sets of twins. Wait until you meet the Sxh`qn Nation. They have litters. I kid you not," he smiled broadly, his white teeth brilliant and dimples deep. "But I have to do a point check won't be long."The Corporal's footsteps crunched over the sand as he walked towards a dark shape near the cliffs to Taelen's left.

Taelen watched the white crests of the three-meter waves thundered down as they treacherously tripped onto the beach. The surf pounding the shore filled his ears. The hypnotic movement had him staring at the ocean and thinking of nothing, his mind void of thought as he watched the white foam and dark green kelp stumble and fall onto the sand.

"Here you are. Do you mind if I sit with you?" The Captain stood; his eyes were not on Taelen but the Corporal as he walked towards them.

Teh`c saluted across his shoulder with a closed fist in the Sz`a`Th discipline of approaching a higher-ranking Warrior.

"Captain, I'm returning to the Garrison as ordered; Taelen will need to be assisted back to the rooms when he's ready."

"Aye, Corporal, you have the orders for the Warriors to prepare for our return; Sergeant Anston and four of our Archers will be assigned to this Garrison."

Teh`c turned and left, walking back up the beach to the Garrison.

"He sent you, didn't he?" asked Taelen without looking at the Warrior who stood next to him as his attention watched the waves pound the coastline.

"Aye, he did, and I'm not sorry he did. I don't know how to be anything but myself and a Warrior; we have lost so much of the past; what I do know is that it is up to us two to begin. No one can help us come to terms with this knowledge we have just learned."

"Maybe something's, are beyond our choosing, are

destined." Shrugged Taelen, "I think it's time I went back. Captain, no ill respect." He raised his left hand to Yassarn; both looked at each other as Yassarn smiled and gripped his son's hand, hauling Taelen to his feet.

"Aye, you are right there." They both walked back to the Garrison. The cold T`hzic Straights boiled as the storm approaching at their backs grew darker.

"Aye…I am, as strange as it may sound, I know for once I feel like I have a purpose."

"Oh…you mean the ledgers that seem more truth than a fable."

"Fables always have some percentage of truth. Your existence is something I have ever prayed for. Your truth means a lot to me. I don't know if I can call you father; something will help me work out that title." He said awkwardly as he looked at the ocean torment with the coastline.

Yassarn smiled. "Captain seems to fit for the moment and will hide your identity and mine. Sometimes what we need for an answer is the last thing we hear, Taelen."

"Aye, you are correct in that." He said as his father helped him climb the rocks that protected the Garrison and the coast from storm surges and king tides that occurred in the season of storms that announced the beginning of winter

The stark black boulders were the most demanding rock formations along the coast and were the only thing that sustained the rugged coastline from total erosion. The thirteen rock monoliths formed a true bastion to the elements, each holding a name. Those names reflected the thirteen full moons of the calendar.

# CHAPTER 3

**Meet me at the Mariners Curse Tavern.**

The Warriors of the coastal Garrison of E`nihs changed their uniforms to depart for the Lake City of Cran`dk.

Taelen was given Lieutenant's rank that Sergeant Anston had said he had attained with his knowledge of Sahn`Frwh and that of the Sz`a`Th.

“I don’t agree,” Taelen argued. The uniform he had been given was of one of the Sz`a`Th Lieutenants who had died in a coastal skirmish two moons before Taelen’s arrival. He had given Teh`c back his.

Teh`c smiled. “I have to agree with the Sergeant here, Taelen. You speak ten languages of the Southern lands and two dialects of the Sz`a`Th, not to mention two sign languages. Your training as a Warrior has been extensive. To be a Sahn`Frwh’ is indeed unique; believe me, you will need those skills. The rank of Lieutenant is required under War Regulations, which as a Scribe you are aware.”

He smiled, and Taelen relaxed as he slid the two matt black blades into his boots. He glanced up and smiled slightly through his dark fringed hair that had fallen forward.

“We shall see, but I prefer the edge of my Quills than the edge of these blades.” He watched the man who was his father turn his back and pull on his shirt. The thick red scare ran two hand spans down his back and was as wide as a Warriors' palm.

“Who gave you that scar?” He asked without thinking.

Yassarn turned a little tentatively as he pulled on his tunic. His expression was unreadable as he glanced at Taelen.

"I disobeyed a direct order." His eyes stared at the Corporal as his fingers deftly buttoned his tunic. Taelen caught the look given to Teh`c and decided not to pursue his question any further.

"Why cannot I go to Cran`dk and register as a Scribe under the Scribes Guild? It would be simpler than going as a Warrior of the Sz`a`Th."

"If it were so simple, Lieutenant, believe me, that is what I would let you go as." Yassarn sat down on the empty bed and began binding the leggings of his boots.

"Mah`sden is well aware that you live, but he looks for a Scribe, not a Sz`a`Th Warrior, especially not one who is Sahn`Frwh trained. There are Warriors of such skills, but they are of the Death Watch and a few coastal Garrisons. This Garrison is manned only by the Death Watch."

"Then, won't he find it strange that I return to Cran`dk with you?"

"No, it is not unusual for Sahn`Frwh to come to Cran`dk to place an edge on their mental skills; all Sahn`Frwh are trained to kill with and without weapon or strength. You would have come there at some time in your life, and it is better to do that training when young."

Taelen went to pick up his backpack; the simple movement dragged his injured arm painfully sharp. The backpack fell with a thud as Taelen's groan drew attention.

Supporting his arm with his other, Taelen acknowledged Yassarn's; he picked up Taelen's things and his own.

"Believe me, we do this for your safety, there is a lot more to this than you realise, and all will be understood once we find the book".

"You mean the first book of the Seven, about the Lore of the Mhyst."

Yassarn looked at Taelen, frowning, shaking his head at the new Lieutenant.

"You know the book, but that's not possible."

"I'm afraid it is, as I have just finished deciphering the text. It is in the Backpack. I packed it as a last-minute thought before we left the Keep."

"I feel we may not have or find the actual book. Nothing is found with ease, and Mah`sden is looking as well." He shrugged. "We may have a few red herrings amongst all these books. I hope you like reading and scribing.

Come, we must leave; some things are happening before they are supposed to. And there are spies within the Sz`a`Th; Mah`sden is in league with the Necromancer Sorcerer Lord Nul`YK."

Two Sahn`Frwh Warriors helped Taelen mount his horse; Supporting his arm, he sat comfortably in the saddle as they rode up the steep black sandy trail that led away from the coast.

The inland sea of yellow-topped S`hyne grasses swayed slightly in a breeze hardly detected upon their skin floated by. Tall, pale grasses bloomed in early autumn with deep blue blossoms. That gave the Plains of S`a a nickname of the Ch`hi, meaning little pond. The 'pond' was, in fact, one thousand kilometres in all directions and boarded by the dark mountain ranges called the F`Hine Ranges.

The horses had no difficulties as they waded through the tall swaying grasses of the savannah. The grasses ended their growth spurt and waited for the winter months to bloom; any trails were now unseen beneath their height.

Captain Yassarn rode as the last Warrior of twelve. Teh`c rode on as Scout as they neared the black stone ranges of F`Hine in the late afternoon of the second day. They skirted the vast lake that held Cran`dk the City of Guilds; the trail snugged the higher regions' vast escarpments. The Lake City of Cran`dk could wait for the moment.

The village of RH`garn, curled like a cowering child beneath the perimeter of the mountains' escarpments was small and quiet. Taelen was intrigued by the warmth and generosity of the villages as they welcomed the Warriors more like family members.

Taelen dismounted with Teh`c's assistance, handing the reigns to an eager young boy to care for. The pain of the ride was etched in his eyes as Teh`c came over to him. Swaying slightly as a hot rush of temperature coloured his face, he said,

"Sorry…Teh`c" and collapsed to the muddied ground on his knees.

Teh`c raised his voice to Captain Yassarn's attention; both lifted the Scribe as the Tavern Keeper guided them down the road that had become a spongy moorland with the early rains.

The cabin they came to was on the fringe of the village, forested heavily by the tall trees called PI`tlyn, known in other regions as Fe`arn or Alder trees which had their protective powers.

These trees rose to enormous heights of forty metres covering the land in a canopy of darkest green. The rain came steadily down, though as a drum roll as a woman opened the dark oak door. At the top of the door was the rune sign of strength and protection. Yassarn looked into the eyes of a woman he had not seen for two winters; she looked from him to the Warrior in his arms.

"IL`ya" was all he said as she ushered them in

through the open door of the stone cabin.

Yassarn, with Teh`c aide, laid Taelen down upon the bed that the woman, IL`ya, had guided them. Yassarn then turned to the Tavern Keeper, who had carried saddlebags and backpacks.

"Here is one hundred B`harda. I know you will look after my men, S`hode. Thank you for this; here is an extra fifty B`harda to put my men up at the 'Mariner's Curse Tavern', not too much ale or wine, S`hode, but just enough." He said with a wink to Tavern Keeper, who pocketed the money and pattered the Captain on the back.

"Your orders, Captain, just enough to make them sleep like babies." He said with an earthy chuckle; he turned to the Captain as he looked at the ill Lieutenant.

"I hope the Lieutenant will recover." The Tavern Keeper left from the yellow glow of the lamps to the black of the night. Taelen drifted in and out of consciousness.

"Captain," she said, curtsying and smiling slightly ", it has been a long time Yassarn".

The room smelled of incense; a wooden wind chime sounded against crystals. The room had not changed much, Yassarn thought to himself.

IL`ya looked at Taelen. She watched as Teh`c removed Taelen's boots.

"I have asked too much of him already," murmured Yassarn's; "It is far too soon for him to travel."

IL`ya eyes of deep earth brown gazed at the youth on the bed, then at Yassarn.

"You will never ask too much of this one, my Lord. But he suffers a sickness from his ordeal. The Mhyst within is raging." She moved towards a locked chest carved in the rune scroll of the Spellcasters.

"If it is 'Mhyst sicknesses, I cannot help him,"

Yassarn murmured low.

"Destiny has brought Father and son together," she said calmly.

"You don't understand." He retorted, throwing his wet tunic off suddenly.

"No, my Lord, it is you who is blind." Her calmness always irritated him. She touched Taelen's marking on his chest after Teh`c had removed his tunic and shirt for comfort.

"This," she said, noting the markings on the youth's chest as the Mhyst flushed a soft grey. "If you do not heal his 'Mhyst sickness', he will die, and his path to you and the path he must walk for all of us are lost forever".

"You may be surprised." Her brown eyes seemed more luminous than Yassarn had recalled.

"No, you are wrong, IL`ya," his frustration hardened. "To satisfy you !'Witch' FINE! I will heal him, but you are wrong," he snarled, cursing her crudely. He placed his hand on Taelen's Mhyst.

Teh`c grimaced at the word witch, a word rarely used out of respect for the Spellcasters, but was not surprised at the no response from the woman before him. The Corporal had to hide his bemusement when she replied.

"If you wish to pass judgment on my craft, do so, but to call me a witch passes insults to a nation you know little of." Her dark eyes tilted towards her temples enough to make Teh`c wonder about her parentage. She caught the look in Teh`c's gaze and smiled at him as Yassarn looked up at her scornfully and grumbled.

"I apologise to those with 'pointy ears' Mistress, but to the craft, well to you, I shall apologise, but the Spellcaster…I don't think so, Mistress." He shook his head at her slowly and smiled, with wry humour, then turned his attention back to his son.

Yassarn closed his eyes and began to speak to Taelen in the ancient tongue of the Sz`a`Th. He could feel the Mhyst calming within the youth beneath his fingertips. The vibration of his aura eased. In the confines of Taelen's mind, Yassarn saw Taelen's mother, as she had been all those winters ago. Her hand held the youths.

Silently she pushed Taelen, urging him to go to Yassarn. He heard her voice as gentle and caring as he had the last time he had held her.

"Go, Taelen, your time is not now. Go, your father must guide the Mhyst I cannot." The purple-blue sprinkling of light particles swirled around the youth as he was alone.

"Taelen, come." The Captain's outstretched hand, as strong and as broad as Taelen's, looked pale in the dusky light of his mind. As their hands touched, Taelen's eyes opened.

"So, it is true". Taelen's voice was low but a whisper as the Scribe looked at Captain Yassarn and fell asleep.

Yassarn's hand trembled as it left Taelen's chest; he glanced at IL`ya. The Spellcaster smiled softly.

"Sometimes, with grief comes happiness; you now have a son." IL`ya placed a ring in his hands and closed hers gently over his.

"This is the boy's heritage, Yassarn; he must know his father's family are linked by the blood of the Elf, Wolf, Raven and realms you know little of. I am sorry; your brother's jealousy has caused so much grief."

He had not heard the word Elf spoken in her language for a long time.

She turned away from them, placed the dark, almost invisible cloth that had kept the ring for so many winters back into the large box made from the ancient wood of Fe`arn and locked it. The wood sighed as if the wind had just passed through leaves. Then the silver lock vanished, and the rune of 'Warrior' appeared embellished in silver ore in the lid's grain.

"It has been ordained, Yassarn. This ring he will wear."

"You …are your people always so sure of what a man will do and what he will accept from the Elves? And how does he explain why he wears a ring of the Elves may I ask, without having his head removed from his shoulders."

"Your blood runs just as red as mine, Captain. You know what is in that blood, do not deny your heritage or your sons."

"Mah`sden knows the boy is not dead Captain." She said, looking over half-moon gold-rimmed glasses.

"Aye, he realises the boy did not die in the Keep." His fair eyebrows arched questioningly at the woman before him.

"For his sake, let us pray that is not so. But Mah`sden is not a fool; it is that cousin of yours who is the council's puppet." She sighed." I am too old for all this again, Yassarn."

"Not that old E`rth Mother, just be careful who you view your political persuasions to; they might not be as swayed towards you as I." His smile warmed the room. "It is time you healed his other side, dear 'witch', I have healed his Mhyst; now you do whatever Spellcasters do" he spoke in mind speak to her, which made her smile inwardly to herself.

She glanced sideways at him. He had not lost his psychic ability. His mind spoke still as articulate as it had always been.

"I do not need the skills of the Coven to heal his

ribs, only the healing of the earth and the sky. I used the Mhyst to heal the Mhyst. Yassarn never doubts my healing skills, for I am Elf, and my alliance is to you, my Lord."

IL`ya began massaging the shoulder and ribs that; she had already healed while Yassarn had been repairing the boys Mhyst.

The following morning the sound of an axe cracking on wood woke Taelen; he slowly moved his arm that was no longer in a sling strapped firmly to his chest. The freedom and lack of pain and stiffness puzzled him as he dressed.

He moved to the other rooms of the cabin and found a woman.

"Excuse me, Mistress, but where am I."

The woman's long dark hair had a blaze of silver-grey coming from both temples. The silver streaks swept up into a long slender braid that ran the length of her spine. Her clothes were a strange colour, blue. Within the gown that held her slender waist in a small clasp of silver, she wore no other adornment except earrings that seemed made of the same ore as the clasp on her waist. They were delicate woven filigree and sat partially clasping the top of her ears, snaking around the ear to the lobe to a more finely woven teardrop.

She turned with her hands still immersed in the suds of the breakfast dishes. The woman wiped her hands on the dishcloth to remove the soapsuds. Then she turned slightly towards him.

Taelen's thoughts froze by her ethereal grace and beauty. Even at her indefinable age, she was desirable. Yet it was her eyes slightly tilted and the deepest earth brown that smiled at him.  Taelen could feel his ears burn; instead, he looked at his fingers to avoid her gaze.

"Come, you must be hungry, Taelen. Sit, and I'll get

you something." She set a place for him amongst baked bread and spice buns at the table.

"Why is he out there chopping you firewood, the pile over there would last all winter."

IL`ya laughed aloud at the obvious statement and patted Taelen on the arm.

"I wouldn't let him know that. Sometimes he feels, well, never mind what he feels, it will help, and that I am only a 'woman' is what covers his thoughts. Helpless, I am not."

She turned to pour him a steaming cup of broth and handed it to him.

"What would he be if all this hadn't happened?" Taelen asked her.

Taelen watched as his father's well-muscled back was only marred by the broad curve of a scar caused by a Mah`s blade.

"King", replied IL`ya simply, as she spread butter on thick fresh bread and sat him down.

He looked up at the woman before him as she busied herself with the dishes left by Teh`c and Yassarn.

"Will you tell me about the scar on his back? I did ask; he said he disobeyed a direct order?"

Taelen sipped the hot broth, enjoying the beef's saltiness that he could taste and began eating the bread. He cut another slice and scooped another cup of the beef broth. The fullness of the flavours seemed to hold him safe.

The Spellcaster gazed out the window, watching Yassarn swing the axe's double-edged blade through the air and split the giant log.

"Yassarn's men had been ordered to push on with a tactical thrust forward through the upper mountains last winter. It would have been suicide to go through with it. When covered in snow and ice, the escarpments are forested, deadly even for us who live here. The area they were to go to is one crevasse after another, even in the mildest winters. He had orders to do so, and as you know, orders are to be carried out. He chose not to. Yassarn knew the village had enough supplies to get through the winter snows, adding supplies for Yassarn's men and the occasional traveller. The winter last was unseasonably brutal. We had animals frozen where they stood." She paused, sighing, again and again, watching the axe swing outside.

"But Yassarn stood his ground, being the stubborn man he is, he said 'No' to Lord Mah`sden. Quite blatantly, I might add. The Lord does not take kindly to having any order ignored. Especially when it is his brother and in front of the Council. A Warrior who had been assigned to your father's Garrison here bladed Yassarn, bladed him from behind, one night as Yassarn stood his watch." She paused, bowing her head slightly.

"The wound was horrendous, Taelen; the Garrison was attacked in the night. How they kept him alive is with the Goddess Oracle above." She ran her slender hand across her hair, more from habit than to tidy loose strands of the dark hair.

"Corporal Teh`c rode here in the night through the worst storm, raising the alarm. He rode with a crossbow bolt in his thigh. The other half of the Garrison was here on leave." She shook her head as she recalled in her mind that night of heroic tragedies.

"Some villages brought Yassarn and the Warriors back to the village of RH`garn. Lord, if you could have seen them, Taelen. The Garrison had suffered heavily. Warriors lay where they fell with the Mah`s blades and their deadly handy work. It took six moons for your father's wound to heal."

"I knew if he died that night, all would be lost." Her

hands reached back and wound the braid into a bun she pinned with finesse. The Warrior who bladed the Captain also died, by whose hand, no one knows." IL`ya turned to him to find a smile on the Scribe's face.

"What"? She asked, embarrassed at his smile and gaze.

"Does he know?" asked Taelen as he dusted the fresh breadcrumbs from his clothes where they had caught.

"Know what, Taelen?" She frowned slightly at the direction of his question.

"How do you feel about him" Taelen watched as the colour rose to her cheeks as she blushed. Her eyes glanced at him.

"Something's are better left alone. If Yassarn gets to be King, the people will not want an unknown, and a Spellcaster sat his side."

"But you're not a Spellcaster, you're a Seer as well, but you are more…more than that Mistress…I just can't, at this moment, think of the word—something tugs at the edges of my mind. The way your eyes tilt upwards slightly, you are not from the islands to the east," he smiled more to himself than at her and said slowly. "And Elves are for children, are they not…because that is all that comes to mind when I see you…it is as if I knew you once, somewhere in time." He laughed, " Sorry, I am. I didn't mean to offend you."

"How do you know that only…" she stopped. "You, my young friend, have not offended me at all, but you will need to learn what you see…" she pointed to her forehead. "?The third eye is something I did not think you would have… and one day, I will explain the Elf theory." She looked back at Yassarn, swinging the axe.

"So, you're a Seer." He shrugged indifferently to her, "I do not see the problem", as he ate more of the broth. "You would make an excellent Queen, and your love for my Father would be important."

She stopped washing the dishes. Sighing deeply at Taelen's comment, IL`ya moved away from the sink.

"Thank you, Taelen. In an ideal world, that may be so. I will always love him; no one can take that love. Beware, you are your father. The Mhyst is stronger in you than even he realised. Dear boy, you will not be short with your body and looks with the company. Just be aware that a man has a woman's needs, but do not sire a child in every town. A child that is not wanted carries a deadly weapon."

"Why" Taelen pushed the plates away as IL`ya took them to wash.

"The Mhyst is a strange bedfellow Taelen; you were conceived of the purest love."

Taelen swallowed the last of the loaf.

"You are quite right there", he replied, standing. "But I'm a Scribe and a Warrior, nothing else, and I prefer to stay that way."

"Oh, and a Scribe doesn't fancy someone besides books?." She asked Taelen smiled the single dimple broadly on his left cheek and brought out a look that reminded IL`ya of his father.

"I understand what you're saying, Mistress, and I have heeded the past warnings. I will not be free with my seed till the time is right."

"Good," she said, "I felt I had to prepare you. Now go and get Yassarn inside before your Captain starts chopping my forest down. The other Warriors will be here soon."

"Aye, Mistress," he said, putting down the dish he had dried.

She watched them greet each other; they both had that smile women would die for. She sighed, they were so much alike, and she genuinely feared for them.

The following day before leaving the village with Teh`c and the other Warriors, IL`ya spoke quietly with Yassarn in the forest.

“The Elves Yassarn will always guard him.”

“I know your people will be watching. But they cannot keep him safe. He is a Warrior, Sahn`Frwh, for god’s sake.” Yassarn leaned against the tree's trunk, feeling the bark against his skin. Somehow, this calmed his frustration.

She smiled at him in a way that tore at his heart. Yassarn cupped her face in his large hands and just stared at her for a silent moment.

“Ah…my Spellcaster, what to do …what to do.” Yassarn smiled wearily.

“No longer are we young, my Lord…. aged and weary would be more precise.”

He held her in his arms. She fought with a vision that kept her mind frosting at the edge of her thoughts and beyond peripheral sight.

“Just stay safe, Tou`hia Yassarnma,y the elements be kind to you, beware Mah`sden’s wrath, he has ‘others’ working for him now.”

He held her close, breathing in the scent of her hair, reminding him of other days he had spent with her here, surrounded by the forest.

Yassarn pulled away slightly rough hands framed her face. His thumbs traced the tilt of her dark brown eyes.

IL`ya found herself wanting to pull away from those eyes of amethyst blue. Eyes she could not shield her heart or soul from, and he knew it. A knowing smile curled at the corners of his mouth.

“You Mistress are safe here in my heart, the hope in my soul.” His voice, husky with the emotional part of him, terrified her. The other part of her loved him eternally. He bent, kissing her deeply with affection.

They stood staring at each other, the touch of the kiss still pressing somewhere locked in their thoughts.

“Why, did you do that?” she asked, a tear escaping, burned at his touch to wipe the tear away.

“I need your heart and have tasted your fear; maybe…just maybe, I need to know that you love me?” Her eyes widened and leapt from Yassarn to Teh`c and Taelen, who were trying to look elsewhere.

“Ah, Captain, we will go on.”

“You will bloody stay where you are, Corporal, for the moment!”

“Aye…” Teh`c replied and shrugged at the Mistress.

Taelen suppressed the urge to grin and failed very well.

IL`ya relaxed, looking up at the Captain. Her eyes traced the lines of life on his face; her hands held him, and she merely said into his thoughts.

‘Have always loved you…always will.’

The Forrest gave them added protection as they made their way on horseback to the Lake City of Cran`dk. The last words of IL`ya weighed heavily in his heart.

Teh`c shifted in his saddle, watching the forest's shadows, an uneasy feeling settling across his own heart. He studied the Captain and the Lieutenant beside him as the other Warriors rode behind them. Something told him these two men would share the same path, and he was being dragged along with them. His thoughts stopped as he caught eyes in the forest, the figure of a young man, a longbow in hand, yet when he blinked, they were gone.

Someone else, it seemed, was along for the same ride as he, finding out who would be more problematic than protecting a Scribe and his Lieutenant. He would worry about the Dominion Lord thing later.

He watched as they rode. A Warrior stepped out of the forest 100 metres before them. He had never seen a uniform that was of mottled earth colours, he had no weaponry that Taelen could see, but that meant nothing.

This Warrior was tall, 6'4", he guessed in bare feet, but boots always made you taller, his hair dark sandy brown but bleached at the tips from time in the sun. His beard was the same colour, but a hint of red was cut short in the Sz`a`Th tradition. He stood legs apart and his arms crossed. He let out three sharp whistles with his fingers, just his thumb and index finger. Captain Yassarn signalled to them to caution, but it was Teh`c who called to Captain Yassarn

"Captain, it is Corporal T`tamu from the R`atogh Pack. I know him."

Yassarn had dismounted warily but relaxed when Teh`c mentioned the Pack with which the Corporal was. He ordered them to dismount and rest in the forested woods on both sides of their path.

"Corporal Teh`c, go order that pup to get his arse here now, my orders, we stop for a break."

"Aye, Captain", Teh`c dismounted, running towards the Corporal, who did not move.

As the small group of Sahn`Frwh Warriors made hot drinks and rested their mounts, Taelen asked his Captain, "Begging your pardon, Captain, was that wise here in this heavily wooded Forest?"

Yassarn smiled as he looked back up the path as both Corporals hugged warmly, slapping each other on the back and talking, for they were old friends.

"The Tal`iz Forest is a friend…one day; you will know that."

He tilted his head and looked back at Taelen.

"Those two have rolled out of every Tavern. Every compass point and borders, coasts and mountains, drunk, in fights, and fighting with each other. Corporal T`tamu is a Tracker of the R`atogh Pack and the Sqh`xn Wolf Nation. His Uncle is Lord Za`qrn – his mother is Za`qrn's sister…."

Taelen looked blankly at the Captain. "Believe me keeping track of family in the Wolf Nation is complicated. It gives me a headache, usually caused by Lord Za`qrn."

"Captain, you said, Wolf…?" Taelen watched the two Corporals cursing at each other for some misdemeanour he presumed involved a Tavern.

Once metres from Captain Yassarn, Corporal T`tamu saluted in the R`atogh tradition. Captain Yassarn returned the salute in the Sahn`Frwh culture.

"Sit, T`tamu, take a hot drink with us and tell me were you successful with negotiations with the Dwarf contingent at their Mines of H`Hgaer for the return of the Warriors that survived the Taayra`Ge Keep attack? And taken prisoner."

T`tamu sat down on his haunches, accepting a mug from Teh`c.

He looked at Taelen and smiled a grin as broad as his shoulders. Taelen had heard of Trackers. This was the first one he had seen. The Warrior's eyes were something Taelen had never seen before, not so much the tan colour but the diagonal slash through the iris. His earth brown eyes were slashed with a silver diagonal colour.

"There is a cost with the Dwarfs of the H`Hgaer mines. All Warriors have been sent to the closest Coven for healing. One was missing, and also a Scribe, female. The Warriors are most concerned with her safety. She has healing I have not seen but have heard of her; they called her Mistress Yhy`h, though the Corporal that is also missing is called Brae, and the opinion I garnered was if I find his corpse, it's not a great loss. Bit of bastard, from all I heard." He gulped the hot spiced tea. "From the intel the Warriors gave, Brae and Mistress Yhy`h, actually at the Lake City of Cran`dk, seems Brae did a deal with the Dwarves – he had to provide a feast – let's hope his kills were quick, the Tree's remember the kills of beasts, they do not forgive lightly."

His earth brown eyes looked at the forests around them, and then he looked up at the canopy. "Trees never forget…ever. Neither do Dwarves…don't ever play cards with Elves…." He smiled wryly. "But a Raven is still as good as their call."

The Warriors with Captain Yassarn looked at the towering trees around them warily.

"And the cost?" asked Captain Yassarn with a wry smile.

"Twenty oak kegs of lager and ten barrels of wine."

"And who is the cost going to can, I ask Corporal?"

T`tamu smiled. "Lord Za`qrn, of course – I have already heard his howl, but as I have other assignments, I am sure his bed is kept warm by a bitch or two."

He drank the rest of the tea, throwing the rest behind him and stood to salute.

"By your leave, Captain, I have other things rather pressing north that I must attend."

"Aye, thank you, you have saved a tedious affair that I owe you one with the Dwarves of the H`Hgaer mines. Nice to see you left with all your kit."

T`tamu drew his blade that circled his waist called AR`q. Captain Yassarn signalled his Warriors to stand down.

"Never leave my den without it, Captain," he slid the curved blade back into the leather band with such ease that Taelen thought anyone else would have needed a lot of stitches. “Besides, they know if I throw this, it always comes back”.

“Teh`c,” he said, raising his chin slightly and winking “, not too many bitches next time, but more lager.”

They watched the R`atogh Tracker walk into the forest and vanish without a sound.

Captain Yassarn gave the single to remount, and they were again riding through the forests with more respect for the trees than they ever thought they would have had.

Taelen spoke silently to Teh`c, ‘He, T`tamu the Tracker, is a bit laid back.’

Teh`c grinned his dimples deep ‘You want someone at your back in a battle, that Wolf will die saving you…and your proverbial arse, I have fought with him at times, in battle. I owe him my life. The bastard will always remind me when we are in a Tavern on leave.’

‘Wolf, I don’t understand?’ replied Taelen silently.

Teh`c glanced at Taelen ‘you will, there are more of the Wolf Nation intertwined in the Sz`a`Th, that even I do not know of, never underestimate them, free with their speech and ways, it’s a learning curve I sense you will take in your stride Taelen. Their terminology can be confronting and confrontational, but it's their language. Never call them a dog in jest, or it will be a full-on brawl and fur and skin will be lost.’

# CHAPTER 4

Before them, the City of Scribes lay. Cran`dk Garrison seemed to float upon the surface of the vast lake. The rectangular, slim-width design of the buildings of high bone towering white stone had the city resembling a cemetery of headstones. The rectangular flags that usually flew from each tall building were missing; their vibrant colour was gone. It made the city starker and chilling.

They rode across the limestone bridge that stretched a full kilometre. Narrow towers in the same design as the buildings supported the bridge. As they rode, their eyes were drawn up.

At spaced intervals were the heads of decapitated Warriors. The silence that shrouded the Garrisons' entrance made Taelen want to run. The stench of decaying flesh had them wrap the scarves of their M`lak delicate chain mail turban over their heads, anchored at each ear around their faces covering their noses and mouths. No one looked down into the water, lapping at the towers; the slow thud of flotsam unnerved even the horses.

Fear teased at the Warriors, as some recognised the faces of men and women they had served alongside Warriors of both genders fought equally in all the Nations of Myth and Sz`a`Th. These were Sz`a`Th Warriors, Spellcasters, not the Garrisons' staff that cared for them.

"This is not the welcome I had hoped for." Mumbled Teh`c as he stared at each head as they gazed down at them.

The Captain looked at him coldly, and Teh`c fell

silent as others. Yassarn stopped them halfway across the bridge. Only the wind and the noise of fighting carrion birds squabbling above the thud, thud against the pylons. No one looked down into the waters; dread told them corpses were making the sickening sound.

Yassarn stood up in the stirrups so the Warriors he faced could see him.

“I know none of you has any interests within this Garrison. I am ordering you to go back, warn the Villages you arrive. Just say the Mhyst has changed within. They will understand. I have prepared them over the past winter to prepare for this.”

He took a deep breath; “You have your orders. Warn Sergeant Anston of what has happened. And four Sahn’Frwh Warriors to be assigned to the Garrison, work out more manning with Sergeant Anston. I do not wish to see his face looking down on me from some spike. You are to go as far south as you can and warn all. Also, send this information to the Covens.”

He sat down slowly. As the sound of his men in retreat, the horse’s hooves finally faded. When they had left the bridge, he saw his Corporal staring at him. Teh`c’s green eyes studied him silently.

“Why Teh`c, did you disobey, and you Taelen?” Yassarn’s eyes looked towards the sand blocks of the Garrison.

“Your orders were pretty clear, Captain, but you see, the rank of the Warriors against you outranks you. We took a majority vote when you brought the term Mhyst has changed within.” Teh`c said with a wry grin.

The Captain frowned at the two remaining Warriors.

Teh`c’s dimples were deep as he grinned broadly at his Captain. “It’s my turn. It seems to disobey a direct order.”

“If anything happens to you, your sisters will never

forgive me," Yassarn said.

"That's the problem, Captain, she will forgive you, but she won't forgive me."

Taelen shrugged as his father looked at him. 'Teh`c has a twin sister and too many siblings.'

"I was coming here for specific reasons, remember? I am the only one who can decipher the runic texts that you need to read."

"Well, it seems I am stuck with you, both. These are orders, and they will be obeyed."

He lent over from his saddle and handed the clasps of Lieutenant to Teh`c. Teh`c disagreed, "I can't just jump from Corporal, with all due respect Captain, there are Sergeants and Staff Sergeants, Warrants. There are exams, stuff…."

"Teh`c, you have a swift promotion to Lieutenant; I can do this because we are technically not within the Council's field of jurisdiction, and we are at War. As a Lieutenant, you will obey orders, do you understand?" Teh`c stared blankly at the silver clasps in his hand. "Put them on, for God's sake, Teh`c. They were coming next winter; I have just brought them forward. No excuses, just put the damn things on and get rid of the Corporal clasps. I am about to use your expertise. If something happens to me, get to the Spellcasters Coven at Dunnh`SA and warn them what is coming."

He grasped his mare's reins in his hands and spurred his horse on. The three lone riders' hooves echoed across the bridge's length.

The Garrison was just as quiet as the bridge; they made their way to the Scribes Hall. They passed through streets that had been once a sea of colours. The many Guilds studied within the Lake City walls all had their colours that coincided with the flags of Scribes and their colourful apprentice cloaks, along with the colours of the people who lived and worked within the Lake City no longer. The streets were vacant.

The air was still within the vast high white-walled corridors of the Scribes Hall. Their booted footsteps echoed their arrival to all; Taelen wondered who would be there while Yassarn and Teh`c stalked slowly behind him, wary of any noise.

They entered the registration room. Light speared down onto the highly polished tiles of pearl white, illuminating the room with natural illumination. The hall was empty except for a young woman who looked to be sixteen winters; her head bowed as she scribed across a large ledger of information about Sz`a`Th Guilds.

She did not raise her head as they stopped at the large desk that dwarfed her.

She wore a grey gown with a square-necked bodice and an embroidered shield in a narrow panel at the centre, falling like an apron.

The cloth embroidered panel was in the deepest sea blue with the Guild rune in silver thread. They were worn over the white tunic and trousers of her Guild of Scribe.

Her hair was traditionally swept up in a white muslin hair wrap with a slight length of cloth that trailed down her back and, if needed, could be used as a veil when required for the visiting regions from the north or, if necessary, to protect her features both genders wore this, for even Scribes had their orders of the Guild.

Taelen stood behind his father, who spoke to the young woman on his behalf.

Without answering, she handed him a registration form for Scribes. She then pointed to the area to her left where the document had been filled out. Taelen followed Yassarn to the desk where they sat. His eyes lifted from the parchment to the young woman at the desk. He knew her; she was the girl on the ship that had healed the Keeps Warriors. She had been his most senior apprentice Scribe. Taelen called to her, silently whispering her name to her thoughts.

Teh`c stood slightly to the left of her. She glanced up at his face. Large oyster grey eyes held him firmly, deep sadness in those eyes that held him silently.

“Did you call me?” she asked. Teh`c turned to look at Yassarn and Taelen, his eyes wide and questioning. Then looked down at her and answered.

“There must be a mistake, Mistress; I’ve never met you before.”

“But you spoke my name Yhy`h, into my mind,” she said, confused and frowned, wrinkling the smooth skin of her forehead.

“It wasn’t the Lieutenant, young Mistress; I called you by your name,” Taelen spoke; her eyes swung to his voice. The fear on her face was not for her but them. She swallowed hard as she heard another enter the hall.

Footsteps resounded down the length of the long Registration room.

“Lieutenant, block the view of the Master Scribe from this Warrior who’s approaching.” Teh`c did as she asked, standing between them, so both were difficult to see.

“Yhy`h” The voice was loud, demanding and arrogant. All three Warriors instantly disliked the young Warrior and his cocky stride as he approached her desk.

“What is it, Brae? I am swamped with ledgers and no time or inclination to speak with you, Corporal.” Her eyes did not lift from the paperwork she was scribing.

“Lieutenant Brae.” He corrected her with a haughty sarcasm that even Yassarn had to control his fists that had turned white with disgust at the young man.

“Lieutenant Brae.” The Scribe answered with such a

chill in her voice even they felt cold the first wind of the Snow Plains of D`zac. "As you say," she said, "I am busy", ,,,,, and she continued to ignore him.

He lent over the table and held her chin firmly in his fingers.

"No, you're not. It's time we talked," Brae's stance was defiant.

"About the Taayra`Ge Keeps Warriors?" she looked at him squarely. "You said you would set them free from the Mines of H`Hgaer when we were brought here."

"But we are free." He said the look of cockiness ground into Teh`c's eyes.

"No, we are not," she stood standing.

"Those Warriors will die in the mines; their wounds have not yet healed."

"Then you should have healed them liked you healed mine."

"I did not heal you. Will you get it through that thick skull of yours? I did not heal you," she said heatedly.

Teh`c turned to the Warrior, leaning over the Scribe and her desk. If there was one thing he hated, it was the man who thought women were just for property and bedding. This one was one of them.

"I hope you aren't bothering the Mistress, Lieutenant?" His eyes narrowed. His voice was loud and cold as he spoke, "the Mistress is not in the least interested in you, and surely even you know when a woman is not interested in a man because where I'm from, even the whores know when they're not wanted. Can't take a hint, Lieutenant or are you just so egotistical?" Teh`c was fighting to control his anger. "The Mistress has made it quite obvious that you're not welcome with her, and I suggest you move on."

Yhy`h blushed as the unknown Warrior winked at

her, his dimples making it more difficult for her as her cheeks blushed deeper. She stacked the loose papers as Brae grabbed her arm; papers suddenly flew into the air and slowly leafed to the floor. She yanked her arm free from Brae's grasp and hissed angrily at him.

"Do not touch me. Don't ever touch me or hear me, Corporal Brae."

Brae backhanded her across the face splitting her lip.

'Oh, that does it', Teh`c spat angrily. "Strike a female with no weapon…you are a Qrenen Rodent. They eat corpses like you in one sitting!" his voice was as sharp as his blade.

Teh`c's patience ended swiftly as he went to her aide. Braes blade swung up, diving deep into his upper thigh.

"You just bloody stabbed at Sz`a`Th Sahn` Frwh Lieutenant! me I will slit you from breakfast to arse hole…." Teh`c felt his energy slipping." or not."

Teh`c could not believe what had just happened. He gripped his thigh hard, the pain having him fall against the Scribes desk. Thick red blood oozed between his fingers, quickly reddening his whole hand. Teh`c paled as he gasped with the movement of muscle against the blade. Ledgers and ink spilt to the floor as he slipped further.

Yassarn had seen enough; he pushed his chair out and went to his Lieutenant. He stepped into Teh`c's thoughts and said, 'This will hurt more than you will ever imagine.' He grasped the blade, pulled the short swordsman's short blade, and then twisted the blade out swiftly.

Teh`c groaned aloud, sharply slipping in his blood. He fell to the floor. His green eyes rolled back into his closing eyelids as he fell into shock at the attack. With the blade's removal, Taelen hastily took off his tunic, making a wad and tied it firmly on the wound, then swung the Lieutenant up onto his shoulder, carrying him. He turned to Yhy`h.

“Where can I tend his wounds, Mistress?” Blood dripped down Taelen’s arm and hand, falling onto the white marble floor. The dark red blood seemed savage and stark upon the white marble floor.

“Here are the Papers of Registration Mistress.” He said before she could answer Taelen.

Yassarn caught Brae's hand as the other blade sliced through the air at the Taelen’s throat.

“I wouldn’t ‘Corporal’ because that is the rank you will use if I have anything to do with it. You have two offences against you, the attack on both my Lieutenants. Not to mention your dealings with the young Mistress here and the detaining of… it, Sz`a`Th Warriors, in the Mines of H`Hgaer well, I’d think it over very carefully if I were you, you are in deep bloody‘shatter’ already. Want to try me, lad? Go ahead because your head will be from your body before you can breathe or blink.”

Brae glared at the Captain. The man gently held out his hand to Yhy`h.

“Mistress, I am Captain Yassarn.” He bowed slightly but kept Brae in his sight.

“She is with me,” Brae said coldly, eyeing all of them with suspicion.

“I will never go with you, traitor”, Yhy`h said, verging on tears. Her hands trembled as she crossed her arms across her chest. Her eyes stared at the blood spots dark on the pale marble floor.

“They are strong words, Mistress.” Replied Yassarn to the young Scribe and then turned to the Lieutenant in front of him. “Your name is Lieutenant Brae, isn’t it? You have a lot to learn about being a Warrior of the

Sz`a`Th. I know you were at the Taayra`Ge Keep."

Yassarn called out to the two Warriors standing at the door to the Registration room.

Both Sz`a`Th Warriors ran into the hall and to where Yassarn stood.

"Thank you for being so prompt, Corporals" he flipped the Braes blade. "I will return these to his Captain", Yassarn looked at the two Corporals. "Take him, please; he is to go to cells, solitary and right now. Or I will carry out the Lieutenant's threat of slicing."

"Aye," they said, leaving the room for the corridors and their Captain.

Yassarn stood with the young Scribe as she fought to compose herself, her hands trembling as she tried to pick up the papers that littered the floor like autumn leaves.

"His Captain is Rq`arnh… the X`n dagger is the choice of weapon," Yhy`h replied.

"Rq`arnh is a good Captain; how did he get that dangerous psychopathic piece of work, I wonder." He glanced at the Scribe. "You have dealt with him before. I can't understand why you did not use your Pal`thic art."

"Brae is under Lord Mah`sden's influence, Captain. My Pal`thic art fades when he is near me," he smiled at the young woman as she straightened the desk from training and habit.

"I wouldn't use that title if I were you when his people are close. They have been known to lose their head." He said sadly, "when did they start the beheading."

"Two moons ago, I'm told, but I found in a ledger that the killing began as soon as you left for the coast one winter gone."

Taelen cleared his throat; the concern on his face and the blood from Teh`c's wound thick on his uniform brought them back from their conversation.

"Oh, God's bloody storms, I completely forgot about you two," Yassarn said quickly.

"Thanks," said Taelen begrudgingly, his hand bloody from staunching the blood from Teh`c's thigh.

"Lay him on the table, and …" started Yhy`h.

"I don't think that would be wise, Mistress. There are many eyes in the Garrison. Here is no different."

"Then follow me."

They quickly followed her to an empty Warriors room and laid Teh`c upon the old reading table. Here Taelen removed the Lieutenants trousers. The wound was dangerously close to the femoral artery, and he cursed angrily.

"Teh`c, can you open your eyes for me."

The Warrior was now in shock and shaking uncontrollably with teeth chattering loudly. He nodded his head, affirming. His green eyes watered as he opened them. He closed his eyes tightly, squinting with the deep pain in his thigh. He was sucking air sharply through his teeth.

"The wound is difficult, I want you to listen to Yhy`h, and she will make the pain go."

Teh`c opened his eyes at the young woman and smiled slightly, his dimples prominent with the concentration. His forehead creased with the intensity of the pain.

"I could look at you all my life, Mistress," he said with difficulty, but the stress was tearing at his soul. The wound burned intensely as if a fire was within. Tears welled in the Warrior's eyes; a deep groan escaped through his clenched teeth.

Taelen nodded at his Scribe to begin. As he felt the Warrior's pulse run rapidly, he tried to slow the blood flow, it was the deep blue-red of a major artery, and he had lost a lot of blood.

Her spoken words flowed in the silken fashion of the Pal`thic into Teh`c's thoughts, relaxing him immediately. Taelen's healing of the Warriors leg began with one hand on the Lieutenant Mhyst design on Teh`c chest. He laid the palm of his right hand on the wound as dark red blood oozed between Taelen's fingers and over his hand.

His words began in a language no one spoke; rune was a language of the ancient healers and mystics that had started the Sz`a`Th Nation. Taelen's Mhyst went from purple to blue, fading to an iridescent white. Yassarn watched his son; he had heard the legends like everyone else of the ancients and their ability to heal in times of death and severe wounds that would leave a healthy person lame if not treated by them. Here, now, he was witness to a legend coming to life.

White light snow flaked down across the wound and deep into Teh`c's thigh, spreading a pale mauve light that pulsed through Teh`c's whole body, healing everything. Taelen removed his blood-coated hand and exhaled deeply as the light faded to blue.

"We are finished; I would like to put him to bed if we have rooms allocated."

Taelen carried Teh`c to the Garrisons living quarters in the guard tower; the narrow steps were steep, but the lake's view surrounding the city was breathtaking once at the top.

Yhy`h showed them to the rooms that the Watch's Sergeant had billeted them in their room slept four. The room was typical of the Garrison. The beds were bunks. Each bed had a separate robe and drawers recessed into the thick limestone stymies.

When Teh`c had settled, she turned to Taelen, asking him.

"Master, why did you heal Brae in the ship's hold?"

Taelen washed his bloody hands in the washbasin; his shoulders sagged from the healing and the arduous climb on the narrow steps leading to their rooms.

His uniform was soaked thickly, with Teh`c's blood that had drenched his chest. The pale shirt under his tunic was blotted angrily with the blood and resembled the wild blood poppies that bloomed in summer on the E`boda Plains to the north.

"One thing Yhy`h, I'm a Lieutenant; you will have to use my rank or name. I am no longer that Scribe at Taayra`Ge Keep" he shrugged. "No longer, you're Master Scribe." He said sadly.

Taelen ran his hands through his black hair and the short beard that had grown when he had left the Keep. He absently thought aloud why he had saved Brae's life on the ship. "One day, I might just need the murdering bastard." His tone was as cold as the blade Brae had stabbed Teh`c.

"Brae terrifies me," she said, turning to the Captain; large grey eyes pooled tears as she buried her head against his chest Yhy`h fell into exhaustive tears.

Her body shook and trembled with the moons of emotional and verbal abuse and physical abuse hidden beneath her gown, bruises that still held Brae's fingerprints that she had withstood.

"It's alright, my young one, you are safe with us. There is a spare bunk, and you are welcome to it tonight. I would rather know that you are safe than …."

Wet grey eyes stared up at him. "Captain, you are very kind. Thank you," she said and sobbed until she could cry no more.

"Please rest. Mistress," Captain Yassarn said, "I need to find Captain Rq`arnh, and Teh`c and Taelen will keep you safe."

She glanced from one Warrior to the other. Taelen was tired of the healing he had completed on his friend and closed his eyes.

Yhy`h curled up on the bed. A pillow hugged tightly to her chest. She rocked silently, saying Pal`thic Prayers.

Her oyster grey eyes stared at the walls, her mind blank from thoughts. Things seen could never be unseen, and the War meant more things that made her mind tired.

Taelen opened his eyes, blinking slowly; the room was silent except for the deep breathing of Teh`c as he healed in a deep sleep brought on by the healing of the Mhyst.

"I didn't know a Pal`thic could feel fear." He said as he watched her pale grey eyes swim in silent tears.

"Do Sahn`Frwh? "Asked in a whisper, noting the sign of the Red Crescent Moon on Taelen's temple. "I think it's healthy to be frightened, Lieutenant."

"Aye, it is, Mistress, but only sometimes…living in fear all the time is not good." He replied quietly and realised she had fallen to sleep.

# CHAPTER 5

Captain Yassarn knocked on the Lake City of Cran`dk, Sz`a`Th Captains' door and entered with the black blades in his hand.

His old friend's bent, the blonde head was still as he wrote a document that seemed to be causing problems, and Yassarn smiled.

"Some things don't change, do they, Rq`arnh?" His broad smile spread across as Yassarn watched his friend's response to his voice.

The man looked up with a reply on his lips to see Yassarn. He pushed the papers away and lent back in his chair.

"Yassarn, it is you?" He questioned with profound relief at the document now discarded, his quill back in the holder on his desk.

"Aye, it's me", he frowned at his old friend, "Have things been that difficult?"

The Captain of the Guards stretched his arms above his head, reaching high into the semi-darkness of his office.

"They are when I have Lieutenants like Brae in my company. By the way, how is Lieutenant Teh`c?"

"After the shock that he'd been stabbed by one of our own," Yassarn offered with his eyebrows arched. "I do not think he will forget Brae's face or blades for a long time; he is asleep. Taelen healed him." He placed the two X`n daggers in the Captains in the tray. "Nasty… choice of blades." He said, staring at the blood on the three-twists blade that held a fishhook design at the point.

"Aye, granted, Brae is a wild one. He is only alive

due to Mars`den's poison – get a cure for that, and I will kill him myself. Brae sliced off the Seafarer's arm; on the ship, Brae was taken prisoner like those taken from the Taayra`Ge Keep. Strange, though he was critically wounded with three crossbow bolts and was near death, someone healed him. It wasn't the female Scribe." He watched his friend's expression, but Yassarn was not about to give any of his thoughts away. "Any ideas as too, who healed him?"

Yassarn had his own, but he was not about to air them in the Watch.

"Word is Mah`sden boy is alive. The Sergeant of the Marines on the ship felt the Mhyst energy."

"I thought the boy died", replied Yassarn, not hinting at the knowledge he held.

Rq`arnh stretched out in the chair. His long legs grew in length as he stretched his feet, pointing them and then relaxed from a cat-like exercise. The leather, highly oiled, did not make a sound. Captain S`en Rq`arnh had begun as an Imperial Archer, a sniper whose aim was said to be a gift from those of the Nations of Elf. He never missed his target; his nickname within the ranks of the Imperial Archers had been Wind Spirit. No one heard him; no one could see him. Snipers have a short life if they live. If they do live, they go through the ranks like S`en Rq`arnh.

Yassarn had sensed his friend's tactics mirrored the Trackers of the Nation of Sqn`xn. A Nation of Warriors who could change their form to large timberwolves. He had never asked him, though.

"Aye, so did everyone else; there's a rumour you have a new Sahn`Frwh Lieutenant?"

"Aye, that is Teh`c," Yassarn answered.

"It's not him I am talking about; Teh`c's promotion is well deserved. That lad reminded me of us a long time ago." He said simply. The Captain's pale blue eyes watched his old friend.

"Why is the Lieutenant being registered as an Imperial Sz`a`Th Scribe Yassarn? I know he is Sahn`Frwh Warrior" The Captain pulled a sheet of paper out of his in-tray, showing Yassarn.

"Because that is what the boy is, his teachings were with the Lord down at the Taayra`Ge Keep."

"Then, why is A`hres on here as his birthplace, was he born at a monastery?"

"Aye he was, but the Lord, being paranoid because of Lord Mah`sden and under orders of the King, had instructions that they are, he was trained as a Sahn`Frwh as well, there are such Scribes thus trained."

He said as he wondered about the Monks and their connection with his son.

"Gods of the storms, he could have killed Brae in a heart's breath." the look on the Captain's face was not sympathetic to Brae's plight. Yassarn laughed at his expression.

"Aye, lucky, aren't you? He didn't; you'd have more paperwork than you already have."

"Well, he has to register, then, doesn't he?" asked the Captain.

"Aye, debatable, more paperwork if he had been killed by one of his own. And he has thanks to young Yhy`h. Just keep Brae away from her, she's young, and I would hate to think what he would do to her."

"Aye, I will make him a eunuch if he touches the lass without a second thought. He can keep his manhood in his trousers permeant or lose it. She knows how to use a blade, but evidently, Pal`thic's Lore prevents it from using them!" he paused, saying absently, "Makes sense why there are so few of them…for shatta's sake, I told her just to stab the bastard…."

Yassarn glanced sideways at S`en's comment with a wry smile.

Yassarn turned away and stepped to the narrow window; the lakes seemed too silent, he thought.

"Alright, now that that is out of the way, I saw your signs of 'greetings' on the bridge. What the bloody hell is going on here, S`en, and I need to know it all," Yassarn said, using his friend's first name.

The Captain's eyes of pale blue narrowed as he tightened his jaw.

"About a week after you left six moons ago, Mah`sden came on one of his fleeting visits. It felt, and I am talking about the Mhyst. There was something wrong, very wrong." He frowned, trying to think of the exact words to tell his friend what had caused so many Warriors and Spellcasters to be executed.

"Hell, it's like the Mhyst is tainted, evil, you know that thing, like enveloping insanity," he shivered at the thought. "When the Mhyst is still within a body that's died, leaving it trapped, suffocating the brain, so death is finally…."

He looked up at Yassarn, "It's like an evil madness that seeps into your soul, mind, body, and you're trapped. The man needs stopping. I know he is your brother, but I cannot keep making excuses for a madman." He stood, pushed his chair away, and leaned over the desk towards his friend standing by the window.

"The genocide atrocities, and that is what they are, have increased over the months, not only here but all along the coast, on the east side. He has yet to cross the vast deserts to the west. Vicious murders and attacks, things that happened when the Sz`a`Th was tainted four hundred winters ago, that we thought had died. Those things are happening again with Mah`sden. I have no explanation for any of this."

He took a deep breath and exhaled slowly. “I have ordered we evacuate, sending all the Garrisons' Warriors that aren’t tainted south to the other Garrisons and Covens.”

“I’ve asked to go to the Death Watch. S'li and the baby were executed four full moons ago.” He said, mentioning the death of his wife and child. “Hell is here, Yassarn. I don’t know what you want, but get it, and get out. I have orders to get the surviving Sz`a`Th Warriors out of the Mines of H`Hgaer, and I intend to do so immediately.”

“Those Warriors have been released. It seems the Wolf Nation is working, shall we say, separately from its present leader.”

“Well,” his friend sighed “, Things in that region are rather…Lord Zar`qn has his contacts and ways; it is a relief that Warriors of the Taray`Ge Keep are on their way to the Coven in the Castle,” he shook his head. “Something has changed on the wind, so to speak.” He said nothing more.

The lines around his friend’s eyes seemed more profound. Circles under the pale brown eyes were as dark as the winter storms. His friend had shelved his intense grief for his family in some hollow recess of his mind.

Yassarn felt a weight of a nation that, if left, would become a war within itself if it already had not

“My sympathy for S`li and the baby. I wish I had returned sooner.” His voice was but a whisper.

“It would not have stopped the killing of Yassarn. When tainted, the fever of the Mhyst is as fast as a lightning strike. They fight it with the Mhyst; their fever inevitably frays into insanity.”

“When do you leave?”

“Tomorrow and even tomorrow is not soon

enough," he said, "don't stay any longer than you have to, Yassarn."

The Captain of the Watch picked up a brown paper parcel, "Come let us walk the Wall; it is empty at this time, and there are things I must speak of."

The Wall was the last defence of the Garrison. Deep blue waters of the lakes lapped at the two-meter-deep white sand stymie six meters wide.

Yassarn stopped on the rampart where only the wind now walked in silent steps. He recalled being crowded with Warriors and market hawkers not long ago. Where the people of the city of Cran`dk moved with grace and contentment, knowing peace was installed.

Their clothes of blues, greens, and mauves of their respective guilds, some wore the white that the young Scribe had dressed. However, all wore shades of amethyst. The colours reflected the deep respect that Cran`dk had for the Mhyst as a belief and the Elementals.

The warm greetings of the past were no longer. Now the wind was cold and had a precise cut to it. The smell of death hung on the lake breeze like invisible flags. The heady scents of flowers, the burning of incense, the gentle tolling of bells, and the taste of spiced meats roasting from the kitchens were missing.

"Things have changed," he said quietly as they walked. Both with their faces in the wind, their hands clasped lightly behind their backs.

"A lot," said Rq`arnh. "But for the better, this," he stated, handing Yassarn the brown parcel. "This is the Ledger on Cran`dk. Should Lord Mah`sden retrieve all Seven Books of the Sz`a`Th, then we might as well slit our throats." Yassarn took the parcel; he glanced at his old friend.

"And what do I do with this? I am no Scribe." his

voice was level.

"Aye, that is true. But the Lieutenant that is with you is."

He stopped and held Yassarn's arm; pale blue eyes held Yassarn.

"The youth, Yassarn, and I want the truth this time, not some fabricated story." Blue eyes narrowed sharply at him.

"You have been a good friend and confidant when I had no one to turn to."

"I know that, so the Scribe that I have just registered, Yassarn? Few are Sahn`Frwh trained to the extent that that youth is."

Yassarn urged them to continue out to one of the flat rooks. The wind bit harder out here as they walked.

"More like 'who'… the youth is my son." He held the brown paper package to his chest.

Rq`arnh stopped walking beside his friend. He stared intently at Yassarn a few steps ahead as he turned around, their eyes locked.

"Stop gaping like a dead trout, Rq`arnh; you sensed his presence as much as I did." Yassarn was irritated with this insight into his past, even to an old friend like Rq`arnh.

"Aye, but I never put him as your son, for shatta's sake. You have to get him out of here. He is a dead man." S`en replied, cursing.

"He was a dead man the moment he was conceived." He ran his fingers through his fair hair with the agitation of a man who had no control over the past. Nor even the present and possibly not even the future.

"I don't know what to say," Rq`arnh said flatly, staring at his friend.

The Captain lent on the limestone stymie, looking down at the slight chop of the lake's dark waters.

"Congratulations, I have a son?" Yassarn's sarcasm bit into his own conscious. "Sorry." He said, surprised at the anger that had surfaced.

"So, do I ask how it happened? Because of a night of passion, for  sake, Tou`hia! were you thinking with your dick, not your head, for crying out loud?" Rq`arnh's crassness slapped his friend's face sharply.

He said, frustrated at his friend's indiscretion seventeen winters ago.

"Well, you're still as diplomatic as ever. Of course, I was thinking with my head. Hell, I loved her from the moment I saw her. I breathed in her scent. I knew all there was to know about her."

"You were widowed, your father murdered and that 'nutter' of a brother of yours..."

"Maybe I wasn't thinking." Yassarn cut in. "I was feeling the short beard that has grown."

"That's the most promising bit of news you've given me so far." He said, raising his eyebrows at Yassarn.

"Hell… I don't know; all I know is I loved her, and it was me who caused her death."

"Your wrong there; Mah'sden slit her throat.  It is time you stopped beating yourself up for something you never had a hand or a heart to do." He paused to steady the anger and frustration that he felt. "Shattas sake…. Yassarn! We all know that." He swore as the breeze on the lake picked up suddenly; the caress across his blonde hair was a welcome relief. He swallowed hard with the added knowledge he was about to tell Yassarn.

"There is no easy way to tell you this, and gods know I have thought of every word and the phrase I know. Your wife did not die in childbirth. Your brother poisoned her, causing the death of your unborn child and hers."

Both were silent; Yassarn stared emptily. The hollowness in his stomach ached. The breeze blew stronger than before, and he wished he could stand and scream until nothing else came with his grief and added knowledge of his wife's death and child.

"I sensed that to be the truth. I just did not want to believe it. Denial is a sad thing."

"So is the treachery of a sibling, who has destroyed our world and all that was the Sz`a`Th. He is not your family. Understand that bad blood is bad blood. I will die for you if I have to. But you must decide the highest mantle of the Sz`a`Th, Yassarn, and you bloody know what I mean."

Staring at his friend, both had joined the Sz`a`Th at the same time, both were now widowers, had lost their first child, and his heart was as heavy as stone. He knew the decision the Captain meant. He wondered whether he dared to do what needed to be done. His friend looked at him.

'Yassarn', he spoke in mind speak, 'Being a Sz`a`Th Warrior, Death Watch, we were told our choices were the hardest of the hard…not the easy of the easiest. Make the decision, or we are lost. I am with you, and when you decide, the hardest of the hard. Contact me use the old way' he smiled. 'Crows are such good messengers.'

Yassarn took a deep breath and just nodded his head once. 'A Coup is one thing, S`en.'

'Nah', he said, falling into the slang of his homelands to the northwest, ' killing Mahs`den may be the easiest thing you or I ever do. It would be quick, not how my wife and son died. You have my oath on that.'

Tou`hia tilted his head slightly, quickly removed a dagger from his boot, and handed it to S`en, who drew a dagger from his boot. Each took the others and returned them to their boots.

'You know we can both be killed in various forms, for this conversation under the boring title of Treason.' Tou`hia replied.

S`en smiled, noting the sarcasm of his friend. 'Aye, we have nearly died for bloody less for the Sz`a`Th, no offence intended – how many Warriors have parted with their dagger to relay an unspoken oath?'

'Too many.' Replied Tou`hia 'too fucking many. No offence was taken.'

'Aye, and you and I shan't be the last.'

They walked back to the Watch Tower that rose into the air. Yassarn entered through the arched façade, his friend still silent.

"The Death Watch, maybe the only haven for him, Yassarn." Their eyes met, "I'll say goodbye now for later on…." Yassarn nodded slowly as Rq`arnh squeezed his shoulder lightly, walked into the dim corridor light towards his office, and closed the door behind him.

"Excuse me, Captain", came a youth at his shoulder.

"Aye, what is it?" he said relatively short; his anger at himself would not pass.

"I've been assigned to you as your Steward."

"I think you're mistaken; that is the last thing I need."

Distracted, he looked at the slim youth with the black cap of a Steward on the back of his head.

"You're rather small to be a Steward, are you not?" his eyes strained in the dim light; Yassarn pulled the youth into the daylight.

"Yhy`h, is this you?" Pale grey eyes twinkled mischievously up at him. She turned slowly so he could see the transformation.

"Stewards don't wear lavender if they can help it." He said, smiling." The ones I know tend to smell of horse stables and pine if you're lucky. But they are a rare breed." His eyes looked her over, and she blushed.

"One thing, how did you know… flatten yourself," he said, trying not to smile at her ingenious transformation.

"Bindings, I used the same webbing as the ones on your legs." She answered proudly about the way she disguised herself.

"Why do these things?"

"Captain, I am old enough to realise that travelling alone as a female will only attract unwanted attention to me. To travel in your company with the two Lieutenants is only natural for you three to be accompanied by a Steward."

"Our female Warriors are leaving with the Captain as we speak. Who said you were coming with us?". Captain Yassarn's eyes smiled down at the young girl, who impressed him.

"Captain, I am not stupid either. Your search for the 'Seven Books of the Mhyst'. Would not two Scribes be faster than one? My Master may know some of the languages that are included in the Books, but I know the one he can never read." grey eyes of Yhy`h never left the Captains.

"Aye, he can never read the sixth book; only a Pal`thic can read words that are not written." He placed his hand on her shoulder.

"It seems we travel as four then not three." His eyes rested on her. "Just do not forget that under this illusion, you have achieved. You are a woman; I know my two Lieutenants will not forget that. Now let us return to our quarters, Steward. You have backpacks to pack and provisions, not to mention four horses to prepare."

The look she gave him was priceless. Yassarn burst into laughter, deep and warm.

No one paid any attention to the young Steward and the Captain; his long stride was kept up by the running of her feet beside him.

Yhy`h opened the door to their quarters But stopped as she knew there had been a lock on her departure.

Yassarn wavered and thrust the package at Yhy`h. His eyes pained as he spoke in 'mind speak' to her.

"Get the horses."

She saw the single blade of the Rapier slide through Yassarn's shoulder. The red of his blood soaked through the Tunic of his uniform.

"Yhy`h… Don't just go" he slipped to the floor in the room's darkness.

Yhy`h dropped to the floor to outmanoeuvre the man she could see in the room as he stalked her.

"I wouldn't try it," she said, "You don't want to hurt anyone, do you? Go, you are just so tired, go and lie down."

The assassin fell to the floor of the corridor. His body hit the stone floor with a thud.

Yhy`h tried to sense what Yassarn was trying to say in telepathy, but his images were incoherent. She could not get through the swarms of images that assailed her in his mind.

Warriors ran to the room. Looked from the Steward to the Warrior as they looked to the Lieutenant, who collapsed out in the corridor, to the Captain lying in his blood in the room. And wondering who stabbed who first.

The young Scribe lit the lamps. With the assistance of a Corporal, she removed the tunic and shirt. Lifting Yassarn onto the bed, she ushered them out, convincing them he would be fine with her Pal`thic insistence.

Teh`c opened his eyes only to close them again as the intensity of his head wound came home with the force of a double-bladed axe.

"What the hell happened, and who in God's name are you?" He groaned from his bed.

"Just stay there; it's me, Yhy`h". Teh`c, eyes followed the Steward's shape but had to look twice when she removed the skullcap from her head.

"Oh, Aye, and I am the bloody Dominion Lord…I'm afraid I have to disagree with you…." his voice seemed confused as his eyes tried to assess the transformation.

"I have never seen a shapely Steward, have you," she asked with a rare smile.

"Not of late and not smelling of lavender," he said, his cheeks dimpling. His eyes tightly scrunch shut with the throbbing in his head.

"What the hell has hit me? I feel like I have been hit with a broad axe."

"I'll heal your head later; I need you to heal the Captain right now. He's been wounded with an X`n."

"Just what I need, their favourite choice of weapon it seems to be, and where the hell is Taelen?" he asked, looking for the Lieutenant.

Yhy`h swung around in a panic. She held his shoulder firmly in her concern. A single crystal lamp lighted the room, and shadows lay in corners, but her senses told her Taelen was not there and not at the Lake City of Cran`dk

"I have to find him, Lieutenant." She said as she tried to pull away.

Teh`c grabbed her by the arm firmly and spun her to face him.

"Just hang on a second." Her eyes glared at him angrily as she tried to release his grip, tugging furiously at his hold on her.

"Let go of my arm," her tone was as icy as a southern gale in winter.

"NO." He said firmly. "Three things Yhy`h, one, the Captain is wounded, and only you can help him. Two, the Mhyst is tainted, and Taelen has gone Gods know where, and three, damn it, Yhy`h, I'd never harm you if anything, my sweet Scribe, I'd probably be stupid enough to die for you, or worse," he sighed angrily.

"That's four, not three" her eyes glared at him from the pits of her soul.

"Are Pal`thic always so bloody stubborn and precise?"

Teh`c, could not reach out to her. She had raised an invisible wall between them in her anger that he could not penetrate. She was as cold as the Snow Plains of D`zac towards him.

"Are you going to let go of my arm?" she said, twisting her arm angrily.

"No, I'm not until you say you will not go off in search of Taelen", gritting his teeth and fighting the pain pounding in his head.

"Will you two stop this arguing and heal this wound before I bleed to death or…just…" he lay back pale, sweat beaded on his forehead.

Both swung around to where the Captain lay. Embarrassed that Yassarn knew how he felt towards the Scribe, Teh`c let go of Yhy`h's arm.

Teh`c pulled himself out of bed. His head pounding, he reached into the trouser pocket of his uniform.

The Sz`a`Th Lore of healing was as intricate and detailed as the delicate veins that ran through the healing stones of his homeland.

Teh`c sat with his hand on Yassarn's chest. His skin tingled as the Mhyst moved from one to the other interacting and healing. Teh`c spoke in the dialect of 'Lin`eh'. The language of his homeland was more in the chanting melody as he said the words. He used the

Crystal Lore of the Sz`a`Th and his island home to heal his Captain.

Yassarn took a deep breath as the Lieutenant's healing finished. It always felt as though his breath had been sucked from him. However, it was only that Teh`c was a Dai`h or Halfling and not full Sz`a`Th, that his healing had such unusual power. Lore held that a Dai`h held the full strength of both parents.

“Even I feel better,” he smiled at Yhy`h, who just glared back from where she sat at the foot of Yassarn’s bed.

“Are you finished?” She asked coldly; as Yassarn looked at them both, he smiled to himself.

“Do you still have that parcel? “He asked, watching her reaction to Teh`c as he stood removing his bloody shirt. The Lieutenant had his woes as a dark gash that he had somehow received stuck to his shirt. He turned to Yassarn, who shook his head.

“You’ll have to ask the Steward to tend to that.”

He smirked, knowing what the Lieutenant would do.

“I would rather sleep with a Wraith Whore; I will seek help elsewhere if you don’t mind, Captain” he gingerly pulled the shirt back on and left.

“Should I go after him or open this?” her fingers ran smoothly over the brown paper that securely wrapped and bound the book.

“Yhy`h, it would do no good to do either; one person can only read the Book of Cran`dk; to all of us, the pages are blank, except to you and Taelen.”

“What about the Lieutenant?” she asked, her eyes on the open door still holding the image of Teh`c and his wounds in her mind’s eye.

“He will find solace with a sympathetic person, who will pander to his temperament simply because of his rank.” Yassarn lay back, breathing slowly, trying to relieve the pain, "He will cool down in his own time." He looked around the room for the first time.

"Where is Taelen?" He asked, staring at the disarray of bedding and belongings that, while showing a scuffle, had left no images he could detect of body heat and pain, not even his.

"I don't know, Captain; when I came in, you were both wounded. Taelen was not here; I assumed he was with you."

"So do I. Are the horses ready?" he said with a grimace at the thought of riding with the wound. Even though it had healed, the pain lingered.

"They are all ready," Yhy`h replied quickly.

"Then go find that hot head, Lieutenant and tell him we leave now."

"But you're not healed; he's not healed."

"And if we don't leave, my young Steward, we along with the Garrison will be dead, now go find him and let the Captain know that we will leave with them for the Death Watch."

She placed the skullcap back on her head, tucking the hair up and leaving when he added. "Yhy`h," he said, opening his blue eyes.

"Be prepared; this will be the hardest and longest ride. It is not something, and I mean no offence when I say it is not a ride for women."

Yhy`h frowned slightly and felt awkward. Deciding not to say anything, her grey eyes met his.

"I am more than just Sz`a`Th; I sense your moon tide phase is soon; you decide to travel either as my Scribe or my Steward. I know moon tides are, well, beyond painful, for a Pal`thic."

Yhy`h blushed slightly at his intimate remark. She began chewing her bottom lip.

"I will return, Captain." She did a nod to him and

left the room.

Yassarn found himself with his thoughts when she returned with the Lieutenant moments later.

Her hair was neat, its dark brown curling ringlets secured back in a single silver clasp. Yhy`h wore the winter pure dark grey over tunic slit to the hips and the black trousers and shirt of the Scribe; across her chest were the runes designed in delicate embroidery. The warded silver thread of the Guild of Scribes ensured that all spells and wards would be cast honestly.

Yassarn sensed she was awkward with her attractiveness as many girls are at fifteen winters; thankfully, he thought it was better than the flirtations and anger at any authority that some did go through. He smiled, recalling the confusion of male Warriors training of the same age.

In her backpack, he instinctively knew she carried the herbs she would need to relieve the pain of her moon tide—her quills and inks and the clothes she would need for such a long journey.

Her black cloak had the same silver and dark grey embroider that denoted the rune Guild of Scribes on the back of the riding cloak. On her black gown, she wore as well as the dark grey panel that was their apron. Thick and warm, she pulled on black leather riding gloves, the crest of the Guild of Scribes on their back.

She stood silently as Teh`c began to change his clothes, and Yhy`h turned her back to him for privacy.

"Lieutenant, have you forgotten there is a young woman present," Yassarn asked him

"With due respect, Captain, last time I looked, she wanted to be male, Captain." He said curtly.

"Not for the ride we all have ahead of us." Teh`c just grunted with indifference

Teh`c dropped his trousers, replacing them with

warmer ones; outside weather had begun quite ominously. He grimaced and swore as he tried to put on the thick undershirt of his tunic.

Yhy`h turned without looking at him and gently guided his arms into the shirt and pulled it over his head, then his shoulders and past the wound that had been healed by someone else.

She again guided stiff and sore arms into the tunic, deftly doing up the buttons and insignia of the Sz`a`Th.

"Thank you." He said quietly, watching the downcast eyes. He glanced at his Captain, who shook his head not to comment on her change of clothes.

"The Captain of the Watch has ordered everyone to leave within ten minutes; the area is to be emptied of all Warriors and staff. We leave for the Death Watch immediately."

Yhy`h dressed him in the same way she had the Lieutenant. Yassarn assisted in groaning from the pain in his shoulder.

"Let's leave; it will take three weeks to get to the Castle Dal`Qeit and the Death Watch." He said, thinking, 'if we get there alive'.

He also noted the drain of colour in the young Scribes' face, and he knew her moon tide had come earlier and more intense, and he felt for the young woman and the journey ahead of them.

They left for the stables in the rush of Warriors readying for the total evacuation of the Garrison. Pushed and shoved by Warriors in a hurry, Yhy`h's footing tripped in the mêlée; the Lieutenant's arm went around her waist as she stumbled close to a squad of running Warriors. She let him guide her to the horses now standing in the light snow.

Mounting horses in the snow flurries seemed ethereal as they all rode as one down along the same bridges that Yassarn had only earlier come across. The darkness made their departure even more intense as the moonlight caught on the death masks of the decapitated heads sitting atop spikes and hung from the flag posts.

A galloping, tight-drilled group of riders, turned away from the platoons' main body as they hastened their horses north and south to Garrisons and Covens along the eastern seaboard roads.

As they entered the not so well travelled forest paths of the vast GA`ryn Forest, the atmosphere seemed shrouded in an air of protectiveness. All Sz`a`Th uniform cloaks were worn so no metal would glint in the darkness to give them away. All grasped the tortured black rectangular scarf and loosely covered their heads to hide the Warriors' features and colouring.

The Warriors wore the fine chainmail Malak that covered their faces leaving only their eyes seen. Now that she understood why the Sahn`Frwh blades were matt black, their cloaks made them shadows and why their movements and training required them to move and track like the Elf in the old stories and language. She looked at the dark giants of the GA`ryn forest that hid them as they rode. The oaks were silent to her thoughts as her eyes searched the shadows around them.

Warriors rode with their black-gloved hands on the hilts of their blades. Yassarn and Teh`c rode on either side of Yhy`h; it had not taken more than a few silent words of explanation for the Lieutenant to be aware that the Pal`thic between them was in more pain than both he and his Captain had anticipated.

What frustrated Teh`c most was that she refused to speak and stared into the darkness and Warriors' backs in front as they rode in squad formation. The horses walked without noise, the forest silencing each step, each breath of man and horse.

Yhy`h's silence was the only way she could survive the deep, tearing pain that seized her deep within her pelvis. Her back ached not from the steady sway of the horse but just from the moon tide that seemed to hold her captive in a painful embrace. With one hand, she hooked the black guild scarf across her face. Teh'c could see the thick black eyelashes and glimpses of those large oyster grey eyes.

The Lieutenant tried to approach her on the first night, but she just curled into a foetal position on the ground where they camped. At times, he noted the palm of her left hand upon the closest tree as if she was listening. Teh`c watched her facial features of concern and slight smiles. He wondered if there was any truth in the language of trees and could those from the E`rth speak; he tucked the thought away and returned to his sweet tea at the fire lit.

The second night he knelt before her and touched her cheek softly; she could feel the roughness of his fingertips from the work he had been doing. His skin was cold, having removed his gloves before.

"Yhy`h," he began bringing a cup to her lips; she felt the heat of the liquid and tried to pull away. "It's a tea," he started sheepishly, embarrassed by his admission of her moon tide. "I've got this; it's to ease the pain."

"Oh, and what would you know of my pain." Her voice croaked as she spoke to him. Her oyster grey eyes stared blankly somewhere, but not where he was.

"Where I come from, what you are experiencing is something my mother experienced all her life. I know Pal`thic suffer the same pain, only three times worse. My mother's mixed heritage gave her no benefits except knowing she was wise."

Her grey eyes glanced up to him from where she lay; she considered the cup he held and whimpered for the first time as she tried to get to a sitting position.

"Here, use me." He said and sat with his back against the tree trunk she lay near. Teh`c arms held her protected as she leaned against his chest.

"Now drink this, my mother swore by it, and also this." He handed her a small pillow that sounded like soft grass, but it was hot, but not too hot. "May I?" he asked as she held the cup to her lips and frowned.

"What are you doing?" She seemed spent.

"You are not sticking that between my legs."

She was fatigued from the continuous pain and dull aching spasms that ripped across her.

He laughed aloud and smiled dimples deep.

"No… put it on your lower stomach; the heat will help with the pain." He said, and she let him place the small pillow beneath the tunic's apron she wore as he wrapped her winter woollen cloak around her.

"Now, just rest in twenty minutes; you will feel some of the discomfort lift. It won't take it all away, but it will take the intensity out."

She lay back on him; his body warmth heated her lower back where the pain was most intense. The tea eased itself by calming her, and when Teh'c mentioned it, the intensity of her moon tide pain had gone, and what was left was manageable.

"Your mother is a wise woman; why did she tell you about this? Why do you carry such a thing?"

"I have five sisters, Y`hyh, and one is my twin – seriously, you don't want to argue when it is their moon tide – besides, my people welcome it as part of nature and sometimes being empathic is not all. To do with gender."

Teh`c laughed short, more to himself than to what she had asked.

"My mother was a wise, warm, loving woman…

sadly suffered my father's misogynistic mentality and culture, that a woman's pain was 'just'. Gratefully and unfortunately, she died."

"She died just from this pain?" Yhy`h was incredulous that a woman could die from her moon tide; she had heard of complications but had never actually known anyone.

She turned gently and looked at Teh`c for the first time, then realised she had not understood him or how the female Warriors and young women and old seemed to hold him in council with their intimacy. She realised now that he was not womanising, as she had thought but actually giving advice. She felt worse now than before.

"Miserably yes, complications set in, and she haemorrhaged to death." He said, his voice strained with the remembrance of his grief. "She told me that no woman should suffer, and through her herbal lore, she taught my sisters and brothers this and that the same can be used for aches, sprains, wounds…but more intense where her teachings with me…She knew I was not going to stay. I miss her a lot." He shrugged at his loss. She shifted slightly and leaned back on him.

"Lieutenant…?" She whispered as the herbal tea began to relax her more, and her body lost its tenseness against his, and the pain eased, and the cramping had stopped.

"Yes"

"Thank you…" she said quietly as her head lolled against his shoulder.

"Yhy`h, do the trees…speak to you before you sleep?" He answered her quietly as he sensed her body fall into the restful sleep he had hoped the herb would bring.

"Not …in words like you and I, but emotions and images…they protect us…others watch…" her voice faded

"Who…?" Teh`c` asked, and he smiled as he heard her sleep rhythm.

Yassarn watched his young Lieutenant and the Scribe, remembering his friend's words of 'we are Sz`a`Th Warriors. We make the hardest of the hard'.

He leaned back against his pack pulling his cloak over his legs. He had just made the hardest of the hard decisions. Not to go into uncharted territories to find his other Lieutenant Imperial Scribe. He was Red Crescent just as all his men were; he was trained as hard or harder than the others to survive. He thought some rank decisions were stupid, some indifferent, and some just tore your heart out. His Mhyst marking tingled, this had never happened before, and his Imperial Scribes' words came to him in the flickering of the firelight 'Death Watch…' and the sense of a smile.

Yassarn sensed somehow that he would see that Lieutenant again and alive. He checked each of the Warriors and the young Scribe. It would be a long ride before they would be where they needed to be, and he needed them all to get there alive.

Sleep came slowly for the Captain; in the end, he slept as deep as any Warrior in a world where war had begun.

# CHAPTER 6

Taelen lay against the cold, damp limestone wall; little light entered the dungeons' domain. Rats as large as squirrels and cockroaches nearly the size of mice scurried through his cell. Their scratching seemed the only reality.

He had no idea who had brought him there or why they wanted him there. He sighed as he watched two dark greys, coated rats, watch him. Their eyes blinked slowly as their long whiskers twitched. The silence was equal to his.

Taelen smiled at these two, who held a small conference between themselves. His understanding of the squeaks intrigued him, which was more bravado than anything else.

Taelen felt the dampness and cold of the floor beneath. The mould and stale air made the bile rise into his throat.

Though dungeons of the Cran`dk Garrison had always been renowned for their coldness, they had their history of infamy; he was not at Cran`dk anymore; he had no idea where he was.

His fingers stretched

painfully as raw and bloody grazes stung in the moist cold air. Taelen looked around the cell, except for the door and the high window bars. Only a rusted iron grate in the corner was the only area of exit that he could see. He sat slowly on the putrid floor.

Two rats stared at him from their corner, not far from his face. Whiskers twitched in a silent language; their black pearl eyes blinked slowly as they watched him.

Taelen slowly sat up, resting his head against the limestone stymie; the pain in his head was sharp and piercing, and salt on the stone stung scrapes on his skin. Spiking him like hot sparks from an angry fire. The gritty texture of the walls felt natural to him as the rats watched him closely.

"So young master, you have laid long on the sacrifice stone. Who hates you so much that they drag you here? Is it the man who kills with no heart and bleeds not?"

"What crime?" Taelen mentally sagged more from the pain that threatened to empty his stomach upon the floor, stabbed sharply in his gut. "It is difficult to say," he said; back in mind, speak startling one of the rats scurrying behind the darker one.

"So you speak to beasts…." The rats' whiskers twitched excitedly.

"You are him… yes, you are him." Dark eyes shone within the rat's intelligence.

Taelen sensed the rat smiling. The thought amused him. But how could he speak to them? He touched the back of his skull, feeling tacky blood and hair, his nose wrinkling with annoyance.

Both rats suddenly scurried to a grate that Taelen had not noticed. In the corner of his cell, hidden by shadows, sat salt corroded bars. Absently he could hear the sound of surf somewhere.

"Young master," they said, darting through the corroded iron bars, "kick with your feet; if you stay, my Lord, the prophecy of the Sz`a`Th, has been nothing but a careless whisper for us, and he who watches you will not be happy with us, who he has trusted."

"Your Uncle wishes you dead," said the other rat as they watched him.

"You state the obvious, my friend, but what is my

prison," Taelen asked.

"To you, this is the dungeons of the Imperial home of the Sz`a`Th firstborn. You have no time, my Liege. Kick the grate."

Taelen shimmied across the filth of his cell, pulled his feet up to his chest, and kicked. The rust snapped where rusted hinges had held the grates drain door. He leant forward and tugged it gently, placing it aside. They scampered into the darkness. The rats were urging him mentally to follow them in haste. He realised rats had no patience, only spontaneity, and he panicked them with his slowness.

Red eyes stared at him. Urgency filled Taelen, cold and hard in his stomach. He crawled through the drain's opening and into the darkness on his elbows. He crawled into a more substantial drain where slime and stench meant decay from the castle's drains and excrement. Taelen entered the sewers of the Imperial Castle Zsr`n`Th, the home of the Sz`a`Th, his father's home and his once; he vaguely recalled the enormous corridors above floors covered in luxurious carpets and walls tortured in beautiful colourful tapestries. Still, it was not his home but his Uncles, and he was his prisoner.

Quickly he emptied his stomach, vomiting yellow bile across the rough stone drain. The three hours it took him to crawl out felt like six.

The cold, damp night air hit his lungs in an avalanche of sharp needles of nerves sprung to life as Taelen coughed violently. He waited until his chest eased back to normal and, in his pain, crawled slowly into the cold wetness that was grass and lay still.

The thick black velvet night stretched out above him. Stars he had never looked at before seemed to hold an exquisite beauty of life itself. He lay slowly regaining his breath; his clothes smelt like death and foul decay.

He was three hundred metres from the west wall that faced the vast expanse of the B`ryndi Forests. He breathed in the smell of the large Beech trees that were the primary growth. It was the snow gums of eucalyptus he needed.

The last time he had this view of the west wall was when he was six winters old, and his mother hurriedly dressed him for the voyage that would see her murdered before his eyes.

"A cabin to the east, she will come to you", spoke the rat to his mind.

"You said 'he watches me'…. who is this man."

"Oh… not a man, young Master no…no, not a man in the sense of appearance, but one who is of 'Homo Fata Alfar' you know who they are."

"You are speaking of childhood tales…Elves do not exist." He said with difficulty as a cough tried to escape the pain of his lungs.

"You still think with the mind of the Nation of Man; you have much to learn…you speak to us…who would believe such a tale…Dominion Lord?"

He rolled and stood to cough slightly. The stench of the subterranean air of the dungeons had poisoned his lungs; the burning in his grazed hands and head told him more than he needed to know. Taelen was tainted with the dark Mhyst of Lord Mah`sden; this chilled the very blood in his veins.

His steps became more onerous as he moved on through the tall trees that forested the lakes. Though the night's air was cold, he knew he was catching an illness. His body burned as he fought the fever that raged within him. Finally, after six hours, his staggered footsteps had brought him to the cabin.

The small stone-built cabin had two rooms. Taelen pushed the door open; the cabin was pitch as he fought to control the Mhyst so his night vision would assist his condition and surroundings.

Closing the Oak door covered in runes and silver inlay on the inside, he glanced at the fireplace someone had already prepared the wood, and he placed the dark crystal touching it lightly using his Mhyst. It glowed hot white, igniting the wood.

Shivering, he stripped, leaving the uniform where it fell on the floor near the door. Padding barefoot to the other room, he found the small bathroom, turned the taps made from dull silver ore, and stepped down into a deep bath carved from the stone. Tipping in salt crystals and oil the colour of deep blue, he smiled as he smelt the eucalyptus breathing in the scent. He lay exhausted; the fever burned deep in him as he weakly scrubbed the stench and filth away.

Slowly he extracted his body from the steaming waters. He fell into the bed that had been made. Nothing added up to the fact that no one was here in his mind. His head, thick with fever, burned his thoughts, curling the edges of his mind in darkness as he crawled into the bed and was asleep.

His fever broke at midday, weak from the illness that had raged within his body for twenty-four hours; he lay and only drank and ate what food and water were in the pantry that he could hold down. He collapsed into a deep sleep just to be woken by a young woman no more than fifteen or sixteen winters old.

She startled him, but he was still too weak to argue. His necked ached along with his ribs, and his boots with their blades were in the other room.

She said something to him, but he closed his eyes. The words he knew as his mind searched for the language of the Sqh`xn Nation.

"You must… go", Taelen opened his eyes, staring at

her.

"My orders are to meet you", her voice caught in the threads of his torn thoughts. The strange lilt to the words she pronounced drew him.

"By who…?" He asked. "And may I ask who are you? You are not Elf?" his eyes watering, blurring, and burning as he tried to focus on her. His own Mhyst was fighting its war with the odorous poison taint that edged like mould on bread into his psyche.

She frowned at the word Elf wondering why he would say such a thing to her.

He wished for nothing except to be left alone. As he opened his eyes, the young woman stood patiently beside the bed again. Her yellow-green eyes were strange and enchanting to him. Her head tilted from side to side slowly as she seemed to contemplate his words. Just like a puppy, he thought.

"No, I am not Elf…I am of the Wolf Nation, the Sqn`xn Nation Lieutenant. My name is Kurr`etun, which means one with silver paws, and no, I am not Elf. I doubt much that there are any Elves in this region. They would not show themselves even if we asked.'

"What? You have paws" his eyes closed; with the dull ache in his body that seemed to have a pulse, his thoughts collided into sparks fracturing the darkness he wished he could find in his mind. Not much was making sense, the only Wolf he had met was T`tamu, and they really hadn't held a conversation.

"My people are of the White Wolf Clan; we are of the mountains, not the plains." She added quietly.

"White Wolf, you said, not Elf, but you have paws…."

"Yes, is something wrong?"

"No Silver-paws, nothing is wrong." His memory seemed to shatter into tiny filaments of cold frames; he felt as if the night world had held him captured or was a 'Dream Caster' hiding in his dreams. "But who told you to meet me? More to the point, why am I here? I recall little except rats?"

Every joint and muscle in his body burned and ached. His body felt as if it was on fire. As if knowing his pain, she began sponging his face and chest. He grasped her wrist slightly in a non-aggressive move.

"You must go; only grief and harm will come to you here." Her eyes did not meet his.

He felt the coolness of the damp cloth sponging him. His skin was pimpled with thousands of goosebumps as he shivered. Kurr`etun ignored him and began again washing his body, cooling the temperature that now, to the Wolf Warrior, seemed to confuse his reality with myth.

"His name is Ariarki-Kika; he has a white blaze through his brown hair. He is the leader of the Sqn`xn Nation. He has ordered me to be your guide and take you to a place; my people call it Pa`le-mn Gap. He said your people call it the Death Watch."

"Also, Deaths Gate the Castle Dal`Qeit has many names", he whispered hoarsely.

"My Lord, I have noted that you wear the Red Crescent Moon of the Sahn`Frwh," she said, "Please drink this; it is not too hot, the drink has a sour taste, but it will give your body the rest it needs."

The liquid tasted like bile, and he could feel his stomach lurch suddenly, then nothing, not even pain, nausea left swiftly, and a headache.

Taelen sensed his head feel light and the sensation of floating high as he fell asleep. His sleep held no dreams, nothing entered his mind, and he slept fitfully for the first time since his escape from Taayra`Ge Keep.

The next morning he found the fever was gone, and

the only ache was a slight one at his temples. Clothes that were his, but it was the ceremonial first dress of the Sahn`Frwh and were laid out on the chest by the small window. He wondered why this uniform and where it would lead him.

Black trousers wore a thin blue stripe, and as the trousers, the loose pale soft woollen shirt was midnight grey fitted perfectly. Taelen pulled the dark grey near black leather boots and wound the webbing around his calf muscles. He felt the growth of four days growth upon his face. The dark black beard had been trimmed neat and close.

Taelen opened the cabin door and followed the sound of the repetitive thud of an archer's practice.

Taelen stopped as the young woman aimed with her bow straight back. Her right arm pulled back in an angle near perfect, and her left arm was straight, but the fingers were loose but comfortable. The twine touched her cheek lightly and was gone.

The arrow flew straight at the target, a tree trunk long dead, with a dull thud. Taelen looked beyond the tree trunk. He sensed others but actually, who they were was confusing him.

The young woman had drawn the shape of a Warrior, and each arrow had been a perfect shot. She aimed to kill, not to maim.

"You are an exceptional archer Silver-paw," he said and smiled as she turned to face him.

"Thank you, but please call me Kurr`etun," she replied as she walked towards the trunk to retrieve her spent arrows. The tree's deadwood only spoke in a wrench after a twist of her wrist and gave up her shaft in defeat.

She wore clothes that were, and he presumed to be ceremonial. Which Wolfpack of the Wolf Nation, he was unsure. He had not seen this uniform before. The Warrior in him noticed her step through the undergrowth, not disturbing or making a sound. Kurr`etun came towards him.

"You have paled my Lord slightly," she said, noting his weakened state.

"I'd rather you didn't say that…I am no Lord and don't intend to be one. I am a Lieutenant of the Sz`a`Th just call me Taelen; it's my name; my uniform gives me away anyway; where did you find this uniform?"

She lowered her eyes. "I cannot call you by your chosen name."

"Well… it's an order, not a request," Taelen caught the look of immediate subservience, "My apologies Kurr`etun, neither of us have asked for any of this." He said, tasting the bitterness in his own spit.

He stopped his amethyst; blue eyes narrowed immediately as they analysed the fall of land before them. Eyes full and brilliant, the mauve in his eyes caught the light, fracturing the colour like a bolt of purple lightning across a blue sky.

"Hand me the bow and an arrow, and do not make it too obvious or too slow, Kurr`etun," he said, "Are you expecting anyone?" His eyes darkened to a mercurial blue. He did not see that another set of eyes, green to his blue, had seen the same thing.

She watched his eyes glanced over the top of her head.

"Just don't move while I nock this arrow." Taelen pulled back on the string until it was taut, she only had to move slightly, and it would pass through her at this length. Kurr`etun's breath was shallow. Her yellow-green eyes stared as he raised the bow up slowly; she could feel the bow against her.

His eyes froze as the arrow flew out. The string

vibrated back into position. Kurr`etun listened for the thud, a short cry and the staggered fall of the Warrior.

"You can breathe now", he handed back the bow. "You stay here," he ordered Kurr`etun.

Kurr`etun crouched down, carefully picked up the bow, drew back the twine, nocked the arrow aimed, and released. Taelen swung quickly around as the arrow hit its mark.

The intake of breath of the second Warrior that had attacked followed the sound of long grass and twigs crushed underfoot. As the Warrior fell dead to the ground, Taelen sensed another close by, walking back to her side.

Taelen slid another arrow out and knelt down on one knee. He looked back to where he had stood previously, checking the fallen Warrior. He could sense the presence of yet another Warrior but could not see him.

The Warrior lying in the bracken was a man of twenty-two winters; Taelen closed the green eyes that stared blankly up the pale sky. Something about the dead Warrior troubled him; the uniform was Sz`a`Th but not what he was accustomed to.

Taelen opened the tunic and shirt to reveal the sign of the Mhyst. Why had a Warrior of the Sz`a`Th wanted to kill him? Unless he had the misfortune to be poisoned by Mahs`den.

His distraction was enough to see a third Warrior not far from him; he knew the young woman at the cabin had not. He stood, making an obvious target of himself. However, another had also seen.

The hair on his neck's back stood prickling his nerve endings as he walked towards the cabin. Goosebumps spread, running across his scalp. Taelen breathed deeply as he sensed the other, a Blade Warrior.

Instead, he cried out to her to get down; running back to the cabin, he tackled her, slowly rolling them repeatedly.

With her between him and the cabin wall, he reached down to the webbing of his boot to grasp his black blade. He heard the sound of the Blade Warrior's dagger pinning his shirt at the waist to the wall. His black sword left his fingertips, cartwheeling through the air.

The soft thud and the sharp air intake were all they heard as the Warrior fell dead to the ground.

"Don't move; I can smell the dagger's taint of poison." He said close to her ear.

Taelen cursed as he suddenly realised two more Warriors. The footsteps came closer as the swish of the dagger Warriors flew with lethal accuracy through the air.

"Shattas!" he swore loudly, "This is going to hurt," Taelen swore more for his benefit than to the young Warrior he shielded; he tensed for the impact of the dagger.

He could not move in any direction; the blade thudded home into his left shoulder and protruded through the skin of his chest cutting through an old scar.

Taelen moaned deeply, and then he felt his Mhyst sing within him.

A grey, purple mist-fogged his mind as heat and pain surged through his thoughts. He twisted painfully as his hand gripped the blade, reefing it out; the sucking sound sickened even him.

An hour later, he heard, somewhere, in his mind, his name. Hands undid his shirt and cut it away.

The wound was ugly as the poison inflamed the stab wound, frilling the edge of the injury black; his skin was dying.

"The Mhyst will heal." Taelen's voice slurred like a drunken Mariner on shore leave. Kurr`etun heaved Taelen away from the cabin. The darkness and safety of the surrounding forest aided in hiding them.

Sitting him down some distance, she began to tend the wound. Kurr`etun grimaced at the smell that permeated the damaged flesh. With the healing techniques of her people, she cleaned and stitched the wound.

She found a thickly wooded area near a creek where they rested.

Taelen sat down with his back against a large grey rock of granite; the sun had heated it through the day and now gave him some comfort as support and helped the wound in his shoulder deaden the ache that pulsed monotonously.

Taelen glanced across the creek's gurgling waters to see a Warrior similar in age. His clothes resembled those that lived in the forest regions called the Ten`ara Territories far to the west. The cloth, the shades of the forest, not the colour of sand.

The dark brown hair was cut short similar to his. The strange turbans scarf scooped beneath his chin and fixed above his ears by ear clasps that sat on the top of his ears. The clasps were matt black in the Warrior style. The Warrior walked through the creek waters to Taelen with a step that reminded him of a silent hunter. Taelen turned to the young woman beside him and realised she had stopped her movements.

"She will not hear my words or see me, my Liege, Lord Yassarn." He bowed to the waist as he reached the shore. "You will recall little of my coming, but it is I who watches over you; it will be I who dies instead of you, for we are linked by blood blended long before the Sz`a`Th became who they are today; your bloodline intertwines those of myth and man, you are he."

"If you are to protect me, you are doing a bloody lousy job. Why, does some Blade Warrior wound me, and why was I taken to the dungeons of Zsr`n`Th? And I am not he, I am no Dominion Lord," he groaned with receptiveness adding, "I am for the last time a Lieutenant of the Sz`a`Th, a Royal Imperial Scribe, and my name is Taelen, for god's sake." Taelen asked, studying the young man, whose eyes tilted slightly to his temples in the deepest forest green he had ever seen.

The youth smiled at him and intentionally ignored Taelen's last verbal outburst, his left eyebrow arched, and he nodded. "Lieutenant, too many questions for this Elf to answer, and I am not permitted to do so. These are for my Father to answer."

Taelen went to stand but found he could not and watched as the youth removed his bow and quivers. He knelt down, half squatting on the sandy soil.

The deep forest green angular eyes looked with gentleness at him. The youth held out his hand, the long fingers elegant and the nails neat.

"You have the hands of a Scribe, my friend," Taelen said weakly as he placed his own rough hand in the youths as a sign of solidarity. The young man smiled again, showing perfect white teeth. There was a white scar across the youth's forehead.

He had the strangest feeling then as they grasped hands that he would heal the youth one day, and he frowned.

"Why do you frown, Lieutenant? Have I offended you by this visit?"

"No…I just saw you wounded your shoulder."

The youth frowned and touched Taelen's own shoulder wound; he felt a lightness in his mind and in his soul. The Warrior spoke in a language so old, so sacred that Taelen felt a breeze through the Veil that separated one belief from the other. You can never comprehend that liminal space unless you sense, see, and think.

"The future is not for me, Lieutenant, but I trust the truth in your vision. I sense you shall heal mine just as I heal your wound." The Warrior fell quiet and seemed sad as he stared at Taelen. "Lieutenant, you must not worry about the future. It is but a breath away from each thought of the present."

Taelen reached out to the youth as he stood to leave. "Why did you show yourself to me?"

"You needed to believe again, in what once was Lieutenant, and to know you are watched…I must go, for I have kept you too long already, she will not remember my coming, and you will think me but a dream to confuse you, but I am not. I leave you with this." He stood, took a small clasp from his clothes, and crouched again. His gentle hands affixed the clasp to the inside of his tunic. He glanced up and smiled again. "Now I must go, Lieutenant. When all this is over, return the clasp to the deep woods surrounding the Castle of Zsr`n`Th, we shall meet, and elements willing, I will be there to accept it. But we will meet often; the Elementals intertwine our destiny path."

"Your name…?" Taelen asked quietly.

"I am called NK`las, Lieutenant… as I said, we will meet many times before the seven return to a protected place. And the Eighth is revealed."

"Thank you, NK`las, I pray I remember you so as not to be rude next time we meet, and I thank you for this gift."

The Warrior turned, walked through the creek's waters, and blended in with the forest on the other side.

"What happened? Why am I here"? He asked, very out of breath; his skin had paled with the touch of the

Elf.

"You don't remember what happened?" she asked, feeling a little confused.

He narrowed his eyes, glancing toward the sound of rapidly flowing water. His eyes only saw dark green boots leaving the water, which were not wet.

Taelen looked back at her; the Warrior's hands shook so much she hugged her knees, drawing them up to her chest.

"I don't even recall very much who I am, let alone who you are."

"You killed them, hacked them to pieces. Like it or not, and you were wounded." She glared at him; tears fell, and her voice cracked with emotion.

"How can I know? I would not do such a thing, Sz`a`Th Lore forbids such atrocities, and I choose to differ, for I am not wounded." Taelen hung his head; his fingers raked through his black hair. As if calming him, he had let the Mhyst control his emotions.

"You know your name and are a Warrior; your memory will return in time." Her voice held contempt for him and his actions. In the space of an hour or less, he had disgusted her; he knew it would take a long time for her to think anything kind about him if she ever did; for some inexplicable reason, this pained him.

Taelen stared at nothing. He knew no words could explain his actions. Taelen took a deep breath and shuddered.

"Well, it seems you are the only one who knows who I am. So lead the way, Kurr`etun."

Fragments of a frenzied Warrior came to him; he knew he had lost control of the Mhyst and felt ashamed of such a weakness that was within him. The anger that welled in him brought a brooding silence between them. A Warrior haunted Taelen's thoughts with green eyes, not the act he had committed to Warriors who wished him dead.

Kurr`etun somehow pushed him along in his dazed state through the Plains of De`hcct and into the sheer escarpment country leading to the Mountains of He`lian.

The beauty that unfolded below them as they climbed higher was a land of grey and brown of plains. Below the escarpment laid the vast forests; the sunset contrasted starkly into a palette of bronzed orange, ochre reds and deep plum purples.

The silhouette of the young woman stood featureless to his left. Her arms folded firmly across her chest in the act of disgust at him. She turned slightly; those yellow-green eyes were still icy as she guardedly watched him.

"We shall spend the night here." She said, "There is enough food."

He did not glance at her voice.

"I'm not that hungry," he said, "but thank you."

"Why thank me, Lieutenant?"

Taelen looked at his hands. How he wished he had stayed an Imperial Scribe, ignored by all. He swallowed hard, angry at the regrets he had.

"It is a need I have." He said, shrugging for his ineptness.

"What for Lieutenant." She replied a second time.

He looked down at his hands. Hands that once only used the blade of a quill to transcribe the written word. Fingertips stained with dark ink. Now he felt he would never feel the beauty of a transcribed document, only the hot stickiness of blood.

"For persevering with me," He replied with a quietness that surprised her.

"Lieutenant, I am obeying an order; that is all. I am a Warrior of the Wolf Nation, and all I am doing is following my orders", her reply was cold.

He stood up and walked over to her, but that seemed comfortable for them both at a forced distance. A cold breeze began to invade the region.

"What is the hottest thing you've ever touched?"

"That would have to be hot orange coals from a campfire."

"Yes," he said with a slight smile.

"When a Sz`a`Th Warrior feels the Mhyst sing within him. It feels like your blood is scorching with those orange coals from the fire. The very breath from your lungs is being sucked away by your blood boiling." he shrugged slightly. "Back near the cabin, I could not control the 'Song of the Mhyst' because the blade poisoned the stab wound."

Taelen watched the sky transform into darker colours as the dusk became night. "What would they have done to you had I not killed them."

"We would have been captured and tortured." Yellow-green eyes glanced sideways at him.

"But they would have kept you alive for their pleasure, and I don't want to think of my existence after that."

She watched the large eagle glide in the air currents swirling high above the escarpment.

"Would they have killed you?" she asked, eyes on the eagle above her.

"No…if anything, my death would have been a slow long death to suit Lord Mah`sden. Torture is a sick necessity to gain truth in War, yet it aids no one. To end torture, you will tell them what they want to hear. Just to stop the pain even if it is death which you know will be the result," he said and watched the eagle as well, wishing he could sometimes escape and fly away from all that had happened to him in the passing moons since the attack on the Taayra`Ge Keep.

"What do your people call this bird?"

"Zey`rnah", she replied, "Swift death."

"Zey`rnah", he repeated, rolling the lilt of her language across his tongue to savour as a vintage wine. "It is a magnificent bird."

"I will keep the first watch," she said to him without taking her eyes off the eagle.

"I would sleep if I were you" Taelen turned his attention to the mountains at their backs.

"You are not me, Lieutenant and I have my orders. I am not under yours."

"Fine." his voice was as cold as the wind suddenly coming down the mountain wall. "Be warned then."

He rolled over, wrapping his cloak around his shoulders and turned his back to her. The wound was healing quickly, but he could not shake the feeling of his Mhyst darkening.

He felt her anger staring him in the back and smiled to himself. He knew he was correct in assuming that she was feeling tired. She knew, too, that he was right.

Taelen woke, his eyes sharp. He had sensed the riders ever so faintly within his mind. He crawled over to Silver Paw; his intuition told him to ask her spirit with the Mhyst. Nevertheless, her sleep was that of exhaustion. Waking her would only startle her from such a deep slumber.

Lifting her across his shoulders, he was surprised at how light she actually was. Taelen began searching along the path ahead and saw alcoves the rocks where the cliff overhang of jutting stone protruded into a lip in the night light.

With the Warrior on his shoulders, he climbed midway with pain and difficulty. The cave he needed was but a small alcove to hide them both from the weather and the riders heading towards the mountains.

He lay down, placing the young woman between him and the rocky wall and covering them with his dark cloak. Within the shadows and under the darkness of late night, his cloak seemed to make them blend with the nights shadows.

The deep thunder roll cracked sharply after the lightning lit up the dark jutting escarpment. Taelen had chosen the height of the rock alcove so he could see and hear all, but in turn, they would lie undetected by those hunting them.

The sounds of horses came, as did more lightning and cracks of thunder so loud, it took his breath away, bringing a child's fear of storms.

A cry from one of the riders as his mount reared suddenly to the storm's ferocity.

"Lieutenant, we must stop", the Warrior yelled above the wind, "This storm is spooking our mounts, and the trail is too treacherous."

Taelen shivered as he recognised the voice of Brae. He shifted the Mhyst to cloak both him and the woman. He smelt the fresh scent of rain pocketing the parched earth of the plains far below them.

"Noted Corporal…. There are caves up ahead. Large enough for the horses, these here are far too small for us to shelter from this storm." The Calvary Lieutenant said, staring into the alcove that Taelen lay in.

Taelen closed his eyes and shut the door between them. He breathed more relaxed, safe within the cloaking Mhyst. As the rain teemed steadily in the darkness, he fell asleep beyond the alcove where they lay dry and protected. The storm dropped across the land with a dark taint that it was no nature's course but that of the Spellcasters.

Morning arrived, and rain fell without wind. The

change in seasons was welcome to those who lived in the vast region. He watched the rain that had replenished an arid land was still falling. The plains held a dark grey haze of moisture.

'Taelen', a voice within the Mhyst, his eyes snapped open. Taelen felt as though Brae's eyes stared coldly at him. A deep feeling of apprehension flowed through

"Who seeks the one called Taelen, for it is a common name," he asked silently, within the veil of the Mhyst.

"I will not answer to a voice with no name" his voice was cold.

Instead, pain surged into his mind, and Taelen coiled tightly, groaning.

The sudden movement woke the startled Warrior next to him, who scrambled to her knees, huddling in the overhang of the rocks escarpment walls.

"Taelen", she whispered as his eyes rolled, showing not the blue she was accustomed to seeing but the whites of his eyes. That had turned blood red.

She cursed as she climbed over him to keep him from falling from their hidden cave.

"Taelen", she tried again, touching his face lightly. He whimpered with the agony that etched deeply across his features.

"I can't", he whimpered to her softly, "A voice within the Mhyst is doing this".

"Damn your secretive bloody Mhyst Lieutenant," she snapped, "It will be your death shroud, Lieutenant. Push it out. Do it?" she ordered angrily, half straddling him. She dragged him onto the wet, muddy cliff ledge. In the pouring rain, she opened his shirt, exposing his chest to the elements. The design, the birthright of the Mhyst, the sign that all Sz`a`Th Warriors wore stared at her.

She placed her palm down upon his wet skin. The Spellcasters rain fell relentlessly. The young woman raised her face to the silver drops of rain falling.

'Rain of the Spellcasters'

'Heal this man of flesh and bone.'

'Warrior, Lord of all Dominions.'

'Within my grasp, heal his moans

'Elementals hear my plea.'

'I of the Wolf Nation beg thee.'

'Bring this Lord of Dominions home.'

'So Mote it be.'

The sharp surge of pain arched Taelen's back violently, burning into the woman's palm and into her blood. Searing into the dark recesses of her mind and his, she screamed in her pain as Mhyst begat Wolf.

The severity of the pain dragged her into the depths of Taelen's Mhyst. She saw him lying inert upon a field of deep purple Mhyst. Her movements were slow as if the Mhyst was holding her, possessing her.

"Taelen", she called out. "You must answer me," she moved closer, staring at him. Tentatively she crouched and rolled him over. Eyes so brilliant in their blueness blinked slowly up at her, endeavouring to focus on her face.

"Taelen," she commanded; frustrated at her inadequacy of Mhyst knowledge, she thumped his chest angrily.

"Wake… UP" tears welled in her eyes. "Damn you! You must wake. I'm here in this cursed Mhyst of yours." Tired, dirty, and soaked with his blood, she bent her head crying, angrier at herself than him.

"He won't answer you, Mistress of the Wolves," The voice, a Warrior's voice that instantly chilled her thoughts. Her instincts made her seek her blade from the webbing. Her hand ran down Taelen's leg finding his dagger.

Kurr`etun straddled his body so she could protect him. The blades held back against the length of her wrists, like a Wolf ready to pounce.

"Who are you?" she demanded, the man was deceptively striking, and he looked nothing like Taelen. Where the youth was dark, this man was fair.

But it was the man's stance, legs parted and arms crossed in front of him, the coldness in his blue eyes devoid of caring that terrified her now. This man before her was predatory, and she was his prey.

"I'm interested in who you are, my little furry friend" his eyes roamed unheeded and invasively over her body. She shivered under his scrutiny.

"So I interest you," he said mockingly,", You dear interest me.' His invasive leer chilled her colder than the weather.

He moved closed to her and Taelen. The young woman sent a silent thought to the Wolf leader. Gritting her teeth, she was not prepared for what had happened.

As she did, the man before her leapt, grabbing both blades. Taelen shifted beneath her weight as her blades touched his skin. The burning of the Mhyst song sent her reeling back off him.

Instantly she was on a cold, snow-covered plateau, still crouched as she had fallen. The blades were gone from her hands. Her hands went to her leggings at her boots. She sat back, relieved to feel the steel beneath the cloth.

She sat back, hugging her knees, with one hand grasping Taelen's just in case he left. Rocking back and forth, tears of exhaustion fell, then as tiredness eased her tension, she felt calm and safe in this strange place. The calmness of the cold icy plateau became a deep sleep and a dream.

She recalled the white Mhyst that was the Lieutenant, then nothing.

The Warrior's voice felt like a dark shroud and stayed with her as she woke. 'You are one, with the Mhyst. When your blades struck this man, his blood mixed with yours. The evil is now hunting two, not one.'

Kurr`etun wiped her hands; his blood had dried on her skin. As she washed them in the puddles from the still falling rain, she saw the cut on her palm.

"Curse my stupidity." Her anger did not diminish as rain-washed her skin free of both blood types. A design appeared. The spiral mark on the Warrior's chest was on her palm.

"Holy Goddess of Beasts, what the hell is this?"

"You shouldn't swear," murmured Taelen.

"I haven't even begun to swear, Lieutenant, and if you start preaching to me about that, I'll deliver you dead, not alive, to the Death Watch and not my father!"

She spun around and stuck her palm in his face.

"What does this mean?"

He pulled back her hand to focus better on it with a slight smile that did not endear himself to her. She snatched her hand back angrily. Taelen's eyes smiled, all the same, pleased that he had managed a reaction from her.

"Well," Yellow-green eyes narrowed impatiently. Still holding her hand, Kurre`tun added with a tone that would cut stone if allowed.

"I don't understand any of this. Who you are, why it's so important that you stay alive and…."

"You have my birthright, "he shrugged ", that in its self-will, probably be enough to make your blood curdle." His look of challenging response was a disappointment when she sat back against the rock wall.

"He said the evil hunts two, not one now" Kurr`etun glanced over at Taelen

"Does this mean I will die keeping you alive?"

Taelen stood up. "It's time we moved on," He looked up at the sheer wall of rock that was the cliff asking.

"How well do you climb?" as he pulled out rope and climbing equipment

Kurr`etun stood wiping her wet hands-on on equally sodden clothes.

"We will have to see, won't we, Lieutenant." She grasped the rope, making a harness for them both. "I shall go first."

Taelen stood as she began climbing vertically as if born to it. His black eyebrows rose in admiration for the Warrior above him.

"So, Lieutenant, who are you really."

"I'm the Dominion Lord" he heard a groan, then soft laughter above his head as he climbed, following her lead.

The black rock face steamed with rain. Both lost their footing on the slick and dangerous surface more than either wished to recall.

"So who are you really"? She asked him.

"Someone who likes a challenge really need to know I'm a Sahn`Frwh Knight and Imperial Scribe," he said, smiling behind and below her.

"Are you going to answer me or just play games?"

He did not answer as he pulled himself up and over the lip of an overhang.

"This thing, on my hand, I don't suppose it will come off, won't it."

"I'm afraid not." Was all he said as they continued to climb in silence and the teeming rain?

The cliff's lip was a welcome respite for both of

them as they hauled their wet and grazed bodies over the black rock.

Concern niggled at Taelen about the location of the Warriors who had passed earlier. He did not have to wonder anymore, not far. They came across their bodies. They had been for dead hours; the rain had drained their blood away from the terrible wounds they had all suffered. He mused the butchery was uncalled for, but this is what War does. He closed his emotions.

Taelen stood staring at their faces; all had a similar look, a question. He then realised that they knew who had killed them. Rain pitted down onto them, diluting blood into the pooling muddy trail.

He had only time to throw both of them into the mud and rocks, covering them as best he could with a Veil of the Mhyst. He and the girl looked as dead as the Warriors they lay beside.

Four Warriors on horses moved through the carnage. The Mhyst appeared over Taelen and the girl distorting their features as if hacked violently to death.

One stopped staring at Taelen and the girl studying their butchered appearance.

"Brae must have killed these two." The others looked over at their bodies.

"Aye," one said, "He's a mean bastard." He looked at the Warriors. "He is one I don't trust or like."

They all murmured their agreement in the rain, urging mounts forward and away from the blood-drained corpses that lay half-submerged in the quagmire.

Taelen and the girl lay silent in the mud and rain until he felt safe moving on.

Soaked to the skin and mud stuck to their clothes and boots, she led them a different way. This was her land; she climbed as agile as the mountain goats that lived there. Taelen was having difficulty keeping up with her intense pace.

She had discarded her cloak into an alcove where it seemed others of her clan had been.

That night she took them to higher ground than he had ever been before. His muscles burned, and his breath scorched in his throat and was short when she finally stopped them.

"Airs thinner up here, Lieutenant." She stated as if he didn't know.

A structure with narrow slit stone windows was carved into the stone into the rock wall's natural fissures. The heavy wooden door had only a carved design upon it. From what Taelen could see, there was no way to open the door, no obvious handle or lever of any description that was evident in the dark black wood.

Kurr`etun went to the thick heavy oak door and placed her forehead upon an inscription carved deeply into the wood. He heard the door open, wood scraping upon the stone floor. Entering into the darkness of a long hall, the only light glowed pale and yellow from a lamp she had lit.

"Welcome, to my home. Please, your room is down the corridor to your left,' she handed him a thick candle.

A man stepped into the light. Taelen eyed the tall man with a wariness that came from intuition. This man wanted something and was not squeamish about how he got it.

"Welcome, Dominion Lord." his voice was deep, and the statement was deliberate to receive a reaction. Taelen's' blue eyes held the man in a cold stare of suspicion.

"Well, that is your first mistake; I am a Sahn`Frwh Knight and an Imperial Scribe of the Sz`a`Th, the Dominion Lord I am not." Taelen groaned again.

Kurr`etun eyes swung to Taelen wide; he smiled and

shrugged to her; her annoyance at his indifference made his smile seem more full than it actually was. She had not caught the look that he had given the man.

"My Lord," said Taelen bowing to the Pack Leader of the Wolf Nation.

"I see my daughter has protected you well, if not a little soiled." Yellow eyes swept across Taelen's mud-sodden uniform.

Taelen instantly disliked the man before him; the arrogance and edging sarcasm had him give the man a questioning glance.

"I am here, thanks to Kurr`etun and her skills, not by anyone else's assistance," Taelen said firmly, not liking this man.

He also felt that father and daughter disagreed on many things; he was one of them.

Two women came in, bowing their heads to him. He gladly let them lead him down the corridor to the rooms. He was amazed at what he'd taken for a cabin. It was, in reality, the front entrance to a fortified Garrison of the Sqh`xn Nation. Cavernous in its nature, it tunnelled off in all directions reminding him of the termite mounds of the red desert region of Zar`it, built like silent towering red monoliths through the region. He mused good eating if you could dig into the impenetrable dirt towers harder than any rock.

The corridor was actually an east wing. Opening onto an open veranda that took the whole side to Taelen's left were impressive courtyard trees and shrubs that came with a well-planned and balanced garden. Enormous with a central pond and pool, Taelen stared as he slowly followed the two women who waited patiently for him.

A door was opened for him; the rooms beyond were spacious with furniture that was crafted in strong primary perspective, defined lines yet beautiful in simplicity. The two women bowed and left him alone. Taelen knew the lock would be unlocked, yet he sealed the lock on the door using the Mhyst.

He found clothes, of soft grey wool trousers that would tuck into the impressive boots and leggings. He stripped and plunged into the tepid waters of a large deep bath run for him. Taelen was soaked in the mud and cold the previous couple of days. Lying in the herb-scented waters, he wondered what the man he had met earlier had in mind for him as he scrubbed the grime. He thought of the Seven Books. His thoughts also lingered for his father.

The clothes fitted perfectly, which did not thrill him at all, as he would have liked to stay awake. The moment he lay down on the bed, his eyes closed. He realised he was not a guest but a prisoner trapped when he awoke.

The window stared out silently onto a cloud-carpeted sky. Jutting black spearheads of the mountainous terrain knifed the deep grey-blue thunderous sky threatening more rain.

Taelen could not shrug off the heavy morbid feeling. He opened the door leading to the expansive stone veranda; cold winds ruffled his shirt and tunic, which he had not bothered to do up. With close ties at the neck, the shirt flew waving in the wind over his shoulder.

Taelen studied the slender figure of the person walking toward him. He felt he knew the person, but the person did not match the person standing a few feet from him.

“My Lord, may I speak with you? Inside,” their eyes downcast, Taelen could not picture them. Her voice frayed by fear masked who she was to him.

“My rank is Lieutenant, and that is how I will be

addressed. Do I know you?"

"Lieutenant, my apologies, I need to speak with you immediately" he felt a tug on his subconscious mind. Frowning, he leaned forward close to their face. Only to see the red tear-shaped tattoo on the cheekbone.

"You're a Pal`thic," he said, frowning.

"Lieutenant," the voice cracked with emotion.

"Come," he turned from the peace and stillness of the garden back into his room and closed the door behind him.

The person began shaking. "Lieutenant," they said again, the voice cracking with emotion. Taelen pulled back the cowl of the dark cloak from their head, the hair was short like a Warrior, but this person was not a Warrior.

"Yhy`h…?" Taelen looked closer, bowing his head down to her height.

She lifted her face to his; those pale, oyster grey eyes and enormous pupils looked up at him. A tear slid slowly down her fair-skinned cheek.

"Your hair, oh Yhy`h, they cut your beautiful long hair." His fingers combed through the dark tufts. She tried to speak at his touch but burst into heart-wrenching sobs. He gently pulled her towards his chest; she felt as fragile as an autumn leaf. He could feel the bindings beneath the woollen gown; the bindings were around her chest, yet she flinched at his touch as he gently stroked her back.

Taelen pulled away from her.

"Show me your back." He ordered her slowly.

Yhy`h lowered her eyes and undid the buttons at the back; she turned to face him holding the gown of grey to her chest in modesty. Taelen cut the bindings free. There against the cream of her skin were the redraw welts of a vicious beating with a whip.

"Stand still while I heal these."

His fingertips traced each welt, each scar. Taelen felt her shiver under his touch. He released his healing Mhyst profound dark purple energy upon Yhy`h, and its light enveloped her.

Tingled sharply as it touched each mark, he traced the scare, and the skin turned silver.

The skin on her back was pure, no scars marred its flawless beauty, and he gently did the buttons up that gathered the gown-marvelling how smooth and pale her skin was. She turned to face him when the last button was finished.

"Yhy`h, I'm sorry for the …all he did" his thumbs wiped her tears away. She smiled sadly; her eyes reminded him of the Tali`z Ocean in winter.

"Do you recall when we were Scribes; we had that rat chew the chronicles we had to transcribe."

"Aye, how could I forget? It took twelve moons to complete," he said, looking at the angle of her chin and delicate high cheekbones. Her large grey eyes always mesmerised him, tilting slightly upwards at the temples. He cleared his throat and tried to concentrate on something else.

"You said it takes time and love to restore something so beautiful to its original beauty. I think it also takes a kind heart and true devotion."

"I did say that," he smiled at the comment. "I get a bit emotional over the art of writing, especially when we were in the Keep. But we're not in the Keep anymore, Yhy`h."

The Pal`thic frowned and walked to the window, her long graceful fingers traced over the dark stone windowsill.

"Taelen, you realised this is a trap we are in. Your father is here, so is Teh`c. He is a little worse for wear, having confronted Brae. He and other Warriors attacked us after we left Cran`dk; we searched as far as we could in the forests, and that is when they ambushed us."

"Aye," sighing heavily, "I realise this is a trap." Yhy`h back straightened as her head tilted to one side.

"How do you feel about his decree and his daughter?"

"I am in a position with no happy ending if I don't marry her; he kills you three. No doubt Brae would be the hand that holds the blade."

He sat down, holding his head in hands that now felt the burden of his destiny. "Hell! Do you think I liked being in such a position? 'Shattas!' he cursed in the tongue of the Keep. "Yhy`h, I feel I'm not in control of anything, not my life, yours, or anyone's."

Yhy`h turned around. Taelen sat, staring at his trembling hands. The white fury of rage shone around him.

"Taelen..." She kneeled before him; her hands clasped his trembling calloused hands. She smiled sadly up at his amethyst, blue eyes

"You are who you are. Destiny is not what we want. Personally, it is what is needed for now and the future. I know that you are who you are meant to be" her large grey eyes held his. Calmness ebbed into his soul as her eyes caught his.

"What 'if' I don't want to be this bloody person? Even the title sounds somewhat archaic" he snapped more from anger at his situation, frowning, confused with the suffocation of all that it entailed, he hung his head. His hands raked through his black hair.

"What if, Taelen 'what if' never comes? It is a bit late to say no, to such a title of destiny. You are kind, caring, and loving. I think the Great Southern Lands are ready for peace, don't you."

He looked back at her. His intense blue eyes held pain and loss and darkness that concerned the Pal`thic, for she had never seen the fringes of his own existence before. The foreboding was like a lengthening shadow; she caught her breath at his fear but said nothing.

“Aye, how many will die for peace at my expense if I choose such a weighty mantle-I don‘t want it, Yhy`h with all my being. I just don‘t want it.”

“That is where you are wrong; those who fight for peace do so with their hearts. No, those who die for peace do so because they believe it’s something worth such a great price as death, like you and me. There are others you know who guard your safety. We are all Warriors of some shape and form and training; we are who we are regardless of our rank, guild, or occupation. It's not the uniform but the person wearing it that is the key.”

Yhy`h smiled at him.

“What…?”

“I hear his daughter is quite lovely.”

Taelen screwed up his nose as she playfully slapped his thigh and stood.

“Oh, I thought you were referring to someone else; besides. I don’t know her.”

“You spent days with her, Taelen. Are you telling me you noticed nothing about the girl, except she’s a deadly aim with the bow!”

He raised an eyebrow and shrugged. Yhy`h rolled her eyes and said.

“I think you spent too long with books and quills Taelen Yassarn.”

Taelen shrugged again, jamming his hands into the pockets of the loose trousers.

“Why the silence? Is it because she is of the Hyarits`h Nation, which is part of the Pack of Sqh`xn

Nation of Wolves?" she shook her head. "Taelen, there are arranged marriages all the time."

"Aye, but it is not you being 'arranged,' is it?" his voice sharp with anger at the things he could not change. "Yhy`h, if you have been sent to pacify me into this marriage, you're not doing an outstanding job at it."

"You're a very rare man, Taelen Yassarn of the Mhysting; whoever you find to love, you will be given a gift, not a burden."

"So you're philosophical now, are we" he looked up with a questioning frown that made her laugh.

"No, I am realistic; you may love her like no other love that comes to you willingly. I would be grateful for one great love in my life."

She turned to the window, watching the wind playing with the crisp autumn leaves within the courtyard before her.

"So, does this mean Teh`c hasn't a chance in hell of falling in love with you?"

"He… well, I think your problem is greater than mine now."

"You are so wrong there, Yhy`h so, so wrong. Teh`c would die for you."

"He does not know my heritage Taelen, but you… Do not know yourself, and you should read up on Pal`thic's. You are the Imperial Scribe, after all."

"And you have no understanding what being a Pal`thic is…we are E`rthn, like Elves…" her eyes pooled. We live longer, change in ways that make people fear and hate us…one day Teh`c will hate me, and then and only then will you ever understand those of liminal space is as invisible as the caress of a breeze."

She turned away from the window, ignoring his comment as he had just ignored her.

"Your father and Teh`c need your healing, but I had

to tell the guards that I was trying to persuade you into this marriage. Taelen, I can't heal them; it is beyond me for some reason."

Taelen stood up and gently held her by her shoulders.

"It would have been nice if you had told me this earlier." He glanced out the window to the veranda to see two Guards glance in simultaneously. "It seems they approve of what you have done, but I think you should take me to them now."

When Taelen entered Teh`c and his father's rooms, he inwardly shuddered at their critical state. He was appalled at the amount of blood soaked up by the sheets in Teh`c bed.

"You should have told me, Yhy`h," the savagery inflicted on Teh`c and his father left him exhausted. Taelen knelt beside their beds; he placed both hands on each of their Sz`a`Th marks and chanted. A second healing like this was dangerous. White mauve light exploded into the room, cocooning both Warriors. He ignored Yhy`h's words as he intuitively healed both of them. His Mhyst energy was increasing, and this scared him. What if he was this god damned prophecy he denied with all his strength, it was the 'what if' that scared him to death.

Taelen sat back onto his haunches, his hands spread in support upon the cold tiled floor, his head hung heavily. Weary, he lay down on the large tiles of grey, feeling the coolness seep into his back as he laid hands clasped across his chest and his eyes closed, resting.

The Mhyst was a deep, dark; purple that swirled within the corridors of his mind. He followed, entranced by its deep velvet contours of liquid Mhyst. In wonderment, he observed, it was as if he was a child again, and his mother was playing hide and seek.

Taelen saw a pale glow from within the folds of purple Mhyst.

The Mhyst swirled around his legs and arms. As he gravitated towards the pale glow, the shape of a woman emerged. Someone he knew. His mother stood before him.

"You have grown into a fine young man, Taelen." She said to him. She was as beautiful as she had been, those last moments on the deck before she was murdered at the hands of a loveless husband. Her dark braided hair, her eyes slightly titled to her temples, now told him of the Elf heritage; he smiled to himself as he realised he was both his mother and father.

"You are your father in looks, but you are not him in thoughts, my son."

"Why have you come to me now, here?" he asked, his heart aching to hold her once more, protect her as the man he was, not the child he had been.

"Your despair has awoken the Mhyst, my child."

"I don't understand; the Mhyst is the Mhyst. There are no in-betweens."

"I speak of the white Mhyst that circles your father and friend. Your Mhyst is that rare one. Dangerous for it, it can be used to heal and to harm. Beware Taelen, the white fury of the Mhyst. It can give so much power to you that it can blind where it should guide. It is why Mah`sden your Uncle wishes you and the Sorcerer and deviates he is encircled by. They will try to entrap you at every move and will not give in until you are their prisoner to mould."

"You didn't come to advise me about the Mhyst; Yassarn can do that type of lecture rather well, Mum." He had not called her that since her death

She nodded her head slightly with a smile that broke his heart.

"Always, I have come to tell you that you will find the Coven of the Spellcasters within these mountains. It is there you must go."

"Why?"

"You are, and you will be Master of the Mhyst child of mine. Just remember, sometimes fate brings another who is a mirror," she added intuitively to his thoughts she asked. "Why are you so withdrawn?"

"We are within the Hyarits`h Nation. Their leader has spoken to me; I am to marry his daughter."

He explained all his fears to her. The Mhyst soothed his frustration at the problem at hand.

"How can I wed someone I do not love? I am but seventeen winters."

"Hush," she said quietly, "You are wise to feel fear, and do you not think this young woman is as terrified of you as you are of her? It would be an idealist to think love is romance and song, smiles and endless dreams. Taelen, love is the most difficult thing in this world to grasp." She took a deep breath and sighed.

"Yet, should you hold it just for a moment, it will give you more joy in that lasting moment than a whole lifetime can give you. However, remember that part of your heart that you gave will always belong to that love. Another can't replace it; every love will differ from the last."

"You're saying I should marry this woman to save Yassarn and Teh`c."

"Eighteen winters past, I married your Uncle to save your Father's life" a tear ran down her cheek as olive as his own olive skin. "I cannot tell you who to love or who to marry. That choice is one thing a parent can't do, for I am not your heart".

"You still love him, don't you?"

"With eternity Taelen, he is my heart's breath, which

has died." She sighed. "Think of the others, my son, but remember love is something undefined to keep, yet even hold for a moment, you must first let it touch you. Sometimes love does not even last eternity. Only our souls do; for a while, I am dead. He lives and just let me go to love again." She began to fade. "Remember, she is afraid. Nurture her, and your reward will be. You 'maybe' the Dominion Lord. Think about the word 'maybe,' for I see more than one." She paused, "Taelen, do not fight this, the Nations of Myth and Man have worried over such a Mhyst, but you are not alone

"Wolves, Elves, Dwarves, and Ravens, Mum, they are creatures of myth, not reality, and I am really quite fed up with this prophecy theory that I am supposed to be."

"My son, you are an Imperial Scribe, you are Sahn`Frwh, and more. You are well educated in history, politics, geography, diplomacy, and more; you will unite Man and Myth's nations like no other. It is decreed, just as Lord Za`qrn will become the enigmatic leader of the Wolf nation. He is your Uncle through the lineage of Wolf."

"I have seen his name in documents. I never realised he was Wolf. It did not occur to me that the man can take the Wolf form?"

"You still have much to learn, my son, your Wolf brothers Ji`rah and JA`rvis will teach, and your destiny does not lie, remember my words when fate happens sooner than you wish, to answer your question, what is Wolf becomes Wolf, what is Raven becomes Raven."

"Can I?"

"No, you are the Dominion Lord, Lord of Man and Myth. Accepting the mantle of the Lord of light and dark is decreed, and we all have an opposite, a twin."

He cried out her name and woke to the concerned

look on his father's face, his clothes damp with cold sweat; his breathing scratched his throat with each breath.

"How long have I slept, and whose bed is this," he asked, looking around the room.

"The floor would have frozen you, six hours you have slept…you dreamed of your mother?"

Taelen sat up, combing his black hair with his fingers and wiping the sleep from his eyes.

"Aye, I did" he was quiet; he thought it was more a nightmare. "Where are the others?" he asked, wishing to distance himself from words still swirling around in his mind.

"If you mean Teh`c and Yhy`h, they have been resting within the gardens of the courtyard,

Taelen swung his legs out of bed and moved to the window, looking at the grey sky outside.

"It still rains. The Spellcasters must have a call for so much lightning and thunder".

"It is said that great change is upon the land when such a spell is cast," Yassarn answered, his eyes studying his son more closely.

Taelen drank the cold water from the earth mug that Yassarn handed him.

"Where is the Coven of the Spellcasters?"

Yassarn looked at him, alarmed. His eyes, a shade paler than his son's blue eyes, were hooded as he glanced away from Taelen's eyes.

"There is only one person who would have said such a thing to you, your mother?"

Yassarn walked out the door to the stymied veranda, the wind as a welcome respite to the Captain. Taelen followed his father and lent on the wet rocks; the garden before him was awash with grey greens and browns, silver and white, as rain fell steadily.

His father spoke slowly as if the words he formed were sacred.

"Your mother was a Spellcaster, Taelen."

"She's a Witch?"

"There are 'witches', and that is a derogatory term. They are Spellcasters. She also had the blood of the Elf in her. What stands between both is a fine line. There is a difference. Subtle as it is, there is one".

"Can I cast spells…Elf, you say as, in the children's fables, she said you have Wolf lineage?" Somewhere he saw deep green eyes smile at him. He frowned, not knowing if this was a memory or a fleeting thought caught.

"Aye, the Sz`a`Th lineage has Wolf, Elf, others, but Spellcasting, I don't know - I've never thought about you like that, but the Elf was always elusive." His tone changed to concern. "I hope this isn't obvious to Mah`sden; my brother is someone who would get the last drop of blood out of you just to see if you really would die." Taelen shivered at the memory of a man he grew up to believe by six winters to be his father.

"Changing the subject, I hear you're getting married." One look at his son's face had the Sz`a`Th Warrior laughing aloud. "Come, Taelen, she can't be that unappealing, can she?" he felt for his son, they were prisoners, and this was Mah`sden's handy work; he hoped the bastard of a brother was not coming.

"I am too young to get married, and arranged marriage sticks like vomit in my throat." He snapped at his father.

"I should tell you, and you're married to her; the Lord took the liberty as you slept."

Taelen threw the mug out into the courtyard in anger. His father remained silent.

The screaming broke the moment as breaking

furniture ripped their thoughts away.

"Teh`c, Yhy`h?" Yassarn shook his head. His feet were already striding into a run. Taelen, following his father, rounded the veranda corner to face two guards as furniture battered the door, and then there was silence.

"Open the door" Taelen glared at them as his voice boomed in a fury. His hands held in tight fists, he growled as he gritted his teeth-baring them.

"Sorry, my Lord, that is not possible. We have tried. It is barred from inside."

"I don't give a shatters in hell if bloody wards bare it; open the bloody thing and now!"

Taelen felt prickling across his skin, numbing his mind as he saw a white flare across his vision. His heart pounded in his chest. Part of him panicked, screaming for it to stop, but the other part of him, through his terror to one side, held him firmly in a grip that he sensed would strangle him if he did not let it flow forward.

Yassarn saw the faint white glow of the Mhyst behind Taelen's eyes. His son did not hear anyone as the Mhyst took control, and the door exploded behind the Guard's backs. The force threw the Guards to either side.

Inside he found the twisted body of Kurr`etun on the tiled floor. Beyond the dark golden eyes glowed coldly, he heard a low guttural growl, and then a leap out of the darkness came directly at him.

The Mhyst swirled darker than it ever had before. Guards and Yassarn, unable to move for what was happening before them, was a battle between Mhyst and Wolf.

The Hyarits`h Lord folded down onto himself, becoming the sizeable black-brown timber Wolf his well-muscled legs and enormous paws padded silently with his head down, and fur rose to the ridge along his spine. He stalked Taelen for death, not life.

Lips drawn back showed enormous canine teeth that would easily dismember the Sz`a`Th Warrior, saliva drooled down in thick threads from the mouth of the Wolf.

Taelen lent down for the two matt black daggers in his boots. His fingers felt nothing but empty pouches where the blades should have been. He sensed the Wolf laugh in his mind.

'So you are the one Mah`sden stalks, a boy of seventeen winters, a Scribe…an easier prey than I could have wished for.' Taelen's skin crawled as the Hyarits`h Lord entered his thoughts

'Again, you show me how your ego has shadowed your intelligence. I am Sz`a`Th, Sahn Frwh Red Crescent, and a Warrior, a Lieutenant Imperial Scribe, and you are nothing but an egotistical fool; you have the wrong information.'

A howling rose through the air. High pitched and long sound had the fine hairs along many a Warrior freeze spines.

Only one would leave the room alive, and all hoped it would be the young Scribe.

Iridescent white light exploded from the room. The oak door where others had taken refuge blew out as wood splinted and rained planks and sawdust down the corridor now exposed.

They peered into the demolished room. Fine grey dust filtered down on one of the Warrior's remains in a twisted, bloodied, unnatural pose over the large tiles that were on the floor. The other stood, his clothes hanging in tatters covered in grey dust, blood covering his body, holding a young woman dead in his arms.

The young Sz`a`Th Warrior was covered in blood from head to boot; Taelen stood, not knowing what to do next.

Yassarn instinctively went to his son, gently prising the young woman from his arms and then nodding for Yhy`h to enter and coax his son from the room.

Taelen moved with wooden steps. His pain drained his energy, his thoughts, and his will. Yhy`h slipped her slender hand into his blood-covered hand and led him from the room that resembled a slaughterhouse without rules.

The remains of the Pack Leader of Hyarits`h Nation lay torn and dismembered across the floor and walls with blood sprays upon everything to the ceiling and windows.

Yassarn closed the door using the Mhyst behind him and ordered that only he was to enter. The Guards had seen the remains of their fanatical leader. They were in no hurry to enter the room and obeyed the words of the Sz`a`Th Captain.

Their eyes noted that the Red Crescent Moon signified Sahn`Frwh of Captain Yassarn, and the Warrior inside the room carried enormous weight and awe to those who had only heard whispers of the Sahn`Frwh Warriors of the Death Watch. They were to be obeyed, not ignored.

What had happened in the room behind them for the Guards that stood by that door? It was something neither of them wished to consider. With light wounds bleeding from their faces, arms, and back, they returned to their station on either side of the debris that clung to their uniforms, skin, and hair.

The Hyarits`h Nation did not mourn their leader, who had brutalised his people and his daughter. He would not receive the traditional sending-off to the Elements. The remains were chucked off the highest part of the stronghold where his remains would be fodder for others whose hunger bit harder in the storm-the greatest of insults for a nation's leader by Captain Yassarn.

The 'howling' ended with the death of the Lord. Word by messenger had been sent to the Wolf Nations' Pack Leader. The man called Lord Za`qrn, Lord of the Sqh`xn Wolves, was now their leader, and all Wolf clans were now as one unifying them for the first time in four hundred winters.

Taelen sat staring at the wood tower as flames licked and crackled, igniting them in the outside fire pit. He could not stop seeing her face. She had died because of him. His mother's words entered his mind as the bells tolled the crowning of Lord Za`qrn not far from the edge of the cliff where he sat staring. He saw the bird spiralling high above him.

'Taelen many will die for freedom. The Raven above cannot have freedom even though he flies high. He still, too, must fight a war that has barely begun. Reunite the Nations of Myth and Man, my son. Freedom comes with the highest cost to all.'

Amethyst blue eyes welled with tears; his shoulders shuddered with the strength of holding the grief he had contained deep within. He felt responsible for Kurr`etun, her body cremated in the traditional funeral pyre in the Castle behind him. The wooden Shi`atr flutes played with the massive drums beating her soul to the paths plains in the sky. The voices of the Sxq`rn Nation rose to thunder in their song of War spread out from the mountain peaks in the declaration of unity.

He stood his legs apart and stared hard and long, and he did not see the young Warrior NK`Las standing within the shadows of the night, nor his words as he cursed the Elemental Lords. The Elf Warrior already knew the price of the Dominion Lord would burden may well just bring the Warrior he watched weep in grief to his knees, turning him to darkness, not the light they all prayed for.

Rain fell as the funeral pyre grew in raging intensity. The celebrations behind Taelen carried on into the night. For one Nation, at least, there was joy in the death of the dictatorial Lord that had just died. For Taelen, his worries had just begun.

# CHAPTER 7

His eyes slowly focused through the palled haze of purple Mhyst. At fleeting moments, he saw his father's face fade and return. Many times the darkness was his only comfort. Yet rain and wind he could feel upon his skin icy and wet. On the other hand, was he with fever or fear? It did not matter. He couldn't recall anything.

The wind was icy and refreshing on the cliff where he sat. He watched the funeral pyre of Kurr`etun. His mind felt spent and empty.

Someone tapped him on the shoulder; the smell of conifer came from their skin. He blinked slowly at Yhy`h.

In a stronghold, leagues from them, a Necromancer laid his spell carefully and watched with a crooked smile as his magic traced through the regions to destroy.

Nothing could have prepared him for what happened next. The blinding blackness, the explosions that knocked him to the ground, was nothing compared to the father's stillness he had just found. Yassarn, mortally wounded by the ambush of a battalion of Dark Sz`a`Th Warriors who had infiltrated the Wolf clan, took all by surprise. He lay where he fell. Eyes that once loved, laughed and cried now stared in a stillness that shattered Taelen's heart into black shards of grief and despair.

Now a Warrior stood before him, near where he stood beside his father's comatose body. He spoke in the silent tongue; the Elf Warrior's voice came to mind. 'Lieutenant, the King, will live, but he must heal within the walls of the Elf in a place known as the undead. He will live to return to you one day.

Taelen stared at the Warrior he knew had been NK`las, the Warrior had haunted Taelen's thoughts from that first day by the stream, and now he was to take his father away to a place unknown to the Nation of Man. The Word was that the Spellcasters had instigated his kidnapping, and the altercation with the Hyarits`h Lord had caused the storms that never abated, yet Taelen did not blame the Spellcasters.

They blamed themselves for his father's un-death and his wife's death. Taelen's grief was enormous and impenetrable. It had been two winters since his father's un-death. Yet the death of Kurr`etun, who had been his wife for unknown hours, had shattered him with guilt. His silence, his shroud. Lord Za'qrn had provided wisdom and comfort; his eclectic, eccentric and unorthodox manner and vanity had brought some relief to the young Warrior and Scribe. It was Lord Za`qrn who had suggested he return to his Imperial Scribes Guild at the Spellcasters Coven.

He had applied himself dutifully, immersing himself in the Elf and Dwarf languages of H`dn and O`pn Earth. He studied hard and was now their Imperial Senior Scribe in the Coven of Szsd`ET in the He`lian Mountains, the central seat of energy for all Spellcasters.

Taelen refused to accept the mantle, which was wise. It made him invisible. It was his job to stay hidden. He was declining the rank of Commander as well. He had only acknowledged the Sahn`Frwh as his devotion and Imperial Senior Scribe. He kept his rank of Lieutenant.

However, all who were in the Coven of Szsd`ET and the attached Garrison of the same name accepted him as the Imperial Senior Scribe.

Teh`c had immediately joined Taelen at the Garrison. His friend's total silence and solitude worried many. Grieving was a personal thing. All hoped the young Lieutenant would awaken from his grief, and soon he was nearing his nineteenth winter.

Teh`c was a formidable Warrior; his swordsmanship was deadly with the weapons he now trained the Garrisons staffing with. Many had joined Teh`c after Yassarn's premature leaving into the folds of the Elf Nation. Yhy`h had helped Taelen control the Mhyst, and now he understood his mother's words about how light could quickly turn to darkness.

The storms of the mountainous region had caused significant flooding and a considerable loss of life that winter. Some assumed that the storms were that of a rogue Spellcaster, for someone had to be there pulling the strings of Lord Mah`sden. For a Spellcaster, he was not a delusional psychopath with a tilt for narcissism; he was definitely.

This morning was peaceful; the storms had ended, and the sun was shining for once. The cold, harsh winds had left for the coasts, and Taelen had taken to strolling alone along the shore of the small blue lake that lay within the fall of the land near the Coven, surrounded by a vast tall forest of thick conifers. Nobody ever bothered him; they knew grief took time to heal. As he walked alone, he would not speak, as was the mourning custom within the Spellcasters and Sz`a`Th. All had accepted his silence.

The rains had brought flooding. Taelen began negotiating a swollen creek as he balanced on the fallen trunk that breached the muddy waters to cross over to the other side.

While halfway across, his thoughts were shattered when a Spellcaster, a second Novice, came running down the slope. Bells tolled within the Coven for the commencement of Lessons.

"Please, Please!" cried a young woman. Startled, Taelen looked up. "Can you move? I'm late. I really must have a free way to pass you, Lieutenant?"

She lifted her long dark, grey straight skirt above her knees as she began balancing her steps on the fallen tree's trunk. Taelen had already passed halfway. Looking behind him, he decided it would be quicker to go on.

He stopped to steady himself as she came hurrying towards him. He was stunned at her forwardness and was lost for words.

"Can you move, please?" Staring at him with large pale green-grey eyes that hinted at something ethereal as they tilted to the temples, he looked at her, saying nothing.

"Are you mute…look, hold these, honestly, you Warriors just go mute when approached, and if I am late, it will be your fault, Lieutenant?" she said, handing her books to him suddenly, thrusting them against his chest.

"I'll move around you," she said and smiled at him shaking her head, for still he said nothing to her, and she knew of no Warrior in the Coven that could not speak. If anything, they never were silent as they went around their duties.

Taelen raised his eyebrows in disbelief as she unceremoniously handed him the books and held him around the waist and up close to him, for the trunk was not wide enough for two, let alone one person. She turned him around on the not-so-full tree trunk.

"Thanks," she said and went to leave, turning back; she laughed." Forgot my books," she said, grinning at him and grabbing them, losing her balance and nearly slipped began to lose her footing on the wet wood of the tree.

Taelen became unbalanced as he went to grab her. The weight of the books was all that was required, as they lost balance. Taelen swung the books so high that they landed free of the swollen creek.

This simple action sent both into the water at awkward angles. The water was deep; both swam strongly to the surface, swimming diagonally with the current.

Both surfaced, shaking their heads of the water, and began to drag themselves through swollen creek waters to the bank.

He expected her to abuse him, but they helped each other out of the flooded creek and up the muddy embankment. The young Spellcasters sat down, wringing out her skirt, sighed slowly, looked at him, and began to laugh.

"I'm so sorry, Lieutenant; you just look so stunned and very wet..." she looked at his bare feet, "and muddy." Leaning over, she removed dead leaves from his hair.

She glanced to where her books lay high and dry. "You throw well, Lieutenant."

He looked at the books high up on the bank and then looked back at her. As she laughed, tears rolled down her pale cheeks.

He slowly spoke for the first time in two winters. The words came freely to him.

"Thank you," he said as he removed his shirt and rung it out, spreading it upon the grass to dry.

"Why?" she asked as she spread her stockings and boots out. "If I hadn't been in such a damn hurry, you wouldn't have your boots, leggings, and shirt off drying. Just don't take your pants off." She said as she combed her fingers through her pale brown hair, trying to dry it.

Taelen's laughter felt good to his ears. She smiled at him. She was so fresh and open.

"Actually, I hadn't thought that far. You are going

to be rather late, you know. Who is your tutor?" he asked, studying her face. How she smiled made him feel alive, and he smiled back. He thought that smile you could not forget; it could light up the darkest of nights.

"Oh, I'm scribing today; Mistress Yhy`h is my Teacher; she has a strange name."

"I suppose it is to you, but she's not strange if you get to know her."

"You know her?" Large pale green-grey eyes stared at him, surprised.

"Aye, that I do," He said, smiling at the infectious young woman wet and bedraggled before him.

"She's pretty." The young Spellcasters said as she rang out the stockings she had removed. She began threading her hair into the braid customary to some of the Spellcasters.

She tugged the pale wet blouse away from her skin so the breeze would dry the material.

"Who... you mean Mistress Yhy`h? I suppose so. Are you always so talkative?" He said, frowning slightly as he glanced at her sideways, then stared at his boots drying alongside the webbing.

She blushed, looking directly at him as her long fingers finished the braid and then let the braid fall to her waist.

"Not always. It's just the end of my studies. Our dedication is soon, and Lord Yassarn is doing the honours."

"An honour, I'm sure," he said slowly, smiling and standing, glancing at the autumn sun warmed them. "If we are too dry off, Mistress, a good way is to walk. By the time we walk around the lake, our clothes will be dry."

He said, looking down at his trousers that were drying.

"But I am below your class, Lieutenant." Her eyes glanced at the red and silver stripe that ran down his trouser leg. Then to his left temple in the hairline was the Red Crescent. "And you are Sahn`Frwh."

"Well, you will be safe with a Sahn`Frwh Warrior, will you not, and I will talk with your tutor. Believe me; she will be pleased that the outcome was so positive."

Their walk was as informative as he had anticipated. Spellcasters belonged to a time when magic and spells had been a necessity. Yet now, he also wondered at their revival. Many a person had a gift that improved with the study.

He wondered why the Spellcaster's art was now needed, more so than any other time in the history of the Sz`a`Th. Why had the old spells and knowledge been dusted off so swiftly to teach a new generation of students?

He also wondered if their fate would mirror their ancestors. He would have to wait.

"So, in two days, you will become a Spellcaster?" He glanced sideways at the young woman who was intent on skirting the sharp angle of rocks that would smart her bare feet. He laughed as she raised her damp skirt above her knees, showing slender, pale legs. She seemed unaware that such bare skin was not something Spellcasters usually showed freely. Yet he did not mind the view at all, no, not at all.

The young woman shrugged indifferently to Taelen's comment. She turned to face him on the rocks. He laughed as she stood with her white blouse hanging over the dark grey skirt and her stockings and black ankle boots in her hands.

"So who is your escort?" he asked, watching her face. The large pale green-grey eyes seemed to be unreadable.

He sat down and pulled on the dry socks and boots, beginning the webbing binding.

"No one who'd want to take me; besides, I'm not pretty, and I talk too much. Most of the Warriors treat me as if I'm their sister." She sat down and pulled on her stockings and boots. "There is no one, Lieutenant; I have things to do after…." She glanced at him as he watched her slide the long stocking socks up to her thigh. "You should not stare when I put these on."

"Well, Mistress, there is a protocol about the leg length you must show; I think I have seen more leg today than my nineteen winters." She stared open-mouthed, then laughed aloud, which he found infectious. "Then Mistress, may I escort you to your Dedication?"

"May you what? Oh," she laughed aloud, then apologised profusely, "I didn't mean to offend you. It is just, well, why feel sorry for me, and oh?" she looked down at her legs drying in the sun, blushed deeply.

"No… you have misunderstood my intentions. I am not offended by you or your actions. They are refreshing; besides, I like you; I haven't laughed for it. Well, a long time, and today is the first time in a long time that I've noticed things. I have not before, like you, and how your smile lights up your face, I am one Warrior Mistress who would not think of you as a sister; I would be honest with you if you do not mind such frankness. I find you enchanting and desirable, and I need to know you more." He stopped. "I have said too much and embarrassed you; it seems we are both breaking archaic rules today."

He watched the pink blush rise from her pale cheeks, smiling from where he sat on the flat rocks.

He lent for his shirt and pulled the sleeve over his arm. "Let me take that as a 'thank you for today." He stood, pulling the shirt over his back. "My name is Taelen, Lieutenant Taelen," he said, not using his last name.

"Sometimes rules are meant to bend, well, at least I think so." She said, standing and brushing the leaves and dirt from her skirt.

"You could say that." He said, realising she thought Lord Yassarn and he had to be two separate people. He began lacing the shirt. "Besides Mistress J`nn, you've just seen more of me than most people I know."

She laughed, "That is true, Lieutenant." She frowned, staring at his chest as his open shirt lay unlaced -the Mhyst marking beneath his dark chest hair that she studied and came closer. "Why is your Mhyst such a deep mauve blue with white sprinkles when mine is pale grey?" her long slender fingers laced through the dark chest hair trailing gently over the Mhyst design, revealing her Mhyst mark just above the rise of her breast. Then blushed as Taelen's eyes moved from the sign of her Mhyst to her face. She smoothed the top of her shirt back in place.

"Are you always so…so forward"? He asked her as she lowered her eyes.

"I…Oh, I'm sorry, I didn't think I just saw yours and showed you mine. I'm not forward, or have I offended you if I have? I am so sorry I didn't mean my mouth gets me into a lot of trouble" she blushed again, slightly flustered. She glanced up at him through long eyelashes.

"I like spontaneity and confusion; you're like my brother Ji`rah. He is now a Lieutenant of the Sqh`xn Nation," He said, removing a leaf from her hair. "I hope you don't cast your spells the same way." He asked, his voice low near a whisper as his eyebrow arched in a silent question to her, his lips smiling. It took a moment for her to answer as her large pale green-grey eyes studied his features. She could not work out why he made her feel at ease.

His amethyst, blue eyes with their mauve fleck seemed brilliant in their colour; his olive skin held scars from battles, she thought, and his dark beard cut close in the Sz`a`Th tradition, with the short hair dark and fringe fell slightly over his forehead.

At his left temple, the Lieutenants Sahn`Frwh Red Crescent moon meant utter devotion to protect and fight at all costs. Discipline and elitist statist with the skills of the Warrior. She should not be talking to him; she knew such fraternisation between Warriors and Spellcasters was severely frowned upon. "No, I'm a bit more refined; my name is 'J`nn' if you still want to escort me to the dedication."

He laughed as she quickly buttoned her white shirt and left the laces loose on his shirt; he left the shirt out as the breeze billowed it slightly and continued to walk with her.

"I'll be outside the Dedication Hall waiting for you then, Mistress J`nn…strange name, no vowel?"

"No, not in my language; maybe you can add some to liven it up, "she laughed, smiling wide and infectious, relaxing in his company. "My other name is Sah`ski."

"Can I call you J`nn?" He asked before they parted, not wishing for their conversation to end.

J`nn's pale green-grey eyes held his for a moment, and smiling, she nodded, gathering up her books, turning she smiled saying goodbye, and ran with her skirt raised, just as she had when he first saw her. Her braid swung wildly as she jumped over rocks and branches.

Taelen was whistling as he entered the buildings. Staff and Warriors stared and stopped as he walked past, greeting them-surprise, tinged with relief. The Warrior had now left his world of grief and into a world that held promises.

He entered the room that was Yhy`h class. She looked up from the lesson she was teaching and was startled to see him with mud and grass stains on his shirt. He smiled at the Spellcasters as she grabbed his arm, whisking him out into the cold corridor.

Her hand went to his forehead, feeling for a temperature. "You're not with fever, are you alright? Where did this mud come from?" Her eyes raced over his body, checking for abrasions that would explain the personality change in her close and dear friend.

"Are you insane, Taelen? What has happened? Did you fall into the flooded creek?"

"Maybe, but actually, I feel just wonderful; why had I forgotten to do something up," he said, glancing at his trousers. He caught the look on Yhy`h's face and burst into laughter. He picked the tutor up, swinging her around in the corridor.

"Put me down, Taelen Yassarn. You're not making any sense!" Taelen placed her down on the stone floor and kissed her cheek.

"So, why are your clothes smelling of muddy creek water, Taelen?"

"I fell in the creek, the flooded one near the lake, no damage done, Yhy`h, I'm fine, really I am…fine, you worry too much, Spellcaster."

"Fine…? You…don't utter a word in two winters. All of a sudden, you're like this." Her arms swirled around his clothes, much to his amusement.

"Oh, before I forget, a Lieutenant asked me to let you know a student of yours, J`nn, might be a bit late."

"No, Student Sah`ski will be fine; she's my most Talented student; if she is late, she will know the work already." She felt his head for bumps. "You're sure you didn't hit your head." Her face looked at him with concern.

He smiled and turned. His back seemed straighter as he walked away from Yhy`h.

"I will see you tomorrow at the Spellcasters Dedication; Yhy'h… bye." He handed her silver pins he had removed from her braid. As her silky hair fell in wisps, she blew the offending hair up, narrowing her eyes at him." You might need them." He winked at her and said, "You know you can throw a spell my way of gracious Mistress of Spells."

"Seriously, right now, you're damn lucky I can't, Lieutenant!" She deftly rebraided her hair, pining in the pins with accuracy and speed, and stood with her hands on her hips, watching him walk down the vast corridor.

Taelen whistled as he left her. The tune was hauntingly beautiful. Yhy`h had only ever heard it once before, and that was in the Taayra`Ge Keep, nearly three winters ago when he was her Master Scribe and she the apprentice.

She sighed as she remembered. So much had happened between that time and now. Taelen would whistle the tune as he walked down the back path to the Taayra`Ge Ocean, and the Apprentices would wait until they heard him and the rest from the tasks he had set them. Yhy`h smiled at the memory.

Yhy`h could not understand the change in him. She decided to wait for tomorrow and re-entered her classroom to a sea of smiling faces who wondered at the Lieutenant's difference.

Dusk's pale grey light filtered through the narrow chiselled windows into the Hall of Dedication. Guests began to arrive from within the fortress of the Spellcasters Coven.

Taelen stood in his uniform as a Lieutenant of the Sz`a`Th. Its deep, dark, near-black purple seemed alive as the light fell upon it. The narrow blaze of blue and silver denoting his Guild, rank, and Sahn`Frwh ran down the entire length of his trousers' outside leg. The runes within the silver ran like drops of rain on the windows. The script of an elemental oath all the Sz`a`Th believed.

The Lieutenant mingled with the guests and Spellcasters, who knew his grieving had come full circle. Their hum of conversation began to give him a throbbing in his temples.

Taelen excused himself and went to the corner of the vast hall. The dedication would not take long. He knew the procedure; the twelve students moved around, and a silver star denoted their interest. Their gowns of the deepest blue heralded the transition from student Spellcasters.

There would only be one who was a specialised Spellcasters. Just one who had excelled beyond what was considered natural Talents in all their fields. That one person he had been told was Mistress J`nn. He was to hand each Spellcaster a silver segment of the twelve points of the Covens star. J`nn would receive all twelve points, an extremely rare dedication.

As he stood in the shadows, he watched as Spellcasters and Warriors mingled; amongst them, Lord Za'qrn had ordered warriors of the Sqh`xn Nation to increase the manning at the Coven.

He had yet to see J`nn enter the hall. Taelen had an hour spare and left and moved to the wide veranda covering the large hall's ground level.

The silence was something he still loved; the sweet smell of garden perfume and their coloured petals of white through to mauve and purple in large earthen pots looked surreal in the complete moonlight pooling into the garden.

He lent upon the stone balustrade and breathed in

their scents. The night sky was clear, with no rain on dedication night. Taelen watched the white moon moths float silently in the dark shrubs of the garden below him. A curse, distinct and abrupt, cut bluntly to his thoughts.

“Touch me, and I’ll….” a sharp slap smacked the night air and whimper, followed by the thud and determined tussle of bodies wrestling on the ground.

Then he felt it a taint, a shift within the Mhyst, the scream was enough, and it brought a cold sharpness to his heart. He yelled the command warning silently into the Guard's minds that stood on duty. Taelen leapt the balustrade into the garden, diving through the manicured shrubs.

He ran, entered a small secluded garden, and saw the pale braid of J`nn’s hair lie on the dark grass.

“I’d think twice, Warrior,” he said. His night vision within the Mhyst showed the Warrior now straddling J`nn in the shadows of the Covens wall. The Warrior had her pinned to the ground Taelen had his blades out; crystal lamps pulsed in the pale white glow on the garden's perimeter. He could hear the sound of running Warriors towards them.

“J`nn?” he commanded, “Move away, towards me.” The terror that he sensed made his stomach want to heave.

“If you want to live, get off the Mistress.” Taelen removed his tunic, throwing it behind him.

“And if I choose not to?” The voice was older but familiar. Taelen frowned, confused at the sound he heard; the accent was of the Tarra`Ge region and of the same-named Keep he had grown up in before the massacre.

“You are in the Spellcasters Coven Warrior; you are under Sz`a`Th Lore of which you have irrevocably broken the law of the Warrior." Taelen's voice was as cold as the winds of the winter ocean he grew up on.

"I know where I am - I came to get a Warrior, a Scribe he's called Taelen."

Taelen knew then that the man was Brae. He felt the spitting of light rain upon his skin.

"Let the Spellcaster go, Lieutenant. She is nothing you need," He ordered levelly.

"That is where you are wrong," Brae hissed his reply. Taelen heard the ripping of J`nn's gown and the small cry of terror as her skin felt his touch.

He then heard a curse from Brae as J`nn drew up her knees to his groin, kicking him brutally hard.

She then stabbed him and slashed her attacker's face with the small silver dagger she always carried.

"Bitch", groaned Brae and slapped the girl hard across the face. J`nn's head twisted. The impact of Brae's strength sharply knocked her to the ground. With her last strength, she pivoted on her back, kicking him sharply in the groin.

Taelen threw his blades at Brae; running hard, he leapt onto the Warrior.

J`nn rolled away from both Warriors grabbing Taelen's discarded tunic. He saw the paleness of her skin. She grabbed his ceremonial tunic and wrapped it tightly around her body; blood spilled from her lips from Brae's blow; it was all he needed to see as his blood sang loudly.

He crashed into Brae's shoulder, knocking him to the ground.

They fought equally as Sahn`Frwh. Taelen restrained his skills and concentrated on Brae's tactical errors, rolling as one as they dived through the undergrowth as other Warriors surrounded them.

Brae dove to grab his blades secured in his boots as

Taelen threw the total weight of his body into Brae's back.

Yhy`h came running towards them. He could feel her Pal`thic powers filter like a soft breeze towards them. He snapped a purpled Mhyst between her and them.

"DO NOT INTERFERE SPELLCASTER – MY ORDERS!" he yelled at her; his psyche slammed her to the ground hard. She lay breathing hard.

Both men stalked the other, black blades in each hand twisting slowly as the other watched each step and each blink of an eyelid; both breathed heavily as sweat beaded across their faces.

"Damn you, Lieutenant." Yhy`h snapped at him.

"Get J`nn to my quarters now!" he yelled, "I'm ordering you, Pal`thic. I am not asking Yhy`h!"

She gritted her teeth, stemming her anger at him and helped J`nn as two Warriors escorted the two women safely back within the Coven walls.

"I do not want you, Lieutenant; I seek a man called Taelen," he said as he avoided the full arc of Taelen's blade.

Taelen laughed. "You are a fool; we are both Sahn`Frwh" he nodded slightly, tilting his head," Doubt much you would come off unscathed; we both know Sz`a`Th Lore requires the witness to kill. So overused these days. Torture is not worth my energy either." He stood legs apart, arms folded but his daggers still in his grip.

"Why should I listen to you when you assaulted one of the Spellcasters not moments before?"

"I didn't attempt …I succeeded, and besides, I need Taelen's help." He said. Taelen felt the Mhyst rise in him. His anger was white as the Mhyst he now controlled.

Warriors appeared from every conceivable vantage

point in the garden as Taelen stared at the Warrior he had once saved.

"You lie. Why harm the girl, Warrior? You know the punishment for such a crime within the Lore of Sz`a`Th. That Lore covers us and the other regions. I have just spoken the Lore you broke."

"I do, but I am a dead man already, Lieutenant. Being killed here and now will not bring me peace. I want death, I can't do it myself, or Dral`north will play his sick game of reviving his dead."

He skirted around Taelen, his steps as precise as a cat's. Both stalked with the intent to kill, not wound.

"Who did you expect? Taelen himself, you are more of a fool than I have been led to believe, Lieutenant". Breathing heavily, Taelen bent down and put his blades away, his hands on his hips as he sighed heavily.

"I refuse to play this game with you, Lieutenant Brae," he said. "Guards, take him, and if he moves, kill him. Sahn`Frwh Warriors detail – six Warriors NOW!" Taelen dispersed the Mhyst that surrounded them.

"How do you know my name, Lieutenant?" Brae asked as the Warriors held him brutally hard.

"Seems your tarnished reputation meant only one Warrior would stoop so pathetically low to break such sacred lore of the Sz`a`Th. I heard the Scribe saved your life once. He should have fed you to the sharks, Lieutenant." He said coldly and spat spittle in disgust at the Lieutenant.

"Lieutenant, what about the Mhyst…his, I mean" asked one of the Warriors securing Brae.

"He was once one of us Sergeant; he knows Mhyst Lore and Sz`a`Th Lore. My orders still stand; if he moves, kill him. I am tired of playing games with a bastard of a fool and traitors to the Sz`a`Th."

Taelen glanced over his shoulder as Sahn`Frwh

Warrior's surrounded a man that had made his own life as a Scribe hell on earth.

Within the Coven, no one had been wise to the disturbance within the garden. Taelen asked for an

hour's delay as he ran up the stone steps and along the corridor to his quarters. He entered quickly.

"Yhy`h", he called out; his quarters were lit only by two oil lamps' blue oil sat still within the crystal lamp base.

"Here, Taelen", came her reply. "She won't move, she is frozen with fear, and I need to…see her wounds to heal." She touched his lips, then his eyebrow "your bleeding; let me heal you."

"Forget it, Yhy`h; you know Sz`a`Th Lore as well as I do. A black eye and split lip and eyebrow are not life-threatening. It was a brawl, nothing more; leave it."

Taelen stepped slowly through the door to the sleeping quarters and knelt at his own bed, where J`nn was curled up. He knew the physical wounds would heal, but he wished the Elementals that the attack had not happened emotionally.

"Sh", he hushed quietly…, "my Mistress, you are safe; I'm here, and no one can harm you here." He smoothed back the light brown hair that had tasselled across her forehead. The angry red abrasion on her left cheek made his fingertips tremble. Her lips had swollen, and the blood congealed dark and red.

"J`nn, all men aren't that, Lieutenant. I'm not." She shook her head and slowly began rocking back and forth. Fiercely she held her knees tightly to her chest. "J`nn… it's Taelen, Lieutenant Taelen; remember the creek, water, and mud? You're pretty deadly with that dagger."

Slowly she stopped rocking herself, her eyes dry; with a haunted openness, she looked at him. The recognition came in a flood of tears. He went to touch the abrasion on her cheek, but she recoiled from his touch. Taelen pained deeply as he saw the darkness in those large pale green-grey eyes.

"I would never harm you, Spellcaster, not ever."

Tears fell in a river down her pale cheeks; she tried to speak but could only cry. Shuddering sobs tripped over emotions, already stumbling to understand what had occurred to her. The shock came soon as teeth chattered uncontrollably.

"Yhy`h, grab something for her to wear, will you, and something hot and sweet to drink."

The doors closed after the Pal`thic, and silence blanketed the room.

"J`nn did he…." He asked with the awkwardness that surprised him.

She just stared at him. He knew that stare and changed tact.

"J`nn, look at me" His voice was a low whisper.

She slowly shifted her gaze to his, her hand trembling, touching his lip bruised and bloody.

"It is you…Lieutenant Taelen. I thought you were a dream that we hadn't met and that…" her voice barely a whisper.

"Aye, it's me, muddy though, and I won't hurt you, J`nn."

The young Spellcaster smiled a little, a sad smile that showed soft kindness within her raw fragility.

"I know that in my heart, funny" she closed her eyes. "I felt your presence on the veranda, I was running, and someone grabbed me; the Warrior touched… my gown is…." J`nn rocked herself. She let his arms hold her as she fell against Taelen's chest, and he gently cradled her to him.

"Your tunic is all muddy again," she said softly. Her pale fingers picked off flakes of mud and bits of grass.

"Sh… J`nn, I'm beginning to like mud. It seems mud and you go together," he said, "When I was little and had nightmares, my mother would sing a lullaby, and all the bad things would go."

"Could you sing it for me" She began to sob into his chest. Taelen began to sing softly, rocking her in his arms.

Yhy`h returned. The look and his caring made J`nn relax, nearly sleeping. She let Yhy`h bath and dress her in a nightgown as Yhy`h healed her internally. Finally sleeping with her arms folded into Taelen's tunic, she smelt his scent and dreamed.

"I'll leave her here if that's alright with you, Taelen. She feels safe here."

"You stay here with her while I go and continue with my duties", he squeezed Yhy`h shoulder.

"Thanks, Yhy`h" the door closed after him, and it was not long while she sat watching the sleeping woman that she heard the bells toll.

Another generation of Spellcasters had entered out of the confines of the Coven. All wore the ceremonial gown of deepest darkest grey with the mauve pentagram surrounded by the thirteen points of the star of the Kh`irz. The male Spellcasters wore ceremonial dark grey with a mauve stripe down the side, the hem of the jacket reached their knees, with the star on each lapel all wore cloaks with the cowls down on their shoulders. The mauve pentagram appeared upon each third eye in dark mauve, and each wore the Silver Star hanging from a long chain around their neck. Each accepted the narrow panelled tunic that slipped over the gown in black with the pure silver thread embroidered intricately at the breast.

Yhy`h sighed and drank the hot brew of sweet herbal tea.

Taelen left the Hall as the bells tolled and walked down to the Warriors Barracks. He removed his ceremonial tunic and hung it with the other tunics in the guardroom.

0"Lieutenant," he said, saluting to the Taelen and then stood at attention. "Den`ah, was that necessary?" asked Taelen saluting in return.

"Yes, it is", the young Corporal replied as he returned to his chair.

"So…" he said, holding a handful of shelled nuts and chewing them.

"How is the good Lieutenant Brae?" the Corporal smirked in the direction of the prisoner's cell.

"Too well, if you want my opinion, Lieutenant" he took a fist full of nuts and the single long key. The Coven keys differed from other keys; these were a series of knots that were the Spellcaster's wards in knot magic. All made of fine silver, the keys were warded and knotted to each lock in the Coven.

Corporal Den`ah lead Taelen down a flight of stone steps. They turned sharp right and entered a brightly lit room with four cells separated by white bars of energy.

Brae sat with his back against the rough wall within the third cell. He stared at nothing in particular and did not change his view when Taelen entered.

"If that is you, Corporal, you will wish you brought me Taelen." Den`ah looked across the Lieutenant, his face permanently unreadable. Except for a slight raise of his eyebrow at the Lieutenant's comment.

He showed nothing of his feelings. They walked to where a torrent of verbal abuse poured. Taelen rolled a sphere of purple Mhyst within his thoughts and hurled it into the cell occupied by Brae.

"Wish I could do that". Den`ah replied to his Lieutenant.

"In time, you will", Said Taelen. "Wait over there out of his sight."

"Why out of his sight, Lieutenant?"

"Who knows what 'gifts' he has been empowered with? He has spent nearly three winters in the folds of the Dark Sz`a`Th. I would rather know you are safe than have you at his whim Den`ah."

Den`ah's dark green eyes looked towards the cell occupied by Brae. He nodded and stayed where Taelen had asked him. The two other Warriors on Guard Duty stood further past the cell in question.

Taelen moved and stood a meter from the cell bars. His steps were one of a man who did not trust the other. The bars glowed with the energy of the wards cast into them.

"Lieutenant Brae, last time I heard of you, you had been demoted to Corporal. Harassment of a Scribe was it not. I thought your rank was Sergeant, Was that rank demotion not for the indiscretions you had while at the Lake City of Cran`dk? Where you not only attacked and wounded Lieutenant Teh`c ." With a slight nod, he said the Warrior was sitting against the wall and did not rise, as was the custom.

"I got promoted. I was expecting, Taelen, not you, Lieutenant" he glanced at Taelen. "You seem to be everywhere. Can't the Lord of the Dominions do without you?" his stern look hid his fear, yet Taelen knew Brae feared the worst.

He pulled a talisman from his shirt. The black filigree cross - held a white stone within its heart. Brae stared for a moment at the cross, then up at Taelen.

"I believed in this. Then it was my world that the Mhyst and the Sz`a`Th tortured. They are nothing but little boys who pretend peace is obtainable."

"So, you just assaulted the young Spellcasters just

now to prove what....” “I’m afraid I choose to disagree with you, Lieutenant. You had the choice to make. You made your decision and now feel that it is this man you have named Taelen who owes you something for your reputation?”

Brae flung himself at the bars and recoiled as the energy bit deep into his mind. Falling to his knees, he gasped and looked up at Taelen.

“So, I was stupid. I need to see Taelen, and I need to do it now; it is his life all this rests on.”

Taelen ignored his plea; his thoughts were still on the attack of J`nn.

“So you attacked her with your touch. Do you do innocents often?”

Brae said nothing, stared at Taelen coldly and sat back on the cold floor. J`nn’s silver dagger thrust had wounded his face across his forehead and cheek.

Blood still dripped from the cut.

“If Sz`a`Th Warriors soil an innocent, the punishment is death, you of all people know that lore, are you so weak you cannot follow what moral right Lieutenant is?.” Taelen stood, arms folded across his chest, legs slightly apart. “But I have to ask why do you seek Taelen? It’s a common name in the southern regions; even my name is Taelen.”

“He chose to save my life once, he’s a Scribe, and I was told the Scribe is here, was here, you are not the Taelen I know, an Imperial Scribe, much younger than you, Taelen is a Warrior, yes, but he is not you.”

He shrugged and rubbed his hands where the energy had penetrated; the skin had begun to blister.

“Sz`a` Th Lore requires payments. I’m here to repay that debt. He saved my life, healed wounds that should have killed me; I am here to warn him.”

“Tell me, how do you know it was him who saved

your life?"

"I've felt many Mhyst's Lieutenant, Mah`sden's is the evilest and putrid it gags my vomit in my throat. I have felt others since I was captured near three winters ago. Yet Taelen's was healing and forgiving Mhyst; he gave me hope. If he cannot stop Mah`sden, then torture will be all you hear, feel and see. The regions, the people and the buildings will all be scared by him. Blood soaks all the regions; skeletons litter the earth already."

"You're talking all-out War, Lieutenant Brae," Taelen said, his eyes hooded." If it has missed your attention, we are at War."

"Isn't that what war does to us, Lieutenant? It tortures us of our humility."

Taelen stood silently looking at the cross of the Faith that Brae was still holding in his fingers. He knew Brae went to devotion when they were both at the Keep, but he never realised how deep Brae's convictions to his faith were till now.

"Lieutenant, all I have left is my faith, I need to believe, and if I can't, there's no point." Brae's talisman was for freedom and peace, hung from the black leather tongue, swinging slowly, and fell against his chest.

"It is late, Lieutenant, your cell has blankets, and the food was given to you earlier. Tomorrow I will tell you what Lord Taelen has decided. You are shackled, Lieutenant, as you should be. You attempt to escape and actually get out of the Spellcasters magic that has entwined itself within the cell? Then you will receive a Faith burial. That is all I am permitted to say under the Sz`a`Th Lore. Do you understand?"

"Aye, Lieutenant, I do."

Brae shackled with an energy Sz`a`Th bracelet stood legs apart, his fists clenched tightly. He ignored the cutting of the magic into his skin. Both men stared silently at each other. It was Brae who turned his back to Taelen.

He spoke silently to Corporal 'Den`ah, kill him if the magic wavers. He has a Necromancer working on him; I don't care what time it is! You send me a mind stab. I know such things have not been used for a long time, but I need you alive, and sometimes rules should be broken.'

'Is that legal the mind stab?'

'Use it. That bastard will kill you and everyone that comes in his view; I will take the consequences.'

Taelen walked back up the stone steps. The Coven was still and dark. The festivities of the Dedication had finished hours ago. It was now late as he entered his room. The soft glow from the crystal lamps made him feel welcome, and he relaxed.

The dark wooden desk held a note; he recognised Yhy`h's script, flowing and graceful. Yhy`h had been called away and would return when she could. If he were here, she would return to her room.

Taelen sighed heavily from the concern, he went to his bed within the glow of lamplight, and J`nn's features seemed at ease. He smiled as he sat opposite her on an extended lounge, where Yhy`h had been, the pillows and quilt in disarray. He wondered what had called the woman away in such a hurry.

Taelen unwound the webbing and eased his boots off; his shirt lay on the floor with the rest of his clothes as he slid into the soft quilt comfort. Yawning, he snuggled down into sleep, his mind filtered elsewhere. His shade hovered over the Spellcasters Coven in protection.

He realised as his mind saw the land in the darkness of night that Brae was right. Brae had the information he needed. Sz'a'Th Veil Walkers had been unable to infiltrate the Dark Sz`a`Th. He needed to glean what Brae had experienced in the three winters with Mah`sden and his followers. He returned to his mind. Tomorrow he thought, could be a time of spells, now was a time for sleep. The rain fell steadily again within the mountains protecting the Spellcasters and their world.

# CHAPTER 8

Taelen stretched in his sleep, slowly waking. His eyes blinked languidly until he stared at the ceiling. He then looked over to find J`nn watching him. Her pale green-grey eyes seemed to pull him in; she blushed slightly at him and gave a small smile.

"Sleep well?" he asked her, for he knew she slept within his Mhyst and a spell.

"I slept, but I do not feel I have rested." She said as she unwound the braid and combed the tangles with the brush he had given her.

"They say hard work is a cure for an un-rested body, or if you are a Warrior, you work through the bruises and pain."

"How hard," she asked with a small smile and sat up, her hair still in disarray and fell like cascading silk. Bruisers had appeared already on her face. She moved within the constrictions of the assault.

"I have to go to 'CLU`Sli.' It is a good half-day journey there."

Changing his thought, he fell quiet.

"Why there?" she asked, frowning as she crossed her legs, sitting up on the bed.

"I have a few questions that I need to answer," he swung his legs out, and she laughed as he stood, realising he had only shorts on that he'd slept in that night- relieved that he was that he was not naked as he was accustomed to.

"Now, I have seen more than the others have seen of you." She said, smiling at him; Taelen pulled his trousers and shirt on. He was absently thankful that he'd remember to sleep in shorts.

"Aye, Mistress, that you have. I'll be back in a moment" he walked to the door to the bathroom.

Running the hot water, Taelen stripped and, at the same time, stepped into the big deep stoned bath. Ornate stone-carved runes inlaid moonstone carved in the walls glowed. The bathwater was hot and relaxed his muscles, but it was all wasted when he heard Yhy`h call out to him. He inwardly groaned. Grabbing a towel secured it around his hips. Coming out, he winked at J`nn as he said to Yhy`h.

"You want me now?" he said, looking sideways at his fellow Scribe.

"You're in a towel!" Yhy`h stared at him; Taelen smiled at her.

"Logically, I'd look a touch naked if I didn't. I was having a bath when you called to me." Yhy`h rolled her eyes at him impatiently.

"Taelen, this is not funny. You're not considering that Mistress J`nn is in your bed."

"She's an adult; sorry to disappoint you, Yhy`h; it is not the first time she has seen this much of me" He could not contain his composure any longer and laughter echoed through the rooms joined by J`nn.

"TAELEN…!" Yhy`h stared at him, seriously knitting a fine wrinkle upon her brow, but he couldn't stop the laughter.

"Yhy`h… nothing has happened. I was having a bath, for God's sake, girl. I slept where you slept last night. You of all people should know me better than that."

"People gossip, Taelen; that is my concern." She said, trying to ignore the cheekiness in his eyes.

"Only if I let them; now let me get my clothes, and I'll get changed."

She watched as he walked across the room. He

had grown into a strong young man; his body was broad-shouldered as well-muscled. His proportions were as they should be for a Warrior. The dark hairs on his chest seemed to accentuate his broadness and muscle definition. Dark hair that feathered softly down beneath the towel made her think.

The Spellcasters had forgotten he was nineteen winters old now as she was just eighteen winters old. She caught the look in Taelen's eyes and blushed furiously.

"What are you thinking, Mistress? Is there something wrong, Yhy`h?" Taelen smiled at her.

"No," she said quietly ", You have changed a lot since we were teenagers. I have never noticed before, that's all."

"I'm sure if I caught you damp and in a towel, I would say the same thing. ; If I could find my voice," Taelen smiled at Yhy`h broadly and caught the meaning in Taelen's eyes. A cheekiness found in many yet had been missing in Taelen for too long Yhy`h thought. "For I am sure the sight of you, like that, would simply take my breath away."

"Your… you're…" she placed the breakfast tray down. "I'll think of something in a minute Taelen." He laughed aloud at her reply.

"I'm sure you will, Mistress, I'm sure you will," he walked back to the bathroom and dressed, sitting down to eat while J`nn disappeared into the bathroom to bath and change.

"I need two packs with enough food for three days should the weather catch us out."

"We?" she looked at him over the rim of the mug of tea she sipped. "Where are you going?" she asked him.

"CLU`Sli," he said as Yhy`h choked on the tea she swallowed.

"Why?"

"Are you in one-word sentences this morning for a reason, or did my nakedness disjoint your words and start your libido."

Yhy`h screwed her nose up at his sarcasm.

"You are…incorrigible this morning, and I will not play word games with a Senior Scribe." Taelen smiled back, her raising eyebrows in a challenge she ignored.

"Wise as always, Yhy`h, Brae is down in the cells if you must know, and believe me, Yhy`h, there will be a day when I can't confide in you." He chewed slowly the grilled meat that he was eating. "You're not to go down there at all. I don't care if the bastard is bleeding to death and screaming the place down. You're to stay away." He swallowed the hot tea and added, "Master L`unh has cast one or two of his special spells. In the prevention of anyone seeking out Brae."

The aged Master L`unh and his silver hair seemed as old as the earth itself. She knew the aged Spellcasters enough to head the warning.

"You have seemed to have made your decision." She said slowly, then asked about orders he had given two days prior. "Is Lieutenant Teh`c travelling with them?" "Lord, I'd forgotten that all the Spellcasters are leaving for the southwest Garrison."

"Charl`HN", she corrected him.

He turned to her and said, leaning back into the chair.

"I'll not send a young girl into a Garrison of eight hundred Warriors."

"You'd send me in the blink of an eye, Lieutenant, and you would not even worry," Yhy`h said with a smile.

"Because you know how to handle eight hundred Warriors, Yhy`h," he grinning.

"You are avoiding my question." She replied, folding her arms across her chest.

"CLU`Sli," he said to her.

"What is so important that you go to ask the Glade of Truths?"

Ignoring her prying, he answered quietly. Taelen turned his back to her for a moment. He knew now was not the time to leave the Coven, yet there were answers he needed, and he would not find them here. He hoped that a diversion of taking the young Spellcaster away for respite would be invisible and cloaked his need.

"I am taking Mistress J`nn to CLU`Sli; a change of scenery will help. Your healing has assisted," he caught the look in his friend's eye. "Yes, I know it won't erase what has happened; all the time in the world won't do that. We will be back in time for the others arriving."

She nodded at him and then smiled, saying. "I am glad your time of 'Mourning' has ended." Yhy`h turned and left, closing the door behind her. She smiled at the look of surprise on his face. She was glad he had begun to move on. Death was so final where life and living were not.

Both Taelen and J`nn had left hours before the Spellcasters' departure. Their half days of travel was precisely what the Spellcaster had needed to move her thoughts away from the assault.

CLU`Sli was a silent and eerie place that was shrouded in opaque white mist for eternity. Taelen stood thigh-deep within the richly growing ferns. Some reached his waist, letting it resemble a sea of green fronds. His fingers combed absently through the frond's softness and coolness.

At CLU`Sli, an old ward, cast by a young man as he lay dying, protected the area. Wounded deep to his heart by a Spellcasters energy shaft, the Warrior, it was said, had lingered for days as his blood-soaked the earth. His crimson life force spilling became the white waves of the mist.

Whispers came within the swirling white mist that caressed in white waves around his waist. Fingers of white fog touched his back and encircled his waist in a lover's embrace. Here he stood.

"Why has this one come to the glade?" The whispering voice was male, but others came to Taelen, joining in the questioning.

"He is many things, this one…not one…not the other." the voices whispered in breezes.

"Spellcasters the mother…. was the mother but was the another…the blood of the Elf's flow in this one… Wolf and Raven, Dwarf as well" voices swirled around Taelen like a vortex; he turned to each whisper, not catching the next that came to his ears, always elusive to him.

Damp and cold, white mist ebbed back and forth in currents flowing around him and the surrounding trees.

"Mhyst was the father…. Mhyst. Mhyst is this one."

"We must answer his questions, Master of the Mhyst". Their voices spoke as one. The hiss of the whispers was deafening. As abruptly, the waves of white fogging mist stilled

The sounds washed over him as he stood. The glade's coolness and the silence of the surroundings made the clearing seem like it existed elsewhere and did not have this world.

"He is the Dominion Lord." He spoke in a male voice to his left. He turned to see Corporal NK`las, but the Warrior was not in the uniform Taelen was accustomed to seeing him in. The Elf Ranger stood legs apart, his arms folded across his chest.

Within the protection of CLU`Sli, NK`las stood

surrounded by the fogging waves of white mist that lapped against their thighs with each breath they took.

His black hair was short, Taelen noticed the white tattoo in the hairline behind his ear, and a silver clasp jewelled with droplets of early morning dew circled his forehead, where silver leaves, delicate and small, hung on his third eye. His clothes were of the most beautiful cloth, light in their weight and dark in the colours of green and night. He had no bow or quivers. Only a stave carved in runes and made of the finest Beith or Birch, as others call the tree.

Taelen did not speak immediately. When he finally did talk, it was of the turmoil in the lands close and far from the Glade. How the Mhyst had become tainted and evil and how he saw the need for peace to return.

"This is more than the Glade knows, Lieutenant," returned the same male voice he knew was NK`las.

The whispers became silent as the one voice spoke to Taelen.

"Within the Coven's Archival records, there is a ledger. This ledger relates to the history of Spellcasters. The Spellcasters you seek are alive. She is half of what you seek; beware the Seven Books of Sz`a`Th, young Master; not all are true. Some are hidden behind what is seen. Each is its own life, each a person."

"Your words are riddles; who is behind Mah`sden? The man is no genius, and why have Spellcasters done such a thing of evil?" asked Taelen quietly.

"It is their Spell that has invoked the evil that has caused the taint within the folds of Sz`a`Th; Lord Dral`north is the Necromancer".

"Why the two, I don't understand," he said, "Am I being punished for something that happened beyond my control and understanding."

"Blood is punishment enough, and a twin is but the

soul's expression. They say we all have a twin. Beware your young Master; he waits within the shade of your thoughts already; only the un-dead understand the concept of a twin."

The voice came in a haunting whisper that lingered and hung in the air.

"Who speaks to me now?" Taelen studied each fold of mist as it flowed towards him. Now thicker, he could no longer see the ground or the fronds of green.

"I do."

A young man stood before him, dressed in the uniform of the Imperial Sz`a`Th Warrior, his markings identical to Taelen's. He held a Spellcasters energy shaft in his left hand that glowed beside him a decree forbidding them to be used after the Four Hundred Winter War. He was mesmerised by the iridescent storm cloud of dark blue, runes lacing around; here, he read inscriptions, smatterings of thought long gone. In his right hand, the Warrior held the Sahn`Frwh sword.

"Lieutenant, I alone know who you are and what is to be… many will fall, in death, many will live. You must become your twin to achieve an end. Beware she, Spellcasters, take a secret oath, given at birth, and it is at her hand you die."

"How do you know such things?"

"To die, you will live..." the Warrior said with a sad smile.

The Warrior smiled, his teeth white and even. Taelen mused; this Warrior would not have had a problem finding a companion; in many ways, he reminded him of Ji`rah's bravado, M`hta's shyness, Teh`c's magnetism and Lord Za`qrn's charismatic stance.

"I gave into my heart, Lieutenant, just as you will; love is one thing, lust is another combined; they cloud your thoughts as thick as this mist. Your heart gives your feelings away for the one with you."

Taelen studied the Warrior, his hair worn in the close-cut crew cut worn four hundred winters past. The Warrior's intricately patterned tattoo laced along his jaw, hidden slightly by his beard trimmed neatly but close to the symbol of the Sz`a`Th, could be seen clearly. A design of knots in the runic text ran down the left side of his strong square jaw, the Red Crescent on his temp interlocked into the tattoo that followed patterns across his skull beneath his short hair. A story of his life to death. His eyes were of the purple-blue of the original Mhyst indigo blue. Once when the Mhyst was pure in essence and blood.

"What is your name, Lieutenant?" he asked the Warrior before him.

"Ne`leat is my name; think on it, Lieutenant, do not make my errors of the heart."

The whispers lapped, sounding like the ocean far away. Taelen glanced around him. A frog croaked somewhere beneath the mist. Now dispersing, the deep green of the ferns surfaced again to the sky.

Unseen NK`las entered the mist, standing beside the Warrior.

'It's time Ne`leat, come, your duty is done, by the Lore of the Sz`a`Th, Wolf, Raven and Dwarf, Elf, you are free. Stand down.'

Ne`leat turned to NK`las, handing him the Spellcasters Staff. Finally, now he could pass over.

NK`las watched as his spirit rose swirling high, free from the mist that had held him so long, too long. With the Spellcasters Staff and the Warriors Sword, he swiftly left.

Taelen clenched his teeth, frustrated gnawed at him like a hungry rodent, and his head ached like a hangover from Meade's too much.

Mistress J`nn saw him emerging from the Glade. She stood brushing the leaves that clung to her dark grey straight skirt.

“Where to now, Lieutenant, were your questions answered?”

“Back to the Coven, it seems, and no, no answer, just more questions too many for my liking, Mistress. I require the ancient ledgers, and I won‘t find them here.” He said; frowning and deep in thought, he bent and lifted his backpack without a second thought.

“J`nn, do you know of anyone who would have reason to delve with the ‘shadows’ in the Coven or a …twin?”

Her hand grabbed his arm firmly. He was surprised; her eyes were large pools of pale green-grey, but the fear fringed those eyes caught his breath.

“You mustn’t ask those things out loud, Lieutenant. “ He could see the pulse in her neck throbbing.

“Why are you so frightened, J`nn? I don’t have a twin.”

“Nothing,” she said, “Just promise me you’ll not ask about evil out loud.”

He touched her cheek, flinching slightly, and her eyes looked at things he could not see. Yet he shivered, from those dark unknown thoughts, thoughts of events he felt would take her from him. Suddenly he did not want to lose her.

“I promise, Mistress.” Her fingers gently touched his firmly. “J`nn, who is Sah`ski.”

“It is my second name.” Pausing, she added, “I do not use it.”

“Why?”

“Sometimes, Lieutenant, we are the same. We ask too many questions.” She said in a low, hushed voice.

Blinking, she released his arm. "Which path, Lieutenant," she asked, looking up at the dark blue-black clouds tinged with white

"The path must be short."

He looked up at the clouds as the wind started in squalls. It was his turn to hold J`nn's arm.

"Whose 'storm' is this Mistress J`nn?" he asked as thunder rolled across above their heads in an angry drum roll.

"We must seek shelter, Lieutenant, and quickly. This is no ordinary storm. This is a Spellcaster Storm".

Taelen's mind raced. He knew of a place Master L`unh had shown him. A blinding jagged ark of white, blue lightning exploded a tree a hundred meters away. Both hit the earth, their hands over their ears, their arms protecting their heads, as they slowly looked up at the burning tree.

"If you are thinking of casting a spell, I will cast right now," he said, taking her arm, pulling her to her feet firmly in the torrent that opened upon them from above.

"RUN… Mistress and don't let go."

Large drops of rain began hammering the earth. Their faces burned as the rain fell upon their skin harder and more substantial. Running down rocky paths overgrown with brush, twisting and lunging through the undergrowth, they raced as the rain fell heavier. Tripping over exposed roots of trees and muddy inclines, they fell and scrambled in haste.

The wind became icy, and hail formed from what was rain hammering down upon them, stinging and bruising as the hail became large and dangerous, blinding their steps and confusing their sense of direction.

Taelen saw the opening to his left as they ran, he

pulled the young Spellcaster abruptly left, and she followed his lead as they kept their pace, running now as lightning bolts speared to the earth as if thrown by god-like Warriors.

"When I say dive, we dive," he yelled in the storm.

Branches whipped at them as hail became as big as quail eggs. J`nn was flagging, but Taelen dragged her behind him relentlessly. He saw the stone cabin dug into the rocks that skirted the cliff. Pulling her, both partially blinded by the darkening storm and lightning strikes, he rammed at the door, falling heavily onto the stone slab floor. The young Spellcaster stumbled onto the floor with him. The door closed hard as the wind caught it, slamming the door heavily into the architrave. The wind ripped the door open.

Fragments of stone and dust fell to the wooden floor as hail pounded and bounced through the doorway. The door slammed shut a second time.

They lay in the darkness, breathing heavily. The hail hammered down as large as Timberwolf's paws, battering everything. Breathing gulps of air. Taelen pushed his wet backpack off. J`nn's had come off as he had pulled her into the cabin. They lay in exhausted silence, soaked and cold. Taelen moved to light a lamp.

"I wouldn't do that. We don't know who has been here." Her voice rasped from her throat as she gulped air in and lay back exhausted.

"I do," he said quietly and touched a lamp in the darkness. The crystal glowed pearl at his touch, then heightened as it felt his Mhyst.

J`nn sat up gingerly; her hair, wet and tangled, brought something to him familiar, and he laughed slightly.

"Cold?" he asked as he stood.

"Aye, very", she answered through white teeth chattered in the chill.

"That room to the left, the water will run hot from the subterranean springs below, get warm", he said, helping her up. "Change in there. I'm sure there'll be something to do for the moment."

As he lit the fire, he thought the small flame played upon the yellow kindling for a moment and then took hold. Gold and cherry-red flames licked upon the wood, giving off the warmth they needed. Taelen's smile left as thoughts of the Seven Books appeared in his mind and the sight of NK`las in the glade. Taelen pushed them aside yet again.

The storm's intensity increased outside, and he wondered who besides Mah`sden wanted him dead. More importantly, they knew the region he was in. He clenched his teeth firmly. He then realised Brae's appearance was not of a desperate Warrior seeking asylum.

Taelen smiled ironically because they had all fallen for the 'little boy lost' drama. It was Brae who had been brought into the Coven. Sitting in the cells, Taelen wondered coldly what would happen next.

To the room's right, the small galley had a fully stocked pantry that proved beneficial. There were preserves in bottles, smoked meat and dried nuts and lentils.

He removed his wet clothing, hanging it on various pieces of furniture. His shorts were dripping from the rain, but his stomach was hungry. He ate as he stood before the fire, warming himself and freezing simultaneously. He would find dried meat and vegetables. Everything went into a pot with lentils; the water slowly reconstituted the food into a stew.

He hadn't noticed J`nn come out; he turned to see a

pair of woollen socks crumpled at her ankles, then slender, pale cream legs to the knee. She wore a deep blue woollen nightshirt buttoned down the front that, had she not held up to walk freely, would have reached the floor.

"You look warm," he said as he ate, hunched next to the fire, and the goosebumps across his back made her smile.

"And you look freezing. Some clothes in there should fit you," J`nn said, taking the spoon off him. "Go before you catch your death, Lieutenant."

Taelen did not have to be told twice that he was shivering in his shorts. He ran the hot springs water into the bath and just soaked off the mud and the forest. He found loose grey trousers and a pale blue, flannel long shirt. The large cream socks warmed him as he walked back out, drying his hair.

"Still cold?" he asked, watching the fire dancing colours of red and gold across her hair as it dried.

She nodded as she stirred the stew in the dark iron pot hanging over the fireplace.

"How did you know of this place"?

"Actually, it's mine. My father left it to me in his will bequeath. I have been using it for study purposes when the Coven is too loud and was out here another day after I was talking to Master L`unh. He says a powerful ancient ward protects it." He shrugged, looking away and at the cabin for the first time.

"Taelen, are you really a Lieutenant of the Sz`a`Th, Imperial Scribe assigned to the Coven to protect the Spellcasters?"

"Aye, that and sometimes other things," he said, refilling two pottery bowls with the stew. "Why?"

"How long have you been at the Coven"? She asked him. She chewed her bottom lip as she waited for his answer.

"Two winters or a little bit longer, I don't remember." He continued to spoon the stew into their respective bowls.

"Truth," she asked him again.

"I always tell the truth. Why do you ask such a thing, J`nn?" He took the spoon back, spooned the stew into the bowls, and sat on the hearth, warming his back. "Why so many questions."

"What are the other things that you do?" She asked, glancing up from the bowl she cradled on her lap.

"Sometimes, it is better to know a little, my Spellcaster, than know a lot, less knowledge of a Sahn`Frwh Warrior's work will keep you alive just that bit longer, Mistress. Unless you would like to be questioned by Lord Mah`sden, I am the Covens Imperial Scribe; you've seen me bringing in ledges after ledges to the study hall." Taelen scooped up a spoon of the stew and ate it quietly as he felt the heat of the fire warm through him.

"Aye, my class thought they worked you too hard…Lieutenant, how well do you know Mistress Yhy`h? She is in love with a Sz`a`Th Warrior, is the talk I have heard."

"Aye, that she is, and I've known her since quite a few winters now."

"You?" she asked, glancing sideways at him as she ate, her beautiful eyebrows arched enquiringly.

Taelen choked on his stew, coughing when he realised she was suggesting it was him that Yhy`h was in love with.

"It's not me! If that's what you're asking. I, Yhy`h and I have a close relationship, and yes, we love each other deeply, but not intimately. Yhy`h is a friend, and with that, friendship comes a heavy load of trust. " He smiled. "Mistress Yhy`h is a very dear friend, Mistress J`nn; we have known each other for nearly four winters. I was a Master Scribe at a southern Taayra`Ge Keep, and she was one of my Apprentices," he ate another spoon full. "The Lieutenant you speak of is not at the Coven. His name is Teh`c; he is a Lieutenant, Sahn`Frwh."

J`nn ate in silence. Taelen realised he knew nothing of her background.

"I was curious, that's all. I haven't seen you with anyone."

"Except you," he said, watching a tide of pink blush at her cheeks and to the roots of her pale brown hair.

"J`nn, some truths can't be told; they will always be secreted away and gnaw at you at 3 am…believe me, I know." He changed the conversation back to her and asked. "What was your speciality at the dedication going to be?"

"I had three, the silver chalice, the blue light and the third eye".

"Mistress Yhy`h said you were very talented. With those gifts, you would already know my truths." Taelen glanced back at her, sitting on the hearth.

"You would like me to tell you what I see?" she asked him.

Taelen nodded as he ate and listened to the storm batter the cabin.

"If I have made an error in 'seeing', I will tell what the truth is if I sense it."

J`nn stood, moving her bowl to the galley and making two hot drinks for them.

"You were raised in privilege and then Apprenticed as an Imperial Scribe to a southern Taayra`Ge Keep. After a family tragedy left you without parents."

"Close…and truths are there," he said, finishing his meal.

"You were widowed nearly three winters past. You were not comfortable with the marriage as it was an arranged marriage. Your responsibilities are more than just a Sz`a`Th Warrior," she frowned, not understanding the extent or depth of his burdens. "You're lineage is of exceptional bloodlines. I sense you are related to Lord Za`qrn, leader of the Sqh`xn Nation" she lowered her eyes at the cup steaming in her hands. "You, Mistress Yhy`h and the Warrior in the cells are somehow connected."

"Very thorough," Taelen looked away from her to the grey rain beyond the cabin's only window; slivers of silver ran down the transparent pane of glass.

"No, I'm not because there is a wall between that and the rest. It is you who is preventing anyone from seeking further information."

"Information…intimate thoughts, memories. I think they can stay hidden for the moment, don't you?" He stated more than asked.

His eyes stared at the window as if he was somewhere else and not there in the cabin. J`nn moved to her backpack and began rummaging, removing wet belongings and throwing out what was soiled by the rain.

The Spellcaster held a silver-segmented thirteen-pointed star that incorporated the first Spellcasters pentagram covered by the new pentagram of renewal.

Each member of a Spellcasters dedication received a segment separately for completed ordained duties and talents. When all sections had connected, their powers were to be used for protective wards. There was a legend that called on the thirteen pointed stars. No one for centuries had seen or heard of this segmented star. He felt J`nn seemed to be entwined with him, but how he just did not know.

An Ogdoadic Knight could only touch the origin deeply warded and surrounded in the myths of time. Taelen researched this particular star out of curiosity. And a niggling thought had entered his mind at his first meeting with J`nn.

Somehow J`nn was linked to the Ogdoadic Knights, and they were just as bloody elusive, he thought to himself. Only Silver Crescents could contact them. Their whereabouts were not known. No one had seen one for hundreds of winters, yet here in front of him was a young woman with an unknown lineage with a thirteen-point star just as the ledger had said.

The Sz`a`Th had only agreed to the Covens' reformation under the strictness of understanding of the twelve segments. Still, even this decision gave an uneasy feeling to the lands that could again see the Four Hundred Winter War scars.

Taelen watched as she placed the silver chain over her head. The segment lay over the nightshirt, resting on the rise of her breasts. Taelen stood and went to the large blanket box; the deep honey grain wood carved with a rune design with silver ore poured into it. Opening the heavy lid, he took out two quilts and handed her one.

“You take the bedroom. I'll sleep out here.”

“But there are two sets of bunk beds.”

“Aye, and I am a Warrior and a Widower, you are neither, and at the moment, I think you should stay that way.”

“Then you are…gracious Lieutenant…thankyou,” she said, looking at the blue quilt in her hands, feeling the soft texture of the material that was not new yet felt loved in its worn way.

“I suppose I am. Others I know would call me an idiot,” he laughed. He held the quilt loosely in his arms, concentrating on the fire and not her. Just her presence was stirring emotions in him that he had thought were not possible.

"That and many other things, it will be gossip enough when we return. I will not give them the satisfaction of finding us in the same bedroom."

"We were in the same bedroom in the Coven."

"Aye, that was different."

"How," she asked, "you wish to wreck your back and sleep on the floor for the reputation of one Spellcasters, which is already questionable." Her anger and repulsion surfaced from the assault."

"Aye, I respect and care for you more deeply than I have realised." He said, "and sleeping here is my way of protecting you. The beds are for you to sleep in." He shrugged awkwardly. "Go, J`nn, I feel foolish enough already. I have said too much too soon."

His amethyst, blue eyes narrowed as he turned his attention to the fire glowing and crackling next to him as he threw the quilt around his shoulders more to separate the air between them.

"If you say so, Lieutenant, I don't understand why you feel awkward; males can be confusing."

"One day, you will understand. I hope why males feel confused in certain company. May the moon protect your dreams, Spellcaster?"

Taelen arranged the large pillows on the floor and lay down. It was a while before his eyes closed. Taelen dreamed dark swirls of magenta coursed around him as he stood somewhere. Earth and stone were the surroundings—a winter's breeze's sharp, bitter chill mingled with the magenta light.

The Mhyst was his; he could feel its fresh touch. The black-grey swirl came slowly; its pungent decayed odour assailed him and made him gag and dry retch. It climbed over the magenta light towards him. Taelen twisted swiftly away, trying to escape.

As sharp as death's own teeth, cold pointed fingers gripped his shoulders, immobilising him. Taelen's fingers trembled from the nerves in his shoulders pinched tightly in the grasp.

Glancing over his shoulder, a face caught his breath. He felt the fear rise and fought it back down, locking it in a deeper part of his mind. He called upon the Mhyst to rise.

“Now, I have you, Bastard”. His Uncle laughed at him. His eyes were not the same amethyst blue that Taelen shared with his father, Yassarn. Mah`sden's were the dark blue of a winter's ocean.

Taelen's Mhyst rose to swirl around him like a large vapour spiralled, ignited into white fire flew, as one Mhyst met another.

Mah'sden's skeletal fingers trembled until, at last, he let go but rose swiftly to Taelen's throat tighter and tighter. He was gagging as stony fingers dug deep around his windpipe. Taelen swung up with his black blade entering under his uncle's chin. The heat emitting from his short sword made him drop it suddenly. His Uncle threw him to the ground, groaning as he fell back sharply onto hard floorboards. Holding his throat and gasping hard for air, he tried to rise.

“Next time, Taelen, it will be your death.” Taelen lay down as tears burned in his eyes.

“Old man, you are a dead man walking. You will die by my hand and no other.”

He woke to cough; the fire's embers were opaque glows of soft orange and yellow in the night's dark velvet cloak.

Though he had been schooled extensively in the Mhyst and some Spell Casting, his tutor Master L`unh had only touched the grey Veil of evil and, just lightly, upon the power of Dream Casting.

The rain fell in a constant song in the cabin's forest. Taelen stood from his bedding and opened the door to the outside. Darkness cloaked the world before him.

He sat on the black stone steps under the awning of the veranda; his thoughts were as blank as the forest before him. His eyes fell upon a familiar shape as he sat there in the dark and cold.

Wolf's speech entered his thoughts; he felt the Wolf's tentative sniff seeking knowledge of his scent. Taelen opened his thoughts.

A coal-black Wolf with no other markings stood suddenly out of the darkness. The eyes, a whitish-blue with a slash of green diagonally through each iris, watched him as if he was prey.

He was substantial for a Timber Wolf; his chest was easily as broad as Taelen's shoulders. Taelen sat, watching the wet black nose twitch, sniffing the air surrounding them.

"Taelen," the Wolf thought, " I have found you."

"Welcome Ji`rah, Pack leader and runner of the night." He replied in greeting. "Why have you sought me after nearly three winters?"

"Evil pursues you, brother of mine and widower of my sister. And I have been a tad busy with Lord Za`qrn." He thought to Taelen. 'You are in great danger.'

"Tell me something I don't already know. Do you know whose magic is propelling the storm, Ji`rah?"

"The storm is that, but the weather is a slave to the Spellcasters."

"Why have you come?" Taelen asked his friend.

"It is safe to travel the forest at night in wolf and not as a man. There is no place for you, Taelen, which is safe. Our Uncle has ordered me here to be your back. I am following his orders and that of the Sz`a`Th."

The Wolf moved closer to him and sniffed his neck. "You have been visited by one of the Dark Sz`a`Th; I smell the taint and the salt of blood."

Taelen's hand went to his shoulder and touched the wet stickiness of his blood and the swelling of his skin. Ji`rah sniffed the wound through the cloth.

"Evil," the Wolf said as he rolled in upon himself and unfolded a form in a deep purple glow from the crouched position. The transformation from Wolf to man had taken a second. "Dream Caster has to be removed" he bent to his boots, removing a narrow blade.

"Just keep bloody still, Taelen; I'm going fishing. And my balls are bloody freezing."

"You hate fishing…just tell me when the blade goes in as you are at my back, and I don't want to hurt…."

"In." That was all Ji'rah said as he attentively fished into Taelen's flesh for what he instinctively knew was there. The blade's touch on the crystal had him brace Taelen with his other arm around Taelen's chest as he secured the crystal hook pulling it out. He flicked the crystal hook into the fire, where it just dissipated to dust and vanished.

Ji`rah stood as tall as Taelen's 6' 4"; his skin was a dark olive tan. Ji`rah uncurled his limbs and twisted his neck from side to side.

His clothes were the black of his Wolf coat and the uniform of the Sqh`xn Nation. He wore a short beard and the short hair of a Warrior. The only difference was the webbing of his boots, woven of herringbone design laced in such a fashion that the cloth of the webbing would not tangle during transformation. Each Wolf pack had their woven design.

"Brother, it seems you have gotten yourself into a bit of trouble; again, I might add, it is seriously forming a habit with you. Stand still while I heal this incision."

Taelen smiled. "It is good to see you too, brother."

"Oh, Aye," He replied, "I'd like to see those bruises inside under a lamp if I can."

Taelen frowned and shrugged slightly at the request. Inside, Ji`rah held the lamp's light close to Taelen's skin.

"Here, sit still." He said and began inspecting the wound's bruising and loose skin and murmuring as he did, gently pressing softly with his fingertips.

"That does hurt, you know!" snapped Taelen rather grimly.

"Hmm, we are testy, aren't we?" Neither heard J`nn appear behind them as both their backs were facing her. He said, finishing the wound healing; blood stained his hand and blade.

However, both heard the silent whisper as her hand went to get his blade.

"Don't touch him." She hissed at Ji`rah, who turned as well as Taelen.

Her eyes widened at the deep purple bruising and gash on his shoulder.

"Well...Excuse me!" Ji`rah said in an indignant tone, "And just who are you? And don't

touch my weapons, Mistress. You may be a Spellcaster, but as a Warrior of Sxn`qn and a

Sz`a`Th Sahn`FwrhWarrior, I would not touch my weapons ever, understand?"

His eyes widened at the silhouette that appeared through the nightshirt as she stood between

them and the fire.

Eyes whitish-blue with a slash of green diagonally through each iris flashed in a spark that

took warned her.

He blinked, slowly cooling his temper.

"Eh! Taelen, she has more curves than a bitch in season. Those legs I could wrap around my shoulders in a breath."

Taelen groaned loudly and said, "I wish you hadn't said that, Ji`rah."

J`nn leapt at him; the crack of her slap made Taelen wince for Ji`rah, who looked at her, his eyes wide open in surprise.

"Fiery little 'bitch', isn't she," he snapped, laughing as he held the blade and her wrist and continued to inspect the wound on Taelen's shoulder. J`nn squirmed, but Ji`rah ignored her, holding her firmly at arm's length.

"I wouldn't if I were you, Ji`rah. Mistress J`nn is a Spellcaster."

"Whoa, there!" and promptly let her go, dropping her to the floor. Ji`rah smiled down at J`nn as she glared at him.

"Nice blade though…yours?" he inquired as J`nn stood angrily and thumped him hard across the shoulder blades.

He swung around, clasping her face in his hands and kissed her. Taelen watched, bemused as he saw the eyes of J`nn rollback.

Ji`rah was lifted into the air and flung hard at the open doorway.

He fell slowly on his back and lay in the mud. The rain fell on him as he smiled at Taelen, who had gone after him.

Taelen realised she had gone just that little bit too far, not that Ji`rah had not deserved it.

"Get him some clothes, J`nn."

"I will not!" she snapped.

"I'm not asking you, I'm telling you, or would you like me to order you?"

"I hope he drowns in it." She turned her back to the room and left.

"Taelen, I'm in love," Cried Ji`rah from outside in the mud and rain. "I'm in love!"

Taelen stood in the doorway, hands on his hips and fell into a rich, deep laugh. He was shaking his head at Ji`rah.

"Not actually. You're in too many centimetres of mud and water; it's time you got back inside." He said, laughing at Ji`rah spread out on the ground resembling a sacrifice and not a Prince of the Wolf Nations.

Ji`rah stood in front of the fire, stripped naked, and caught the towel Taelen threw his way, wrapping it around his hips just as J`nn entered.

Her eyes travelled down his body.

Dark hair fanned across his chest and down his muscled stomach disappearing beneath the cover of the towel at his hips.

Ji`rah winked at her as she blushed.

The Spellcasters gave him clothes of those who would work in the forest she had found. She watched him closely.

"I am sorry, Lieutenant, "she added, "I didn't mean…."

"AH! I understand now, brother; she is your 'bitch'. You are a lucky bastard!" Ji`rah said as he dressed with no shame, dropping the towel as he pulled on his trousers.

"Ji`rah...!" Taelen rolled his eyes as Ji`rah dropped the towel pulling on the trousers.

"Oh Gods of the bloody Elements, what now? I'm trying to get dressed." He said indifferently, then noticed the look on the Spellcaster's face.

"Ji`rah, she's not Wolf or pack. Watch the phrases, will you, just for once." Taelen pleaded.

"Different worlds, brother, but the pack is the pack. I understand and apologise for any offence it was not intended." He shrugged, but his thoughts were elsewhere.

Taelen looked in disbelief at his friend. Ji'rah was known never to apologise for anything.

"Fine, I will go have a steaming bath while you explain. No, that will take too bloody long, so Mistress J`nn. Five minutes, I still have your mud on me."

Ji`rah returned as they drank the spiced tea, and Taelen shook his head at Ji`rah.

"I must explain to you, Mistress J`nn, that this person is my brother by marriage and blood and is a close friend. His manners are less than perfect, but I think his heart and soul are in the right place". He said, smiling at Ji`rah, whose own eyes were lowered as he pulled soft boots onto his socked feet.

He shrugged and glanced at the Spellcaster's young face's bemused look.

Ji`rah pulled the soft cream shirt over his head and smoothed it down over the dark blue pants.

"These have to be your clothes, Taelen; I'd never wear these colours, oh and I just saved his proverbial arse – he has been visited by a Dream Caster…no thanks needed." He said, frowning. He picked up the towel and began drying his hair.

Taelen smiled; Ji'rah was also known for his vanity; he mused a family trait considering Lord Za`qrn.

"He is your brother?... Dream Casting had been banished after the Four Hundred Winters War," she asked, looking at Ji`rah, his pale white eyes with the green blaze set in the dusky skin that was his made J`nn blush.

"His eyes are Wolf where yours are not," she said, tilting her head slightly in thought.

"She's quick-minded this one. How is she in the den? The banishment seems to have ended," he said, raised his eyebrow and added, "so who Dream Casts these day's Mistress? Spellcasters are the only ones who had that insidious skill?" Ji`rah said

"Ji`rah… enough," looking at him. "She was talking more of your flirtatious nature. That cheek side," raising his eyebrows, "that we love or hate."

"What? Please don't confuse me, Taelen. Where was I? Oh yes! attitude, not, you're breeding, but a good breeder isn't something to be scoffed at!" Taelen laughed at Ji`rah's words.

"Could be why you are still single, Ji`rah."

"Well!" He raised his dark eyebrows, "You'd better tell her. This should be good, Taelen, because the girl has no idea who you are, let alone who I am and what it means to us."

Taelen looked at Ji`rah. Some days he could strangle this lovable, rude and genuine friend. He slowly stood and retrieved his shirt and slipped it on.

"This is Lord Ji`rah, a Prince of the Wolf Nation of Sqh`xn. He is Sz`a`Th and is Sahn`Frwh trained, amongst other things."

"Well pronounced, brother, your diction of my mother tongue is improving."

Taelen's eyes slid beneath lids, then focused again. Ji`rah did push his patience at times, most times.

"I married his sister in circumstances and actions

that brought a new leader to the Pack. His sister, Kurr`etun, was murdered by their father." His voice tightened with the sound of her name on his lips.

Taelen took a deep breath and continued but looked not at them but at the flames and shadows of the fire, which had caught his thoughts.

"But Sz`a`Th Lore forbids the intermarriages of Wolf, so does Wolf Lore."

"I'm impressed, but you see, sweet Mistress, politics always overrules any written lore, no matter which nation it belongs. Besides, it's never stopped anyone from doing what comes with sex, basically. Naturally, Taelen's paternal grandmother was Wolf." Smiled Ji`rah, Taelen rubbed his forehead, trying to relieve the stress. "His maternal now that's an entirely another matter."

"How did this happen? Why was it allowed," she asked impatiently.

"Now that's an easy answer.  Taelen killed the Pack Leader when he attacked my sister, relative wise; he was our father and an absolute psychopathic narcissistic and psychotic bastard; Taelen, well, he's dead. One less arse of the Wolf Nation is one dead Wolf our Nation is glad to be rid of."

"But the Lieutenant killed your father."

"Was a misty experience, I can tell you!" He replied, laughing at his brand of humour.

"The bastard deserved the death he got; believe me, Mistress, we do not choose who sires us, given a chance. I am not the only one of the Nation of Wolves that wanted him dead."

"JI`RAH…."

"Bad pun, sorry. Dark military humour, I'm afraid, always gets you through the worst that happens. We did not mourn the Lord's death; we drank way too much mead and ate."

“Lieutenant is he always like this?” she asked him, already worn with the Warrior.

“Only when I’m in love,” Ji`rah said, gazing wide-eyed at her.

Taelen narrowed his eyes at Ji`rah. “I’m afraid he is,” he sighed “, and I’d have to say, he has become seriously worse in the last three winters since I last saw him. It’s a family trait, and if you ever meet our Uncle, you will understand which side of the family it comes from.”

“I’ll return to bed”. J`nn replied, tired by Ji`rah’s antics.

“Can I come?” he purred to her with a lopsided grin and a look that brought a full blush of sunset red to her neck and cheeks.

“When Hell freezes over, Lieutenant.” Her voice lowered toward him.

“That’s alright. I can wait.” He said, smiling and raising his eyebrows questioningly.

The door to her room slammed loudly, and he grinned at Taelen.

“I’m wearing her down. I can feel it…. she loves me”.

“I think she’d love you to leave, and it’s me that you’re wearing out, not down.”

Ji`rah sighed, sitting down on the hearth.

“Actually, it is you she likes, but I’d doubt, and I’d wager my moons pay rather heavily that you haven’t even noticed.” He grinned ruefully and mischievously at Taelen. “Or have you taken a vow of celibacy since we last met?” His eyebrow rose questioningly.

“I’ll ignore that comment, brother. I am more concerned about what you can tell me about this. Is it Dream Casting, and if it is who Dream Cast these days or better still, what can Dream Cast?”

Ji`rah again studied the bruising deep purple to black on Taelen's shoulder.

"It's Dream Casting, but I'll not give you a name until I know why. Was it him? It will leave some dreams in your mind, but the barb is destroyed."

"So you know who did this do you."

"Aye, your Uncle somehow was in the Dream. The dream world is at night, Taelen, but a Spellcaster has to help them get there. Someone is using them as a medium to travel to your dream?"

"Since when have the Sqh`xn been privy to Sz`a`Th Lore and Spellcasters Lore? Do you now understand the tides of Mhyst and dreaming?" he asked as he pulled the shoulder of his shirt back up.

Ji`rah felt tired. "Tomorrow, I will philosophise with you. But now, I must sleep. I have run for two days and three nights to get to you, my brother."

"Aye, there are bunks in the room adjacent to J`nn. Just be quiet for once. This floor is not as comfortable as I would have wished. I feel I shall be sleeping on the ground for a while once we leave here.

Both slept soundly and without dreams. Ji`rah was the first to rise and slipped out of the room. Stirring the embers, he rebuilt the fire and sat on the veranda drinking his tea. The storm had gone. Only the strips of loose bark, leaves, and the odd downed branch were to show for the storm.

Ji`rah was thinking of his sister when J`nn interrupted his thoughts.

"May I," she asked him.

"If you wish, Mistress," he said, removed and stared out at the light mist of grey dawn.

"My apologies for last night", her words were quietly spoken.

"I should apologise," he said, throwing a fallen

branch from the veranda. He fell into an uncomfortable silence.

"Are your burdens so heavy you can't speak of them?"

"Aye, Mistress, they are. This war has cost me, friends, and family, but I will tell you of young Taelen. He is in danger, great danger."

"Why? He is a Lieutenant of the Sz`a`Th; he is Sahn`Frwh."

Ji`rah looked at her and frowned slightly.

"He told you that."

"Yes"

"It is a half-truth, and Sahn`Frwh do get killed, remember that," he said, shrugging and taking a deep breath leaning back against the pole supporting the veranda's roof.

"And the rest of the truth is what, Lieutenant?"

"Is not for me to say; you will have to ask him that, Mistress."

"Ask me what?" asked Taelen as he stepped out of the doorway and onto the veranda with them.

"The other half of the truth," J`nn answered as she drank the sweet hot spiced tea.

Taelen looked at his hands as he held the mug. He was glancing at Ji`rah. Both had heavy hearts.

"It is time then, is it not, brother."

Ji`rah looked at the pain behind his brother's words.

"I will stay," he said just as Taelen took a deep breath and began.

"In truth, I have not lied to you, Mistress. Some truths are harder to bring from the shadows of the Mhyst than others are. You know the story of Lord Yassarn and how he came to the Coven."

"Yes, Lieutenant. You are in his service. He is your Lord. All know of the Lord's Imperial Scribe and that you represent him in all matters."

Ji`rah looked back at Taelen. He saw how difficult it was for him. Taelen did not want to lose the genuine friendship he had with J`nn.

"I am him, Yassarn was my father's name, and my real father was a Sz`a`Th Captain."

"I know, in your grief, you never saw those in the Coven, but I saw you."

"Why didn't you say something?"

"Why our friendship was, is more important to me than 'politics and protocol.' Besides, who would have believed me had I told them how we met."

Ji`rah smirked, eyes danced with delight. He forgot his melancholy mood of early dawn.

"She has you there, brother," he said, laughing, then stopped. His eyes looked to the tree line. "Are you expecting visitors, for there are four Warriors two minutes ride from here, coming in this direction?"

Ji`rah's hearing was acute; essentially, he was human, yet he had the senses of a Wolf blood lineage.

"No," Taelen said, searching the fringes of the dark green forest and the many hidden shadows that played in the early morning light.

"Then let's expect the unexpected, Taelen." Ji`rah checked his boots for the blades secreted there.

"I usually do when you're around Ji`rah; J'nn gets inside now!."

"I will not," she said, "They will not expect a husband and wife here."

"A who?" he said, his eyes wide.

"Don't worry, brother. They do not know of me. They are your Warriors, not Sqh`xn. One is a Sergeant from the Coven, the others Dark Sz`a`Th."

"Oh Hell," he said, "I hope you two can act well", answered Taelen.

The riders halted in the misting rain. Taelen knew immediately something was amiss.

"Lieutenant Taelen," said the young Sergeant at Arms, saluting; Taelen did not recognise the other three Warriors. The intense stress behind the Sergeant's eyes had all three wary and prepared.

Taelen was never addressed with his full title; this was a well-known order, but the Sergeant had masked his title, addressing him in the way he would a Sahn`Frwh Knight. He saw Ji`rah walk to the end of the veranda as if strolling and lent over the rail.

The Sergeant glanced at Ji`rah. Taelen caught the hidden fear in the young Warrior's eyes.

"You're wanted at the Coven Lieutenant, immediately."

"The reason?" asked Taelen watching the other Warriors closely.

The young Warrior frowned. Taelen smelt the taint of the Mhyst while Ji`rah leapt the railing; two blades left his hands. The thud as they hit the chest of the two Warriors was not as surprising as the third. J`nn let fly her dagger, striking a lethal blow to the third Warrior.

The young Sergeant sat still as the dead Warriors slipped to the wet ground from their saddles.

"Get rid of the bodies, Ji`rah. Dek`hlan tether the horses and go inside when you're finished; J'nn help my brother."

Strangely, he felt she would argue, but there was no argument. He quietly wondered how a Spellcasters managed the art of killing, and the blade's skill seemed to contradict all Lore's. It would be something he would research later. The distinctive dagger she had used was something he had never seen in any of the armouries or the Guilds.

The dagger she had used was engraved in the runic

script from tip to the grip. The pommel was 'T' barred to protect the hand, and so the dagger could be used in any defensive move, and more than just the blade, it was the use of the blade by the Spellcasters as they were forbidden to carry any form of weapon, their spells it was said was weapon enough.

A silversmith and a very skilled Master of the Guild made the dagger. The colour of white to mauve lightning sleek and precise, and silver ore itched at his psyche. Half filigree runic swirls than the blade itself, beautiful with engraving in a language Ji`rah had seen once before.

Ji`rah's sister, Silver Crescent, Sergeant Ry`arma, Sahn`Frwh, taken from the Lake City of Cran`dk three winters past, had one similar if not identical to the Spellcaster's dagger. He swallowed hard; her body was never found; he was told she killed in action, yet Ry`arma was not dead, and he could not shake the feeling of his younger sister. Losing Kurr`etun, his youngest sister was challenging but losing Ry`arma haunted him.

Dek`hlan entered the cabin. The Sergeant removed the oilskin-riding cloak and hung it on the hook.

"Too much has happened in the twelve hours you have been absent, Lieutenant. Master L`unh is missing. We felt the taint of the Mhyst, and this was all we found in his quarters." He handed Taelen the paper. The Master Spellcasters script flowed across the grey paper. The language was that of the Tali`z Coast that Taelen grew up on, an antiquated runic script that few used and less spoke because of the difficultness in the speech and the text-only those of the Scribes Guild painfully persevered, but even their numbers were dwindling.

Taelen read the note and knew Master L`unh would be alive. In the letter, he was a devious old man and stated he loved a challenge.

"How did the Master let this happen?"

"The Healer Maikim said someone poisoned her. Drugged him"

"Who is left at the Coven?"

Dek`hlan looked away from Taelen; the pain the young man was carrying was tremendously weighty; he rested his head in his hands, shielding his eyes, as his hands began to shake.

"It is not the Sergeant. It is the Coven itself," said Ji`rah

Dek`hlan took a deep breath. His voice trembled as he spoke. His eyes could not hold theirs for the violence, and the horror was his alone. He wrapped his arms close to his chest to stop the trembling.

"Everything happened so fast. As you had ordered, Lieutenant, we dispatched the Spellcasters and Warriors to the southwest Covens. The remaining Warriors stood the night guard upon the parapets of the Coven walls." He steadied himself and stared at the fire. Then took a deep breath and began again.

"Last night the storm hit, it...it was if something far deeper within the Coven had shifted, it was as if the Coven wept like a child fearing the worse. Something slipped between the Veils."

"Something…what do you mean?" J`nn asked, her forehead frowning slightly. "A spell, you mean?"

He shrugged. "If it was a spell, the Sz`a`Th Lieutenant caused the incantation to waver. We have no prisoners in the cell. Lieutenant Brae is now Lord of the Coven."

"When Hell freezes the Great Lakes of Nost`ra, will that mongrel bastard sit as Lord of the Coven? Where is Yhy`h." Taelen said, gritting his teeth with anger.

"Mistress Yhy`h left with a detachment of Warriors

before the attack."

Ji`rah cursed in his Wolf pack tongue. His guttural speech and noises only Taelen understood made him smile slightly at his brother.

"Dek`hlan, where hides your family."

"Everyone heeded your plan. Three-quarters of the Coven have hurried through the night down in the maze of underground passages like rats in a sewer," he said bitterly. "My family is north to freedom."

Taelen knew many would have died as well. He also knew Dek`hlan was saying his wife had perished along with their infant daughter. His wife was one of the most skilled Archers; her loss would ripple through the Sz`a`Th. An amazing Sz`a`Th Warrior, his heart tightened. They had been married only one winter. Taelen recalled how thrilled he was at being a father.

Dek`hlan's grief would come in anger. Taelen knew that much of the Warrior before him. Ji`rah realised that too.

"Sergeant," Taelen said, "My grief is yours. We shall honour their deaths swiftly". He let Dek`hlan step into his mind. Here Taelen let his Mhyst glide upon the Sergeant. The young Warrior was grateful for the respite, allowing him to grieve, as he would have, though only fleeting in its moment.

"Do they expect you to return to the Coven with me in tow, Dek`hlan?"

"They expect me to lie rotting for the picking of the forest scavengers," he said coldly, his green eyes still and haunted by his grief, staring blankly at the fire.

"Dek`hlan, you know the passages better than anyone I know."

"Aye, Lieutenant, I do."

"Good, I will return with you to the Coven alone."

"NO!" growled Ji`rah. "He will torture you, and if

you're lucky, he'll kill you after. No, you are not going!" He shook his head adamantly, looking at Taelen angrily; anger and frustration prickled across his skin.

"You have not heard what I am about to ask you, Ji`rah." Ji`rah smiled and stroked his trim black beard with strong hands, making J`nn shiver.

"Ah, brother, you always jump to my defence. What can I do for you?"

"You are to find Master L`unh," he said. "Be warned, Ji`rah, he may be old, frail and silver hair, but watch your manners and ears. J`nn will accompany you. He is alive; just find him."

"I will not go with him," She said decisively.

"You will do as I have asked!" he said; his voice held an authority that stung her, bringing a flush of pink to her cheeks. "For without a Spellcaster, he cannot find a Spellcaster."

"He is a Wolf" she wished she had kept her mouth shut. "He has an 'attitude' problem" as if apologising for her outburst.

"It may well be that damn 'attitude' Mistress that will save both of your lives. Never underestimate him. He is Pack Leader of the Sqh`xn Nation and has more contacts than a Drargon`H Mariner has whores of all genres."

"Eloquently put, brother, couldn't have put it smoother than that." Ji`rah grinned from ear to ear.

"Oh, shut up", J`nn snapped exasperatedly as she caught the look in Ji`rah's eyes. She would end up killing him. She was sure of that, even if it was for peace.

"Pack now; get what you need from here and go. Where you smell that rotting Mhyst odour, you will find our Master. Take two horses as well."

"Dek`hlan, where is Den`ah?"

"All captured Warriors are in the cells. Brae has dealt his punishments". Dek`hlan voice was hard and cold as if hiding the vision his mind held of those captured.

"Mah`sden will kill you, Lieutenant."

Taelen shrugged with the reality that it was a constant threat, always on the fringes of his thought.

"It will not be the first time he has tried to do it, Dek`hlan; it won't be the last." he finished the brew he was drinking. "At the moment, my need is greater than his."

Ji`rah entered with the packs. "You remember how to call the pack if your needs are such, brother."

"Aye, I know." Replied Taelen, his thoughts running swifter than Ji`rah could in Wolf form.

"Then use it, stubborn one. Our gift to you has been," Ji`rah eyed Taelen carefully." Your lineage as Wolf is long; being married to my sister counts to use the howling if you need to."

"I'm not all 'pack' Ji`rah; my guilt over your sister will never leave." "Then find another to breathe with, one that beats the song of your heart and mind."

"Maybe, one day." He said, gathering his pack and rechecking it. "It will take time; I just can't fall in love". Taelen sighed and became quiet, glancing sideways at his brother.

"Sometimes, I say too much?" he said and added, "and sometimes you cannot see what is in your grasp, brother; you are sometimes deaf and blind to those around you."

"Sometimes, you do, but sometimes I must be reminded that everything has a cost."

"Pack", Ji`rah thumped his chest; his whitish-blue eyes, with their diagonal slash of green, held Taelen's amethyst, blue ones in silent, knowing what was ahead of them would not be easy, but both knew it would belong.

"Pack," said Taelen. "Be careful, Ji`rah."

They watched Ji`rah and Mistress J`nn solemnly. Taelen wondered if he would ever see those two again. He knew he would have difficulty forgiving himself if anything happened to them. He had a nagging feeling a lot would die for a cause that had decreed in stone that it was he alone who had been chosen to lead.

Outside, Taelen stood by the Spellcaster; he turned slowly and gently held her face in both his hands, his lips closed upon hers and within the falling rain. Taelen kissed the Spellcaster deeply; desire for her burned through him, scorching his thoughts.

The touch of her skin, softness, and scent woke the primaeval desire channelling through him. His need was to take her there and then on the ground. His pulse pounded in his temples. Achingly he removed his thoughts from the needs of his body and later reluctantly released the Spellcaster.

Holding his breath and pulling away from a spell of nature, he slowly walked back into the cabin. He knew those pale green-grey eyes would haunt him for a long time. Her taste would be forever locked into his memory; taking a deep breath, he tried to extinguish the need in his loins.

Ji`rah smiled wryly as she mounted in silence. The young Spellcaster touched her lips at times as if they were burnt. They rested by midday, their journey long and arduous. The Spellcaster ate in silence, as did Ji`rah.

The trees towered green and silent sentinels. Leaves were quiet, watching; another had begun for every whisper they shared. The leaves glanced against each other in sounds that resembled silent codes.

"The scent is still strong, my Lord," She asked,

using her magic gifts.

"Aye, Mistress, but calling me Lord will get me skinned alive, and I am not ready to be a floor rug, Lieutenant, or just Ji`rah might save my arse " Ji`rah's eyes slid through the trees watching shadows no one else could see.

"Why did he do that?" she asked Ji`rah, whose thoughts were elsewhere.

Frowning at the question, he breathed in the forest's scents, sensed nothing he was not looking for and replied.

"Excuse me? I don't know what you are talking about." Replied Ji`rah, his thoughts on the long path ahead for them both.

"Kissed… me," She said quietly and slowly.

"Oh!" he glanced at her, smiling at the blush upon her cheeks.

"He genuinely cares for you." He said, eating the dried meats in his hand and offering her some, which she took gratefully as they rode. "Have you mated yet?" He asked with the bluntness that had him looking down the point of a sword more than once.

J`nn choked on the dried meat the Warrior had given her. "What did you say?"

"Mated, you know… " he asked with a questioningly raised eyebrow and a look in his eyes that she could have slapped away had she not been on the horse.

"I know, Lieutenant; you are so blunt and crass, even for a Wolf."

Ji`rah shrugged, then sighed as he realised his inept bluntness.

"Then you have not met many of the Wolf Nations. Accept my apologies when you are part of two cultures or more. What will offend one does not know the other. I am Wolf, we are rowdy and unpredictable, but we protect, remember that. And we die without regret understand that is a powerful thing to have in allegiance or friendship."

He stood upon the stirrups as the hair on his neck rose sharply. J`nn led her horse closer to him; she felt the thunder, too silent above them. Yet the earth trembled deep within the part of her that was Spellcasters.

"Riders," he said, "Six of them- Mistress, cloak yourself invisible, and do it now unless you wish to be at their mercy."

"But you" She grabbed his forearm, trying to make sense of what was happening.

"Ah, you care for me! So kind, cloak yourself, Mistress." Yet even within his bravado that she was coming to understand, she saw a skilled Warrior. He watched the air melt like a wave in the heat, and she was no more.

Ji`rah rolled his eyes and curled down onto himself. His clothes became fur.  A large, timber Wolf replaced the Warrior form and slowly backed into the undergrowth with the Spellcasters by his side.

The Warriors stopped.  The horses became restless and disturbed as they could sense Wolf's presence somewhere in the forest's undergrowth. Rearing their heads, the horses pulled on the reins and stamped their hooves. Those on their mounts were trying their hardest to calm their horses.

"Why have two horses tethered? There are scraps of food on the ground as well?" One of them asked aloud as another dismounted and crouched at the footprints in the soft earth.

"A Warrior and a young woman, there are also the largest Wolf prints I've ever seen." His dark brown eyes stared into the forest warily. He said to the other with his hand on the hilt of his black dagger.

"Then they will be dead. Why would they have gone into the forest."

"Not to pick mushrooms; use your imagination!" The reply from the Sergeant was worn and short.

The Sergeant mounted his horse, his eyes still on the forest. Ji`rah and the Spellcaster breathed low into their chests for fear of disturbing the essence surrounding them within shroud and transformation of 'cloaking'.

The party rode off, laughing at the Sergeant's reply at the expense of the Blade Man at Arms.

Ji`rah rolled his eyes and his body back into human form. He twisted his neck from side to side; vertebrae clicked loudly.

"Shattas…" he cursed aloud and complained, "That gives me a crick in the neck!" He rubbed the muscles that had knotted low near his shoulders.

He felt the delicate, slender fingers of the Spellcasters touch, his hands pushing them away gently as she sensed the area in his neck that he had cricked.

"Here, let me. You are so stubborn and tense." She said, watching his head tilted slightly.

Her fingers kneaded and massaged his neck and shoulders until she felt him relax.

"Will they come back, do you think." She asked as her eyes searched for the fading sounds of the riders.

"Maybe… we will be safe here. Can you cast a spell to protect us for tonight?"

He breathed profoundly, looking over the top of her head at the darkening light of the forest; the white fog of his breath was stark in the shadows and chilled air of the giant oak trees that now shielded them from view.

"They will not return as they seek others, not us." His thoughts flew silently through the forest to his brother, warning him.

J`nn wove a web of black and silver over and around them. He watched as she murmured ancient text; her eyes slid back beneath her eyelids in the dusk. Ji`rah made his own, but he prayed for them, mainly his pack brother Taelen. He mentally concentrated on his Pack as he drifted off to sleep.

The Warriors were leagues from them, where the day's death had yet to bring darkness and chill of the night.

# CHAPTER 9

His name was JA`rvis, a high-ranking member of the Sqh`xn Nation of Wolves. Sz`a`Th trained and held Captain's rank as a Sahn`Frwh Warrior. He had chosen to travel as a Wolf. The winter coat of fir was silver-white, and as a Timber Wolf, he was large. Ji`rah's' howl for assistance had reverberated through the Packs at all compass points throughout the regions.

He had heard the howl of Ji`rah regarding their brother Taelen and the attack on the Coven of Szsd`ET.

The Wolf had not been far from the Coven area and proceeded through the massive snowdrifts that had arrived, bringing an unseasonably early winter. He may have been a bit older than Taelen by ten winters; sometimes, the winters brought knowledge not easily experienced by the young.

Taelen was his brother through marriage and blood lineage. This was one request he would not refuse, could not ignore. Too much hinged on the Scribe to stay alive. Also, too many had held their breath for this young man to be found.

While Ji`rah and Mistress J`nn slept, protected by her ward and the silent understanding of the trees around them, the silver timber Wolf was making his way to the Spellcasters Coven of Szsd`ET.

As he moved through the regions, the weather was light and misting rain, and snow flurries fell like fine cobwebs, flowing with the breeze that accompanied the overcast day. The brutal snowstorms he passed would soon be here, carpeting the land in a white shroud.

Deep in the shadows of the He`lian Forests, a large Wolf rolled down upon himself. Again, as he stood, the figure of a man with a broad chest and big-boned but not overly large in build was visual from the shadows.

The man's dark uniform gave the impression of a shadow as he stepped out upon the gravel path. Lantern light pooled from his waist in yellow light as he held the lantern.

The Backpack carrying his kit upon his back ached and felt travel-worn. The Starve in his left hand was dark thunder and strong, but not straight. That was unusual. JA`rvis belonged to the Wolf Guild of Trackers. His Starve symbolised everything that could be seen and found. Nothing was hidden from a Tracker; JA'rvis was one of their best.

The top of the stave held a metal ornament fixed into the wood like a cork in a wine bottle. The delicate lace of silver netted over the metal ornament glowed as he held it high above his head. His lips moved as his breath fogged in whispered words of a pack oath. The Orb of the Sqh`xn flashed brilliantly once, and then only the lamp was his only light.

His footsteps were silent. His feet were enclosed in the softest deer hide and were the darkest blues. His trousers were deerskin and darkest grey, but not black.

The man's shirt was as black as his cloak. However, it was his hair that the Warriors first noticed when he approached the Coven of Szsd'ET black wrought Iron Gate. His hair was silver-white as the moon on a black still night and flecked dark in places, and so was the beard he wore, short and precisely trimmed in Sqh`xn Wolf regulations.

Dark eyebrows arched slightly over smooth dark olive skin with a velvety texture that hid his age. No lines were on his face, almond-shaped eyes that held deep pools of the palest blue with a silver diagonal fleck at the gates of Szsd`ET, and a nose not angular but smooth and shaped gently took the scent that pervaded the Coven.

The Warriors that stood guard thought he must have come from the island nations to the west. His ancestors did once, but this man was no more an Islander than they were. They watched as the lantern he held swung slowly as he stopped at the Coven iron gates.

"Hail, traveller, what is your business?" cried a Warrior leaning over the parapet

"I am Captain JA`rvis Sqh`xn Warrior sent by Lord Za`qrn", he called back up to them. "I have heard the howl of my brother Lieutenant Ji`rah of the Sqn`xn Nation on the 'T`kf Plains' he has told me that the Coven's needs are significant, and it is my healing that I will offer for respite from this weather."

Murmuring from behind the stone parapets, footsteps on the flagstone steps broke the night stillness as muffled as secrets.

Yellow light spilt suddenly onto the traveller from a second door behind the iron gates. His eyes blinked as they adjusted to the light's sudden illumination.

Towering Iron gates screeched as metal passed over metal, and the large wrought iron gate opened.

"Enter…" rasped a Warrior, his clothes bloodied and grimed with sweat, and the battle dirt staggered towards him. The young man's blue-mauve eyes were red and weary, dark black circles pooling beneath the skin of an old-young man. He wavered slightly as speech staggered to his dry and cracked lips. The pale blonde hair was stiff with grime yellow with old blood and a gaping wound bound weakly.

"If what you say is true, I need confirmation that you are indeed who you say you are," the Warrior sagged and held the Iron Gate bars for support, breathing heavily as beads of sweat appeared over his skin.

JA`rvis moved closer so he could define the Warrior's grimy fatigued features.

“PA`Lin… is it you, lad? It’s Master JA`rvis; open the gate.”

Concern creased his features as he assisted in pushing the iron gates open. PA`Lin came from the southern Regions; he was the best horseman and could heal their injuries and illnesses. Also, most skilled in Ah`niqtar, particularly martial arts used by all Warriors, male and female. Simple but deadly.

“Open the Gates; it is Lord JA`rvis of Sqh`xn…my apologies, my Lord, these are dangerous times….” The young Warrior’s speech ended in slurs and mumbles as he slumped slowly to the snow-covered flagstones.

JA`rvis stopped, only to lift the ill Warrior to his shoulders. He stepped into the small courtyard of the entrance as a door opened near him, and a woman’s haunted eyes stared at him.

“How many are ill as PA`Lin?” He gently asked her, lifting PA`Lin’s fevered body into his arms. “I need a fresh bed, table, stretcher to lie the lad on.”

JA`rvis followed her up the stairs and to an empty room. He laid PA`Lin down and removed his leg webbings, boots and uniform.

Unlatching the large windows, he pushed them open, fastening their hooks to the Castle's wall.

“Fifteen, my Lieutenant”, she replied, seeing his insignia in silver on the cuff of his tunic. Her eyes were as worn and bloodshot as the Warrior now lying under the sheets.

“My name is JA`rvis”. The healer’s voice soft, brogues lilt seemed to dispel her fears. He passed through the doorway and said as she guided him to a room with stretches, each held an ill Warrior.

“I need all these men cleaned, strip them, wash them

in hot soapy water, each a clean dish and clean water, and place them in clean beds. Open every window in this building or break them open I don't care how it is done." His voice was angry and level.

"I am only one. Master JA`rvis," She mumbled through exhaustion.

He turned to two young Warriors who watched him from the open door. His arms opened wide as he spoke to her and them.

"These men will die in twelve hours, and then it will be you. Who will then follow alternatively, you may wish to live. You have a choice to make and make it quickly. Too much time has passed, and the sickness has gained strength."

They moved towards him. His pale blue-white eyes drew them closer.

"Assist the Mistress here with clean bedding and clean clothes. Cut their hair, this short, in the Sz`a`Th regulations, beards, do all and adhere to their soul lore, be it Wolf or Man, Woman and in others, I am unaware of their secondment to the Castle. This is a Coven and a damn Garrison!"

JA`rvis said, showing centimetres between finger and thumb for the haircuts and beards. "Burn every soiled cloth in the place, take it all to the furnaces. Now Mistress, show me the others that have fallen to this poison, that is of Lord Mah`sden's doing."

That night he tended eighteen Warriors, stripped, scrubbed, cleaned, and placed them into beds. He had buried five. He had not encountered Taelen, which concerned him greatly. He needed to find the young Warrior and soon.

Master JA`rvis stood at the sizeable cast-iron pot hanging above the fireplace. He had just eaten the hearty, thick beef and vegetable stew and was about to go. He heard a woman's moan.

The woman's head rested on her arms as she sat slumped against the pine trestle table. He gently touched her forehead. Her skin was hot to his cold touch. He cursed loudly for his ineptness, he had been so busy, and he had neglected to notice she was just as ill as the others were. She did not move at his touch. JA`rvis knew she was not of the Coven but was a stranger, dangerously caught in a War she knew nothing of.

The Healer found a spare bed amongst those already sleeping with the illness and two Warriors not yet in bed.

They sat in the cold wind that brought clean air with it through the corridors.

"The woman is fever. Prepare a bed for her and help me tend her". He said his pale white-blue eyes did not want, no, for an answer. Sighing with the exhaustion that left them numb from head to toe, they obeyed his orders.

Master JA`rvis was shocked at the bruisers upon the woman's skin with all his thirty winters behind him.

Abrasions were many; bruises were deep blues, some yellow. He gently placed her into a deep stone-carved bath with oils and herbs, scrubbing her clean and apologising for the pain. Her moans and whimpers came within the fever.

The two Warriors averted their eyes until he ordered them not to.

"How can you tend without looking, "he said coldly." Or did you attack her?" he was angry.

"Not, by our hands, Master JA`rvis' one whispered. "We are Knights of Sz`a`Th. We were prisoners until the sickness took the others."

"You are Sahn`Frwh then? Good then, tell me, who did this?"

Both Knights washed her long deep, burgundy

brown hair without speaking.

“Aye, my Lord, we are Sahn`Frwh. Do we cut her hair”? He asked as the other rinsed the long dark wavy hair. “We only heard the name Brae.”

Master JA`rvis sighed as he lifted her out of the hip-bath, and they wrapped the towel around her drying her.

“Maybe not” he applied ointments to her scathed body and found a grey shirt too long. He handed her limp form to them.

“Find a bed for her; she will sleep until her body and soul are healed, be gentle. I have had to do internal healing for her body. She needs no sudden movements.” Silently he wondered whether her mind would ever heal from the ordeal that had left scars visible and mental.

JA`rvis was exhausted, but he continued lighting every candle within the walls and outer walls of the Coven. The candles belonging to the Coven of Szsd`ET were the thickness of two hand spans, with six thick tree branch-like wicks and the colour of the sun shadows filtered between the foliage. Each Coven made candles reflecting the elements of the region. Each warded, blessed and new spells. These were candles of the E`rth beliefs.

Both Knights, weak from fatigue, obeyed the stranger; both lifted booted feet with muscles that tore at joints and bones, and bodies ached from head to toe.

“You have checked the cells where the Spellcasters keep their records?” He asked them quietly.

The two Knights looked at one another, shoulders sagged, and they cursed under their breaths. A cold wind draft slowly passed around their ankles.

“I gather there is, by that use of language, take me down there.”

He followed at a slower pace, looking at the handcrafted stone blocks that were the walls of the

Coven corridors.

He lit more candles as they walked from the light into the darkness of unlit corridors. He could feel the anxiety of the two Warriors that walked in front of him. The walls and floor wore the angry graffiti of blood spilt and sprayed in a battle of unbelievable ferocity.

Swords, blades, and all forms of weaponry lay littered where they fell. Discarded passions, cold, lost empty. All three stood silently. He found himself alone and followed where the other two had gone.

The silence of the past battle for possession of the castle hung a silent song of loss.

"Master JA`rvis, come quickly."

He heard old cell bars connect sharply with the flat of a sword. The sound of metal on metal was sharp yet dead. Magic had been here. Evil magic hung a blanketing sound.

"Please". JA`rvis said. "Let me."

His hand touched the lock; cold metal, rust texture, scratched his fingertips as his talent unlocked the fixture. The lock clicked quite loudly, and the door silently opened.

Both Knights fell to their knees to the Warrior, who lay twisted, still, and bloody. One felt for a pulse. The Sz`a`Th Warrior lay where he had fallen in his deep crimson blood, stained dark as night on the rough stone floor.

"Not... Den`ah!" the Knight said, his voice was thick and coarse with emotions for the Corporal who lay still at his bent knees.

Master JA`rvis went down on one knee and felt the young Warrior's ankle for a pulse. His eyes held both of the Warriors before him. With the training, only one gets in close combat and wars.

JA`rvis was their anchor, and while he had not been

there for the fight, he would get them mentally and physically where they needed to be if it killed him.

“He lives just… by a fine life thread. Carry him as if he was your child. He has experienced horrors that will be difficult to remove.” Master JA`rvis led the way back through the dim, silent corridors and to the kitchen.

JA`rvis healed what he could. There, they slid his battered body into a healing bath. The assault on the young Warrior was horrific; whoever had tortured him wanted a long and painful death. The Corporals torture, whoever did this had tried to extract something from the young man that did not make sense to JA`rvis. Each point of Chakra had been torched and twisted as if trying to wring something out of the lad. One can’t tear the soul from the living.

His eyes tightened with emotion as he whispered under his breath in his language but was the same in any ‘ you who did this I know your scent, your handprint, your goal, it will be by my hand you die bastard or bitch, every step I take will be to stalk you like the coward you are be warned.’ His guttural growl had the young Warriors assisting glance at each other swiftly.

Whoever had done his torture was trying to withdraw Den`ah’s soul. How the Corporal had lived was impossible for JA`rvis to contemplate. He had seen many acts of torture, some of which defied thought. This was another such one. This, which stilled the Warrior's hearts; to remove someone’s soul while alive was just incomprehensible to these Warriors, and it was against all lore of man and myth that JA`rvis knew.

Captain JA`rvis healed his internal organs, then the burns of torture. He shook his head with tears in his eyes.

“I do not know if this will succeed.”

“Why? Please, Captain JA`rvis, I have heard that he

may become one with another to heal totally if one is so damaged. Is not Den`ah's life worth that?"

"He would become Pack, but will his mind heal from the horrors of such an assault with his attack?"

"You healed the woman…? It does not matter what sex you are, does it? He may already be Pack Captain; he grew up with Wolves where he lived, from birth I presume to ten winters old."

JA`rvis looked at the two young Warriors, he had to smile, and they were so young.

"Aye, it is no different … I will heal him. Maybe the silence of my Wolf blood will ease his soul; only time and good friends will tell. Do you know Den`ah well?"

"He does not play cards well, Captain," The young Sergeant mused, " he told me; Den'ah comes from Qlee`han, the wetlands of the south; he has no close relatives. They died in the Battle of Zira`taq – it means 'flames on water. Few survived that Necromancers work. Village after village burned, and the swamps burned. Once asked how the hell he got out, he said the strangest thing…' when the trees walk, you run like fuck pardon my cursing Captain JA`rvis' The Warrior paused. 'He also mentioned a Wolf Pack from that …Ten`qkn Wolves grew up with them, he said. He is a Veil Walker and Speaker of Tongue's and reads the forests well – I'm not privy to his missions. Veil Walkers, as you know, have a high-security clearance all to themselves, which I deeply respect."

He called silently for any Wolf of the Ten`qrn Pack or Warrior of the Qlee`han region to contact him immediately. He did not expect a swift reply.

'Aye, Captain JA`rvis, you asked for Ten`qrn Pack?'

'How far are you from Szsd`ET Castle?'

‘Five minutes in Wolf form Captain, I heard the howl and was in the vicinity; I am Corporal Aq`ten, Scout Ninth Degree. I am at the Gates now.’

JA`rvis ran and was down the flights of stairs and corridors in Wolf form, then rolled up into his human form.’

Breathing heavily at the Gate arguing with the Guard was a young woman, her black hair with its blaze of blue-white denoting her Ten`qrn Pack. The delicate white tattoo that was on the left side of her temple with the mark of the Green man, three lines three dots now glowing green on her left inside of the wrist was the brand of her Wolfpack, the tattoo of the Swamp Wolf burned into her skin of light olive colouring glowed blue ice in colour.

“Seriously, if you do not let me in, Corporal. I will have your fucking balls on a stick and barbeque them with spices, nuts and fruit,” Before the exhausted Warrior could reply, she had her blade through the bars of the gate at his temple and her other hand firmly gripping the Warriors balls. JA`rvis had a great urge to laugh. It took a lot of willpower to contain him. Instead, he sighed.

Corporal Sar`tq deep brown, dark eyes were exhausted from the snow, wind and long shifts. He raised eyebrows to say, ‘actually, you would be doing me a favour.’ He saw Captain Jarvis and thought not saying anything was saying everything. This was one of those times. He ruffled his black hair of snowflakes and waited.

“Corporal Aq`ten, release Corporal Sar`tq. You’re making his eyes water and mine as well. Corporal Sar`tq let the Ten`qrn Warrior in before she followed through with the threat of the Barbeque. She has travelled the hardest trails to get here, and she is all I have to save

Corporal Den`ah." She released her grip on the Warriors balls and slid her dagger into a hidden sheath on her back.

The Gates opened with a screech that JA`rvis and Aq`ten winced with their acute Wolf hearing. It was painful.

"Corporal Sar`tq, oil those bloody gates, or I will have every Guards blood to oil them understand?"

"Aye, Captain, on it immediately." He saluted and gave the younger Wolf Warrior a glance of thunder, but she said in reply to his look.

Her dark brown eyes slashed with an iridescent green across the pupils, and iris were hypnotising, and her eyes framed in long black eyelashes smiled at him.

"Really, Corporal? Think I would rather runt a tree than you, but nice balls – it's a Wolf thing, and I have no idea why." She winked at him and smiled, and he stood speechless, her smile he thought would and could light a fire in the deadest of men. He cleared his throat and adjusted his crotch, shaking his head. In a silent speech to her, he mused, 'I never runt as it is overrated even for a Wolf' he blinked slowly as the diagonal white slash through the dark brown wolf eyes smiled back at her.

'I shall be wary of your blades, Corporal. Be aware our next meeting might need snow.'

"Come, Corporal, I need you're ..." he sighed and studied her. Trackers wore the same uniform changing the region's colours of the land. She had come a long way. He knew that her Backpack and weapons were secure. Her black hair, now in a braid he had only seen in history books, was so intricate that it made his fingers and hands ache just thinking of its dexterity. He shook his head.

She followed him into the building, passing Warriors changing shifts; they glanced at her uniform of darkest black-green.

"Billet the Corporal on the East Wing Corporal Js`yah"

"Aye, Captain, I can take Corporals Backpack up."

"I take my own kit up, Corporal, Captain. I need to see this Warrior who is wounded. If he is from the region you speak of, very few of us survived the Battle of Zira`taq. I have no Wolf pack living and have met no one since."

The other Warriors were silent, the Battle of Zira`taq they all had heard of in their training, air and water on fire. Their skin goosebumped as hair rose in fear.

When did Warriors become so young, JA`rvis mused and knew because War was a young person's mantle, the old, if they survived War knew the cost, and it haunted all who had experienced it.

Master JA`rvis healed with the howling that came with the different path the Corporal would now walk. He left the two Warriors to tend the Corporal as he had done all which was possible.

He was exhausted and walked back to the cells below as the Warriors tended the young Corporal upstairs in the kitchen.

A shadow moved without any density, silently echoed, its distorted shadows upon the walls and bars as it left the underground that was the dungeon.

He turned once only and rolled a green lime. The fruit rolled down the corridor before him as he walked. The lime moved into the darkness that was just pooled yellow with candlelight.

JA`rvis walked briskly through the silence to the kitchen where the two Knights were bathing the Corporal.

"Captain JA`rvis," he said as he scrubbed the young

Corporal's limbs; the other, as if knowing the strength of his friend's illness, shaved his dark head of dark hair and beard trimmed in the Wolf regulations. His dark green eyes opened, glazed as he stared at JA`rvis.

Master JA`rvis opened the young man's mouth, trickling a potent herbal spiced liquid the colour of blood, thought one of the Knights.

"It is not blood", he looked at the Sahn`Frwh Knight. "Tell me, now what happened and your names." He stroked the young man under the chin as he would a newborn babe to get him to drink.

The Knights had eyes of different shades of amethyst. Jarek's eyes were a milky pale green where Ln`sahr were mauve deep near violet-blue.

Ln`sahr hair was as black as soot, his skin a deep dark velvet brown. Jarek's was the opposite yellow and blonde as those who lived east in the lands where ice and snow lay ten winter moons. Both wore the red crescent of a moons quarter. They were Sahn`Frwh. The mark of the Red Crescent Moon was also on others that now lay healing in the Coven

The crescent lay halfway tattooed at the corner of the left eye near the creases of laughter but not the temple. They were the Knights of the Death Watch and far from the Drakk`n Mountains. JA`rvis wondered why they were here; he also wondered where Taelen was.

They lifted the young Warrior out of the bath.

Corporal Aq`ten glanced at Den`ah's tortured body and saw something very familiar.

"No stop, you can't use the same healing, no clothes, only the sheet…if we were home, I would heal him in the earth with the swamp mud, but I can't; not all earth is the same."

Exasperated, she took the blade from her boot and

sliced the clothes from Den`ah "little time, Captain JA`Rvis, he is not dying on my bloody watch, not ever", returning her blade with speed only brought by her extensive training.

Tending to him in a gentleness that split sharply from the appearance of Knights of the Death–Watch and Wolf Tracker no older than Den`ah himself. JA`rvis sewed and bandaged, spread ointment and poultices onto the body before him.

Den`ah laid in the clean bed; JA'rvis positioned him so that the new moon spilt white across the Warrior's birthright of the Mhyst sprinkled blue and purple, not beginning or ending.

He watched the birthright spit and hiss as if a candlewick damp and cold tried to ignite. Slowly the moonlight ignited the power of the Mhyst; the room exploded in mauve particles of light.

"Please, Captain JA`rvis, the moon must spill on both our marks" she showed Den`ah's mark, a small paw on his chest hidden by dark hair.

"Please, Lieutenant."

"Whose paw print is this, Corporal."

Her dark brown eyes stared at Den`ah. She frowned and took a deep breath, her hand stroking his forehead, smoothing his eyebrows.

"We were just puppies, children. I had been sent to gather herbs from the wetlands and just rare ones we needed that day, and Den`ah, older, was told he had to go with me – he would have rather sucked sour swamp geese eggs than look out for me. Snakes I could kill, but the Cah`nu is a nasty large killing lizard that could take a horse and think it was a snack" a tear fell, and she wiped it away angrily.

"The smell of burning flesh, your world burning human, animal, aquatic, is something you gag on. The trees were walking from the swamplands, the flames like liquid fire flowed, a Wolf old was burning she placed her red paw on my wrist, she was our Elder, one who knew all. By doing what she did, she gave me her knowledge. The fire caught my paw, and Den`ah went to save me, but I put my paw on his chest. He was ten winters. I was seven winters but small for my age."

She parted the chest hair and said simply, "Watch, Lieutenants, this is what pack means, Den`ah became pack when I tried to stop him and save him, and the Tree scooped both up as they walked fast as they could from the flames. I have not met anyone and did not know Den`ah's existence until Captain JA`rvis called me."

The moonlight pooled onto the paw marks and burned into their skin's arteries and veins lit up in an iridescent blue light; tiny particles of the same light flowed around the room in a breeze. An ancient voice sang so exquisitely in its pitch that only after the light dimmed they realised it was the Corporal who sang the Swamp Region's healing song. Her blaze across her iris lit the room in pain she was in with the moon healing.

She pulled her kit towards her and curled up, singing the healing song. He knew she would rather die than go to her billeted room. She was doing this for someone who had saved her once.

"I'm afraid Den`ah, you are now part of the Pack of Ten`kqn and Sqn`xn Wolves. Forgive me. "

He said and closed the door. It was one thing to join the Pack willingly, another to wake and be a member of a nation you knew little of. He bowed his head with regret and what he had been forced to do to save the young Warrior's life.

He found the two Knights had bathed and were resting on stretches outside Den`ah's door in the corridor. He was too weary to sleep; Jarek opened his eyes.

"Sleep in this room next to his Corporal Aq`ten is in there, do not disturb her on your life. Understand that is my order; you need not sleep in this cold and draughty corridor." They walked to the room and collapsed into the fresh cold sheets, not even feeling the cloth's chill.

"I need to know what happened here in the Coven." His palest of blue eyes held theirs steadily.

"Someone undermined the 'Spell of Protection', Dark Sz`a`Th Warriors stormed the Garrison and Coven. They overpowered those here and rescued Lieutenant Brae. We arrived just before they left the Dark Sz`a`Th when our orders were to proceed here immediately. We surrendered our weapons on the threat of them murdering who was left here at the Coven."

"There was no Spellcaster; could it have been the woman?" JA`rvis asked as Jarek's eyes shut to sleep; the Warrior's chest rose and fell gently into and fatigued sleep.

Ln`sahr eyes strained to keep awake stinging; he blinked them slowly.

"They dragged her screaming and kicking, Captain JA`rvis. We were all in the dungeons after; we could hear everything they did to her torture was not as thorough as Corporal Den`ah's but just as sickening; Brae is someone I would like to get my hands on."

"Who found her?" He asked, covering Jarek as if he was a son.

"The Lieutenant that you saw collapsed in the doorway. Someone said that she was called Jy`atis; her satchel carried a book with the name. We presume it to be hers." He looked at the man who had healed all, amazed at his strength and patience.

"You must rest, Captain JA`rvis or the sickness will take you."

"In time, Jarek, I will rest."

"Thank you. It's Corporal Aq`ten we need to thank."

"Why?"

"Healing…us, it is she who is healing us", He murmured and fell asleep. JA`rvis smiled tiredly. He sighed with weariness, the bed creaking with relief as his body left it.

JA`rvis moved silently through the corridors. He followed the steps to the cells. His mind's eye, the images still flickering in the darkness of each cell.

The brutality out by Mah`sden Warriors upon those in the Castle haunted his thoughts. He walked down to the cell that had held the young Warrior called Den`ah.

"You may come out, child."He said. "I'm not about to harm you."

"I'm not a child."

A young boy replied; his voice gave him away as it trembled within the darkness.

"No, you are not tonight; you have seen more than any child should."

The boy was covered in filth from hiding for his life—the lime he had half-eaten held firmly with nails black with grime.

"Come, all are asleep."

"Will Den`ah live?" He asked, trailing behind the stature of the Healer as they climbed up the steps to the kitchen.

"When you are clean, you can see him; he is within the Mhyst. How do you know the Corporal?"

"He hid me, as we were herded into the cells, hid me with the aid of his Mhyst, it left him defenceless as they tortured him…and the woman is she alive?" as they continued to walk past the sleeping bodies on stretchers. He glanced at the door ajar, trying to see the woman's figure on the bed.

"You may see her too."

The boy grabbed his arm, stopping JA`rvis as they returned to the kitchen.

"I saw.... I can't stop seeing and hearing all the prisoner's screams." Wide with horrors unspoken, the boy's eyes stared up at JA`rvis.

"Then come, and I'll scrub you clean, and you can eat and talk." JA`rvis could not forget what the boy had said, that Den`ah had cloaked him with his Mhyst; his heart chilled, and he prayed that something that was Den`ah remained intact to save.

The boy shed his filth and soaked in the herbal bath waters. JA`rvis cut the boy's dark brown hair short, but as he scrubbed the child's back and up to the nape of his neck hidden within the dark hairline, he saw the dark green ornate tattoo of a Dragon's head.

Frowning, he scrubbed the hand that still held tight the lime. His nails were black with grime.

The boy's pale olive skin had him wondering at his origin. JA'rvis guessed him to be at least ten or twelve winters old. He had long dark eyelashes and eyes that were large pools of colour, the deep green of forests.

JA`rvis wondered how a boy his age had arrived at the Coven. The Dragonhead on the boy's hairline showed him to be of the Drargon`H Imperial Legion. Nothing made sense, and he wondered how Taelen and Ji`rah were fairing.

"Here, wrap this around you and stand near the fire. I'll find a clean shirt for you." JA`rvis, while rummaging for a fitting shirt, had guardedly read his thoughts.

Returning, he found the boy eating a large bowl of the stew he would feed the others.

"My name is Captain JA`rvis, and you are of the Imperial House of G`Sharell? And you are called

K`lton." He said to the boy.

The boy looked up at him with eyes that hid all emotion.

"I have never heard of G`Sharell?" He said in a whisper. "I do not even know where G`Sharell is, and how do you know so much."

JA`rvis smiled, "As my station requires me, my young Warrior, I must know such things. And now it is time for sleep K`lton." The boy did not argue for exhaustion swept across him with the darkness of the night.

JA`rvis worked late into the early morning; only then did the Sqn`xn Warrior rest when the last sprig of rosemary lay on his chest.

"Corporal Aq`ten," he said as her eyes opened immediately, and she went for her blades, her stance in crouch attack. "Den`ah will sleep another twelve hours, time for you to go back to your billeted room, when rested return, my orders but sleep."

She looked at Den`ah; tears welled as she hooked an escaped snake length of hair behind her ear. "With all due respect Captain JA`rvis whoever did this, I will kill."

"Then you are standing in a long line, Corporal, and I appreciate the sentiment, but to heal, you need to rest, and I need every Warriior walking to do a Drakk`or's share of the workload on this Castle. Go," His hand touched her shoulder slightly, and she nodded, touching his shoulder the same way. She appreciated this, for it was an informal salute from the Ten`qrn Pack. Something she had not had for half a lifetime.

The Coven lay asleep for twelve long hours. The candles, large and thick as a Warrior's torso and tall, burned on through the night.

"Captain JA`rvis, wake up" A small hand rested on the rosemary on his chest. JA`rvis opened his eyes to see K`lton's deep green eyes intently. It was as if the boy was looking into his mind. As did his eyes, a smile curled at the corner of his mouth.

"I'm awake, K`lton." He said, breathing deeply the cold morning air that had entered through the open windows, which seemed to bring a breath of anticipation.

The Warrior wondered silently, making a mental note to seek the forests beyond the Coven walls. He may be many things, but there were other things to take care of as a member of the Wolf nation.

"The lady is awake." The boy's dark hair, near black, lifted slightly at the cowlick on the left side of his forehead. Eyes young but old stared widely at the Healer; the excitement and unknowing flowed through him.

"Ah, good, then let us welcome her." He said as his eyes mirrored the pale pink-grey coals of the heat.

"I need you to start the fires, K`lton." His eyes glanced down to K`lton's feet. "Don't get those socks burnt, K`lton," he added as an afterthought. "When the waters boiled, make a hot drink for the lady and see if anyone else is awake."

The boy nodded. His green eyes opened wide as his mind intended to remember the Healer's words.

"Are you good with names?" asked JA`rvis tilting his head towards the boy inquiringly.

"Aye, I have remembered yours, haven't I?" The boy's willingness was hard not to laugh at. The Healer sighed slightly and wondered what happened in the winters between trust and distrust that made all men lose some essence that only children could hold.

"Good, people like to be called by their names. You must find who is well and ask them to lift that black pot onto the fire you build. The pot is breakfast."

JA`rvis dressed, splashed the cold water over his face with a hint of pine, and dried his skin.

Many were still asleep. Some dozed. Others lay staring at the open windows where large candles continued and burned. The grey dawn brought rain and snow.

The weather, in its strange way, was a respite. He walked to the young woman's bed.

"Mistress Jy`atis..." Saluting in the tradition of the Sqh`xn Nation.

The woman's eyes held his in a hold that froze his emotions.

"You are mistaken; my name is Iz`sen." She replied slowly. "And I'm far from being a Mistress." Her voice trembled, straining acutely with emotion.

JA`rvis glanced from the woman to the falling rain moving within the stone border of the window's rectangular stone architrave. The sound of rain on stone seemed to soothe the mood within the room.

"Then, I will use the common title of Mistress."

Faint rumblings of thunder skittled through the rain-snow-filled heavens above them as if river pebbles had been thrown upon the roof.

Others within the Coven looked up to an unseen storm, a storm that resembled one of magic.

K`lton's soft knock on the oak door distracted them from the sounds of the approaching storm. JA`rvis smiled with his eyes softly on the boy.

"So K`lton, is the whole Coven still in their nightclothes?"

"Aye, Captain JA`rvis." the boy looked through dark eyelashes that threw shadowed lines across his eyes. He smiled for the first time. His teeth were pure white, his eye teeth had yet come down, and there were gaps where adult teeth still had to grow.

The Warrior waved the boy to enter and close the door.

“This is Mistress Iz`sen of G`Sharell.” He said, naming the alias that he knew she was using and for the simple reason that he had read her thoughts, and G`Sharell was her birthplace.

She smiled at the boy; he bowed his head and smiled slightly, and a dimple in his smooth cheek blinked at them.

Seeing her bruised face so close collapsed the boy’s mental defences, vividly bringing the past torture back; K'lton shuddered.

“I saw Mistress…. In he an.” The boy fell into a deluge of tears as his emotions stumbled and tripped. Sobs from deep within his soul tore out into the daylight of morning. Wiry dark-skinned arms hugged his chest as he tried to control the emotions that he needed to release.

“Sit with the Mistress, K`lton.”

Outside dark billows of grey smoke hung as rain sifted through the clouds from burning contaminated clothes and bedding.

A necessity if he was to contain the taint cast upon the Coven, he was deep cleaning a Castle and a Covern in the oldest and simplistic of ways.

K`lton climbed onto the bed, crawling on all fours to the open arms of the Mistress. The boy lay silent in her arms.

“Where did you find him?” She asked, stroking the forehead until no frowns resurfaced, then tentatively and with care rocked him in her arms, cooing him a lullaby.

“Within the cells below, he has seen too many terrors.”

He observed as she began rocking the boy softly; he smiled slightly. They would be suitable for each other, he thought. They would heal.

"I'll bring you breakfast". The door closed without them noticing.

JA`rvis had four Knights helping in the kitchen. They Cooked to his instructions; they learned the art of healing foods and hotly spiced brews.

He had brought their breakfasts back to them, both emotionally worn; they ate and fell back asleep in the one bed.

He was in the kitchen serving more dishes when a voice behind him spoke.

"Captain JA`rvis…is it you?" came a voice familiar. JA`rvis stood and turned slowly; he was unprepared for the young man before him.

"Taelen! By the Elementals, it is you," he said, standing as they embraced warmly.

The Knights were relieved to see their Lieutenant had returned safely to the Coven.

"Tell me, did Ji`rah send you?" He asked as he and JA`rvis checked each Warrior and Knight. JA`rvis glanced sideways, smiling.

"Aye, and just as well, he did howl. There is not one Spellcaster here, Taelen, and whoever tainted the Ward over the Coven knew the 'ancients' with their sicknesses and their in-depth knowledge of the 'chill' that pervades the halls."

His palest blue eyes looked directly at Taelen.

"Do they remember anything?" He said, looking around at faces he knew.

"If anyone does, it will be the boy K`lton."

Taelen raised his dark eyebrows; his forehead wrinkled slightly.

"What would a boy with a name of the Drargon`H Imperial Legion be doing here? He is thousands of leagues from home. That's if he is, as you say."

"Come, I shall show you the boy; he has the

Dragons head tattoo on his hairline at the neck."

JA`rvis motioned to Taelen at the boy in the woman's arms, both asleep. Within the hairline was the distinct tattoo of a Dragons head, a symbol of the coastal region's nobility known as Drargon`H.

"Who is she?" he asked, inclining his head towards the sleeping woman. Though the room was semi-dark, he could see the rise and fall of her breathing- a shaft of grey twilight that halved the room as if liquid.

"Her name is..." He led Taelen away by the elbow down through the door and into the corridor. The Healers' voice lowered to a murmur as JA`rvis told all he knew of the young woman, which was negligible.

They stood silently within the stone corridors of the Coven. JA`rvis guided him to the young Corporals room.

Den`ah lay as he had for two days, his eyes flickered beneath closed dark eyelids, and his chest rose and fell with the rhythm of his breathing

"I need to find a 'Dream Caster' to coax Den`ah back to us," JA`rvis said quietly. "I will continue to heal his body, but his mind is another thing." His hand rubbed the new beard that had seemed to take over his face.

"Beware Dream Caster JA`rvis, some bastard threw one my way, and it was Ji`rah's love of fishing that had him remove it from my shoulder…dark is the magic now that falls fog like on the lands."

Taelen walked through the purple Mhyst particles that flowed within the room.

"Brave you are to let Ji`rah fish for a Dream Caster's Lure. Don't try to reach him, Taelen." Urged JA`rvis warned as the young man pulled back his hand at his friend's request.

Corporal Aq`ten knocked on the door in the uniform of the Ten`qrn Pack.

"Ji`rah was correct in 'calling' you 'JA`rvis," Taelen said quietly, his eyes seeing the bandages and what lay beneath them pained him.

"Corporal Aq`ten, enter; this is Lieutenant Taelen; this is Corporal Aq`ten, Ten`qrn Pack Tracker I mentioned."

She saluted both Warriors, glancing quickly at Den`ah.

"Pardon my intrusion; I have orders to return to my mission. Has Den`ah regained consciousness yet?"

"No, not yet, Corporal."

"Then please give him this letter. He will know what it means. I must leave now and continue my orders." She handed the letter in a sealed envelope to Captain JA`rvis, kneeled, placing her forehead and nose touching Corporal Den`ah, her eyes closed. Speaking silently in their language, she said, 'call me if you need saving again…come find me."

Turning, she saluted both JA`rvis and Taelen. "I am sorry I could not have stayed longer; I have too many kilometres to catch up, but Den`ah was worth the detour, he will live, and he will actually like being part of the Wolf Nation."

Corporal Aq`ten marched from the room.

"We need more Warriors like her; my skills, attitude, and empathy are someone I shall miss," JA`rvis said quietly.

"Is there any word on Lord Mah`sden," JA`rvis asked. His thoughts were within the forests out beyond the stone window; grey misting rain fell diagonally framed in the dark stone of the Covent's stone wall.

"The rising of the Mhyst is what 'it's' being called. There are blood and bone from one Kingdom to another; Spellcasters and Warriors alike are just cut down where they stand, no interrogation that I know of except here, it would have been Braes handy work." He said, his hand on JA`rvis's shoulder. "Not a clever mix. But then your grandmother never was tactful."

"How can I stop something that I don't know how to stop?" Taelen held the Healers arm. "You are mistaken; she is dead," he said coldly. "So who is in the Coven?"

Thunder grumbled with anger overhead; the rain felt against the windows as the fires crickling and crackling gave some normalcy.

JA`rvis smiled inwardly and thought, 'if only she were.'

"I counted eighteen and five dead. The initial headcount was incorrect but expected. There are two Knights who helped me, Jarek and Ln`sahr, who have not been taken with this sickness. They sleep on either side of Den`ah's door, as you saw earlier. There is also the boy K`lton and the Mistress Iz`sen," Jarvis sighed, rubbing his aching neck.

"And what else should I know" questioned Taelen.

His eyes stared at the rain and snow that showed through a long narrow window to his left. It made him wish for peace.

"There are cells of archives below us. You are the Imperial Scribe. Wolf instinct tells me the answer lies there."

"You're the second person who has hinted at that."

"Oh, Aye, and who may I ask, Lieutenant, was the first." His raised eyebrow made Taelen smile.

"It is not a woman JA`rvis…" he scratched the back of his neck, trying to picture the person who had said those words. However, no vision came.

Taelen looked from the rain to the healer blankly, then frowned.

"I wish I could recall," He said doubtfully.

"Taelen, excuse me, I need to be 'free'" he looked

down the empty corridor to their left. Then folded down onto himself as he walked away, transforming into the silver-white Timber Wolf.

Taelen did not comment and walked with the Wolf that was JA`rvis, who took one side glance at the Sz`a`Th Warrior as he stepped to the veranda. Grey misting rain-smeared with snow smudged the view of the valley as washed-out watercolours on an artist's canvas.

"Pack," said Taelen in the coldness of the falling rain more substantial and heavier. The Wolf leapt from the stone veranda and blended into the forest's drab green and grey-brown palate beyond.

There was the solitary figure of Taelen standing alone, seeing but not, and wondered actually what was in the archives. His fingers scratched at the three-day-old growth of beard upon his chin.

If only he knew what he was looking for and what it would mean to him.

# CHAPTER 10

Dek`hlan stood contemplating the cells a few steps away from him. Candles glowed from all directions—the soft yellow light-pooled areas interloping other areas forming pools of light hopscotching one to the other.

Why had he come here? He heard the howl of a lone Timber Wolf. Dek`hlan turned his head as he did. He saw someone; then he heard his voice scream out as cold singing steel collided with his ribs, scraping the bone as both connected.

Dek`hlan's last thought was the Mhyst and Taelen.

All heard the Wolf howl, followed by a Warrior's agonised cry. Padded stocking feet ran to corridors Taelen's feet were the first to breach the cells' steps.

"Dek`hlan", Taelen's voice carried through the empty cells where darkness seemed to hold tightly. Every candle was extinguished. Warriors appeared weary and worn.

"Stay here," Taelen asked more than command. His eyes looked back at them as he stepped into the ink-coloured environment.

"Lieutenant…" A young Corporal handed him a flaming torch. Its stem of wood felt natural in the world of darkness. Taelen nodded in appreciation; grasping the long handle, he preceded and stepped down onto the level floor from the stone steps.

K`lton tugged from behind. Taelen was about to reprimand the boy.

"You must light the candles, Lieutenant," said the boy. Stocking feet and the oversized shirt made K`lton pull at emotions within the Sz`a`Th Lieutenant.

"On your wisdom, my young friend. Bar that door should...." A Warriors moan cut him short as all stared into the blackness Taelen turned; a flaming torch illuminated the ground as he walked cautiously, the yellow pool showing dark, crimson splashes across the stone floor; the angry drag marks astounded everyone. Only the rain sounded above their breathing.

"Dek`hlan, are you...can you hear me?"

He heard a faint rasping' Lieutenant' as he ignored the blood's direction, lighting candles as many as possible.

Then they heard the sharp intake of his breath.

"Shattas..." Taelen swore loudly.

Taelen called for K`lton to find JA`rvis. What lay before him had been a man.

"He's here, Lieutenant", called the young boy.

JA`rvis ran past them, kneeling in the gloom. He said

"Get a stretcher to carry the Sergeant on and six Warriors."

"JA`rvis in here" urged Taelen.

"I'll attend him here; to move will kill him outright. I need buckets of hot water. Towels K`lton, boyo, I need a sharp needle and fishing line. Can you do that for me?" The boy nodded in silence and left quickly.

Warriors ran to fetch items; lamps of all forms were brought down to the cells. Most paled at what they saw. K`lton stood handing JA`rvis all he needed; deep dark red and wet with blood. His socks did not bother him.

Dek`hlan skin had been sliced and torn from his chest and stomach; the membrane, muscle, flesh, and sinew were all on view. The intestines sat coiled in place by the membrane, which was all that was stopping disembowelment.

JA`rvis stitched and stitched, then washed, bandaged and gave the still thankfully unconscious Warrior the white milk of poppy drink.

Taelen then used the Mhyst; none had ever witnessed the Mhyst used in critical healing, and none had seen Taelen's in use like this.

As a purple, white aura cocooned the Sergeant, Particles of blue light, the colour of the Lieutenant's eyes, floated within the cocoon of purple and white light. The blue lights shimmered as they fell, soaking into the Sergeant's body. They gently placed him on the stretcher and carried him to a room upstairs in the main living quarters of the Coven.

A woman's voice called from the top steps that led out of the cells they were in, asking the whereabouts of the young boy K`lton

"He is here, Mistress; if you would clean him up, I think all of us, including K`lton, would be relieved."

K`lton smiled sadly. "Will the Sergeant live?" he asked, helping JA`rvis put things back in his Healers box.

"A normal man wouldn't, K`lton; Dek`hlan is an Imperial Warrior of the Mhyst. He is Sahn`Frwh trained. This type of wound that the Death Watch are taught to contain for survival. He will live."

Even though Dek`hlan was a seasoned Sergeant of the Arches and Night Guard, JA`rvis saw the concern on the young boys' face. He smiled a little, sadly. "Dek`hlan is strong. His body will heal." But he thought to himself, wondering if the young Warriors mind would heal.

"K`lton come," she said but would not go down to the cells to get him; the cells were a reminder of the torture.

"Take the socks off before you go", Taelen reminded him.

JA`rvis stood up, wiping his hands on the blood-stained towel.

"That blood out there is not Dek`hlan's." As others came to clean with hot water and the citreous fruit, he said. The dark crimson bloody water ran down the central drain as buckets sloshed and dispersed the blood into the stone-slanting floor.

"I heard your call. It coincided with Dek`hlan's scream." He replied.

"What was Dek`hlan doing down here, anyway?" asked JA`rvis.

"My question first…Pack Lore", Said Taelen. He watched the water vortex at the drains gaping in his mouth.

"Pack!" Answered JA`rvis, slightly worn by the formality of his people. "But not here; there are too many spells and counter-spells… the air prickles my skin like a temperate night on the E`boda Plains to the north…."

Instead, they stood on the highest buttress of the Coven; the stairs left both Warriors breathless. They sat within the protection of a stone alcove in the open.

Protected from the elements, the dome shape was open on all sides and made of black onyx.

"Even in this wet weather, you can see the sharp black peaks of the Dom`sh. They resemble the black edge of a L`kus blade in full thrust." Said Taelen. His thoughts were of the Warrior's souls that had died at every peak attempt. A depressing reminder that war only left many headstones. They would bury their dead there in ice and stone.

JA`rvis glanced at them as the icy plains' winds blew a strong northerly in their direction. To the east lay the impenetrable Dom`sh. To the south lay an ocean as cold and as forbidding in winter. Storms of Ice raged in ocean blizzards that tore at the coastline had begun.

Yet, Taelen, he thought, might well have fond thoughts of his life at the coastal 'Keep' that had protected his life for ten winters. The north and the west were lands uncharted, their distances so vast that only stories of the people and their cultures filtered through to the vast majority of the populated lands they were now on.

"Whose blood did you find?" Standing in the winds, he said its strength on the buttress pushed hard at him.

Taelen hung his head, and his hands clasped over his neck. His dark hair threaded through his fingers, forming a human weave of despair. JA`rvis turned to the 'Unknown Lands'.

"Dek`hlan was tainted with Mah`sden Mhyst, slightly may something…."

"Maybe the Sergeant was set a trap."

"More than likely", he shrugged. "He was opened from chest to groin like some animal slaughter."

"Sacrifice?" asked JA`rvis, his eyes watered from the sharp coldness of the wind.

Taelen lay down on the stone bench he was sitting upon. His knees bent, and his arms twisted, supporting his head. He sighed.

"Why sacrifice an Imperial Warrior of the Mhyst? Dek`hlan is a Sergeant of the Archers and Night Guard. His knowledge is just that. It is not the knowledge that one would disembowel a man for."

"He would have been the only survivor of the Coven. He is the only witness to what happened. For I was the bait and had I not ordered here by Ji`rah, he is a witness to the atrocities that occurred here; he said Brae was here and released as well," Said JA`rvis, still looking at the Unknown Lands. The wind was chilling, but neither seemed to feel her icy embrace.

"He was the only one I know of, besides the two Warriors you came across here, the woman and the boy." replied Taelen, then "JA`rvis, there's a lot of writing underneath this dome. And Den`ah, who is still recovering."

JA`rvis turned around to see the dome glow a dull grey.

"Hell... Taelen, get up NOW!" his precise cold demand froze Taelen. The Warrior's blue eyes questioned the Sqn`xn Warrior Healer silently.

"What?"

JA`rvis stared at the swirling clouds high above the black onyx dome. He grabbed Taelen by the arm, reefing the stunned Warrior to his feet.

"Are you mad?"

JA`rvis pulled him to the ground outside the Dome, throwing them both to the wet and cold stones of the parapet.

"Sh. something is happening, and I have an ill feeling about this, Taelen."

"I was starting to feel quite comfortable." He replied, looking sideways at his brother.

"You looked like some bloody sacrifice, now…shut up."

Both men drew their blades from their boots as they lay flat on the wet stones. The rain had begun to fall, pouring from the heavens. They had to fight to hold on to footings as the wind cyclically surrounded them. Their fingers scoured for the edges of the square flagstones as they gripped for security within the crumbling mortar.

Their faces stung as rain and wind whipped at them.

The dome was still; a pale glow of white light began to pulse within the dome's centre through the top and into the clouds on an ark that vanished into the horizon and the Unknown Lands. The noise this made screamed into their minds.

Their ears pained deeply from the whistle and the cold. They squinted through the downpour with uncertainty as the light changed, slipping from white to mauve to purple, not black. The slight figure of a woman of sixty winters lay on the dome's limestone bench.

The wind ended as the rain and snow flurries continued to fall endlessly.

Taelen and JA`rvis lay wet and cold. Hardly breathing, they glanced sideways at each other. Then, the woman lying where they had been was breathing, still and silent on the stone bench.

Slowly getting to their feet, both drew their daggers and made their way to the woman.

Both stood on either side of the stone bench. Her skin was olive smooth and barely showed a sign of age. Silver grey hair hung in a long fishbone plait down over the bench. Her high cheekbones and elegant black eyebrows arched slightly. No jewellery. She wore a grey shift and black pants; the straight gown was slit to her waist.

"She is beautiful," said Taelen. His mind imagined how beautiful she must have been when she was much younger. To be that beautiful, he thought, would have been a curse, not a gift.

"Aye, that she is, " replied his friend as he angrily swung Taelen around by the arm. "What the hell were you thinking of when you were on the bench?"

"I'd like to know that too," the woman said, opening her eyes. Strange eyes that the iris shares two colours. The top part of the iris was an amethyst blue in their brilliance like Taelen's, yet the bottom was the deepest amethyst green he had ever seen.

"Please put those daggers away," she sighed, "If I

were to harm you, it would have been earlier, not now." Both quickly put their blades away and helped her to sit up.

She looked at them both. Her eye colourings made them feel like she probed deep into their most secret thoughts.

The woman smiled at JA`rvis kindly. She glanced to Taelen, who looked at JA`rvis, raising a questioning eyebrow, and laughed slightly.

"I see I should be answering your questions. But first, please tell me what you were thinking as you lay here".

"I will not discuss the conversation, but," he said, looking at his hands", I felt devoid of emotion, lost, unsure."

"Who were you thinking of?" she asked, "It is important; I need to know why someone needs me now after so long."

"I was actually seeking my father's advice," Taelen said as he tried to sense the woman's thoughts with his Mhyst.

"Which one?" asked JA`rvis; Taelen narrowed his eyes at his friend for the cynicism.

The woman patted them maternally on their knees, making them both jump slightly with awkwardness.

"Sh...Why is it a Wolf always speaks from a cold heart?"

JA`rvis just stared at her; she looked at him as if telling him to be quiet, then spoke to Taelen.

"It is complicated. Mistress," Taelen replied, "I was thinking of my Father. I wished him here; I need his thoughts on my problem."

She touched Taelen's face. "His name?" she asked, her fingertips trembling.

"My father's name is Yassarn. It is all I will say, for

I know you not." The woman shivered as if from the cold or of long-suppressed grief.

"If my shirt were dry, I would offer it to you. It is cold up here," said JA`rvis.

The woman took a deep breath. Shaking her head slowly and became very quiet.

"So you are telling me Lord Yassarn is dead." She whispered.

"You are mistaken, Mistress; Yassarn was a Captain. His brother Mah`sden is the Lord. And I will not give you further information unless I know who the hell you are,' cocked his head slightly, raising both eyebrows at her adding without respect in his voice ", Mistress."

"I have been gone too long," she said softly," Who rules the Wolf Nation?"

"Lord Za`qrn", JA`rvis replied, "But he is researching at present."

"Ah, so the puppy triumphed over his brother."

"No mistress, the Lieutenant here killed him." JA`rvis watched her. He felt he knew her. He looked out upon the rain-drenched land to another time in his life.

Though ten winters are older than Taelen, JA`rvis recalled something vaguely familiar about the woman and decided to keep his own counsel.

"Who are you?" asked Taelen, even though he had familiar feelings for the woman.

"Someone, it seems, you have in need of." she looked over the Unknown Lands that existed over the horizon. She felt torn in two.

"Mistress?" asked Taelen. "You knew of Yassarn, didn't you."

"Am I correct in saying he is dead?" She replied, not answering him.

Taelen stood and walked where rain sprinkled

across his front, he sighed deeply, and his shoulders sagged as he abruptly shoved his hands in cold, wet pockets. The icy wind did not even raise a shiver across his skin.

"Aye, Mistress, my father is dead now two winters." He did not wish to discuss the intricacies of his connection with the Nation of Elves with a Spellcasters. "Along with my wife, my Uncles blade and Mhyst rips and poisons all in his bloody dark path, and I just don't know how to tackle him." Taelen took a deep breath to help with the burden he carried in his soul. He turned around and faced the woman.

"One of my finest Sergeants was nearly skinned and gutted hours earlier and fights for his life within the Mhyst. And if that's is not enough, I fear I may have sent not only two dear friends to their slaughter but every last Spellcaster and Mhyst Warrior to their blood-sodden graves. They tell me that all I can do is somewhere in the Coven, a book lies with an answer."

"We are all books, Lieutenant. Maybe it is a person you seek, not a book of parchments and ink?" her eyebrow raised in a quiet question to him.

JA`rvis watched her as the cold wind caught wisps of the silver-grey hair catching strands and letting them waltz, a silent dance with the wind as their partner.

"LH`nejah?" he whispered, her eyes slowly closed, and the silver path of a tear trailed down her cheek.

The woman glanced sideways at him. She gripped his sizeable callused hand with long slender fingers that he recalled combing through his hair, black as night, when a boy.

"You remember," she said in a whisper.

"Aye, Mistress, I have never forgotten, only kept safe your memory."

"You are kind, JA`rvis."

Taelen watched them both. His eyes searched the clouds boiling above them angrily.

"Before you two get too close and friendly, I think we should go down, the weather is deepening, and those clouds are filled with energy. This would be a dangerous place to be." Lightning forked blue-white above the He`lian Mountains as thunder cracked angrily like a stone on metal.

"It is time we left, come, Mistress," he said, and they quickly descended the 'Stairs of Forgiveness' down through the Coven.

They rested occasionally. The five hundred steps were not to be ridiculed but respected. Each step held a carved rune and ancient text. Stopping halfway down, Taelen said to the woman.

"You are a Spellcaster, are you not?" his eyes held hers. His intensity made her glance away.

"I am a Spellcaster", she replied as she studied his face. His father's eyes haunted her soul.

"My mother was a 'Spellcaster' well, that's what I was told."

"NH`dya", her voice trembled with raw emotion and sadness as she uttered his mother's name.

Taelen stopped and nearly fell at the sound of his mother's name aloud. He eyed her suspiciously.

"What name did you utter?" He asked quietly as the edge in his voice grew hard.

JA`rvis was cautious behind both of them; Taelen's tone with the woman was not friendly.

"Ah …Taelen, I think we can discuss this at the bottom of these steps, don't you? Even I am having trouble gauging my steps." He said with a touch of awkwardness.

Wind spirited around them. Its silent buffeting and nudging picked up age-old dust from the grouted lime stymies. Without a spoken word, they again continued down the rune-etched steps.

"What did you call him JA`rvis," asked the woman beside him.

"Taelen", answered the young man, as Taelen looked back over his shoulder at his friend with a frown that would have frozen time.

"It is a common name, nothing special," commented Taelen as they continued.

Thunder echoed loudly down the length of the staircase as they entered the kitchen.

The woman beside became quiet. The kitchen was large. Warriors and Knights recovering from duties and battle looked warily at the woman who came in with Taelen and JA`rvis, who were sodden from the rain that now teamed down outside.

While they were given a steamy spiced tea to drink, both Taelen and JA`rvis removed the wet leggings and boots and then left, returning in dry clothes. Both men were still carrying over shirts when they returned to the table that four Warriors now occupied, all talking at once.

If Taelen had looked, these men were JA`rvis's age and well-seasoned Warriors of more than ten Battles, but he did not.

He stood with his back to the fire as JA`rvis joined the table. K`lton came and stood beside the Lieutenant and looked up at the man beside him.

"Who is she, Taelen?" he asked, forgetting he was eating a biscuit. He then looked at the woman as she smiled at him as if entranced with her. He forgot his words.

"She's very…" the boy tilted his head and moved to where she sat. The young boy toyed with her long silver-grey braid that hung down the chair's back to the floor.

Taelen smiled despite his misgivings of the woman as both her hands slowly crept around and grasped the boy tickling him. K`lton laughed in childish delight as she swung him onto the bench seat between her and another Warrior. The rest joined the child's laughter.

Taelen turned to the fire again, warming his body. As he drank, he had a vague memory. Was it his mother who played that same game? His recollection of her was fuzzy. At nineteen winters, he recalled little of her. Yet just now, he remembered the same laughter. It was his own.

This woman felt like an echo in time in the autumn of her life.

He absently pulled the shirt on but unbuttoned it. Its brushed blue material highlighted the colour of his eyes. He wore dark blue loose pants and thick woollen socks.

JA`rvis watched the woman he had called Mistress Iz`sen move towards the fireplace where Taelen stood.

Taelen went to leave so she would feel more comfortable not being close to a Warrior.

"Please, Lieutenant, I'd rather you keep me company. I feel all your Warriors are avoiding me."

Taelen slid his hand into his trouser pocket and glanced around the room as he continued to drink his hot tea. Those Warriors who were still ill were beginning to heal slowly. They would again be themselves, standing Guard and defending their beliefs.

'MyWarriors Mistress are dealing possibly in the only way they know how to. They are men and women, not the ones who assaulted and tortured you. While they realise you understand this. Maybe if you spoke to them as you did to me, their awkwardness might go." He shrugged, hiding in his ineptitude, not knowing what to say next.

His eyes stayed on the other woman talking freely with the Warriors at the table. Their laughter caught in his throat. Suddenly he wished he could be so relaxed with them and her.

"And you, Lieutenant?" Looking up at him from where she stood.

"I am a Warrior, Mistress Iz`sen. For your pain is mine, Mistress. I am Sahn`Frwh, nothing more."

"Well put, Lieutenant," she said, taking his cup. "If you trust me. I have found something that may lift the despair I see in your eyes."

Taelen took back the cup and finished the sweet herbal tea placing it on the mantle shelf, the wood as wide as a Warrior's thigh. In the adjoining room, she opened the doors to the balcony. Thunder and lightning sheeted through the heavens above, casting abstract angles to the features of shadows and faces in the kitchen.

He followed her as she led him into a corridor and then down a flight of stairs. This area of the Coven was unknown to him. The closeted feeling made his senses acute as they continued down at least four flights of stairs along another corridor lit with mauve crystal lamps.

The glow of the beautiful crystals gave an ethereal feeling to the part of the Coven. The sensation of magic, ancient and powerful, prickled at their skin, goose-bumping and caused them to shiver as if shaking off something that had touched them unknowingly.

The woman stood silently before a wall that later became liquid. Taelen listened as she spoke in her first language and then in the style of Drargon`H, which was the primary tongue of the Drargon`H Empire. A faint sound of murmurings and whispers came to his ears.

He could not understand the woman's conversation

before him with the voices that had no form. The woman then held out her hands into which two books appeared.

Turning to face Taelen, she took a deep breath, and he could see the exhaustion upon her face that held a subtle sheen of sweat.

"I believe these are what you have been looking for, my Lord" her eyes did not leave his as he glanced down at the two leather-bound ledgers she held.

Holding out the ledgers to him, the strain drained her energy, exhausting LH`Nejah.

"Please take the ledgers, my Lord, they are for you, not me, and with each second I hold them, something more is taken from me."

Taelen grasped both ledgers from her to his touch. The magic tingled and burned with the raw magic up his arms from his fingertips.

Turning, she paused.

"We cannot return the way we came, for each path ends and begins again."

Taelen frowned at her, and as if he did not believe her, he turned to find the corridor behind him going. Blocking his steps was the Coven foundations, and he knew they were at least six meters thick.

"Lieutenant, if you follow me, the path has opened for us; it seems you are the true Lord of the Mhyst."

He now understood the derogatory term 'witch', and she was one amongst the wariness that clawed his thoughts.

He turned to see her walking down another mauve-lit corridor. He noted that her feet unseen beneath her gown made no noise. There was no sashay of her hips. It was as if she floated.

He began following her down a corridor that seemed endless-so many sharp twists and turns, so many staircases to ascend.

Even though his feet seemed to walk upon the stone floor, he sensed that his own feet did not touch the ground that seemingly was beneath him.

The reality of the thunderstorm still raging around the Spellcasters Coven broke the spell if that was what he had just experienced. Thunder cracked like an angry whip above him as he flinched from the sound.

They both stood outside his study, the two ledgers firmly in his grasp. Taelen opened the door and asked her to step in.

"There are things I need to ask Mistress, and you are the only one who can answer them." Taelen stood aside to let her into the study before them. She nodded and entered, worn and tired from the experience they both had just had.

Rain pitted against the long and meter-wide windows, two of which were in the study. The rhythm of the rain soothed Taelen's mind and nerves.

Outside, all was a grey smudge of the landscape.

Taelen placed the ledgers down onto the desk with the Covens ledger he was scribing in the quill neatly thoroughly cleaned as the blotting cloth testified next to a crystal ink jar. With its brass lid screwed on firmly to prevent the spill of ink.

Parchments lay scattered, with the black lettering now dried. The cream parchment paper curled on the corners and was ready to be rolled and slid into the brass cylinders corked with crystal stoppers, sealed with green wax and then warded by spells that only Taelen was privy to, sat patiently waiting.

Their engraved runic wards stared blankly at him, reminding him he still had work to be finished and more essential things to be begun in the mantle of Dominion Lord. He again vehemently denied the title.

Taelen glanced back at the large limestone fireplace where the early morning lit fire's soft orange and white coals now opaquely pulsed.

The ledger's magic still could be felt at his fingertips. He moved his fingers, but the sensation stayed tingling across the skin.

“Begin from your arrival.” He said, trying not to bring attention to her torture.

Mistress Iz`sen stared at the window, watching the rain pimple the pane and drizzle down. She took a deep breath and began

“Lieutenant”, she started with his rank, much to his relief. This formality was more of an incident report, which seemed to suit them both at that moment.

“My people”, she began “, please look”, she beckoned “, the Dormas Mountains; you can see the fourth peak as a veiled shadow in the mist, to the right.” She said as she pointed to the black shear blade of rock jutted into the icy air surrounding the Dormas.

Taelen made out the fourth peak and looked back at her, the pale cream skin seemed unblemished, but he knew from a discussion he’d had with JA`rvis that it was not so. There were many scares upon her back.

Her voice came back to him.

“That was my home. We were attacked and herded, worse than animals, into the dungeons of Castle SA`djle. Some were taken prisoner, some died, and the others were slaves. The enslaved people were being brought to the coast.” She swallowed hard; he watched her fingers tremble as her eyes were downcast. Her memory creased inwards painfully as she went to continue.

Taelen felt the prickliness of her discomfort.

“You don’t need to tell me, Mistress.” His hand reached and held hers. Taelen was impressed by her inner strength. Yet sensed she would crumble into insanity at any given moment.

"Here come to sit," he said tiredly, sitting on the large brown leather settee that was just the right length for his body should he need to lay it full range.

"I'll stand a bit," she said. "You are tired and do not need to listen to me" she went to leave. The books on the bench could wait, Taelen thought angrily.

He stood before she blocked the door. His hands gently held her shoulders holding her firmly.

"Yes, I am tired of many things, but many things I must do, and one right now is to listen to you. Because it is simple, Mistress, I may miss something important if I do not listen to you. Now please continue".

Taelen closed the door and sat on the long couch, swinging his left leg and resting his foot on his knee. He arched his back and rested his arms along the top of the settee

"My father was a high-ranking officer within the Castle. His bravery cost him his head,"

She recalled the events so clearly how her father was marched to the centre of the castle ramparts for his execution. How he glanced once at her then bent his head.

His head bounced down the ramparts and off the cliff into the mountains, air slowly whistling down; she recalled she never heard his headland below, any thud, and no skittle of rocks as it touched, just absolute silence.

The pulsing blood gushed from the severed torso and how the blood spread around seemed to be sucked down into the stones it pooled thick and sticky upon.

"Who was your father?" Taelen asked quietly, stretching out on the settee.

"Imperial Lord Jy`atis S`lton of the Dormas", she began again as if to shed the shroud that had just covered her mind. “They attacked ten days ago. Then chose which males and females they wanted for themselves.” She shuddered, hugged her arms tightly across her breasts, and took a deep breath.

“But it was the Mhyst that began to poison us”. She shuddered again and took a deep breath, “when they came here.”

“I don’t understand. Do you mean the Mhyst when you arrived here affected you?” She looked back over her shoulder to where Taelen now lay on the settee. “They found a Lieutenant; his first name was Brae. I don’t recall his last name, he had come with others, but he is not like you.”

“The man you speak of is not like me. He is the ‘one, isn’t he?” Taelen closed his eyes as he saw her attack and those who instigated it within his mind's eye. Lightning split the room brightly. The thunder made both react.

“That was close,” she murmured more to herself than the Lieutenant before her.

“They also did the attack on Corporal Den`ah” as the lightning arrow into the room, she covered her ears and scrunched her eyes shut. Taelen stood flinching as the thunder deafened them and the Coven.

He looked out the window from where he stood and wondered if the protection wards would hold under such an onslaught of magic-induced nature.

“I know the man you speak of,” he said.

“But how you were not there”, she replied, hunching her shoulders up with the next lightning and thunder splitting only seconds apart.

“That dear lady is something only our Dominion Lord knows. No, I wasn’t there and have seen what was done. It is one of the less palatable traits of Lieutenant of the Mhyst. And an Imperial Scribe – I must illustrate the wounds, record the healing etc."

Her eyes were wide, and from where he stood, he could see the deep mahogany brown colour flecked with purple velvet as the light caught her irises.

"But how"? She asked again, her forehead creased with vulnerability; she turned swiftly away from his glance, trying to hide deep in her mind.

"The Mhyst sees many things, Mistress Iz`sen. I don't know how or why."

"The young boy was there when it all happened," she said quietly.

"Aye, he has seen more than he lets on or wants to remember." He stood at his desk, absently, touching the documents he had signed. The crisp parchment sand-papered across each other with his shuffle of them.

"You said you had found something within the ledgers. I'd also like to know how you had such knowledge to navigate the Coven's hidden passages."

"You don't know? But does not the Mhyst tell you?"

He smiled slightly and looked up from the desk. He studied Iz`sen more closely and wondered what linked the boy to her.

"The Mhyst is not a portal for answers hidden, especially those hidden by magic, Mistress Iz`sen. You forget I am Mhyst," he said

"Then I have heard wrong, for I was told you were Mhyst, Spellcasters and Scribe."

Taelen said nothing and sat at the solid oak desk with its rune inscriptions. For some reason, he doubted the woman in front of him. What that doubt was, he had no idea.

"Seriously, whoever informed you has just described possible every Warrior. We all fall under those three titles. I am not the only one, Mistress, and you said you had found something?" he asked quietly.

"I was able to leave with one thing," she said, "I left with a chronicled History of the Dormas region. I was in my last winter of studies. I wanted to teach. My brother, S`Ellen, would be the next Imperial Lord as he was the only male heir." She took another deep breath, "While it was quiet, I went back to the dungeons." He frowned, looking at her finely chiselled profile, the high cheekbones. He could imagine her chin jutting out as she stubbornly argued with males and females.

"Was that wise after such an attack?"

"My father said once that the only way to face fear was to conquer it. So, I went back to the place of the attack. The dungeons smelt of lemons, limes, incense, and candles, as your Warriors had just cleaned them."

She stopped her hand star-fished against the cold of the windowpane when she removed her hand; her body heat had fogged the stencilled mark of her hand, leaving the imprint there.

Taelen watched as the handprint faded, leaving nothing to show what the window had held moments before. He vaguely recalled doing the same thing as a child and that his mother had played the same game with him. He cleared his throat and said.

"You were saying, Mistress" He frowned, trying to shake the impression of the handprint that seemed to disturb him for some reason.

Lady Iz`sen rubbed her nose with the back of her hand more from the cold than any emotion she kept in place.

"The dungeons smelt clean, the candles gave it a different look," she said," I found myself down in there, reading one book, looking through others until I found this."

The Mistress Iz`sen of G`Sharell handed him the

first ledger; Taelen accepted the sizeable leather-bound file. The runes again sent fire tingling up his arm from his fingertips. His mind raced with images of folklore creatures, the like that had never been seen for aeons. The Scribe in him took over as he turned the leather cover over.

The words were ancient in their text; the quill's flow was the hallmark of a Scribe with intimate knowledge and the potency of the words he wrote.

There was no rush to the quill; each letter was as fluid in its blend with the other forming words as an eagle is born to fly the air currents of the blue ocean of sky they lived in.

This particular Scribe had a harmony with the four elements of life, so balanced was the quill in this Scribes hand that even Taelen felt a twinge of envy.

Taelen's fingertips gently stepped from one word to the other. Turning the page, he found himself smiling, slightly impressed by the hand that had scribed. The Scribe was an artist. His mind saw the young man; he was ethereal in his mannerisms and physical statue. Taelen frowned as in his mind's eye he also saw the Warrior called NK`las was this Scribe of the Elf Nation, again trying to warn him.

Taelen's heartbeat seemed to trip as both glanced his way. They smiled knowingly, and then both vanished from this thought.

"Who taught you to read this?" he frowned as his voice cracked with the emotions that scorched his psyche. "Why do you have this ancient book of 'Shadows'? You spoke that dialect."

Alarms sent tingling sensations to him, the book in his hands as he could not get the word to form. The woman's voice came to him faded, and he looked up.

"As Dormas, we are taught to read from an early

age; we are multilingual, Lieutenant, our region is landlocked by four other lands with whom we are friendly. We speak each language fluently with each land that borders our domain. The first is the ancient language, the second the present and third the colloquial slang of each land."

"Are there any languages you can't speak?" he asked, impressed and boggled with such a learning curve that would be daunting to others.

"Only two, my Lord, I cannot speak the language of the Mhyst or Sahn`Frwh."

It was for some reason that Taelen was relieved. He wished by all the Gods of the Four Elements to know why though his sixth sense just did not trust her.

"But what is written here is the script of 'Spellcasters', and you can speak that."

"Read the books, Lieutenant," she said, crossing her arms across her breasts. "And read this one also." Mistress Iz`sen went to the bookcase and pulled out a ledger similar if not identical in appearance to the other two that now lay before Taelen.

The Mistress laid the book atop the other two and said: "Read this."

"I am not of the 'Dormas' Mistress. These words mean nothing to me." He said as he felt the embossing on the leather cover.

"That's true, but you grew up upon the ocean. Your Warrior's and staff think highly of you, Lieutenant. They said you grew up on the cold coast of what my people call the 'Winters Kiss', your people call the ocean 'Taayra`Ge' both have the same meaning of a slow and icy death."

"It is common knowledge that I lived there for ten winters. I was Senior Scribe for ten of those winters." Taelen then fell quiet and added. "Then, Mah`sden came butchering, and I escaped with three friends." He eyed her, "But everyone knows that part of my history, you could have asked anyone in the Coven, and they would have told you the same story, so what is your point, Mistress?"

He heard JA`rvis calling him within his mind. The Wolf's haunting thought interrupted his own. JA`rvis seemed always to know when to call.

"It is time we returned to the others. The rain will be turning to sleet tonight. I dare say the evening meal is ready." He rose from the chair, picked up the three ledgers, and moved to the study's door.

"After you, Mistress Iz`sen." He turned to leave the door to his study open. He knew somehow she was laying a trap, but for who?

# CHAPTER 11

Taelen accepted a plate of hot spicy casseroled meats from one of his men. He smiled, for he knew which of them was Chef for that day. He hoped no one tired of the Sergeant at Arms, an Imperial Knight of the Mhyst Sahn`Frwh.

He doubted anyone would tell a member of the Death Watch that some of their Cooking really needed improving.

It also adds to the knowledge that Lieutenant JA'rvis ruled that the hot spicy casserole is eaten with iced water as a healing brew.

With the ledgers in one arm and his meal balanced in the other, he looked around to see heads down, Warriors sitting and relaxing their conversation, an inaudible sound that was more a dull hum.

He decided to return to his study. Once back, he sat at his desk, quills and ink prepared, and he wondered whether he would use or just read. The latter seemed more comfortable, and he learned as he ate and drank as one.

He had jotted notes down just as fast as he had read without knowing. He lent into the back of the oversized leather chair and swung his booted feet up onto the corner of the oak desk. He began reading intensely; he moved the crystal lamp closer to him for better light.

Absently he heard the knock at his door to see the woman LH'Nejah standing in the doorway.

"K`lton is not bothering you, is he?" Glancing up from the large ledger, he was reading.

"No, the boy is inquisitive and helps me…may I enter?" she asked quietly.

"Please do, sit; there are things unsaid that we must both hear. Close the door."

"It is unwise to close doors, Lieutenant. It ensures people to listen."

She sat down, watching him as he continued to read.

"To answer your question, no, K`lton is not a bother. No child is. But you must remember under all that bravado; he is just that, a child of ten or twelve winters with no parents."

Taelen pushed his chair back and closed the ledgers sliding them into a lower drawer. He placed a protection ward on the drawer. Standing, he leaned on the desk; his hands splayed for support. His eyes stared at her with his emotional pain. His anger and frustration lay smouldering below his thoughts.

"Do you think I don't know what it's like to be ten winters without parents?" he said. The edge coldly in his voice made her flinch. "I watched a man I thought I knew slit my mother's throat from ear to ear. I heard the blood bubbling as she tried to breathe. He then threw her in the Taayra`Ge Ocean." His eyes narrowed, "I was trying to swim after being thrown in by someone who wanted my throat intact. Yet I swam, to her, the ocean red with her blood at six winters.

Taelen did not see JA`rvis and Mistress Iz`sen standing at the door to the study. The tone in Taelen's voice was seething with anger.

"I don't have a clue in hell who… you are, Mistress. I did not ask to be born with the bloody Mhyst birthright. "He then angrily ripped the shirt and stepped closer to her.

"See this!" he said, jabbing at the birthright on his chest. The Dormas woman held his eyes as he spoke.

"Nothing but grief has brought me, I understand, K`lton. Because Mistress, I was and am like him.

She calmly stood and looked from his birthright to his brilliant blue eyes. Both were the same colour.

"Your birthright is the white Mhyst."

"So!" he snapped angrily. "I've seen Mhyst's of purple, and I've seen grey. Blue is just another colour in the scheme of the Mhyst. I don't see the attraction for what is my Mhyst Mistress!"

"But you have never seen white, except your own", she answered calmly, and even JA`rvis, still smarting from Taelen's angry outburst, realised that this woman had a lot to teach Taelen if he would only listen.

"You are your Grandfather all over again; he was the same but pale, pale blue."

"I am nothing if you do not already know; my mother was a Spellcaster?"

"NH`dya was a very skilled Spellcaster and a good mother."

"OH, is that so, then why did she." He cut himself off; his footsteps took him to stand near the bookcase; its vastness took up three walls from floor to ceiling.

"Say it, Taelen slept with your father, Yassarn," she said, "You were born of deep, tender love. That night…"

"I don't want to discuss this anymore. How do you know so much?   A Witch in your spare time?" he added cuttingly, and even JA`rvis was about to enter the room but was caught by the arm of the Mistress by his side shaking her head no.

"No, I am no 'witch' Taelen," she said softly. "I'm NH`dya's mother."

Taelen frowned, shaking his head and closing his eyes.

"I'm your Grandmother."

Neither of them spoke for a few moments. Taelen tried to fathom all he had said and all this woman before him had said.

"Why did you come?" He said flatly, emotionally spent. "Because of some emotive thought by me on the stone bench up there."

She took a deep breath, trying to control her own emotions.

"Life happens, Taelen." She said quietly.

K`lton ran through the door, surprising both the two adults standing there.

"Lieutenant Taelen," he said, rushing in and sliding on socked feet. "Its…" and stopped realising he had interrupted something between the older woman and the Lieutenant.

"I'm sorry…. I did not. "He stopped looking at the two adults.

"It's fine, K`lton. We had finished our discussion." He said, looking at the woman with contempt. "What has excited you?"

"It is snowing…I have never seen snowfall!" His large golden-green eyes were luminous. "It's beautiful, oh Mistress, please come and see," He pleaded to look at Taelen.

"I will come later." He said, "and I'll say goodnight then." The boy grinned and held LH`Nejah's hand. Taelen and his Grandmother looked at each other, and both knew this discussion had only begun. As they left his study, Taelen threw off the torn shirt.

He was angrier with himself for losing his temper and ripping a perfectly good shirt and stood in front of the fire, warming himself and lost in a myriad of thoughts.

The tentative knock at his door had him snap angrily. "What! It had better be bloody good," he then looked up from the yellow-orange coals to see Mistress Iz'sen's form framed within the architrave. The steam from the pottery mug in her hand sent silent grey mist into the air. It seemed to surround her face.

She stammered with his sudden abruptness.

"I …um…" her hands began to tremble, and she held the mug with both hands to stop spillage. " I brought up a hot brew. Something your men called a 'Knights kisses."

"Mistress," he said more levelly and, looking at her, added, "Thank you."

His hand took the mug from her but not by the handle.

"Your men said it would hit the spot. You're not going to throw it, are you?"

He stared at the dark hot liquid in the pottery mug and smiled only slightly.

"I could throw it at someone right now." He sighed, and his eyes glanced at her. "Hit the spot means it relieves the tension. I gather I was heard."

She raised her eyebrows. "You could say these rooms carry words and emotions, but your Warriors understand. Otherwise, they wouldn't have mixed this for you."

Taelen rubbed his eyes with his free hand wearily, then the nape of his neck.

"I suppose not." He noticed she was staring at his torso; the Mhyst birthright seemed to glow in the light of the fire.

He looked down at his naked chest. My apologies, Mistress; I'll just put another shirt back on. I wasn't expecting anyone up here at late this hour."

"No…," she said, shaking her head and frowning, realising what he was feeling. "Lieutenant, it is just I have never seen anything like it. It's not the same as the blue and grey Mhyst birthrights I have seen on your men, as Master JA`rvis and I bathed them after the attack."

"It's no different to theirs," he said, looking down at the birthright.

"But it is, do you not see, theirs is like a ripple in a pond. Yours" Iz`sen finger slowly touched Taelen's skin, and the nail traced the Mhyst marking. "Yours is like a spiral of air currents going up into the sky; yours rises." She said, smiling quietly at him. "Your element is air; theirs is water."

She removed her touch from his olive-skinned chest, and the dark hair curled around her fingers fell back into place. Her touch unnerved him as his skin was covered in goose pimples. He was unsure how innocent her touch was on his olive skin and moved away from her closeness and put another shirt on.

"You must be tired, "she said, walking to his desk and breaking the spell.

Taelen, in turn, moved to the window, watching the snow flurries dance upon the blackness of night.

"You are left-handed." She said, her head tilted in the light of the large candles that brought out the dark colour of her hair.

He heard the quill as it scratched with a right hand guiding ink and design across the parchment. He sat down on the daybed next to the window someone had made that day.

"What are you writing?" he asked as he drank the now cold liquid in the mug.

"Something my father, said to me before his death." She replied and walked to his bedside, where she knelt upon the richly woven rug on the floor. Tiredness lined her face. She rested her head on the side of the bed, where she sat against it. The proximity of her confused him.

"It may be something or nothing."

Her smile brought out feelings he had not felt in a

long time and angered him. He had to stop himself from touching her hair of burgundy; its coolness seemed silky in the half-light of the candles. Yet the heat burned part of him.

"Lieutenant." Her voice seemed as silky as the texture of her dark hair.

"Hmmm?" he murmured

She looked up at him from her sitting position on the floor. "I'm sorry, you're tired. I'll leave and let you rest." She rose, and his fingers ached to touch her hair.

"It's late; I'll put this on your desk." She said and took the mug not empty and said: "Goodnight, Lieutenant, sleep well." She left his room, closing the door.

He flung his arm over his eyes, groaning as he lay down on the daybed.

"Sleep", he moaned ", is one thing I'll not get tonight", and rose from the daybed he was casually lying on. Putting on his boots and coat, he walked out of his room. The corridor led to the vast parapets surrounding the castle.

On the parapets, where snow was making a strange crown upon his dark hair and shoulders, JA`rvis saw him, legs apart and hands in the deep pockets of his trousers.

"Unable to sleep?" he heard JA'rvis's voice coming from behind him.

"You could say that," Taelen replied without turning, needing to avoid eye contact with his Wolf brother.

"Iz`sen…?" JA`rvis inquired casually as he stared into the snowscape.

Taelen ignored him, closed his eyes and breathed deeply. Warriors saluted to acknowledge their rank as they continued their rotational guard shift. Taelen knew they needed a lot more Warriors. He tried to shift his thoughts of the vision of Iz`sen face before him out of his mind.

"Let us walk, Lieutenant Taelen." Said JA`rvis with duty.

Taelen raised his eyebrows, glancing sideways at his friend, who had already begun to walk. Taelen had to take significant strides to catch up with the Sqh`xn Warrior.

"So…" he left it to hang. "Where has Lord Mah`sden's path taken him?"

"I wish to speak about your Grandmother."

"I don't wish to!" he snapped and wondered why he felt that way. Having now changed his mind, he added, "She is a Spellcaster, is she not."

"Aye, she is." JA`rvis knew Taelen's resentment of Spellcasters. It was true they were aloof and living gifted lives. Until recently, he thought. Spellcasters rarely married below their station. This was common knowledge. To marry someone of the Mhyst had caused a great scandal at the time. Pity, he thought, that no one knew the whole truth. Yet, he began to tell Taelen something his friend needed to hear.

"When I was ten winters, the Spellcasters were many; thousands seemed to be their numbers." The wind tipped with fingers of ice streaked through his short silver hair. Spikes of hair tufted to the design of the wind stood where the wet strands of hair tangled together.

"Is there a point to your story, JA`rvis?" Taelen asked, bored with the whole history.

"Yes, there is, and you will hear me out. Wolf age is not the same as human winters," JA`rvis said coolly, raising his eyebrow. "They were at War with the Mhyst. There was and possibly still a group of Warriors 'The Duq`tung, pronounced Dq`tng.' say it fast because it's a curse, a secret. There was one for each Nation of O`pn and H`dn E`rth. One Warrior in a War can dispose of many where many Warriors have difficulty finding one Warrior."

Taelen looked at JA`rvis as they walked in the snow that filtered through the darkness.

"Only one stood up to them. That woman is below."

Taelen frowned. "Where was she when my uncle tortured my mother? Where was she when her daughter was murdered?"

JA`rvis looked at him.

"Where was she when you needed her, you mean?"

Taelen looked away from his friend; his anger and abandonment boiled beneath his skin.

"Your Grandmother could not save everyone. Not even the ones who meant her life's heartbeat. Taelen, when a Spellcaster dies violently. Sadly, your mother tears at the fabric of time and motion because they are the four major elements. Spellcasters and Covens are linked inexplicably by earth magic, which is why this Coven, even though warded by spells, was open to Brae." He said to his good friend.

"Lord Za`qrn spoke to the elements the night of Den`ah's attack. Master L`unh is missing. Mistress J`nn is wounded. Two Spellcasters of the latest dedication were drowned in their blood. You Taelen must call the Spellcasters back to their Covens, and they must bring the Warriors with them."

He paused, looking at the weather, the lightning reflected in JA`rvis's eyes.

"Teh`c and Yhy`h are halfway here, with three hundred strong Warriors and Knights of the Mhyst." He looked at his friend, "also, consider your feelings towards Mistress Iz`sen. A woman tortured makes a man feel a need to protect her. She is not what she seems,

Taelen. Yes, she has experienced something horrific and revolting; no word in any language describes rape. But beware of her revenge. It may cost more than even she realises. She will shred every person that comes within scent distance."

Taelen stood. His eyes stung and burned as he tried to take in all he had been told, but what pained him most was that J`nn was wounded. He wondered if Lord Za`qrn would forgive him.

"There are Warriors here, who are now Pack because of their wounds," he added.

"Then they are yours for protection of the Wolf Nation of Sqh`xn," Taelen said. The sadness and burden of his title seemed to drag his emotions down.

"Payment for services, aye Pack is Pact, is it not."

"They will leave when Lord Za`qrn arrives," said Taelen.

"They know this, my Lord?"

"Yes"

"Pack," he said quietly

"Pact," said JA`rvis, his arm across his broad chest. JA`rvis went to leave.

"One question," Taelen asked, "Why not the woman Iz`sen, K`lton and Cpl Den`ah?"

JA`rvis smiled. "Brother, I mend bodies, not hearts and souls. That has always been your forte since I saw you as a pup. Do me a favour next time your balls tighten near a woman, go roll in the snow, and believe me, it will cool the heat you feel."

"Oh, will it now, and you're an expert on balls?" He replied with a bemused grin.

JA`rvis laughed aloud and patted Taelen on the back.

"Aye, I am thirty winters old, Taelen, and I know there are no pups out there or a woman that is mine."

"So the roll in the snow works?" Taelen asked, smirking.

"Not always… there are other ways of adjusting your crotch." He laughed again and said, "You are one person who just can't go relieving his balls every time they tighten…."

He ran his hands over his wet hair in a vain attempt to dry it.

"It's time I went in… a 'mate' will come when the time is right…" he turned, and they looked at each other silently, and he nodded his head. JA`rvis left Taelen standing alone with the snow and the vastness of the landscape before him.

The Lieutenant stood a solitary figure with a burden that threatened to crush his psyche if he let it. The cold icy tendrils of the wind and snow finally pushed him into the protection of the Coven. Taelen's footsteps moved inside to the hearth of the kitchen.

Only the next night shift sat playing cards quietly. He did not see his Grandmother at the sideboard doing what he mused she had always done, making sure things were right, small things that meant a lot but mostly fell unnoticed.

"You're up late," he said to her, pouring two hot brews and sitting on a chair near the hearth for warmth.

"They say the old never need as much sleep as the young, Lieutenant," she answered using his title; he said nothing to acknowledge her words.

"Was I named after my Grandfather?" he asked, not looking at her.

She smiled wistfully at the memory of her husband. Her eyes watered, and she frowned.

Emotions came as swift as the morning tide. Feelings she had permanently closed behind a large door in her mind now fluttered free. She took a deep breath and closed the door, her eyes stinging with the tears she did not wish to come.

"You are named after him… aye. You are he, in many ways, just as your mother and father. And I even see myself in you sometimes, which is the way of children."

He handed her the mug filled with the spiced tea typical to the Coven and the Garrison that permanently wattled in the same dwellings.

He'd not thought about that before, but now he wondered why both still existed with the other; her voice interrupted his deliberations but irritatingly.

"You have Yassarn's eyes and your Grandfathers eyes," she said quietly.

"Aye, I have met my father. Thankfully, you look nothing like them." he smiled slightly, and she could not determine whether this was insult or flattery on his behalf.

She looped strands of silver hair over her ear that had escaped the long braid that fell to her knees, snaking down her back and continued.

"Yet you are taller than both of them and have their smile. There is a small crease at your brow when you think deeply, just like your Grandfathers." She shrugged lightly and sipped her spiced tea. "Your shoulders are broad like theirs. You are the Mhyst Lieutenant; it is that simple you are the breaker and maker of hearts and souls. I see now why my daughter fell in love with Yassarn."

"I am nothing, I am not my father or grandfather, just as I am not you or my mother, and I wish others would see just that to the gods. You forgot to include that you are part Wolf too." With a carelessness that showed his internal pain, he knew his words would wound her, and that was their intention.

"Yes, you are not the first and will not be the last. You have the gift of many cultures, which is their gift to you."

"Is that why you see so clearly?" he said as JA`rvis walked in and stopped as he glanced at the two in conversation.

"Only one who has walked such a path can relate to it. The Sqh`xn Nation is great and powerful. You share the ways of the Wolf Nation through your paternal line," She said, looking at both her grandsons.

"So, Grandmother, when would you tell me you are also part Wolf and part Dream Caster?" He asked her, still not trusting her. "This brings me back to the fact, Mistress. You are a Dream Caster, which I forgot. I need your gift to assist in bringing Corporal Den`ah back to the land of the living, not the dreaming." He paused and added, "Being of the Pack will aid in his recovery, as sadly that was JA`rvis and my only source to use when I tried to heal the lad."

"How did you both know this?" She asked, sipping the tea again.

"Your name was on my wife's lips as she died, something about a past debt paid in full."

She smiled silently.

"Dream Casters are rare, Taelen. It is not a mantle I wear with comfort. It is part of the Lore of the Spellcasters and Sqh`xn, a link between the elements. Even you could Dream Cast if you knew how."

"You are going back with JA`rvis, aren't you?" He said as he watched the Warriors at the table play the game of cards known as G`cqa, which meant cheating hearts. He glanced back at her and took another sip of the tea.

"There are things shall we say…that were left hanging before I was removed from the Coven, that I can only rectify. As you said earlier, I am part Wolf. "

Taelen was silent as he looked at the embers, their heat warming his eyes.

"Why didn't you…?"

"Why didn't I save my daughter and you? I was exiled to Cha`dor, a place far away. Lore of Sqh`xn and Cha`dor bound me. The price you pay for being a 'halfling' is that your loyalties cross over to guide you, undo you."

"The Spellcasters Citadel, I thought that was a nasty tale for children." Said Taelen as he drank the dregs of cold tea; the heat of the fire prickled his back in its glow.

"No, I am afraid it exists." She said grimly." My husband and anyone connected to me were killed. You see, I defied them because they were in the wrong. But I knew too much, and knowing too much means being perceptive enough to know that no one would listen to a compromise."

"Mistress, Lieutenant Taelen, "said JA`rvis ", pardon my interruption, but…." Taelen, too, felt the shudder within his psyche. A single gasp of life extinguished like a candle. It was more than that.

Simultaneously the screams of Iz`sen and K`lton were what caused the ensuing chaos. Warriors ran, knocking mugs over, chairs skittled across the stone floor, and the card game stopped spilling their 'hands' upon the table into the direction of the battlements while Taelen had thrown his mug and had run towards their rooms. They were both found cowering in the corridor outside Den`ah's room.

Iz`sen was holding K`lton tightly to her body. The boy hung onto her, both screaming.

JA`rvis and the others were mystified; LH'Nejah was not. The Spellcaster crept down onto her knees and spoke between the screams.

"Iz`sen put the blade down; no one will touch you or K`lton." She was breathing heavily, blood streaming from wounds that JA`rvis had healed.

"Get… them… away," she screamed, verging on hysteria. K`lton was crying uncontrollably.

"Iz1sen-K`lton, you will look at me, NOW, at my eyes. Look at me," she ordered. Both stopped screaming as their eyes made contact. The blade that Iz`sen held fell with a clatter to the stone floor.

"Catch them as they fall." She ordered Taelen and JA`rvis. "Wait till their eyes close."

Eyes red from crying and swollen from tears flittered and closed; both fell Taelen caught them with JA`rvis.

"Take them to your rooms, Lieutenant. You must not touch them in any way. I will be there very soon."

"Where are you going?" he asked his Grandmother.

"To the Corporal's room", and she left them all, and all that could be heard was her stockinged feet padding purposefully down the length of the carpet down the corridor. "He needs to awaken and now."

LH'Nejah entered the Den`ah's room; he lay still cocooned within the Mhyst.

It was here as Dream Caster that she uttered the following spell.

"The 'four elements' will be renewed within what was and is."

"Within the hour, what has been will be gone."

"Within the hour, what has killed will be killed."

"Within the hour, blood is blood, and the pack is the pact."

"Within the hour, what was Mhyst Lord will be gone."

"Within the hour, what was Lord will be scribed by quill."

"Within the hour of the new moon, all that was old will be gone."

"Within the hour, what was wounded will be healed."

"Within the hour, what was a nightmare will be a dream."

"So mote it be."

She then turned to the window and opened it. A sharp white light long as a sword left the Corporal's body. He arched his back, groaning excruciatingly and sagged, exhaling.

"Go back to your Master, but take this with you." From the wounds still raw within the Corporal came red practicals that leapt upon the white light as it vanished out the window.

Without turning, she addressed the young Lieutenant that was guarding the door.

"Lieutenant Jarek."

"Yes, Mistress," he said; having seen her Spell Casting and the Dream Casting, he wasn't about to say no to her.

"The Corporal will wake in the hour; he will be starving; make sure he doesn't gulp his food down or be sick." She said, grinning slightly.

"Yes, Mistress… That thing, what was it?"

"A reminder for me not to forget the past and never turn my back on a Sorcerer. However, magnetic his personality is." She said coldly.

"I don't understand." Replied Lieutenant Jarek, watching her closely. His eyes slipped to the Corporal's sleeping form in the room.

"You don't have to, Lieutenant. I do." Her smile said more to him than he wished to know.

She said, patting him on the chest. "Just watch the Corporal." She left then to find her Grandsons.

# CHAPTER 12

LH`Nejah's socked feet walked quickly along the carpet that ran the length of the corridors of the Coven. Though tired, she knew more than she wished about the young woman and the boy.

She was grateful to the Goddess, her insight with those two had been invaluable, and it was the second insight that had flowed cold down within her like a barb she would never be able to retrieve.

For she now knew who had sent Mah`sden to kill Yassarn and who was, in fact, the assassin, some Spellcasters. She mused, just did not know when not to interfere. Her cousin Dash`un image came into her thoughts. She mused it was nothing but a tart when they were younger, tart. The word was too kind for her. Having played too many games with the Warriors to get her way, she was now in league with Lord Mah`sden. So much for trusting family, she thought. Lord Mah`sden and Dash`un suited each other down to their fetid Mhyst.

She stopped at one of the long windows that let light flood the corridor's stone floor and the long carpet. Lightning flashed across the night sky. She watched the windowpane dappled in a hard rain peppering the surface loudly. Thunder fractured the darkness. Her reflection stared back at her. The face of a woman, rain shadowed down her cheeks, leaving the impression of tears that seemed endless in their grief.

LH`Nejah shivered, her hand cupping her mouth as she leaned against the frame. Her tears welled in her eyes as she steadied herself. Slender shoulders rose as she breathed deeply, a resolve within her now-fired contempt for her cousin, there would be blood on her hands this time, and she didn't care if it was her cousins or Mah`sden. This time there would not be a compromise. She shook her head. No, not this time.

She began again down the corridor rubbing her hands from the cold. A cold she could not keep warm from. LH'Nejah entered her Grandsons room.

"What happened to them?" Taelen asked her as she came in.

"Past", she answered, "It was part of their past."

"You're saying those two know each other?" Asked JA`rvis, swearing and frowning at the implications that he knew would surface.

"Look at them closely, and tell me what you see while I tend them." Her voice was exhausted, but there was now a finality about it that concerned both men.

She healed with the power of a very high Spell Caste and found a change of clothes.

"You can both help me. I can't dress them myself, it won't be the first time you have seen a woman naked, and it won't be the last."

Both were relieved when she had finished dressing the open wounds.

"They will stay in the Eastern Wing but the Axes room." LH'Nejah frowned, knitting her slender eyebrows together with her heart heavy like a lodestone to her emotions.

"When you have done that, I need to talk to you both."

Both men returned to find her staring out into the darkness of the room's only long window. It was moments before she spoke to them. Their reflections mirrored in the night on the glass of the large long window. She touched her lip with one slender finger and thought quietly about the tiredness of stress and the late hour.

"It's late, "Is it vitally important?."

"They are related somehow, but she is far too young to be his mother," JA`rvis said.

"Is she?" LH'Nejah turned to face them. Her slender body silhouetted against and only showed light with the storm's electricity pounded the mountains like a war drum to the gods above and the men and women below.

"I've heard of child brides, but she would have been twelve or thirteen to have mothered K`lton."

Their grandmother raised her eyebrows, sensing both their feelings on the subject. She smiled at them with her love for these two Warriors before her.

"The Dormas had an understanding with the region of Drargon`H. To some, the belief of early marriage is ancient, brutal, and some believe the spirit is not free and only benefits pain." Pausing, she added, "how can I put this?"

"Not delicately," said Taelen raising his eyebrows and shoving his hands into his pockets roughly.

His discomfort made him fidget, and he moved only a few feet instead of JA`rvis, who was pacing the floor like a father worried about a child.

"No, I can't. The Dormas use the royal children, females, mainly as 'breeders' with the Drargon`H Nation. K`lton is the result of that act. Politically, Iz`sen is merely property to bargain between the two nations. Kolton separated at birth. The child is taken and given to its father. Somehow she found K`lton, or he saw her. This is punishable by death on either side. I do not know how or what the connection between mother and son is. The spell or ward is ancient and complicated. To answer your question of what happened, just when a spell reflects," She frowned. "This is difficult, so bear with me for a moment."

Simultaneously as lightning illuminated the room,

an electrical current of mauve light tentacle slightly through the room, as it appeared, the air crackled, and thunder deafened in the storm's climactic explosion.

"Close..." Taelen said. His eyes scanned the room; the long window now seemed a portal to another world parallel to theirs.

"Maybe, I can help with what you need to convey." He said. "When a spell is cast, whether verbal, written, or signed, it is for good, not evil, or the old belief of returning threefold to the Caster is invoked. Somehow K`lton has fractured the Lore of Spells, reversing the effect; their worlds are tilted now and not parallel, causing a ripple through the elemental levels of space and time."

JA`rvis glanced at his pack brother.

"So… to put it simply?" He asked, arching both eyebrows with an explanation he had just heard. He shook his head; he never did understand complicated replies.

"The Lore of Spells is missing its mark. It doesn't even have a bloody target by all that has been said."

"You could have said that to start with, you know. Without all that waffle, you just sprouted.

It makes you sound like the Dominion Lord." JA`rvis scoffed teasingly at his friend Taelen.

"If the cap fits JA`rvis, then it's what I am to wear."

Changing the course of the conversation, JA`rvis asked, shaking his head at his brother

"How old was she when she had K`lton?" His deep blue eyes steeled to grey.

"She was twelve winters old." LH'Nejah answered quietly, adding, "K`lton is twelve winters. He hasn't started his maturing yet."

JA`rvis cursed openly." That is my world is classed as child torture."

"But in theirs, it is not; you see, that is where and why worlds collide and Lands war."

“How old is K`lton’s father?” asked Taelen; his thoughts of the woman a winter older than he and what she had experienced chilled his soul.

“He would be the reigning Lord, his age would be that of any monarch, and I am not aware who the Lord of the Drargon`H Region is. We will undoubtedly hear from them when they realise their heir is alive.”

“Do they still practice this…breeding?” asked Taelen, feeling quite sick.

“Not anymore. I am afraid Mah`sden and his murdering disciples have torched every town, village, and seaport. Both nations are in chaotic decline. Mah`sden leaves very few alive, as you both well know.”

“Do you know if they recalled anything?” Taelen asked quietly.

“No,” she said, “my capacity as Spell and Dream Caster is chronicled. My perimeters are strict.” She stood. “It is too late, and I am tired, watch over them tonight. The Coven is clear of spells, and I have a covering ward network.” She nodded slightly at them. “Goodnight,” she said. They noticed her walk was purposeful; both knew she would not sleep.

JA`rvis said his leave, and Taelen listened to his brother and friend's departing footsteps down the long carpeted corridor.

He fell onto his bed, arms spread out, his mind confused.

‘If I am supposed to be Lord of the Mhyst, why don’t know I feel like it?’ He thought to himself and had an ill feeling about his future.

Taelen knew he would not sleep; he entered the other room joined by a single door and walked to his desk, sitting in the leather chair. The array of parchments and his ink and quill seemed the comfort he needed. He hand-picked up the parchment that Iz`sen had quilled earlier.

The Master Scribe in him was impressed by her dexterity at using left-handed nibs, not easy for someone who was predominantly right-handed. A left-hander could only use the cut on the nibs. He used as the right-hander had nibs cut in the opposite direction. She had deftly mastered a problematic technique.

Taelen sat up, now swinging his legs over the end of the corner of the desk. The chair's leather creaked with his shift in position as he lent back. Studying the script on the open pages, he leaned and opened the warded drawer and brought the three books to the desktop. He lit the large candles on his desk and opened the ledger. His fingertips turned pages. At three in the morning, he found himself in the kitchen.

The next shift of the Knights and Warriors was changing over.

"M`hta," he said, pouring a hot drink, only this one was strong, black and bitter to keep him awake.

"Yes, Lieutenant," he said, looking up from the card game that had commenced as Taelen came over.

"You were the Historical Scribe at Ch`nel, weren't you?" Taelen asked as he drank the hot, bitter coffee the shifts drank to keep them alert.

"Aye, that I was; why do you ask Lieutenant?" His green eyes were flecked with gold and brown, surrounded by black eyelashes. He blinked slowly as he glanced up from the fan of cards he held in his hands.

Taelen scoured the notes he had jotted down earlier and placed them in front of M`hta.

"I've been researching these ledges, have a look, and I'd like your opinion as a Scribe based on the

Historical side." As their eyes met, he smiled, "I will play your hand."

The Guard Shift's Warrant looked up from his cards at Taelen as he dealt more cards. Js'yah's brilliant cornflower blue eyes always startled Taelen in their directness

"That was not a fair offer, Lieutenant; last time I played with you, I lost, and may I add, I lost heavily." He smiled and looked at M`hta. "You owe me for this sacrifice M`hta."

Cards were dealt with and lost as M`hta sat down and studied Taelen's notes. It was much later when the Corporal looked up at Taelen.

"May I speak freely?" M`hta asked as he watched the cards placed in the centre of the table, hands reached out, taking which cards they needed.

"Aye, I see no reason why this can't be shared," Taelen said as he won that round of cards.

M`hta's reading of the jottings that Taelen had taken down came fast and precise. It had to be for the workload he would have been under as a Scribe. Collating, deciphering and translating facts in a historical context would have been difficult and time-consuming. Considering that, the text they were studying was only written in Rune.

He took a deep breath and kept his eyes on the original parchment that Taelen had also brought down to the kitchen with him. M`hta lent to his backpack and pulled out his quill and ink secured in an oak box with runic embossing crystals. Having removed the ink and quill, he slid the nib into place.

"Ah! The hidden talents of M`hta" said the Warrant winking at him with eyes of brilliant blue that always without fail landed him in trouble. His penchant for putting his foot in the obvious was one reason he had stayed a Warrant.

M`hta laughed aloud and shook his head at his Warrant, then said. “Throw my hand in, Lieutenant; I need to show you something.”

His quill moved with the grace of someone who had been apprenticed young the intense training as a Scribe. Taelen noted that the sound of the nib was smooth and not scratching.

“Here is the ‘Guardians of O`rath’; we are centred within a two-league radius of the Guardians. But in the second millennium, a massive earthquake shifted the ‘A`rlon Plateau’ five leagues to the east, and it was moved three leagues down into the earth, its name changed to the ‘Plains of Etta’.”

The Warrant closed his hand and said. “Some earthquake.”

“Aye, it was.” Replied M`hta. He placed the parchment in the centre of the long kitchen table as the others forgot their cards and held the corners down with now cold tea and coffee mugs. All leant forward with renewed interest. The card game was overlooked for the moment.

“Etta means grief, in O`rathian, the O`rathian civilisation, and was the second millennium's richest, most powerful city. In short, they ruled unopposed over the vast dominions that surrounded them. Their domain was coast to coast in all directions. They were tyrannical and believed in slavery and sacrificing to the Gods. Pillaging and plundering every region they could – a bit tiresome.”

“What is in that area now?” asked T`Aogh, an Imperial Archer and Blades man, as the Warrant glanced over the rim of the coffee mug.

Ez'rhn was still holding his cards in one hand, put them down and looked up at them all. He was a strikingly handsome young man. His dark skin and laconic grin were part of him like the Sergeant's lightning blue eyes. Ez`rhn dark lashes shadowed the green pastel iris that resembled pale jade. The Corporal was one of those Warriors that any weapon was easy, skilled in many that even Taelen had no training.

"The 'Plains of Etta' are the most productive agricultural area in the region; they are the plains west from here, about three leagues from here. Brutal in winter, they are just one vast white landscape of death. The twin cities of 'P`ntoz and S`zryn on the coast, the North West coast, or the Western Seaboard if you wish."

Taelen smiled as Ez`rhn continued. As a trained Cartographer, he knew the lay of the land the same way he knew his own heart.

"But this here," his dark fingers traced the Plains of Etta. "Through here," he pointed and retraced the perimeter. "Are immense chasms, they fill with water during the 'wet season and the 'The Plains of Etta' are more an island than a Plain. Erosion over the past millennium has caused it to form an isolated escarpment plateau."

"What you have found, Lieutenant, may well be the 'Fourth book of Sz`a`Th" in the six volumes. The other names for the two pillars called the Guardians of O`rath are 'Fate and Destiny", said M`hta standing and straightening his back with fatigue.

"You've lost me," said T`Aogh, his hands rubbing his head vigorously with frustration and confusion.

"And me." Added Js`yah as he drained his mug and poured more coffee.

"Lieutenant, the floor is yours." The Sergeant said, spreading his arms gracefully and dramatically as he leant back in the chair with a wink and laconic grin.

"Eloquently put as always, Js`yah", replied M`hta,

smiling at the man at the opposite side of the table.

"Each civilisation had one book. Out of the six to; use their constitution of government under the Lores of the Sz`a`Th. But the seventh…."

"There is always a seventh," said Js`yah "let me guess, death, destruction, torture, pillage, plunder, all the fun things that invaders do. Why do I feel suddenly so depressed?" He said flatly and reached for a biscuit baked only an hour before. He sat passively eating the nutmeg and cinnamon biscuit and let the crumbs fall to his chest.

"Your insight is sometimes staggering, Js`yah," said Taelen smiling at the Sergeant.

"It's not, Lieutenant; I'm a bloody pessimist." He grabbed three more biscuits and ate silently.

T`Aogh brought the sizeable hot pot of bitter black coffee over to the table.

"I think we will need this," he said, refilling everyone's mugs.

"I have a feeling Lord Mah`sden has the Seventh Book. The imbalance of the Seventh Book is undermining the Mhyst." T`Aogh said quietly, placing the coffee pot down on the table.

"But we all know the Book of Shadows pertains to the Mhyst but isn't the Mhyst," said T`Aogh

"Aye, the Book of Shadows implements Spellcasters and the Lore of the Sz`a`Th. One cannot move without the other it is like a game of checkers. The Lore of Elements is the Sixth Book; somehow, they all interlock with the other," said Taelen.

"The Book of Shadows is the fifth book. It contains what is opposite in the other six books. It is the mirror of the seventh book." Taelen added.

"Now, I may be a bit thick sometimes, so bear with me for a moment. You are saying that the Book of

Shadows reflects the Seventh Book. Now, if I know anything about spellcasting, it is that you only send out good, not bad, or the old thing about coming back three times worse apply." Said Js`yah. He took a large cup of coffee and grimaced at the bitter taste.

"Lord, that's awful," he said, commenting on the coffee. Then added

"So it's simple we find the all Seven Books without getting our heads separated from our bodies or some other gruesome pastime that Mah`sden and his men have thought up. Hold the book in the Mirror and chant the Book of Shadows backwards three times." He took another swig of coffee he had complained about and looked at Taelen. He raised his eyebrows and said in an exhausted voice.

"If you thought I was depressed before, think again. I may just slit my own throat and save Mah`sden the time." He said, shaking his head and putting down the table's mug. Js`yah's brilliant cornflower blue eyes closed for the moment in weariness.

M`hta's eyes swept around the table to the men he knew well. "This design here," he said, pointing to the intricate rune flourish at the top of the page of each Ledger that Taelen was studying. "Shows how each book's mosaic fits into the other. If then hypothetically, we manage to obtain."

"Steal you mean, let's not mince our words M`hta. Some of us will spill our blood and guts for these bloody books." The Warrant of the Guard had cold determination now and a realistic outlook. He scratched at the rough of a beard that he had not intended to grow to its annoying length. He was a man who knew the actual cost of war.

It was T`Aogh who spoke next. His earth brown eyes, fair skin, and freckles made him seem youthful at thirty winters. He was just younger than the Warrant by three winters.

"Even should Lord Mah`sden manage to collect the Seventh Book? There is something that hopefully, he is unaware of."

They all looked at him and then at the Warrant, who looked back at them with a 'what?' expression across his face.

"Warrant, your no fool; look at the design; your people use this."

He tapped his finger on the design in the runic scroll. Js`yah looked at the design turning the parchment round so it faced him. He then set it where the Axes of the five elements would sit. Then those brilliant blue eyes stared at Taelen.

"It's only you, Lieutenant, he needs, only you to give him ultimate power, and he has to do it before your twenty-first winter or on your day of birth, not a great present, do you know your day of birth?."

Taelen glanced up at the Warrant and asked.

"Alive or dead, or shouldn't I ask the obvious?" Taelen asked those Warriors at the table. "My birthday is hazy; there is no explicit confirmation of the date or time."

"Alive preferably, because although the power of the Mhyst will linger in you at death, disperse to the four elements." He paused and swallowed the last of his coffee. "While alive, he will drain you of the Mhyst, but it will kill him unless he has something we aren't aware of. His Mhyst is not white, purple or blue. Those three are compatible; he is something I never wish to see again. His Mhyst is a sea green near black, like something insidious, which seeps into your soul." Js`yah continued, "See how the Ancients interlocked the runic design. The Mhyst Lore is one of creation. That we know. Read the design as creation; see how the runic scroll rolls skyward." His finger spiralled up. "That is how your Mhyst behaves, Lieutenant; I'm sorry, simply Mah`sden will want you at all costs and milk the last drop of Mhyst from your soul."

Taelen pushed his empty cup away from him, remembering Iz'sen's prophetic words that his own Mhyst swirled upwards.

"You are the key, Lieutenant," He said, tapping at the design. "A Spellcasters phrase wards it. Unless that phrase is uttered, the books won't unleash the full power of the Seventh Book."

Taelen took a deep breath. His eyes rested on the Warrant of the Guard. Both knew that to stall would cause death more death than if they went ahead and searched for all the books.

"Well, we're safe. I have no idea what the phrase is." He said, shaking his head.

He rubbed his eyes with his left hand; he was tired and felt it.

"But Lieutenant, if Lord Mah`sden knows the phrase and somehow you utter it unknowingly…" he opened his hands in surrender.

Taelen saw the danger instantaneously. Everyone was silent at the table.

"Thanks, Js`yah, you know how to make my self-esteem plummet," he said as the other Guards' dawn shift came into the kitchen.

Taelen pushed back his chair and stood up; he glanced at the other Warriors as they waited.

"One other thing, my Lord, that no one has bothered to mention or realises, there is one other person needed…." Js`yah said, staring at him.

"And why is this person needed?"

"Legend tells of a Kh`irz…" He straightened his

back and legs from fatigue and glanced at the empty coffee pot, hoping someone would take the hint and refill the silver pot full of piping hot black coffee.

"Kh`irz are only legends Warrant, nothing else. What could a group of secular monks have to do with the Seven Books of the Sz`a`Th? Kh`irz, the most powerful of healers, is written in the ancient runic script of the Sz`a`Th that a member of the Kh`irz will bring the Dominion Lord back to the living and that it will be by her hand that he dies." T`Aogh said as he replaced the coffee pot with full steaming hot coffee; its aroma seemed to lift the fatigue they were all feeling.

"Not so. " Said M`hta. "If we are to believe in the Legend that the Warrant has touched on. It means someone else, somewhere, is the opposite of the Lieutenant. Fate and Destiny… the other person is a woman, and she will be a lot younger than your nineteen winters Lieutenant, and she's a Spellcaster of maybe sixteen or seventeen winters." M`hta took a deep breath and exhaled slowly. "You are Fate, and she is your Destiny. Another version is that by the Kh`irz hand, he shall die, but he shall live by the heart. Who is to say what is truth and what is lie?"

"Very poetic…romantic even, but what if it's not me and another Scribe who is Sahn`Frwh trained…there is that possibility." Taelen grimly said and sat down heavily in the chair.

JA`rvis had just come in from his shift with others trickling in for the changeover and handover of the Night Guard. He stood by the large fireplace warming frozen limbs.

"I know her name." He said as they all riveted towards him with their eyes.

"Aye, and how do you know this?" asked Taelen frowning at JA`rvis.

“The Spellcasters healing within the protection of the Sqh`xn Nation is the other Guardian of O`rath.” His voice was low and nearly a whisper to them.

Taelen’s eyes narrowed at JA`rvis; J'nn was the only Spellcasters he knew that was with the Sqh`xn pack.

“Is this true?” His amethyst, blue eyes pained with the thought that this was one person he did not need to be on Lord Mah`sden's prowling list of would-be corpses.

“Aye… this is not something I would tell an untruth about.” Was all JA`rvis said; the look in his eyes told Taelen that this news was the truth. His shoulders sagged, and he stood and seemed lost for a moment as he stared at nothing. Then as other Warriors entered, he turned to them all.

“While you wait for the rosters, Js`yah will explain this to you,” he said, indicating the scroll on the table. Taelen’s feet felt like lead.

“I’ll be out on the battlements if anyone needs me, Lieutenant M`hta. I just promoted you; allocate someone my room. I won’t be using my bed today.”

He grabbed his cloak and stepped onto the parapet leading to the eastern battlements. He did not need guards where he stood, as the only access beside the route he took was from the air and a six hundred-metre vertical drop. It was for its remoteness and solitary atmosphere that Taelen had chosen to walk the narrow parapet with its metre and half-high protection wall. The winds battered there constantly.

M'hta found him alone on the bleak fortifications; snow and wind lashed at him, but he did not notice the elements.

The young man walked over to Lieutenant Taelen, standing quietly to his left.

“Lieutenant,” he said, acknowledging Taelen’s

overwhelming responsibility.

Snow lay on his shoulders and within the folds of the cloak. His dark hair sprinkled the magic of the white crystal flakes with his beard.

"It is time you rested, tomorrow dawns," he quietly said as a faint pale glow came upon the world of snow-covered forests below them.

Taelen glanced sideways at his Lieutenant; he nodded and turned, slowly moving frozen limbs and stamping his boots. He shook the snow from his shoulders and cloak in one slow movement.

M`hta walked in silence with Taelen and through the side door. The oak door took them to the heated bathing pool. He helped Taelen remove his cloak and tunic jacket. Taelen removed his uniform and plunged into the pool.

"So I now have my own Steward?" Taelen said as he felt the tepid water burn his skin, tingling frozen nerves back into life.

"Yes, if that is what you require, but most I am a friend, Taelen", Replied M`hta sitting on the worn oak bench. The wood is polished after many winters of use.

"M`hta, you should have a wife and children, why don't you."

"What? Me! No, it is easier without a partner. I'd rather not have someone left alone to grieve for me in my absences and death; it would not be fair on either of us."

"I can't promise those men and women of the Sz`a`Th in there or you anything." He closed his eyes, resting his head on the edge of the deep pool. Steam rose around him as bubbles rose and burst from the deep thermal pool beneath the Coven.

"They know that my Lord, my error Lieutenant," said M`hta wishing he could lighten the burden that seemed to be forever on his friend's shoulders.

“Have things changed so much that even you call me Lord?”

M`hta smiled as he removed his cloak, which was very humid within the confines of the bathing pool.

“Aye, the Mhyst rules whether we like it or not.”

“So things have changed much between those who see me as that title I avoid?”

“Yes and no,” he said sadly, “you have loyal friends, not just Warriors. That is something that has altered; in there lies the difference. Another is, for the first time in many winters, we now have hope,” M`hta said as he turned to go out.

“Would you eat if I brought you something?”

“Aye, why not? It might help me think a little better.” Replied Taelen as he swam the tepid waters.

"Then I’ll take it to your rooms.”

“M`hta,” he said, his eyes opening, the pain a deep chasm within him of what lay ahead.

“Yes, Taelen.”

“I promise with my heart's blood oath to destroy Mah`sden.” He said quietly, " I promise no one will ever grieve for you.”

“I know, Lieutenant” M`hta smiled slightly and left, praying it would not take Taelen’s heart's blood oath to achieve just that.

# CHAPTER 13

Darkness enveloped his room except for the squat yellow candles at his desk. He wondered how long he had slept. Taelen rolled over and smiled at the curled form of K`lton upon the large lounge chair beside his bed. The boy's face was peaceful and relaxed; his dark eyelashes formed long shadows across the smooth olive skin of his cheeks. K`lton had Taelen's dark cloak over him for warmth from the icy chills that had pervaded the room in the late dusk. The Lieutenant silently rose out of his bed and, lifting the boy, placed him in the bed where the warmth from his own body still lay within the covers of the large bed he slept in.

"Sleep, little Dragon," he said. Taelen put on thick woollen socks. He kept the dark blue uniform trousers on that he had slept in the night before. He moved to the long window and opened it slightly ajar, and let the icy winds caress his body; he loved the feeling of cold air across his skin.

His left hand held the warm, soft cream shirt he had picked up from the chair K`lton had been curled upon. Stretching as far as his fingertips could reach, he stood in that position as he called on the four elements to give him strength.

The Lieutenant felt the energy reaching up from the earth star and prickling the souls of his feet and his inner core. The sensation ran the entire length to his fingertips, and the soul star then ran down as the cold air fanned through his fingers and cascaded down his tree of life within him. His Chakra was renewed.

He did not turn as he sensed someone entered the room and continued his morning ritual. He listened to the woollen socks cushion as they walked upon the stone floor.

"Pardon, Lieutenant, I didn't realise you'd woken," she said quietly. "The light in this room is low. My apologies. I have brought you hot food."

He could smell the aroma of the roast lamb and spiced vegetables slowly roasted over the hot coals in the kitchen earlier; his mouth began to salivate, much to his chagrin. He ended his routine to answer the calling in his stomach.

"K`lton will sleep while we eat." He said and pulled himself away from the window, closing it to the elements. The white world outside only worried him more as he knew that commands. His command had meant that people of the Sz`a`Th, were now out in that weather trying to return to the Covens, Keeps and Garrisons. He said a silent prayer to the Goddess for their safety.

"Sit, Mistress Iz`sen," he said, then added, "Please" she nodded and sat opposite him. Both of them were quiet.

"Your Hospitality will not go unnoticed, my Lieutenant. But I must return to the Dormas." Taelen looked up from his hot meal.

"And what of K`lton? He is your son." He ate and glanced up from the food.

"Better here with you…if you will care for him."

"He is the heir to the Drargon`H Nation surely…" began Taelen sipping the hot tea.

"He is as good as dead, my Lord…how did you know he is my son?" Iz`sen asked, confused as panic ran through her like the cold steel of a sword.

"I know enough, Iz`sen, but you must tell me."

"I can't." She said as she stared at the boy asleep in the bed, not meters from them.

"Can't? You know all there is to know of me." Said Taelen as he finished his meal. He shivered and recalled he'd forgotten to put his shirt on.

"Come to my study. It is just through that door. If K`lton wakes, he knows where I will be."

Standing, he slipped the thick shirt on. Its softness and warmth was instant. He grabbed the black boots on his way through the room as he entered the study.

Taelen opened the long window to let the smell of candle wax and incense to be free and stood looking at the desk.

He noted M`hta had been at work on the parchments; his elegant scrolling letters were in code, code apprentices used to pass notes. Something had not changed as he looked at the note from M`hta to himself upon the desk. He placed the ledger that held the Guard Roster and placement orders for the Garrison attached to the Coven over M`hta's early morning notes.

He looked at the rest of the desk and smiled as M`hta had left his beloved Scribes tools behind.

"What time of day is it?" He asked, turning his attention to the light outside that seemed faded.

"Actually, it's very late in the evening, just after dusk. You have slept for two days, Lieutenant."

"I think we can dispense with rank. Taelen will be fine." He said coolly.

Mistress Iz`sen rose from the chair in front of the large oak desk, with its runic script down each leg and along the front. She knew the top of the desk held an ancient runic design, tugging at her senses for some reason.

"I leave tomorrow at dawn." She said, distracted by the large oak desk.

Taelen glanced at the window to his left. He could see the white flecks of snow highlighted from the glow of lamps in the Coven.

"You leave in this weather? Why?" he asked. The paleness in his eyes reflected the snow's dim bluish glow that enhanced their colour.

She looked away from those eyes.

"I think you should reconsider, Mistress. The blizzards have hit the Dormas region, and to get even a day's travel from here, would cost me two fresh horses, feed, clothes and at least four Warriors as your escort.

She narrowed her eyes and clenched her jaw.

"My people need guidance."

"Your brother is in that position."

"My brother is a liar, money user, and a manipulator, my Lieutenant."

"So you are going back to overthrow him and throw your region into chaos."

"I… what I do does not concern you; the politics of the Dormas region concerns only me."

"You are wrong there, Mistress. What happens in one region affects all regions." His voice inflection rose, "You are talking treason, Mistress; the penalty for treason is…Death. I think you should reconsider your actions and weigh up the consequences. For your actions will only bring a stain of blood and deceit to you and all you touch."

Taelen noticed the guard at his door look in, his hand resting on the pommel of his short flat-bladed sword, which was called a L`kus. Taelen knew he only had to look one way at the Guard, and the woman before him would not have time for an intake of breath.

He shook his head ever so slightly. The Guard nodded in recognition and stepped back where he stood unnoticed moments before.

"K`lton will stay with you, Lieutenant. He idolises you, wants nothing more than to be a Sz`a`Th Warrior."

She frowned slightly as if something else held her thoughts.

"Let us walk, there are things that need to be said, and I'd rather say them with the elements as my confidant."

They both walked past the Guard, who acknowledged them with a salute. Taelen knew that others would monitor his moves within the Castle and out upon the ramparts. However, he chose a side door that led down a narrow stairwell to a private courtyard below them.

He yawned as the darkness of the stairwell surrounded them; all that could be heard was his footsteps and the soft ones of the Mistress beside him.

The narrow oak door he came to at the base of the stairwell easily opened for him, offering only a soft icy breeze that held no whispers. The courtyard had only a slight snow cover. The evergreen shrubs and winter flowers that bloomed seemed surreal to them both. They both sat in an alcove built into the walls of the Coven. Here only one Warrior could notice them, and he stood sentry on the far western rampart that faced the plains, now an ocean of white.

"You're deep in thought, my Lieutenant."

"It is not deep; believe me, but the burden you have asked me to consider and the proposed actions you will take on your return to the Dormas…."

"K`lton is not a burden," she said indignantly, her hands clasped tightly together.

"My apologies for my use of words is not eloquent, but you have asked me to become a father figure. That is something I do not take Mistress lightly. I am still trying to understand why you now wish to abandon your son."

"Do you understand the Dormas lore, my Lord?" She quietly looked into the garden, lightly dusted with snow, not glancing at him.

"Understand is a comprehensive term. Do I agree with the Lore you were under at that time, if you're asking? I would try because a bridge would gap my ignorance, and I would accept, but may not feel comfortable with some aspects of Dormas and Drargon`H tradition."

Taelen knew that once she was back within the Dormas, she would wage war built on a deep-seated loathing. Her hand touched his, and he flinched without thinking.

JA'rvis's words sat oddly cold within his thoughts as a warning of the woman next to him.

He looked at the pale hand on his own olive skin and removed it back to sit on her lap with her other hand.

He stood brushing the light fall of snow that had landed on his boots as he had sat with his legs stretched out in front of him.

"Go to the Dormas. I will raise K`lton as a Knight of the Mhyst. Or a Scribe or a Cook if he desires if that is where his passion lies. For whatever the gift that lies dormant within the boy. It will be I with the Mhyst that will offer guidance to him. Nevertheless, he will know why you left and who his parents are; you will not burden me with that grief I leave within your domain. You know the way back."

Taelen did not look back; his steps took him up the narrow stairwell to the large corridor he had left earlier. As he walked back to his room, he felt like hitting out at something. The Guard nodded once to him, and Taelen shrugged his shoulders.

"Lieutenant, the woman?" he asked diplomatically. His coal-black, brown eyes were steady and never wavered from Taelen's.

"Aye… escort the Mistress from the courtyard and

prepare her for the journey back to the Dormas. Choose four Scouts. They volunteer for this; I cannot guarantee their safety with this."

"Aye, Lieutenant, I would suggest 'Sahn`Frwh'." His eyes looked once towards the window in Taelen's study and added: "and of the 'Sqh`xn' brotherhood."

"Aye, your advice is a good counsel, X`ysta, at least they will have protection, arrange that now, and their departure is at midnight. X`ysta, she is to be left at the border, but what I give to you must be given to the Imperial Scribe, Rior`dan. He is to meet the Mistress at the border."

"Lieutenant as you command." The young Corporal saluted sharply across his heart, turned and left.

Taelen nodded, entered his study and stood at his desk. 'Aye on my command', he said to himself. He knew that X`ysta had just volunteered his services. He silently prayed to the four elements for their protection and sat heavily in his desk chair. The leather crackled softly as he reached for the familiarity of his quill, feeling its weight of balance crystal as he held the shaft. He habitually placed a nib into the cylinder and unscrewed the brass top that sealed the black ink.

Reaching towards the crystal jar, he gently dipped the nib into the black ink and began writing a document that one of the Warriors assigned to Mistress Iz`sen would take with him. He addressed the document to the Imperial Scribe Rior`dan and the Council of the Dormas. The report would be opened on the seventh day, after the arrival of Mistress Iz`sen Jy`atis.

Taelen and Rior`dan began their Apprenticeships when both were six at the Taayra`Ge Keep. Rior'dan's father was then the Warrant Officer of the Keep, training Warriors in the Sahn`Frwh, just as Anston had trained him through the winters that followed.

Rior`dan's father had been transferred to Cran`dk Garrison, where Rior`dan had continued his Apprenticeship under the Lake City's Guilds. Taelen shook his head more to himself for his jealousy when Rior`dan had come excitedly to him to say the Guild Master had accepted him.

Now he was asking the Imperial Scribe of the Dormas to spy. The 'Dominion Lord' had ordered his friend to spy. He wondered if it was he who would receive such orders, would he? Taelen also wondered whether Rior`dan would recall the boy with the amethyst eyes and no parents from the Taayra`Ge Keep all those winters past. Only time would tell, and time is what he was running critically short of very quickly.

After the document had dried and was now in the brass cylinder that would carry it safely to the Dormas, Taelen cast a ward to protect what he had composed. Only one could would be able to read the document.

Taelen hoped that the person he addressed in the document was still alive and had enough influence to realise that a bloody war between the two regions was to follow. The Sz`a`Th Nation had declared total neutrality in the matter at the document's sealing.

He lent back and let out a sigh of relief. His thoughts ran in many directions at the implications surrounding the young woman returning to her native region.

"You're awake. Lieutenant Taelen," K`lton's voice croaked with sleep as he stood between the study and bedroom doorway.

"Aye, and it's near your dinner time. I am about to eat. Are you hungry?"

K`lton nodded sleepily.

"I just have to give this to one of my Warriors, you hop back into bed, and I'll bring us something from the kitchen." He said; K'lton nodded and returned to Taelen's bed.

As Taelen entered the kitchen, he saw the five Warriors he knew had volunteered to be Mistress Iz'sen's escort. They were all scouts and trained and seasoned 'Sahn`Frwh' Warriors; they were the 'Death Watch' elite.

All five were specialised Sz`a`Th and 'Sahn`Frwh'. More importantly, they were of the Wolf Nation. The weapon was a sword named after them that unsheathed, measured two metres sheathed it measured two and a half metres.

The sheath had its weaponry with two half-moon filigree blades. The end blade had a double-sided axe head. At hand, the guard sat with a broad curved edge that came out like the head of a scarab beetle. The end spikes of the sword were warded for death. This scarab curve protected the 'Sahn`Frwh' trained Warrior virtually to his shoulder. The blade was a weapon used for death; no one survived its cut.

They were highly trained to kill without weapons of any kind, only their body. Sahn`Frwh were taught in the darker side of Spell Casting.

Taelen knew them all as well as they knew him.

Once a Warrior had completed their training, as 'Sahn`Frwh', they wore the tattoo on the inside of their wrists. The tattoo was simple; it was the 'Tree of Life' reversed; the Tree of Death meant they were under the Lores of the Lord of Death. The Red Crescent Moon was the other they wore on their left temple close to the space between eyebrow and temple.

Taelen went over to the four Warriors and handed the document sealed in the brass cylinder to the Warrant. He had played cards with the same Warrant three nights ago and had won - much to the delight of those Warrior that sat with them playing cards.

No words were spoken between the five Warriors; Taelen pulled the sleeve that covered their left wrist; the tattoo in red of the Tree of Life on their wrist was reversed.

Aside from them stood Mistress Iz`sen dressed and ready she pulled the cowl of her cloak over her head and stepped into the courtyard, mounting her horse with ease.

All six Warriors walked out into the courtyard, and six mounted their horses, already packed and equipped for the terrain they would meet as soon as they left the gates of the Coven.

Taelen spoke silently to the six Warriors in mind speak. 'You are protected, by me, should.... you have your orders. May the Gods answer my prayers for your safe return?'

He then turned to Mistress Iz`sen and gave her a small minute canister; she did not have to ask what was in it. She stared at it and then slid the cartridge onto a small chain on her neck, placing it within her cleavage. She would use the poison; this poison would only work for her, not killing another.

"Forever grateful...Taelen," she said, using his birth name. He did not smile, but the corners of his eyes crinkled with that short statement. He was more concerned with his Warriors and the sacrifice he gave

"Forever can be a long time, Mistress." That was all he said in a cold-levelled voice.

As if on a silent cue, the five Warriors screamed a war cry as ancient as the runes inscribed on the large swords they held across the front of the saddle, resting in a notch especially made for the sword on the horn.

With the deep blue-black of their cloaks tortured over the rear of their horses for protection, they pulled the cowls over their heads. The M`lak, a chain mail face scarf, fell across their features, only allowing the eyes to be seen hid any recognisable features of the Warriors. The chain mail was intricately woven so as not to catch on beards but had strength. So fine was the metal it felt as soft as cloth.

They left, galloping out of the Coven gate. Taelen stood in the falling snow until he could no longer hear the beat of the horse's hooves upon the earth. It was only then that he ordered the gates closed, and even then, it was a while before he re-entered the kitchen door.

He said nothing as he accepted a food tray for K`lton and his needs. He smiled slightly as a deep red wine glass and a carafe were added to the tray. When he glanced up, he saw M'hta's eyes, and all M`hta said was.

"For later, when you are overthinking the orders you just gave, such as the weight of hardest hard decisions, we are Sz`a`Th. That is what we must remember through all we must go through. Everything has its cost Taelen."

"As always, you know what my thoughts are."

"It is not hard, Lieutenant, the whole of the Sz`a`Th realise the enormity of your decisions," M`hta replied quietly.

Taelen shrugged his shoulders slightly and turned to leave. He stopped and asked.

"When does Lord Za`qrn arrive, do you know?"

"Tomorrow morning at the first light of dawn, intel tells, Teh`c is with them."

Taelen nodded; he wanted to ask about the Spellcaster J`nn; there had been intel report that she was injured as if reading his friend's mind, M`hta added.

"There is no word on Mistress J`nn." He said the concern in M`hta's voice betrayed him.

"Wake me when they arrive." Taelen couldn't say anymore, so he left and returned to his room.

K`lton's eyes opened as soon as Taelen had placed his foot in the door.

"You have the hearing of a Dragon," Taelen said, smiling as he brought the tray of food over to the young boy.

Both sat crossed-legged on the large bed, backs against a mound of pillows, with the quilts pulled up and a mug each of hot sweet tea.

"K`lton, would you like it if I became your Guardian? It means I'd be responsible for your education and training. You would live here until you came of age, and if you still wanted to, you could stay here after that time."

Taelen was leapt upon and barely managed to save his cup of tea as K`lton hugged him; that single hug from K`lton answered every question Taelen had been running through his mind.

"I gather you don't mind." He said, smiling and laughing as K`lton let go and sat in front of him, legs crossed and full of his questions.

"Oh no, Lieutenant, but I can't call you that; what can I call you?" He said excitedly. "I can't call you Taelen…."

Taelen smiled as K`lton frowned over something so simple.

"You know you will have to study and learn politics, defence, and religion."

"Can I be a Warrior?"

"You can be whatever you wish."

K`lton looked at him solemnly." I don't want to know about them, my birth parents. I saw what they did."

"Yes, I do, K`lton. I know of them."

" I saw my Uncles heads on spikes; your Uncle is terrible, isn't he."

"I am afraid he is… he killed my mother when I was younger than you, he killed my father and wife …I know what it is to hate someone K`lton, enough to want them dead. I hope you are not at that stage."

"Can I be a 'Sahn`Frwh' and be a Scribe too?

Taelen took the mug from the boy and said, "Right now, you must go to sleep, tomorrow is a new day, and you must choose your room with a study if you want."

"Can I sleep here just for tonight?"

"Yes, only for tonight 'Little Dragon'"

"Why do you call me that?"

"You don't like it."

"Yes, I do; it means that I have Dragon magic in me. I like that. It is something to be wise about."

Wisdom of children thought Taelen. K`loton was at that cusp of winters, child verging on the precipice of teenager winters, training as a Warrior would begin tomorrow Taelen glanced down at the lad, for he was sometimes a boy. Yes, he thought so could Ji`rah.

Taelen sat next to him on the bed and hummed a lullaby he had not remembered for the first time in winters but now, this night, it came back to him.

His voice did its haunting beauty justice, and K`lton soon was fast asleep. Taelen left him and returned to his desk but not before leaving a purpled Mhyst that floated across the boy. It would take eight hours for the Mhyst to be absorbed into the boy's soul, and with the full moon already rising, the power that K`lton would hold at the time of his Mhysting would be equal to that of Yassarn. K`lton's heritage was involved; Taelen knew instinctively that the boy would be a great leader and would inevitably unite many nations and regions that were now ripping each other to bloody pieces in their own twisted versions of peace.

Now he was a boy of twelve winters caught between

childlike dreams and the unknown path of youth to manhood. He wondered about a difficult time in anyone's life as he watched the boy sleep. Would K`lton be the one to bring peace to his homeland, or would he be like his mother and walk away to his personal vengeance? He bowed his head and sighed; a child's heart's hurt never left. It stayed and would wait for the moment to hand the emotional pain back to that parent. Raising his eyebrows, he prayed it would not be him.

# CHAPTER 14

"Lieutenant," a woman's voice entered into his realm of sleep. His blue eyes opened, his mind still foggy from dreams he uttered croakily.

"J`nn?" his eyes focussed. His Grandmother placed a single slender finger upon her Grandson's lips.

She gestured to the study door that led to the corridor, and they both moved to that area.

"What wakes you early, G`rnah," he said using the Sz`a`Th word for Grandmother, which it seemed the whole Coven had adopted instead of her title.

She smiled thankfully as she accepted his title of Grandmother to her. Her silver hair was not in the braid he had become accustomed to; her hair fell to her knees in straight stresses.

"M`hta has asked me to wake you; Lieutenant Teh`c and Lord Za`qrn have arrived with three hundred Sz`a`Th Warriors and the fifty Spellcasters. They are settling into their own wings at this moment."

"Where is Teh`c?" He said sleepily, stretching his entire body length. He asked as he tentatively looked into the room K`lton slept in.

"I will stay with him if you wish, Taelen?" She pulled out a brass cylinder from her sleeve.

"Mistress Iz`sen asked me to place this in your hands. You must read it to K`lton, and it must bear both your signatures and seals." She handed him the brass seal and the green wax of the Drargon`H Empire.

He held the brass cylinder and the seal and wax in the other.

"She thinks of everything, doesn't she?" His sarcasm was cutting.

"Not all, Taelen. Her child is not important. You and your Ward, your emotions and thoughts towards each other as the progress of the winter and K`lton becomes the man you are."

"I don't play games." He growled.

"That I am glad, for K`lton will need someone to be his confidant and someone who knows when to step out of such an emotive picture."

"I know," he said in the half-darkness of the corridor.

He tapped the brass cylinder against his thigh and saw Teh`c walking towards him.

Even though he had changed and had refreshed himself, his friend was exhausted.

The circles under his eyes and the fatigue clawed at each step that took him closer to Taelen showed how long and arduous the time apart had been.

The Spellcaster took her to leave and went to K`lton's side.

"Lieutenant…" Sighed Teh`c, then added, "Taelen." his fatigue grinded him to a sudden halt. Taelen greeted him, guiding him to the vast walled library that was but two doors from his own rooms. The walls held the text of millions of spells, their listings, and origins. The library smelled of leather books and aged parchments, a tomb of knowledge and silent thoughts.

The floor was stone but also covered in rich greys, greens, and mauves, with blue as the primary colour on the floor. The stone had been mined eons ago from beneath the Mountains of D`lrth, which had been the seat of power for the Dwarfs long ago. Some said D`lrth was also a place. No one could remember where the city was, and few had seen a Dwarf for hundreds of winters.

Taelen sat at one of the few reading corners where one could read without disturbance. The seats were large, firm, comfortable, and dark grey leather.

"Please, Teh`c sit. I would just read this first." He said. Teh`c was grateful and sat slowly, sore from the saddle and the earth he had slept on for the past months. He sighed as he sat. It had been a very long and cold night.

He watched his friend read from the parchment within his hands. His jaw edged firmly as lips pressed against one another in discontent at the written words he was reading. Eventually, he sighed.

"Problems?" asked his friend. Taelen rubbed his eyes with weariness.

"No, not really; it's a complicated issue that sees me as the lone Guardian of a young boy in the Coven. His mother has relinquished all parental ties, denying the birth father any parental power over the boy." Taelen looked again at the parchment. "I didn't realise this boy's lineage was as powerful and prominent as it is."

"Does it alter anything? Because she has denied him as her son. The boy loses all rights to his maternal heritage. How old is he?"

"Twelve winters and recalls nothing of his home."

Teh`c lent back, tucking his feet under his legs; the leather creaked from his movement. "Taelen, you have the soul to give this boy all he has lost. That is love, caring, food, learning, and understanding. But are you able to, will you be able to accept his mother's decision? Can you understand her abandonment of him, as he was conceived by what our beliefs call child torture?"

"His seal must be on the document and mine, and both must overlap." Replied Taelen, scratching his eyebrow wearily and rubbing his stubble on his chin in thought.

"What's his status when he is of age?"

"He becomes the Imperial High Lord of Drargon`H,

with knowledge of Sz`a`Th and whatever else his teachings include over the winters that he is with the Sz`a`Th."

Teh`c swore and shook his head; the thought of someone not of the Mhyst knowing so much was something he did not particularly like.

"You know how to pick them, don't you? Has his mother asked for a third party on the paper?"

"Why?" asked Taelen wiping the sleep from his eyes and wishing for a hot, bitter black coffee with more than one sugar. He frowned, looking at the world outside, which was still in darkness.

"What time is it?"

"I think last time I looked, it was just after four in the morning, a bit early, but we had no choice the way things are." His own eyes were bloodshot from icy winds and lack of sleep. "By the law of all the lands. His mother must have a third party agreeing with the signing over of parental rights." Teh`c yawned loudly, "I'm sorry, Taelen, just tired to the soul; it's enough to start a war without the third party."

"Oh… she'd love that!" he said sarcastically, his anger simmering beneath the surface.

"Aye, she probably would. Look, I'll take on the third party, but you must scribe for me, for it is only an opinion, but it could stop a war. What Lands does this entail?"

"Dormas and the Drargon`H Nation," Taelen answered as if it meant death for the young ward now to be in his sole care.

"Hell! Taelen, the boy was conceived for war, not peace." Rolling his eyes, "Lord, how you managed this is beyond my imagination. You didn't bed her, did you by any chance." He asked. He was stretching his back, which seemed so tight and sore.

"Believe me, the balls tightened, but not with wanton desire, more a wary prickling feeling that she had to be avoided at all costs besides JA`rvis warned me earlier about such a thing. Not to mention the lad is twelve winters, and I am nineteen winters mathematically an impossible conception, thank the gods."

Taelen smiled and began to report what had transpired since the attack on the Coven. Teh`c, who listened intently even though his body and mind ached and wanted nothing but sleep, was mute.

"JA`rvis is an astute bastard when you least need it," groaned Teh`c with fatigue.

"Teh`c…" Taelen asked as he watched his friend try to fight fatigue that was winning.

"Hmm…' he replied, tired and fighting the sleep that tugged relentlessly at his eyelids.

"Will you teach the boy, Blade, crossbow, in short, all things that will keep him alive?"

"He is that important?" asked Teh`c raising his dark eyebrows. Taelen knew what he was insinuating. "People will be suspicious."

"Not if it is common knowledge that I am the boy's legal guardian. That he is also of the plains region that reaches from the Dormas and the Drargon`H coast."

Teh`c yawned loudly and leaned his head against the wall where they sat.

"Tactical shift there, Taelen; you've just swung the quandary back onto the maternal side." He said, rubbing at the beard stubble upon his face and distracted by the fact that a beard would have protected his face in the changeable weather he had lived through these past months.

"More political than anything, it will save us from being drawn into a war where no one wins."

“We just have to keep the boy alive now,” Teh`c said, battling to stay awake.

“Aye, I will teach him Sahn`Frwh; the death Watch’ will keep him hidden. As we must keep you incognito.”

Taelen pulled a low table closer to them and began the third party with ink and quill when his Grandmother knocked softly. Taelen did not look up but nodded and kept scribing.

“Please come in, Mistress,” said Teh`c, beginning to rise as the custom was.

“Sit, Lieutenant; your battles have been longer and harder than mine; rest.” She said more than ordered, and Teh`c stretched his body entirely and glanced back in a tired smile at her.

“I doubt that, Mistress, but thank you.” He replied, sinking into the seat. His eyes closed for a moment, stung by the burns of wind and snow.

“So, she has asked for a third party guardianship.”

“Aye, Teh`c has just offered, just as you would for someone legally orphaned,” he murmured as his nib glided across the parchment from left to right. He spun the parchment to Teh`c, tapping him on the leg to wake him. The Lieutenant glanced at the document and held the quill signing it swiftly.

“May I offer my signatory to this? The child will require Spell Casting and Runes, which will ward off his location and disguise the tattoo on his nape. This will keep him hidden except the one person who sired him.”

“You're saying that only his father has the gift to penetrate that of the Sz`a`Th and Spellcasters?”

“He is a child of the Dragon; nothing can hide the child from the father or father from the child.”

"’That is too heavy a lodestone for one so young,” Teh`c added, turning the document over to the Spellcasters to sign.

"Not necessarily; I've been researching insignias of the Sz`a`Th, Sqh`xn, and Spellcasters and the paternity region on both sides. All Sz`a`Th will wear it if they agree to this."

She pulled out a parchment with a design in the ancient runic text; Taelen had seen this somewhere before. The only difference he could detect was this one had a tilt to one of the plains above the one he recalled was more elaborate, and he could sense the magic intrinsically woven within it.

"A triple bind rune," murmured Taelen and Teh`c. Together they glanced at each other than at the woman before them.

"This means K`lton is now a 'Ward of the Mhyst,'" Taelen said, glancing at the document as the black ink slowly evaporated in its moisture, like a shrinking secret. He slid the parchment onto the table, exhaling slowly at the magnitude of the document before him.

"So, Mistress, if we are all to incorporate this triple bind rune upon the nape of our necks, I will also need a document to incorporate such a design into the Lore of the Sz`a`Th," glanced at her, smiling as she produced such a document. "Seems you have looked into a crystal ball, my Grandmother?"

"No, my Lord, I haven't; remember, such things are not permitted, and scrying can be time-consuming and gives me a dull head for twelve hours. The only time I have used a crystal ball is as a weapon; the target was knocked unconscious.  I might add that it does the trick if your aim is true."

She smiled at them both as she handed the document to Taelen.

As he read the script, his frown became more profound, and his stance shifted more serious. "When was this written? The date here is close to that of my birth."

"Scrying was permitted then, my Lord, and as you have noted, the signature and wax seal is that…."

"Is that of my Grandfather? Why was such a document ordered then, and who did scry to see the future?"

"Things were done around the time of your birth that I had no control over, Taelen, I wish to the Goddess that I could have had, but it was not allowed. You were Sz`a`Th. I am not. It was that simple. It was deemed that such a document be drawn and handed to you at this adoption."

"So they knew what was going to happen?" He asked as anger steamed within him.

"No, scrying does not show the whole event, only a moment, only a movement."

"What of this bindrune?" asked Teh`c, forgotten by the other two, with their concerns about the past and the implication of the document that Taelen held.

LH`Nejah glanced across to the Warrior, exhausted and nearly asleep. She was relieved from his distraction and stood to straighten the folds of her deep purple-grey gown.

"Del`qt will do the design on our people."

Taelen pictured the large Warrior, big-boned, his hands large, engulfing Taelen's own. The young man was imposing in height and girth but the most gifted tactician Taelen had ever met.

"Del`qt is an accomplished artist. He uses all the mediums, and this design will also be with a subtly strong ward."

"Del`qt is…" began Teh`c stumbling for the pronunciation of the term used for an artist who could use the artisans' gift that could use 'elementals' and the inner talent of the Sz`a`Th that also permitted the balance of alchemy.

"You're telling me Corporal Del`qt is a Qkt`ilht or close." He finally answered as the others floundered with the problematic clicking and lilt of the ancient world that was rarely used.

"I think how you pronounced it is the closest we will get." Taelen added, "Even with this document you brought to light, how do I explain this all to the Mhyst?"

His Grandmother turned to him and smiled slightly. "That my Grandson comes from the heart. You will ask them to accept a child that may well, many winters from now, cast us into a war from which there is no return. Or he may save us all with his life. "

"Trust," Taelen said.

"Aye," said Teh`c, "The Mhyst must trust your decision, and the boy must trust you."

"What will you tell young K`lton?" His Grandmother asked, grasping a wisp of grey silver hair behind her ear.

"Truth and love are more important, don't you think? So it is decided."

"Aye, trust is one you missed, but there are more pressing issues now. These books and Mah`sden…."

"You and only you must know how many of the books you have." She said, "Only you can collect them."

"Why?"

She smiled. "You have not been burnt by those books you have already transcribed, have you?"

Taelen said nothing, for he had heard that for those of the 'Spellcasters', the Seven Books of Sz`a`Th were death for them; even their book, the 'Book of Shadows' could cause the death of a 'Spellcaster.'

He had presumed it to be an old tale to shroud the Seven Books in more mystery than they deserved.

"Believe me, Taelen, should I or others of my

persuasion touch one of those books that are not of our heritage? She showed them the inside of her wrist. The white scar tissues showed an angry and deep burn that scooped into her skin. “As a novice, I accidentally touched such a book. My arm smouldered for six days; the pain lasted six months.”

“Why, then?”

“The reasons are many, Taelen.” She said quietly, not looking at either of them as she spoke. “Sometimes, the truth is not found, Taelen, or it is as if those who know the catalyst hold their breath. They hold their breath because of uncertainty and fear. You are not Mah`sden son, those who have held their breath for those sixteen winters waiting for your Mhysting may well breathe a sigh of relief, or maybe they still hold their breath in dread. Their concern was that if you are not the son of Mah`sden, your power is unknown and unlimited, some say.”

“So they all wait for me to make the first move, and who are these people.”

“Only if they can detect you, your Spellcaster wards are still as strong as the day this document was declared. These people were chosen many winters ago when I was not even born; they are from the Nations of Myth and include the Lords of the Elements.”

Teh`c yawned rather loudly and excused himself rather absently.

“I have to lie down…I am knackered to death.” Taelen frowned at the statement, but his Grandmother left a bemused look at the now sleeping Warrior. Lying on his back, his knees bent and fell against the end of the bench seat he had sat on, slowly his chest breathing in exhausted sleep.

“I knew you lived these past nineteen winters,” she said, passing her hand across them, leaving a trail of purple Mhyst through the early morning air. The particles glowed white as they intercepted Taelen's aura. "See the Mhyst, and you can see its path because you are trained, and I let you see it. A spell cloaked you at birth by your mother.  But it could not hold you hidden from me. Even though I was in exile, I felt the Mhyst, your Mhyst." She emphasised the latter the sighed more with emotion than the tiredness she felt at such an early hour.

"Taelen, there is more to the mantle of Mhyst Lord than you realise. " She stated, "your birthmark will become white on the winter of your twenty-first day of birth; no one knows when a child with the colour of blue becomes white, as we are told. There is no other marking that lives or has lived for a very long time." She drew in a deep breath. "You are in all reality, the Dominions Monarch."

As she spoke, the thunder rolled like a million war drums across the land. Teh`c shivered. Taelen felt that iced steel had sliced his bravado, and he winced.

"This is why Mah`sden will kill you at all costs. This is why you called me through the 'Gates of Da`ryton'."

"Aptly named." He replied, distracted by Teh`c loud snoring. He nudged his friend awake. "Go and get some sleep. You can use my rooms."

Teh`c snuffled awake and was startled at the Taelen's words replied. "I wasn't asleep. I was going over next moon's roster if you really must know," he said, yawning. He stood up, bowing stiffly to the Mistress and scratched his face irritatingly. He said grumpily that he would never grow a beard and staggered as if he was drunk out the door and down the corridor to Taelen's rooms.

Taelen rolled the parchments and sealed them within brass cylinders. The wax seal of Sz`a`Th oozed thick and green down the sides. He then handed it to his grandmother.

He glanced at her as she moved toward the door.

"The Gates of Da`ryton, can I access the Seven Books through that portal?"

LH'Nejah stopped with her back to him. The bowed head straightened, as did her shoulders. Without turning around, she asked him why.

"Those Gates have never been activated before, have they?"

Still, she did not turn around, he could sense a deep-seated fear, and he needed to know why.

"No, they have never been activated before." She turned with tears welling in her eyes but continued. "No one in the history of the Covens has been able to use them; to my knowledge, only you have been able to melt somehow the acute wards placed on that form of travel. Taelen, they are used to expel Spellcasters to the other world, not bring them home."

Taelen stood and stepped towards her; she seemed so frail and scared.

"What will happen when they realise you have left and left through the Gates of Da`ryton?"

"Death will hunt me, for the Custodians will search for me, for I have defied the Lore of Spellcasters. I am classed as 'property' by them."

"But you are a Dream Caster, could not that have been my chosen path? G`rnah, whoever they are, I will not let them take you. You have brought sanity to Den`ah; without your help, insanity would have been him. Besides, am I not the Dominion Lord?" He said with a wry grin. His eyes crinkled at the sides.

She laughed slightly and patted his chest, her hand resting on his heart.

"Here is where the truth lies, and my life is in your

hands. I, like all the others trust you."

She reached out for his hand and went to speak when a sharp rap on the door to the Library had them both look up. Lieutenant M`hta stood as if in obedience as that of a servant than that of a Warrior.

Taelen knew of the young Warrior that he was from a region called Ch`nel.

"Aye, Lieutenant, what news do you bring me? Taelen acknowledged the young man who had been more his counsel and advisor as the days had turned to weeks.

"Lord Za`qrn awaits my Lord." He said wearily; M`hta had just finished a week of Guard shifts on the West Ramparts, the coldest and windiest part of the Garrison; he was so cold through to his bones he could not get warm.

"I will see him now; you go and soak in the bathing rooms where your bones can warm; you must be bloody frozen through M`hta."

"Aye, I shall, your leave, Lieutenant." Replied M`hta and turned his leaden steps dragged down the hall.

Taelen stretched his back and felt tired from his early awakening; the audience with Lord Za`qrn of the Sqh`xn Nation of Wolves was the last thing he needed.

He lent back and closed his eyes for a moment. Lord Za`qrn was fluent in all languages and was enigmatic, spontaneous, and intense. Before he had time to extinguish those thoughts, Lord Za`qrn swaggered into the Library with a huge smile and perfect white teeth.

He stood hands on hips, then bowed with exaggeration sweeping his left arm down in an ark to his knee and looking up at Taelen, who stood passively shaking his head.

"My Liege, Lord Taelen, Dominion Lord and Lieutenant…" He stood up and smiled. "I didn't miss any titles, did I?" he asked with a smirk and continued

"So, 'puppy' seems you've got a bit of a mess within the Dominions, and that's saying it mildly."

"Welcome, Uncle. It seems travel enhances you." Taelen shook his head. It was hard not to like this man before him, and it was easy to tire of him. His intense personality moved swiftly, leaving others exhausted in his wake.

Both moved and hugged warmly as Lord Za`qrn pulled back and looked at him closely.

"Ji`rah was correct; you've become wiser and more stressed. You need a 'bitch' to get distracted with." Taelen rolled his eyes and laughed.

"Just as well, I do not take offence when you and Ji`rah speak like that, so how is Ji`rah and J`nn did they find Master L`unh."

The smile dropped immediately from Lord Za'qrn's lips, and he took a deep breath; a deep frown scratched his forehead painfully as he looked back up to meet Taelen's eyes.

"Ji`rah is with me; he is in the kitchen eating breakfast." He said flatly.

"And J`nn?" asked Taelen. His eyes could not read the Lord of the Wolves. Their black intensity shadowed.

Lord Za`qrn paced the library floor with agitated steps; his hands swept up to the ceiling in exasperation.

"They found old L`unh… Shattas! Taelen, we tried so damn hard to get near old L`unh and young J`nn." He turned and held Taelen's shoulders firmly; his eyes caught him as Taelen felt his soul sink deep within his being.

"It was a bloody trap. Lord bloody Mah`sden had sent some Lieutenant called…."

"Brae..." Taelen said, his voice gravelly. Lord Za`qrn looked at Taelen, questioning his perception.

"It was a maelstrom of magic. I have never seen a Spellcaster with such power as her. You know she's a Kh`irz, don't you?"

"Kh`irz… I have had such thoughts, and you are sure about this. The monks were celibate." He said, frowning.

"Look, the monk's bloody libido", he threw his hands to his hips dramatically "that aside I don't care who they runted for god's sake Taelen." He said, nodding his head. "J`nn is Kh`irz whether you accept it or not."

Taelen did not know whether to laugh or walk out with that comment from a man who seemed to have a higher sex rate than anyone. It was so hard being in this family; he thought so bloody hard. He has scratched his forehead in utter exhaustion.

"What… happened to her?" Taelen looked at the Lord before him; for all his womanising and bravado, Lord Za`qrn was reliable and had always told him the truth even if at times when Taelen had not wished to know the truth.

"Oh, she's alive, just; from what Ji`rah has been able to tell me but… old L`unh, hell…Taelen, Brae and his Warriors committed murders and other nefarious acts." The Wolf Lord's shoulders sagged, and he sat down suddenly in one of the large leather chairs near the fire. Taelen stood his arm resting on the mantelpiece above the large fireplace.

"Where is she?"

"That we don't know. After rescuing Ji`rah through the maelstrom of magic that that girl unleashed, she torched Warriors to charcoal statues, Taelen. You sure she is on our side because if she is not…." He shook his head. "Both her and old L`unh vanished, yes vanished, you know 'poof!' gone. No scent, not a trail of Mhyst, not even a ripple in the vision happened. She's nullah' if you ask me, and so is old L`unh. I'm sorry, 'puppy' so is Ji`rah." His colloquial term eased the tension. It had been a long time since Taelen had heard the Wolf word for nothing as nullah.

He dug into his trouser pocket, pulled out a silver chain and handed it to Taelen.

"This was left with a message to you. You are evidently to put the chain on with the Spellcasters, Star Ji`rah said. The message J`nn left for you is connected to this, and your touch activates it." He said, shrugging. "It was the last words she spoke to Ji`rah before she let fly with her magic. Are we sure there is only one chosen as the prophecy? "

Taelen took the silver chain with the ten segmented stars. He held the star and noticed a three-pointed star enclosed within its centre. There the star was purple, white and blue crystal. His heart froze. He held it up to see the thirteen points of a star.

"This is J`nn's, the three-pointed star of the Kh`irz was there but not like this."

"You're sure of this."

"Aye, Uncle, I was the one who gave her the last segment at her Spellcaster's Graduation."

He slipped the silver chain over his head and let the now thirteen-pointed filigree star fall, touching his chest's skin. He immediately fell to his knees and gasped, gulping air like drowning.

His Uncle went to assist but was prevented from moving by an unseen force.

"Master Taelen." Mistress J`nn's voice entered the Library, but not a person or a vision with it. He wondered why she used the term of Apprentice to him.

Taelen found his voice finally and answered painfully; he staggered.

"You have him, Mistress; just release your pressure so that I can stand." Taelen felt instant relief as the constriction bound his chest dissolved, causing his vision to ripple. He stood gingerly, holding his ribs, and gripped the mantelpiece for stability.

"Mistress, what is it you must tell me."

"Master L`unh and I have escaped to Hid`n E`rth, only just, but I fear Lord Mah`sden will follow. You must contact those of the Nations of Myth. With their knowledge and gifts, we may win over Mah`sden. I tried to save Ji`rah, but he is hurt, and I could not heal him. You must research the thirteenth star for our destiny is one, and " Her voice cracked with weariness and emotion rarely noticed.

"And…?" Queried Taelen, confused at the emotion he felt from the start.

"And let Lieutenant Taelen know I wish him safe journeys. I miss him." She added awkwardly and hurriedly.

"J`nn?" his voice was hardly audible.

Nothing but silence; Taelen touched the star feeling its lightweight in his hand. He fell quiet.

Za`qrn, his Uncle, stood finally and touched his shoulder slightly. He welcomed the silent understanding from this man he had respected and admired for so long.

Lord Za`qrn's intense black eyes did not waver; as he stared into Taelen's blue eyes, the amethyst and mauve seemed to resemble turmoil in his nephew. With the weight of this War and the toll it would take, Lord Za`qrn prayed to the moons that those he had met, his people all of Man and Myth, those who survived would have the heart and strength to rebuild peace, the peace he mused, how elusive a woman it would be if it was in that form.

"She's a strong 'bitch' she'll survive; Taelen, you

must hold onto that hope. She has gone to Hid`n E`rth and will be safe there."

Taelen stared at his Uncle, Hid`n E`rth. He felt he was going mad slowly.

"Hid`n E`rth Uncle, I am not a child anymore to be told fables of Elves and Dwarves who live beneath the surface in a land called Hid`n E`rth!"

"Don't be daft, Taelen. It exists; you have already had contact with an Elf; Lieutenant NK`las has been protecting you."

"What?" Taelen shook his head. "That aside, J`nn, she is alive, you tell me now, but for how long with Lord Mah`sden following her, and what more can they do to her that has not already destroyed her innocence." He looked intently at his Uncle.

"Hid`n E`rth is somewhere Lord Mah`sden and his Warriors cannot go, lad. Something's Taelen cannot be answered; you must have faith that whatever Lord Mah`sden has in store for that young one will make her stronger than any of us could ever imagine. I have not had breakfast yet, and I do not think you have either; Ji`rah waits for both of us…."

"And Hid`n E`rth am I to believe in Elves, Dwarves and Trolls now am I, to save us," he asked, getting his strength back.

"If they let us, Taelen, if they let us…they're A tetchy bloody lot. Who assumes we exist because of their unwavering sacrifice in the Three Hundred Winter War? Believe me, there is nothing more irritating than an Elf, Dwarf or damn Troll with an ego," was all Lord Za`qrn would say.

"Trolls? I can't imagine a Troll with an ego."

"Love a good drink." Lord Za`qrn said with a wink. "But I would duck when the burp or." He shuddered

"Vomit?" asked Taelen

"Vomit! Know they like their buckets close, but when they fart! Oh, by the two moons in our sky…it's something I can't describe, and as soon as one fart, they think it's a bloody competition."

"Like a few Warriors after a few drinks and burping?" mused Taelen to himself.

"Taelen you have no idea. I must rest. I feel a tad nauseous."

# CHAPTER 15

The Coven's kitchen lay on the ground floor; its expanse covered the north wing entirely. Pantries are as large as some of the rooms on the upper floors were filled with bottled preserves of fruits, jams, chutneys and honey. Dried staples covered many lower shelves from flours of all descriptions, nuts and lentils, spices and herbs. Long jars of garlic, chilli and herb oils were stored with fruits and vegetables in other pantries. Pickled fish, eels, crab meats, many salts and freshwater dwellers. Dried, smoked meats and a culinary utopia of food that many did not venture into due to the deviled eyes and other offal placed strategically at the front of each storeroom pantry. Cooks can be rather evil when keeping light-fingered staff away from rations.

With the Covens staff returning for roster change, it was a hive of activity. Chefs, for there, were sixteen apprentice chefs, then the Speciality Chefs and the Senior Chefs. Their jackets, scarves, and caps were black, and only the colour patches on their right arms denoting the type of Chef Apprenticeships and Kitchen staff; all Warriors and Spellcasters did a rotational shift there in the mainstay of the whole Garrison. Assistance staff members for other areas of housekeeping of the Garrison and Coven also were in the Kitchen. It was organised chaos. But full of respect as a Chef could throw their knives with more accuracy than a Bladesman.

It was noisy, but then Taelen did not know if the catering staff could be quiet; he smiled wherever he looked; they were busy and laughing; he knew they were renowned for practical jokes. If anything, they lived life and were genuine people; he loved their warmth and hard work. When they worked, they worked long hours, and he would find them reading or talking or playing cards in the quiet moments.

Nobody took notice of rank in the kitchen, not as one would out on the battlements. The quiet respect they held for others was natural respect; not one forced on them by politics and protocol.

Ji`rah waved to them over a sea of heads that seemed to move in all directions as different meals were being prepared, pots banged, and utensils appeared to bring an orchestrated din to the room.

Ji`rah sat on a well-worn bench facing windows showing escarpments to the north. Their red walls reminded Taelen of ocean waves, only red and frozen suddenly into the rock as the wave had swollen to crest. They caught the early evening sun in summer, which transformed the kitchen to a red essence if the shutters were not closed. But now, it looked like sharp reminders of open wounds in winter.

Lord Za`qrn and Taelen sat opposite Ji`rah; he noticed the silver chain around Taelen's neck. He picked up the silver coffee pot and poured them both a drink.

"So brother, you wear the 'bitches' star."

His voice was quiet and restrained, which was unlike him. Taelen looked over the cup's rim at his friend and brother and wondered why his voice had such an edge.

He heard Lord Za'qrn's guttural growl to his nephew, and the dark eyes narrowed alarmingly. Ji`rah did not cower in submission but lowered his eyes, having been reprimanded severely and openly by his Uncle.

Warily Taelen placed his mug of coffee back onto the well-worn pine table and studied Ji`rah closely. He noticed the livid scar that ran around his wrists as he did this.

“I am glad you are safe, brother.” He said, “Our Uncle tells me you have more information to tell me.” As he acknowledged the young woman, sixteen winters old, on Kitchen duties, he knew from the Taayra`Ge Keep who brought him and Lord Za`qrn dishes of cooked meats and hot buns for their breakfast.

“It was a trap; we entered the area where Master L`unh had secluded him and Mistress J`nn and was not herself. It was surreal, Taelen. I still don’t know if what I experienced was illusion or reality but tell me, is this reality or illusion.” He said, pulling up his shirt; the savage scaring was angry. The skin burned away, now heavily scarred, and resembled a melted skin of keloid cording, discoloured and uneven all over his chest and abdomen.

“You are still my brother. I see you no differently.” He said quietly, knowing no words could take Ji`rah’s pain away or comfort his anger.

“He held me up in burning bonds while he slit my belly open and let my entrails slide to the ground.”

Taelen and Lord Za`qrn pushed their dishes away, and he motioned to her to remove them from the table. They had suddenly lost their appetite for breakfast.

As the young woman cleared the table, Ji`rah grabbed her wrists, firmly holding her. The young woman had seen and had heard their conversation. She had stood quietly to the side being rostered to their table.

“What do you think ‘missy’,” Ji`rah said coldly, his anger rising to the surface. “Would you love a man with this, to touch as you mate in the heat of passion? Would you run your hands over this body and tell me you love me?”

Ji`rah’s eyes drilled into the young woman who was

winter or two younger than he was. Her pale brown eyes were framed by wavy honey brown hair tied up in a braid but seemed to escape its bindings at any avenue that was not securely pinned.

Lord Za`qrn went to move, but Taelen held his arm firmly, shaking his head. He nodded to the young woman's feet. Lord Za`qrn's lips smiled, but his eyes watered in emotion. He only saw one foot.

She did not flinch; her pale honey brown eyes looked at him for a while, then she glanced back at his eyes.

"You want my honest opinion, Lieutenant? Firstly I don't answer to Missy!" she said in the lilting brogue of the people from the southern coastal region that was the Taayra`Ge Ocean. Her delicate left eyebrow raised questioningly.

Ji`rah was taken back at her reply, slightly confused; she had doused his anger in her acceptance of his wounds and in a calm way of ignoring his force.

"Ah…yes." He replied both Taelen and Lord Za`qrn tried not to smile.

"Personally…" she paused, looking into his whitish-blue eyes slashed diagonally with green. "If you release me, I'd like to find out, and then if you permit, I will ask you something just as personal."

Ji`rah released her hands and was sorry for holding her so firmly. His nails left indents in her fair skin, red and angry. She leant down, touching the skin, angry and raw and smiled. Her cheeks blushed slightly, as did her neck.

"I think I wouldn't mind at all." She said at him, still touching his skin; her touch was calm and soothing and quelled his anger.

"And I would kiss you like this" both her hands cupped his bearded face. Her kiss was deep and sensual;

Ji'rah's hands held her waist; she ended the kiss by removing his hands from her and smiling a little sadly, which confused him.

"Now it's my turn, Lieutenant, for 'show and tells', and I am not facetious when I say that." She added with a slight edge. She removed her hands from his stomach.

"Now, Lieutenant, you tell me, would you touch me?" she asked, her pale brown eyes holding him gently but firmly. "May I? ...Lieutenant Taelen." She said quietly, asking Taelen for permission.

"Aye, Ki`arya, you have my permission." He said, smiling at her and knowing that Ji`rah may well look the other way.

"You, too, can touch if you like." She said with a cheeky grin that brought out a dimple on her right cheek.

She glanced at Taelen more for security than anything, and he nodded and smiled at her.

With a slight tremble in her hands, she raised the straight dark blue-grey shift that she wore, raising it to her thighs where the muslin slip finished.

Her right leg was amputated at the thigh; her left leg was scared more deeply than Ji`rah's stomach and chest and seemed withered and brittle in structure.

"So in your words, Lieutenant, would you mate with me and touch this...Would you touch this without hesitation as you made love to me? I would think about it hard, Lieutenant. Scars are just like tattoos only. A tattoo is a choice; scars are not because you worked through the horrendous pain to gain the courage to survive." She swallowed hard and lowered her shift. She curtsied to Lord Za`qrn, nodded to both Ji`rah and Taelen and removed the meat dishes.

Ji`rah was quiet. His eyes stared after the young woman walking away from them, one of the Cooks pinched her arm cheekily, and her laughter spilt across them like a warm wave.

"What happened to her?" Ji`rah asked more in a whisper.

"Who Ki`arya?" asked Taelen as his eyes glanced to where she had gone and turned back to Ji`rah, "Before we left the Taayra`Ge Keep, when I was sixteen winters, there was a massacre."

"Aye, I know that." Ji`rah's reply did not have the edge it had earlier.

"Ki`arya was tortured, saving me. I could not stop what was happening. You might say I was pinned to the ground by a blade and wounded. Sergeant Anston healed me and did what he could for all the others. We returned to bury the dead. They hung her by her hair and set alight, and she revealed nothing of me."

Taelen drank another mouthful of the bitter coffee and wished he'd put sugar in it. "I had to amputate her leg and try and heal, but it turned out messy as you saw - I was entering my Mhysting."

Ji`rah frowned at the thought of Ki`arya's pain and watched her return to the table with more coffee and sugar.

"Lieutenant Taelen, Lord Za`qrn, Lieutenant Ji`rah, Cook needs your taste opinion on these." She placed a large tray with warm apple, walnut and cinnamon buns.

"May I answer your question?" Ji`rah asked.

"No," she said quietly, "Because I know Lieutenant Taelen would have now told you why I am like this, and I see the sadness in your eyes. You see, Lieutenant, I do not want your pity, just your acceptance and maybe your liking and understanding for what I have survived. I admire your strength, for your burns were caused by magic. She did not mean to harm you. When you have mastered your bitterness and anger, and realise Mistress J`nn saved you from a much worse fate, then maybe you won't be so vain about how you now look."

"Have you finished?" He asked, hurt.

"No, just remember pain is personal, and I was about to ask you something else."

"Aye, what is it?" His bravado and ego burned within his soul.

"Isn't it this?" she said, holding his bearded face, her fingers laced through his beard in her hands, holding him mesmerised as she kissed him a second time profoundly and pulled away, leaving Ji`rah lost for words. "Isn't it what counts most and not what you and I both now share in this War...love is of the heart, soul and mind…not looks?" Her eyes watered as her brow knitted in emotion. "Even if the person I love is scarred physically, mentally or the soul and heart…that, they could not see their reflection. I would love them more deeply. Love does not see; it feels as if blinded."

"My leave, Lieutenant Taelen, please." She asked, visibly upset, more at herself than anything Ji`rah had said or implied.

"Aye, Ki`arya, your leave; you may go." He said, nodding.

She bobbed quickly and left, running from the kitchen. One of the Cooks glanced at her exit and approached Taelen, wiping his hands on his apron.

"No problems, I hope, Lieutenant?" he asked.

"No, actually, I'll go see to her. We were reminiscing, and she became a bit upset; that is all; I am afraid it is partially my fault."

"If that's all, Lieutenants, Lord Za`qrn… she's a good lass."

"I know M`ykn; she is that. I won't be long." He nodded and walked back to the large stove he was working at.

"My leave Lord Za`qrn. I won't be long Ki`arya is

only out on the veranda."

Taelen passed the busy staff onto the smaller veranda attached to the kitchen.

He found her with her face in the corner of a stonewall sobbing uncontrollably.

"Ki`arya… It's only me, Taelen." He gently touched her shoulders and turned her to him. He held her as she sobbed hard into his shoulder until she regained control.

"I'm sorry, Lieutenant, I just can't, it all hurts too much, and I'm so sick of those sad looks people give me." Ki`arya's hurt was sincere, and he knew there was nothing he could do to help except hold her and listen.

"I'm afraid my brother is not all that subtle. But what you did say was what he needed to hear, and neither our Uncle nor I knew how to say it. Yet you did. I am grateful to you, but I wish I could just stop the hurt in you."

He tilted her chin gently and wiped the tears with his thumbs across her cheeks. He was kissing her lightly on her forehead.

'Sh, Ki, you did well.'

His silent speech and nickname for her from when they were children at the Tarra`Ge Keep had her look at him in her eyes, so honey brown reminded him of the colour of autumn leaves. Golden brown, and he mused one could slip easily over the same way.

She shrugged, wiped her tears and nose, and sniffed. Her pale, honey-brown eyes looked up at Taelen. She held his hand with her chin; he was like a big brother to her.

"You know, I think he's rather nice if only I didn't have ."

"Sh…Ji`rah may just surprise you. Now come back before Cook thinks I've run off with you."

"Aye, I will in a moment. Let M`ykn know I will be

no longer than ten minutes."

Taelen smiled at her and turned back to the kitchen. He found Lord Za`qrn and Ji`rah at the stove, talking in-depth with M`ykn.

"Give her ten minutes, M`ykn; she won't be long. She is just collecting her thoughts." The Cook looked up at Taelen and nodded.

It seemed Lord Za`qrn was discussing the use of certain herbs with certain meats, which appeared to interest the Cook and the Lord. Taelen smiled and returned to his table, where Ji`rah met him.

"I deserved that." He said openly to him as Taelen stirred the spoon of sugar into his coffee.

"Maybe…better than a slap, believe me." Replied Taelen shrugging off Ji`rah's acknowledgement of his weakness, "Let's face it, Ji`rah, it had to come from someone who knows the pain; it couldn't come from our Uncle or me." He said, sipping his coffee, leaning back, relaxing, eating the bun he was pulling apart and letting the crumbs fall freely. He chewed the bun still warm from the oven enjoying the taste of spices and apple.

"She's different to the others here in the Coven," Ji`rah said, glancing around at the kitchen staff.

"How so is she different?" Asked Taelen, swallowing a mouthful of warm fruit bun.

Ji`rah shrugged. "Just something about her, she's not…." he struggled to find the adequate description he was looking for.

"I think you mean she's not a Warrior who would give you back just as hard, though," he recalled a time at the Garrison, "having taught her self defence, she can swing that stump with fury. And cheeky to win a heart, no, and she doesn't make you her target. She's more at home with males than females, by the way. And I have never seen Ki`arya kiss anyone." Stretching and scratching his neck. "Actually, until now, strange she picked you," Taelen said, eyebrows raised. He knew Ji`rah would remember that comment and come back at him in his eclectic Wolf manner.

"You amputated the leg above the knee?" He asked as Taelen swallowed the mouth full of the sweet bun he was chewing.

"Aye, I did. It was difficult because I was experiencing my first Mhysting then. We thought she would surely die, but she didn't, and I'm relieved."

"Why?" asked Ji`rah as he ate the warm nut and fruit bun and reached for another.

"She is different, but not in the ways we have discussed just now. You see, Ki`arya has a gift that many of us have lost. She guides those who are lost in their pain back to the living. Be it physical, emotional, or trauma pain. I watched her at the Keep, We were I must have been seven winters, and she was four or five winters old. " Taelen frowned at the memory of watching her convince a Warrior not to take his life. "Anyway, she has healing in a way that we do not."

He dusted off the crumbs from his trousers. "Usually, when Ki`arya finishes her shift in the kitchen, she goes to the infirmary to see if the 'Healers' require her."

"And when she's not in the infirmary or here in the Kitchen?" asked vaguely where the young woman relaxed.

Taelen laughed aloud at the sheepish look on Ji`rah's face.

"She likes to walk on the ramparts of the East Wing."

"That's a lonely place." He said, sipping the hot, bitter coffee.

"Not for her. I know about Ki`arya that she likes her

own space and does not suffer fools easily. Life in any Garrison or Coven, for that matter, is claustrophobic. Just don't push too much, Ji`rah; for some reason, she likes you." He said, smiling as Ji`rah's eyes followed Ki`arya as she re-entered the kitchen and spoke to M`ykn and Lord Za`qrn.

"Promise me one thing, brother." Said Taelen standing and dusting off the remainder of the bun from his uniform

"Aye… and what's that?"

"Get her to safety if we are attacked. With the wooden stump, ' Pack', she can't move as fast as the others."

"Aye, Pact. But we are not going to be under attack Taelen."

"That is something I have an ill feeling over at the moment." He shivered. "Something just isn't quite right at the moment." He leant over and poured himself another coffee and stirred the sugar in. "I'll be up in my study if anyone wants me, Ji`rah."

Ji`rah nodded to him as he left. He, too, had paperwork that needed to be filled out. He stood to leave as Lord Za`qrn approached him with a pleasing look.

"Taelen is in his study if you require him, Uncle."

"Aye, I will go to him soon. It seems the Cook has a recipe for Mead," he said, smiling with a spark of cheekiness in that irascible grin. Lord Za`qrn seemed more interested in the promise of Meade and what devilishness it would bring.

Ji`rah stretched out his body on the chair and grimaced, "Last time you drank Meade, you had a sore head for a week." He said, screwing his face up at the memory.

"Don't you mean the last time we drank Mead together, we had one hell of a hangover?"

"Aye, how could I not remember?" He said, "I had fur on my tongue for a month and a day."

Lord Za`qrn burst into laughter because his nephew had not been able to transform into the Wolf form after drinking the Meade, and for that matter, neither had he been able to.

"Aye, we were just a touch tetchy with everyone." His Uncle replied.

"Before I drink this one, I prefer to see the recipe on paper to know what I am drinking."

"Wise decision always pays to know what one swallows." He said, smiling.

Ji`rah grimaced as he stretched the entire length of his body out under the table.

His Uncle could drink a ship's company under the table without even a slight pain to his head or stomach the morning after. The Lord had proved his staying power more than once to his nephew.

He pulled himself up in the chair and found he was suddenly tired; he excused himself and left to see where he had been billeted.

His head was down as he walked up the stairs to the Guardroom. The wind whistled down the stairwell, stirring up dust and leaves that had snuck in through the doors opened by those of the Coven.

The Guardroom was just as busy as the kitchen as he squeezed in to look at the list on the board where they were billeted.

"No good looking for us, Ji`rah. We have been placed on the top floor of the East Wing." He turned to see one of his people. H`ta was an Imperial Archer, and she belonged to one of the desert regions pack of X`qwet.

Large bone desert Wolves, the men especially, yet the females were a slighter build but equal to a Warrior in human terms. H`ta had blazing red hair cut short with a design that showed the tattoo of her pack on her skull. He mused she could scare some of her own Warriors, and her bluntness he swore could crack crystals.

Ji`rah was waiting for the derogatory comments that usually came when the Wolf Nation were billeted separately from the others. But it didn't happen this time.

"East Wing is a solitary place," the woman's deep green eyes glanced away from one of the Sz`a`Th Warriors. She eyed both closely.

"I know it is good for howling." She winked at him mischievously and moved with stealth towards the Sergeant standing near the stairs sorting papers out he had in his hands. Ji`rah smiled; H'ta never did get a chance to slip by her. 'Poor bastard', he thought and thought or 'Lucky bastard', heaving sighing and grabbed his backpack and started climbing the four flights of stairs that would bring him to the top of the East Wing.

Once there, he threw his backpack into the empty room with his name written in the strange scratches of the Sqh`xn script at the end of the long corridor.

Ji`rah tilted his head, sniffing the air, knowing why the Wolf Nation had been billeted in the East Wing.

East was the Element of Air and the Power of the Mind. Its natural forms were the winds, the atmosphere, and the breath. This was a place to heal the mind.

His hand gripped the brass latch opening the door onto the ramparts outside. Though tired, he would not sleep and stepped out into the cold blast of air that astounded him.

Rain pitted down on him, but he did not mind; he began walking to the rampart's end. Along the wall were small alcove areas where Guards on duty could step out of the weather and still see clearly.

At the furthest end, he walked and stood to take in

the vast view of the plains one hundred meters below him. It was cold, but he could be himself here, he stretched up, and his eyes rolled back as Ji`rah folded down onto himself. The movement was slower than even he had anticipated. The burns on his chest constricted, making breathing difficult; Ji'rah whimpered in the form of the black timber Wolf that he was.

The pain hurt in sharp pulses, and he yelped. Ji`rah was stranded in the Wolf form.

Angrier at his stupidity, Ji`rah had been told this would hurt; he used all his energy to transform back into his human form. The pain tore a primal scream from his lips. He lay on the wet, cold black limestone gasping and coughing up blood.

Someone was running towards him, calling out to others who happened to be now on the fourth floor to assist.

"Ji`rah, what the hell have you done? You're covered in blood."

He groaned at their foresight.

"Oh aye, what gave that away?"

"Don't fret", he heard H`ta's voice ", it's his own blood."

He tried not to laugh; the pain tore at him again as they lifted and moved him as gently as they could inside his room.

"Shattas, Ji`rah, how much blood do you want to lose? Have you forgotten your Wolf? Ease the flow. Damn, you concentrate!"

Someone else spoke through his pain. "He can't, this is magic, and only someone else can heal him."

"You then heal him now!" H`ta snapped at the young woman in anger.

"I can't; I'm not a Spellcaster."

Ji`rah felt his skin tear. The scream that tore from

his lips was something that had those who had brought him in standing back, afraid.

"This is not working." A voice familiar to him said, but he could not place a face with the name and closed his eyes, glistening. "We have to put him back out in the rain. It is the only thing that will stop the magic fire burning within him."

"Do as the lady says, get him back out in the rain, and you, Lg`jen, get down those bloody stairs as fast as you can and get Lord Za`qrn, and I don't care who you disturb, do it."

Lg`jen saluted across in the Wolf tradition; his dark brown eyes were lighter than his skin, and his hair had a blaze of blue through them, the same colour as the blaze across his dark brown eyes. Trained in sword, crossbow and axe, he was powerfully built.

Sergeant Lg`jen ran. Others lifted Ji`rah back out onto the rampart.

"We have to remove his tunic and shirt."

H`ta's face swam into view with a grin, she said.

"At last, Ji`rah, I get to take your clothes off." Ji`rah grimaced and growled at her, which immediately wiped the smile from her face. Instead, she produced a blade with a black hilt; its name was a 'Darku'. The Warrior deftly sliced his tunic and shirt from his body and then his skin.

The other woman, whose familiar voice bent over him, for she stood slightly apart from the others.

"Could someone get one of the Cooks to peel some potatoes finely, very finely and bring them up here?"

H`ta snarled at her," You look fit enough to me, Mistress. Why don't you go down those stairs."

"Because I can't go down as fast as you."

Ji`rah tried to focus on the woman who spoke, H`ta always got on his nerves, and she did it again.

"Oh, and give me a good reason why." H`ta snapped.

"You have two legs. If you want to save this Lieutenant, I suggest you go to the Cook M`ykn. Tell him Ki`arya needs the box for burns and potatoes, and he will know what you mean."

"Oh, Aye, you don't have two legs." H`ta snatched up Ki`arya shift to the muslin slip."

Her green eyes glanced back up at the young woman, who did not say a word or react to the encroachment on her person by H`ta. Instead, she gently held the hand that held her knee-length shift up so high and said with a small smile.

"My legs are a bit cold, and I think the Lieutenant has just seen a wee bit too much of me." H`ta released her hold on the shift, and it fell quickly, already very wet in the rain.

"I won't be long." She said, frowning, not knowing what to say and do.

"Sergeant, he'll need herbal painkillers that you use for your 'season'."

H`ta nodded and ran through the rain.

Ji`rah was shaking more from shock; Ki'arya removed her coat and placed it over his legs and arms, bare his chest. The rain was easing the burning as blood ran off his skin and diluted onto the pale grey limestone.

She shielded his head from the rain with her upper torso as she removed the wooden stump and sat down in the rain, gently placing the wad she used for her stump under his head.

"It'll stop the rain drowning your ears and running into your nose." She said, shivering. Her light brown curly hair curled and hung in long ringlets in the rain.

"Lieutenant, I'm going to touch the burns with my fingertips. I need to know the intensity of the magic."

M`ykn the Cook came panting over to her. The Cook had the box she had requested with the potatoes.

"No, lassie, you can't. You'll burn." He said, kneeling and grasping her wrist. H`ta kneeled next to him as Lord Za'qrn's voice came to him.

"Ji`rah…pup." His Uncles voice held that rare emotion of deep caring and love.

"We can't move him yet," Ki`arya said, shivering, and glanced at M`ykn. "I must touch the burns; you know I know that." She looked over at H`ta and smiled slightly in the rain, and her coldness brought out a rare stutter. "When It…t…touch the burn I will kn…kn…know the depth of the magic, what you must do is determining the thickness of the potatoes that you peel, you must put it where my fingertips are, the thinner, the better. You have the herbs for your 'season,' Sergeant?"

"Here," she said. "I have diluted the herb to my strength."

"Then quadruple the strength." She glanced down at Ji`rah "Believe me; you will need it." She looked up to see Taelen also dripping wet in the rain. "Lieutenant, I shall require your Mhyst to dilute the m…m…magic."

"That isn't going to work." He said as a squall hit the ramparts. She smiled, rain dripping down her face and her teeth chattering. Her white blouse clung to her like a second skin.

"Trust me, Lieutenant Taelen, it will."

As her fingertips touched each burn on Ji`rah's chest, he moaned. She nodded to M`ykn and H`ta as they precisely cut slices of potato with his Cooks knife, her with the black hilted blade. Taelen concentrated on the Mhyst. It sprinkled down onto Ji`rah's burns and did as Ki`arya had predicted. The Magic rose in spirals of steam and was carried away by the wind and diluted by the rain.

Only she knew how much pain he was in because it coursed through her fingertips and into her mind. M`ykn glanced at her.

"You can't keep this up, lass; look at your fingers."

Ji`rah reached for her wrist and held her hand close; the skin was burned away. Blood, her blood ran down his forearm and hers. She pulled her hand away and continued.

Lord Za`qrn touched her shoulder and knelt in the rain. His dark brown eyes held hers. Rain streamed off the skin on his head, but he did not mind.

"Lass the Cook is right. You can't keep going. Let me help. You use my hands as a medium to work through." She looked at his dark-skinned hands with elegant long fingers and almond-shaped nails. His hands were similar to hers. Gently she held his, closed her eyes, concentrated, and began finishing the small amount she had to go.

Lord Za`qrn growled as the pain she had experienced for nearly all the healing hit him full force as it had done to her. His eyes watched her, and he realised not all the wetness on her face was rain; a lot of it was tears.

When she stopped, she looked down at Ji`rah and then at H`ta and nodded for her to give him the herbs.

"Now he can go inside the elements that have assisted in his healing as much as we have. He can't eat meat for a week, only vegetable dishes and lentils and rice."

The others lifted the exhausted and bloody Ji`rah into the corridor and down to his room.

Only M`ykn, Taelen, and Lord Za`qrn were left in the rain. They lifted the young Ki`arya and carried her down to Taelen's floor.

The West Wing was silent, they bandaged her hands, and Taelen's Grandmother helped the young woman change into a nightshirt.

She lay back silent against the pillows, tears streaming down her cheeks. The pain only eased when she took the herbal drink that was infused with a potent spell by LH`Nejah's magic.

Taelen entered, having changed his wet clothes, and sat beside her on the bed. He looked at her closely as a shudder of pain shook her whole body.

"It seems you have caused quite a few tongues wagging, my dear one." He smiled at her. Her pale brown eyes looked back at him from her bandages.

"Why I heal all the burns in the kitchen, Lieutenant, you know I do."

"Not quite how you did up on the East Wing; my brother is resting."

"He will heal." Ki`arya stared at him; her delicate eyebrows rose in concern.

"That's just it, Ki`arya. He has healed."

She frowned at him, her own hands bandaged.

"That's impossible. It takes days, and dressing changes, and…." She looked at her bandages where the blood had soaked through. She knew that her own body would take long weeks ahead to heal. Why had the Sqh`xn Warrior healed instantaneously?

"My Grandmother is curious to know your heritage. I only knew from what I had heard at the Taayra`Ge Keep, which seems so long ago. That even then, you could heal all manner of ailments and injuries. That like me, your only parent was killed and drowned by Mah`sden and his men." He paused, looking at the bloody bandages and continued. "I know you were on the same ship I was on, but we were so young then. I remember we played a lot together when we could." He smiled at the memory that came from the boy of six winters that he once was.

"I was only four winters old, Lieutenant, I remember, though, but I have never understood why I was saved." She looked from his amethyst, blue eyes with their purple fleck back to the bandages that blood now stained heavy and dark.

"Mistress LH`Nejah has gone back through the archives. She found the list of passengers for that ship. The documents say you travelled on the ship with your father."

"I sadly don't recall him; his face is featureless to me." She said, still staring at the blood that was hers. "I know that my mother died when I was a babe."

Lord Za`qrn stood quietly and spoke.

"Your father was, what is called in the Sz`a`Th Lore, a 'Soul Healer' or for want of the ancient term 'LZ`rqks'. His name was Kr`s Tah`n. His lineage was that of all Nations of Man and Lord Za`qrn through his family. He said slowly. The name brought images reeling back through memories she had hidden and ones Taelen had hidden.

Taelen closed his eyes, for the man was his own Uncle, and he had forgotten. He now had a cousin of his own blood, someone from whom he had had to amputate a leg, and those he had had to leave behind on that day three winters ago.

He opened his eyes to see her wiping her own eyes with the blood-stained bandages she wore on her burned fingertips.

"Ki`arya, can you forgive me? We are family. I don't you think I am a good cousin?" he asked, a tear escaping his eyes.

"I did a long time ago. Can you forgive me for pestering you all those hours to learn to scribe like you and getting underfoot in the Keep?"

"Aye, you know what this means now, don't you LH`Nejah will fuss and hound you."

Both laughed; Taelen held her bandaged hands and kissed the bandages lightly.

"Welcome home to the Sz`a`Th Mistress Ki`arya Tah`n." He said, smiling and remembering when their childish laughter and running footsteps were heard throughout the Imperial Castle of the Sz`a`Th that his Uncle now occupied. He saw her fragility then and excused himself, closing the door he left.

She slept until dusk when Taelen knocked and entered with a tray of food for her for the evening meal that had been served throughout the Coven.

"Well, it seems like I shall have to feed you. M`ykn said you didn't have to have a strict diet of vegetables like Ji`rah. This must be your lucky night." He recalled that she did not have a great love of vegetables.

They were halfway through her meal when another knock came at the door.

"May we enter?" asked Lord Za`qrn, sweeping into the room as always; Ji'rah smiled a little as his Uncles arm dragged him in and the firm grasp on his own forearm also meant he had no alternative but to follow.

"How is the Mead coming along, Lord Za`qrn?" she asked, smiling at the Sqh'xn Nation's men.

"Oh superbly, my lovely, it's doing its thing in those wonderful jugs that M`ykn has down in his pantry. Just can't wait till we can do a taste test." His eyes widened at the prospect of tasting the elixir. His hand slipped into his tunic breast pocket and pulled out a carefully folded list of items.

"You must listen to this; it is the Cook's recipe for Meade." He said quite seriously. His dark eyes glanced back at the door with an edge of secrecy that she hid her smile behind her bloodied, bandaged hands.

Lord Za`qrn began squinting at the notes. He pulled out fine gold and black rectangular reading glasses from his pocket. They sat neatly on his nose, which was not angular or long like some wolves would have but neat and just slightly 'flat', he called it; the noise came from his mother's side of the family, where their lineage could be followed high into the mountains where such 'flat noses' were common.

He glanced over the glasses to see if all were listening and began.

"Jugs and pots, of course, it says here to use six-quart size…one…. I think I will double the quantity one will not last." Ji`rah rolled his eyes into the back of his head in defeat.

"Hmm, I won't go into the apparatus used…now; here is the interesting part of the recipe. Yeast must be wine yeast—no cheating with ale or yeast for bread. My goodness, two pounds of clover or orange blossom honey, and well, I think I will put in more than just two whole cloves crushed into this, cinnamon sticks and the sliced root of ginger, orange peel and water from the springs. I think I will add other spices like nutmeg and other honey." He neatly folded the list and patted it into his tunic breast pocket.

"Just can't wait to make some Mead." He said, smiling with the thought.

"I can." Groaned, Ji`rah wished he had not been dragged down here to the West Wing by his Uncle.

Lord Za`qrn swept his arm through the air dramatically as he said to her taking his glasses off and placing them safely away.

"No more Lord this, Lord that, my lovely, I've just found out your family, so you just must call me Uncle." He bent over, kissed her on both cheeks, and said, hugging her tightly.

"Just one less female I must flirt with," he said, winking, knowing the reaction he would get from the other two men in the room beside him

Both Taelen and Ji`rah groaned so loudly that Lord Za`qrn swept out of the place dramatically but with the widest of his grins as he heard her say.

"I think he is sweet under all that bravado." She said, looking at Taelen, who smiled, nodding in agreement. He then looked at Ji`rah and said

"Take over with the food, will you? I have a mound of paperwork that must be done before midnight."

He leaned over, kissed Ki`arya on the head, and handed Ji`rah the fork he had used to feed Ki`arya.

"She eats slowly…unlike some Warriors I know!" he said and left the room, closing the door behind them.

Ji`rah sat down where Taelen sat and placed some food on the fork. She opened her mouth, gently tugged the Cooked meat off the fork, and chewed slowly, self-consciously.

"Uncle is all bravado. You are right there," said Ji`rah, slowly adding more food to the fork. "So…they say your Taelen's cousin. How does it feel to be landed in our extended family?"

"No different to the one I have down in the Kitchen. People are themselves where ever or whoever they are. Actually, it's a nice warm feeling to have blood family." She frowned slightly and glanced back at him.

"Taelen said your burns are completely healed."

"Aye, Mistress, I am, and sometimes blood family can be a big pain in the arse." He put down the fork and pulled his shirt off completely.

His chest showed no signs of scaring; it was as if the magic had never burned him though Ki`arya could tell he had been. The scars were still there, burned down deep in the crevasses of his mind and would always be there behind his eyes.

She touched his skin but realised her own hands were heavily bandaged.

"How long will it take for your hands to heal?" he asked, wincing as he gently turned them over her blood-red where it had seeped through.

She shrugged.

"Usually, burns take a few weeks to heal," she said, looking at them with a frown. "I don't know this magic burns deep, Lieutenant, very deep." She leant back into the mound of pillows behind her back.

"It's very late. I should get this tray back to the kitchen. Do you need anything else?"

"If you can braid hair, I wouldn't mind this mop of hair that I have tied in one, I'm afraid it is a pain to brush, and I can't deal with these hands."

Ji`rah put down the tray and brushed her very wavy light brown hair that would have reached her thighs had it been straight, but the wave made it coil up; Ji'rah then braided it quickly, which even surprised him.

"Thank you, Lieutenant. One other thing, do you know where my leg went? I can't seem to see it here?"

"I'll go ask and hopefully come back with it."

He took the tray and closed her door. She listened to his footsteps, and once she could no longer hear them began to cry from the pain in her hands. Exhaustion dragged her head back, and in moments, she was asleep.

Ji`rah had found her 'leg' where she had used it to support his head on the ramparts of the East Wing.

He knocked gently but, hearing no answer, walked away when Taelen called him in the corridor. He turned to see his brother walk tiredly towards him; his hands shoved into the trousers.

Taelen looked up, smiling wearily and nodded to

Ji`rah.

"I see you found her 'leg' I was wondering where it had got to." He opened the door, knowing she was in a deep sleep produced by his Grandmothers magic.

"She will sleep to morning." He said as he walked in; Ji'rah looked around the door to see her curled up, the long braid snaked down the quilt. The blankets lay flat where her other leg should have been.

"She is in pain?" asked Ji`rah as he watched her hands twitch now and then.

"Aye, she will be for a few days. G`rnah is looking at spells to quicken the healing, but there is nothing that is covering for an 'LZ`rqks'. It seems 'Soul Healers' are in their own realm. That is why I could not save her leg three winters ago; it was impossible even though we are blood." He took the wooden stump from Ji`rah and placed it in the cabinet next to the bed.

"She may be all that can heal you one day, Taelen." Ji`rah's voice was just audible. "I hope you realise that." He said, studying both her and Taelen.

"Why did she heal me? I have been a complete arse to her," Ji`rah asked bluntly.

"Ki`arya doesn't suffer fools lightly, Ji`rah; she sensed your pain just as she sensed H`ta's own deep pain."

"H`ta is a pain in the arse," Ji`rah said, remembering moments not long ago upon the rampart. "One day, that 'bitch' will go too far, and it will be fur flying all over the place."

Taelen stretched his back; he was tired when he remembered something important he needed to show Ji`rah. "There is a good reason for her attitude."

He replied, recalling the massacre that H`ta and another were the only survivors of horrible injuries.

He tapped him on the shoulder, nodding at him that

they were to leave. Ji`rah glanced at the 'Soul Healer' and closed the door after him.

# CHAPTER 16

Ji`rah's footsteps dragged behind Taelen down to his study on the right side of the corridor adjacent to Taelen's own room. The crystal lamps lit up as they entered, illuminating the room in a pale white glow.

"Your Spells are improving, Taelen; the crystals exploded last time you tried this." Teh`c acknowledged his dark eyebrows smiling at the memory.

"You remember that?" Taelen cringed from the embarrassment.

"How could I forget, the whole east wing had to be lit with oil lamps for three moons while new crystals were found and…."

"You do not have to remind me, Teh`c…I am still picking up crystal fragments in this room." He sighed at the thought of crystal shards throughout the east wing.

The giant oak mantle clock chimed softly at 2:45 am. It was quiet besides the soft ticking of the clock in the room. Ji`rah suddenly felt tiredness flow over him as he read the time.

"Ji`rah, I need you to look at this," Taelen said as he lit the lamp at his desk. The soft blue-white light of the clear quartz crystal spilt suddenly onto the table. Prisms of purple and mauve hues pierced the dark of the room.

"Aye, nice desk Taelen, smooth lines in the oak, dark honey colour with a runic design the…." He stopped with his mordant commentary as he now leant over the desk. His fingertips touched the centre's design, where blue, mauve and white crystals sat embossed into the wood.

Glancing up, Ji`rah stared into his brother's eyes. Taelen lent upon the desk opposite him. Their eyes met as Ji`rah asked him.

"When did you notice this?" His fingertips touched the embossing.

"I was suspicious about the woman who was here when we arrived. The Dormas woman hovered over the desk when I worked the night before she left."

"Aye, you sure it wasn't you she was interested in?" he asked, smirking.

"Seems the burns didn't improve your sense of humour, none," Taelen replied sarcastically. Though pleased, his brother was not sulking anymore.

Ji`rah raised his dark eyebrows; his thoughts went to the young Spellcasters in his care when they were looking for the Spellcasters Master L`unh.

"Seems Mistress J`nn and I were led into a trap." He replied, smoothing his dark beard as his mind took in the many scenarios that led to her capture, including the kaleidoscope of magic.

"Aye, and so was Master L`unh. Or was Master L`unh the trap?" His blue amethyst eyes glanced from the now cleared desk to the floor.

Ji`rah instead looked up and tapped him on the shoulder.

"You're looking in the wrong direction Taelen. It's the ceiling you need to see."

Directly above his desk, the ceiling held an identical design.

Taelen swore loudly. Slamming his fist down onto the table, smacking the wooden surface hard, he swung away from the desk.

"If that was supposed to make you feel better, I choose to differ," Ji`rah said as Taelen rubbed his now-smarting hand. Taelen grinned with disdain at the Warrior with him.

"I forgot about the other elements." He said, looking

through designs.

"There are only four elements." Replied Ji`rah, now lying on the floor and looking at the design. "Do you know that the light from outside forms a design?" Pausing, he added. "Extinguish the lamps, and let's see what we get, Taelen."

"There are four elements of nature, yes. However, when talking of the elements, there are seven elements, Up, Down and Centre. Those are the ones here embossed with crystals."

"Look, I believe you…." Ji`rah said painfully and lay down on the floor; Taelen glanced at Teh`c questioningly. "My back is screaming, and this floor is hard and flat, and just what it needs…continue, I'm not moving for a while."

Taelen clicked his fingers, and the lamps went out. He lay on the floor with Ji`rah above them was a runic design, identical to the pendant Taelen had around his neck.

"I really don't know what to make of this," Ji`rah said, his eyes narrowed as they followed the flow of the lines of the rune. "Is it a bind rune with a pentacle scroll of the Spellcasters Star?" He rubbed his bloodshot eyes, sore from snow and winds, then stroked his beard brusquely in the hope of waking himself up. He then took a deep breath and glanced at Taelen's writing.

"Seven Books and Seven Elements…by gods, I am tired." He blinked his eyes firmly but without much success and lent back into the seat, staring at the ceiling.

Taelen traced the flow with his mind, reading as he went.

"Why do Spellcasters always write on the ceiling…." His voice trailed as Taelen said.

"Will you just shut up…I am deciphering the writing, and your gibberish is not helping one bit." Ji`rah twisted his head around to look at Taelen, who had crawled over to the roughly stacked ledges and the quill case.

"What are you doing?" Ji`rah asked as his brother began to lie back down and draw simultaneously.

"Sh…" Taelen curtly whispered. Ji`rah raised his eyebrow in contempt.

"Fine, I'll talk to myself." Replied Ji`rah just as curtly and returned to staring at the design on the ceiling.

Taelen abruptly stood up and went to the desk.

"Ji`rah, look at the design." The Warrior groaned because he was exhausted. He stood and leaned on the desk.

"This had better be worth my lack of sleep. I haven't actually slept now for 48 hours."

"You nag you to know, Ji`rah!" replied Taelen.

The large oak mantle clock chimed at three am. Ji`rah shivered and glanced at Taelen and back to the clock.

"It's 3 am," murmured Taelen looking back at his notes and the mess on his desk.

"Aye… Let us leave this, don't you?" Ji`rah said, his eyes nervously glancing around Taelen's study.

"Ji`rah…you don't believe in 'the howling hour'?" he said, his voice giving away how he felt.

"Aye, and so do you; Spellcasters have it all wrong. It is not midnight that opens the door to the darkness. It is 3 am." He swallowed hard as the hair along his spine rose to prickle his skin as the shiver climbed his spine. He glanced to the ceiling.

"Taelen…I really think we need to get out of here…and now." He said, backing away from the desk and towards the door. His footsteps stopped as his hand clasped the brass door handle. It would not turn. His eyes were still on the ceiling. The clock ticked and then stopped. Ji`rah swallowed hard. All he could hear was his pulse and heartbeat.

“Shattas…” Ji`rah’s voice rose slightly. “Taelen, get over here and do it now.”

Taelen hurriedly stuffed the notes into his trouser pockets and returned to the door.

“It won’t open. I’ve tried it.” Said Ji`rah as Taelen’s hand found his on the latch.

Lightning lit down through the design on the ceiling and made a three-pointed star on the floor. Both Warriors froze and held their breath in the semi-darkness of the study. The clap of thunder was instantaneous.

Particles of dark blue light fell shimmering to their form on the floor before them stood a man. His features were refined, and he moved away from the column of light emitted from the ceiling design. His moves were predatory.

Taelen and Ji`rah did not move. They hardly breathed. The beat of their pulse throbbed loudly in their ears that burned hot. Before them stood a male Spellcaster; only this one did not practice the same as the Covens. This one was a Necromancer.

A deep pervading sense of death hung in the room. He glanced at the desk; his hands ran seductively over the design and stopped on the three-pointed star. His eyes slowly looked up and saw the two Warriors standing at the door. His black eyes went to Ji`rah.

“Wolf.” His voice sounded like the last gasp of air expelled from the body at death.

Ji`rah did not move. Instead, he instinctively folded down into himself and stood beside Taelen as the black timber Wolf that he was. He dropped to the floor submissively.

Dark blue, black eyes swung slowly to Taelen; cold air appeared frosty, floating across the floor. The room took on a deathly appearance.

"Only Guards stand at this hour." His voice trailed ice down Taelen's spine.

"So the Lord of the Dominions is a youth of nineteen winters." His eyes dived deep into Taelen's psyche. Instinct made Taelen gag and choke with the taste of death from the Sorcerer into his thoughts and senses.

Taelen blinked slowly; he could feel the Mhyst within him sing softly, warning him, guarding him, stopping the Sorcerer's touch.

"Your thoughts can be of the 'shadow'." He smiled quite serenely at Taelen.

"We all have shadows, My Lord Nul`YK; what do you want."

Both stared at the necromancer, Lord of the dead and undead.

"So you know my name. I am impressed. Not all know of the 'shade world' that we all share."

He was not as tall as Taelen or Ji`rah, and his age was indefinable. Taelen could have guessed sixty winters, but how do you gauge the devil's age? He looked thirty.

"You have an unanswered question; should I answer it for you." He asked cockily. He fanned his hand out and clicked his fingers. A vision of the Spellcasters appeared within the column of light.

"J`nn…?" He said, tilting his head and raising his eyebrows.

"Isn't she the one that is your 'heart's breath'?" His smile was all baseness. Taelen clenched his fists as the Mhyst sang even stronger, tingling his birthmark.

"She lives; sadly, L`unh doesn't." The decapitated head of the older man rolled around the form of J`nn, who stood silently. The thick red ring that was left by the blood of the dead Spellcasters gave Taelen a sliver of hope as all Spellcasters made a magic ring when casting a spell. Using blood made the circle impenetrable.

"You see, young Taelen, the Spellcasters are different, a rare find within the Covens. Your Uncle seems to have taken a fancy to the young lass." He said, smiling. "Such a dark side has he, impressive really, no qualms at all has the man. Especially regarding females and how they should be his entertainment."

"You have broken the Lore of the Spellcasters by killing one of your own." Snapped Taelen as he tried to calm the singing of the Mhyst, heating his veins. His ears roared with the sound of blood coursing through him.

Ji`rah growled low; he crept up on his paws, his head down low, his ears flat against his head as he bared his teeth at the Sorcerer.

"You see, my young friend, even 'Spellcasters' needed evil. That is why this Coven exists. Why not go and ask your Grandmother? She knows. She's quite tasty, you know."

Ji`rah lost his self-control and flew at the Lord. Taelen yelled at Ji`rah to stop. He instead leapt for Ji`rah as the Sorcerer laughed. His fingertips held dark red energy that sliced through the air at them both. Igniting the ancient Lore of Death, this was his domain.

Their training as Sahn`Frwh was all that saved them both. The common bond that was as fine as a heartbeat between the Sahn`Frwh and the Lord of Death was impenetrable. Ji`rah now stood in his human form, blood flowing through a gash to his upper thigh, the Sahn`Frwh sword protecting him.

"Shatta's, that's going to leave a scar!" Ji`rah groaned out loud. Taelen just looked at him as he crouched.

Taelen knelt on one knee. His blood dripped to the floor from the wound across his back where Lord Nul`YK magic had sliced the air, cutting them deeply.

Their Red Crescent moons appeared on their temples near their left eye glowing dully, pulsing as it slowed the blood flow.

"So…you are both Sahn`Frwh…be warned," he said, sending another red slice of energy towards them; the current hit their swords, sending a sound like the crack of a whip through the air swords ringing loudly in their ears.

"Your trial has just only begun. And so has the young Spellcasters." He then strolled back to the centre of the light and vanished.

Thunder rolled angrily, cracking deafeningly above them and the Coven; sweat stung the open wounds that had formed dark blood spots on the floor. They did not move their stance for a while, both breathing heavily, fogging the air and not saying a word.

Rain poured outside, flooding swollen rivers as the two Warriors slowly moved taut muscles from the defence position they had held.

The clock chimed four am and ticked in the silence.

Ji`rah was the first to speak as he put the Sahn`Frwh sword to the side, leaning the length of the intricate blade against the desk.

"I think next time, I will go to bed early. These early morning sojourns are a tad wearing, you know." He glanced down at the wound on his thigh and swore crudely.

"It's wearing on my damn uniforms too." He gingerly pulled the shredded material away from the wound. Screwing his nose up at the same time realising the extent of his injury, he nodded in agreement and said.

"I think we need a healer Taelen."

"Hmm..." he murmured as he pulled out the hastily hidden notes now smeared with blood. "Can you walk with that... mess you call a leg?" he asked as he gingerly turned his own attention to the stinging on his back.

"What's this look like?"

Ji`rah sucked in air through his teeth as he gently pulled the sliced shirt from the wound on Taelen's back.

"By the gods, Taelen, I can with this leg if you can walk with that gaping wound on your back."

Taelen began to shiver as he moved towards the door. It would be an arduous walk from the study.

"Who's awake at this hour? There are no sentries rostered here tonight" he glanced at the clock. "I stand corrected this morning. This wing is empty except for Ki`arya, and she is no help; G'rnah herbal mixture has her asleep for another two hours at the least." He shook his head as he watched Ji`rah limp out the door.

"Then let's stop talking because this hurts more than I want to admit; let's find anyone." Ji`rah cursed, "Who the hell decided that once you call on the Red Crescent, you can't heal for an hour."

"Ask the Death Watch. It is their Lore."

"Well, that bloody figures." Grumbled Ji`rah as he limped slowly with Taelen. They arrived at an entrance to the ground floor, intersecting the Coven's North, South, East and West Wings.

Ji`rah lent against the cold wall, breathing heavily. The wound had widened, and the blood flow had begun again bubbling out from under the congealed seal of old blood that had formed.

Taelen stood still, shivering. With teeth chattering, he glanced at his brother.

"Ji`rah, you have to keep moving. The Kitchen staff are usually up at this hour and were bound to run into one of them here. The Sentry duty is not changing for another two hours."

"Shattas…Taelen, in another two hours, we will be dead." Ji`rah's answer fell as he did sliding down the wall. "I just don't feel very well at the moment."

He had gone deathly pale, the last twenty-four hours had been too much for him, and he slid further, his face smacking the stone floor sharply. His eyes stared ahead and slowly closed.

Voices close by in the darkened corridors rippled through the half-light as they readied themselves for the morning shift.

Taelen had no energy to call out and waited for support as he gripped the wall.

The call to arms of a Warrior on Kitchen duties brought him around; Taelen, too, had slipped to the floor in Ji`rah's blood. His eyes opened to see the Cook, M`ykn, lift Ji`rah up onto his shoulder as he shouted orders to the staff. The large hands of two of the Cooks lifted him quickly; he closed his eyes to ease the feeling of nausea that curdled in the pit of his stomach.

Hardwood replaced the hands that held him, the lights were blinding, and his eyes watered from the intense glare as he was laid on his side. On the opposite table lay Ji`rah.

"Lieutenant, it M`ykn, I need to know how to deal with the wounds and who did it. I am a Cook, that's all; I'm no Spellcasters."

"You need to find Lord Za`qrn. Especially for Ji`rah in case even needle and thread irritate that hard Wolf head of his. I would suggest just sewing the wounds to start with. Lord Nul`YK was our adversary," He said, breathing quickly. "M`ykn… I'm going to throw up."

A bucket was held below the table, and M`ykn held Taelen's head over the side of the table.

“Not in my kitchen; you’re not, Lieutenant; just aim for the bucket; I’ll send out someone to search for the Wolf Lord.”

A Sahn`Frwh Warrior entered, having just come down on shift.

“Cook, you have my assistance with the two Lieutenants.”

He glanced at the young woman no older than eighteen winters; she was Sahn’Frwh.

“I am Lieutenant Dan`e of the Southern Covens. I arrived with Lord Za`qrn.”

“Welcome to these two fools Dan`e, buckets and strip them of their clothes. I need to know how much I can heal and how much you can heal, girl?”

She removed her cloak and tunic jacket, rolled up her sleeves, sliced their uniforms from them, and began immediately healing as her skills were of the southern region of the Sz`a`Th. Her brown eyes sprinkled green, and her Mhyst birthright was glowing with runes symbols as she healed.

Straight black hair was in a long plait to her waist, and she had been on an already long shift on the Northern Ramparts. She wore the Red Crescent and an intricate tattoo in black that ran from her left jaw down her neck along her whole arm in a sleeve of symbols only the Warrior knew their profound meaning.

He felt the hot, bitter taste of bile rise up as he threw up into the bucket until nothing was left in his stomach. He lay now on his side, exhausted and felt the warm wet cloths cleaning his back, and someone began sewing the wound together.

‘Buckets are for heaving the poison coursing through your veins. Aim for the buckets, not my fucking boots, Lieutenants!”. Dan`e said, smiling at them.

The sensation and pain of the needle and line that

was threading and knotting at each joint made his head swing, and he dry retched repeatedly.

"Lieutenant, you must control the urge to vomit. Each spasm of vomiting stretches your skin." Her voice was low and so coldly commanding.

Ji'rah caught a glimpse of this female Sz`a`Th Warrior. Dan`e eyes were tilted slightly to her temples. They were brown sprinkled green, but the blaze across the iris in gold had him wondering why he had missed her, for he noted that she was close to his age and a bloody good healer. The Wolves on the Zyn`a Pack were close, and all wore the chin to sleeve tattoo denoting clans and guilds. Even with her cross bolt and bolts in her back and thigh harness.

"Aye, that is easy for you to tell gods I feel so bloody ill," He said, laying his head on the table, feeling his temperature rise and fall. Finally, he was cleaned and the wound bound firmly. The shirt he wore was thrown in the bin.

He lay on his side, watching the Cook sew up Ji`rah's leg wound firmly, then bathing it and bandage the thigh tightly.

Ji`rah lay now on his back; his boots were on the floor. And his trousers had been thrown in the bin. Ji`rah lay in his black undershorts; all Warriors wore the same black uniform shorts. His shirt also had been discarded.

"Lieutenant, we have been told that the clothing must be burnt." M`ykn, "I'm afraid your trousers must come off; the Mistress said anything with your blood on it must go."

"Well, you will have to take them off, M`ykn. I just can't move."

"I'm not surprised. You had fifty stitches put in to hold your back together; Ji'rah has sixty used sewing that thigh together. I'm not surprised at all that you can't move. Where is the sensibility in the Mhyst if you can't heal something that needs to have so many stitches is beyond me, it's nonsensical, and I am being fucking polite."

M`ykn quickly changed Taelen's clothes and redressed him along with Ji`rah. With the help of Lieutenant Dan`e.

"We will move you out of here in a moment, you're in our other staff room, and if you're ready, we found your Uncle, Lord Za`qrn."

"I won't ask where you found him." Said Taelen as a moan escaped Ji`rah's mouth. M`ykn quickly picked up a bucket and moved Ji`rah's head to it.

"Aim for the bucket, Lieutenant, not on the floor."

Ji`rah repeatedly vomited until he was entirely spent. He lay panting and shivering uncontrollably.

"Gods, I am dead…someone tell me I'm dead…." Ji`rah groaned loudly.

"Sorry to disappoint you, Ji`rah, your Pack…I am obliged by Lore to heal you." Dan`e said to him, patting him on the shoulder. "Your Uncle is on his way, and I am going to bed." He watched the long black plait swing as she stood up. "You owe me an ale remember!" Ji`rah vaguely recalled training with her. He swore it had been a long time. While he had saved her life, she had saved his arse. Taking the discipline, he groaned inwardly.

Another Kitchen staff entered and covered them both with blankets as Lord Za`qrn's voice sliced through the air. Ji`rah sensed the displeasure in his Uncle immediately and braced himself for the verbal onslaught that was coming.

He stood at the door to the Staff Room, his hands on his hips and a look that would have frozen hell itself; Ji'rah closed his eyes as his Uncle opened his mouth.

"What the hell were you two 'puppies' thinking

when you entertained the Sorcerer of bloody Death? Not to mention calling on the Sahn`Frwh inside a Coven as well. Have you lost your mind? Have you two got a brain between you, and another thing…" he said, his voice rising in anger and agitation. He stood glaring at both of them. Part of him was furious with them; the other part of him wanted to hug them.

M`ykn raised his eyebrows at the Lord of the Wolf Nation. Then at the two men he had just sewed up. Only Ji`rah noticed the Cook squaring off his rather broad shoulders.

"Nobody yells in my Kitchen, my Lord, not Cook, not Warrior and not you."

His voice was level and not threatening but persuasive in his tone as he spoke.

"I'll be moving them to the Lieutenant's double rooms in his wing. But right now, I'm going to open a jar of Meade; the recipe is also down on parchment for you to read, my Lord, something to take with you." He said with a look in his eye just as mischievous as Lord Za`qrn had the other night. Ji`rah wanted to laugh at the cunning of the Cook.

"Did you say, Mead? Well, let's not waste a moment more." With his arm around the Cooks' shoulders and a hushed voice discussing the merits of opening a jar so soon, they left, closing the door behind them. It was as if nothing had happened.

"I now know why our Uncle has never been married." Groaned Ji`rah as his leg throbbed.

"Why is that?"

"Because the man has no sympathy and is an absolute prick." Said Ji`rah. Taelen laughed aloud and whimpered as the stitches drew against the bandage. He had to agree.

Lord Za`qrn was self-centred, ostentatious and vain.

Many other descriptions came to Taelen just as the door reopened, and he saw Lieutenant M`hta with disbelief across his face.

"I'm not going to ask how you two have managed this. M`ykn has asked that you both be taken to your guest room, Lieutenant Taelen and Ji`rah. I've sent for Mistress LH`Nejah."

He winced as he glanced at the wound on Ji`rah's thigh." I forward my apologies for the ear thrashing she has threatened to deliver." M`hta stepped to one side, and as he nodded to those waiting.

"Why bother M`hta? It seems we are the whipping boys of the hour. Lord Za`qrn spun in but was persuaded by mead just as he was about to tan our arses" Ji`rah tried his humour, but his laugh sounded more like a groan as his leg twitched.

Four Sz`a`Th Warriors entered with two stretches; they were Archers from the North Wing. Taelen and Ji`rah were then carried up the flight of stairs and down long corridors to the guest room at the end of his wing.

Once in bed, and only their boots with them, they both realised they were at Lady LH`Nejah's mercy.

Lieutenant Dan`e knocked on the door, standing to attention.

Taelen lay on his side, facing Ji`rah. His back prickled and burned, and he wanted to sleep. Ji`rah lay on his back. Exhaustion had thankfully taken over, and the Lieutenant was sleeping. He had thrown off the bed cloths covering his thigh for just that amount of weight brought too much pressure on his wound.

Taelen was restless; as he heard the bells toll the early morning devotions that brought the Spellcasters to separate rooms in each wing of the Coven.

This meant his grandmother would not see them until devotion had ended in an hour.

She cleared her throat to get their attention.

Both glanced at the Warrior still in her Warrior Uniform and crossbows.

'Aye? Lieutenant enter." He had not met this Lieutenant before. Her markings – the tattoo, her eyes showing of the Wolf Nation and her eyes slightly titled to her temples told him there was Elf in her lineage. Yet the Raven tattoo on her nape of the neck ran in runes to her collar bones in the symbol told him this was one Lieutenant whose skills were like nothing anyone had seen. The tiredness in her eyes as she lowered them was telling.

A slight breeze caught a wisp of the long black hair in the traditional plait of the Southern Regions of the Sz`a`Th, which floated ethereally for a second, bringing something about her to be trusted. She let the wisp fall lightly down her cheek and left the eye. She was looking slowly, directly back to Taelen.

She stood at attention and spoke quietly, "Lieutenants, the Raven Nation has ordered me to form an allegiance with the Sz`a`Th immediately. It is paramount this gets signed, and I leave immediately for the Southern Regions that only the Nation of Ravens knows.

"Seriously, Lieutenant…were you not just down in the Kitchens stripping, bathing, healing, and redressing us?'

"Aye, Lieutenant, but my orders are under secrecy by Lore of Lord Za`qrn and others you have yet to meet. It is imperative."

Slowly and holding his breath, he moved crab-like out of bed; as cold as he was, he went to the bathroom, running the water in the shoulder bath, he gingerly eased his body sitting on the small step inside the tub, water lapped at his waist any higher on the bandage would have become wet. He knew by experience to not get the Cooks angry, his Uncle yes, his anger he could handle the Cooks, no, upset a Cook, and you did not know precisely what you were eating, he had seen too many a Warrior caught out with offal and other unsavoury meals after inadvertently upsetting the Cook.

He eased his body out of the water. His body had turned pink with his blood; he tucked a towel around his waist and began the steps that would take him to his study.

The study was still the way they had left it, and the blood was now soaked on the stone floor. With little thought, he held out his left palm, and white light blurred the room. And he thought he might be wise to keep that cleaning bit of magic to himself.

He went to his room and gingerly dressed his lower half; getting a shirt on was out of the question. White bandages had been firmly wrapped around his chest from just under his arm to his waist and over his right shoulder. He was holding his back together where the stitches were.

Now he was dressed in warm uniform trousers and socks. Taelen picked up some clothes for Ji`rah and returned to the study. He picked up the ledges he had been working on and his quill box and returned slowly to the room he shared with Ji`rah.

"Come, Lieutenant Dan`e, show me the parchment. I have only heard of you in the most secret of conversations. You live a dangerous life, Lieutenant Dan`e."

She smiled ever so slightly "So do all of you Lieutenant."

He read the parchment and signed it immediately, sliding it into the brass cylinder and sealing it with his wax stamp.

"Lieutenant, I may not arrive at my destination. If I do not, then one of the Raven Nation will contact you. If I do, then you will have saved us. We are small in numbers but have lived a secretive life...makes us, loyal spies. If the Sz`a`Th require anything, we will do so for you."

He handed the cylinder to Dan`e, who placed it securely in her Backpack..." I must leave the way I came...have a handy door to an open parapet?" she smiled slightly – "Tell Lieutenant M'hta that I will meet him one day." He watched her stretch out her arms in the black Sz`a`Th uniform, form merely into a Raven, and fly into the night sky.

"Ji`rah is not going to believe this has just happened...not sure if I understand it, but...parchments don't lie."

Ji`rah slept deeply, his leg twitching from time to time. Groans escaped Ji`rah when the leg twitched as nerves knitted and muscles mended.

Taelen sat at the desk opposite the window that was on the north wall facing the densely wooded forests of N`qwina Forrest.

The N`qwina Forrest's enormous expanse literally went from the east coast to the west coast. The towering D`roin conifers gave the impression of a sea of green-capped white with snow. Winter had arrived unseasonably early. Tree limbs were still too young for snow's weight splitting and crashing within the forest's fold.

Taelen sat at straight as he could without hurting himself. He opened the ledger from the Taayra`Ge Keep he had picked up at the last minute on his escape. The first book of the Seven sat open. He knew this book from front to back.

It pervaded memories for him, vivid memories.

Since escaping, he had not opened this book that day so long ago.

Yet, he wondered if it was the first book or a decoy ledger. The second book was for the Four Elements; he closed it and placed it beside the first book. He glanced from the two ledges beside the blood-smeared and creased notes he had taken down the previous night.

There, on the parchment, was a silver segment of the star design. The sketch in the ledger was identical to the segment design of the ceiling design and the desk design.

He took off the pendant that belonged to J`nn. Thirteen-segmented Spellcasters star. The silver filigree was in that particular segment identical. He laid the KH`irz star on the books. Taelen was looking at the Ogdoadic Star within the thirteen sections. The Knights were elusive, if not invisible. He wondered who was behind all this, and he now doubted that the books were actually ink and parchment. He chewed his nail in deep thought.

Taelen went to lean back in the chair he was sitting in, forgetting the pain in his back. The sharp twinge astounded him. He swore softly, trying to sit in the same position he had previously done with some respite.

He gingerly stood up and moved to the side of the desk. There he opened the glass window that led to a small narrow veranda. He stepped out into the icy breeze. The light sweat that misted his skin immediately cooled him with the cold snap.

Out here, his thoughts ignored the expansive view of snow-covered forests. He glanced at the fine misting rain falling across his vision.

He never heard the knock at the door. His thoughts twisted and turned around last night and the Lord of Death. Why would the Lord travel through the Veil to the world of elements and people? What was he looking for in the study Taelen used? It was not the ledgers. The man could have tripped over them had he wanted.

"Why stand in the cold, Lieutenant." The voice was Ki`arya's. He went to turn and stopped at the stitches, and skin reminded him that he bore a twelve-inch wound down the left side of his back.

"It's easier than sitting." He turned stiffly; she was still in the nightshirt that his Grandmother had dressed her in.

"Couldn't my Grandmother find you something more…?"

"Feminine? No, I am not one for that design in clothing. I'm at ease. Your nightshirt suits me fine and is similar to my own." She smiled, bowing her head slightly at his attention.

Taelen stepped back into the room and closed the weather from them with the windows.

"How are the hands?" He asked, glancing at the darkened bloodstains on them.

"I think I should ask how your back is and the Lieutenants leg." Her eyes widened as Taelen turned.

"OH!" exclaimed and went to touch where the blood had seeped over time.

"It's not as bad as it looks. It's a clean-cut." He said, motioning her to go back into the room as he moved.

"Who healed you? No Covens Healers were in the Coven last night. It was a Night of Harvests, but I think winter's dissension caused the herbs to have perished in the harsh frosts and early heavy snows."

"That explains a lot; M'ykn found us downstairs. He stitched. And Lieutenant Dan`e an excellent healer within the Wolf Nation."

"I'd like to sense the wounds to allay my own fears."

"Start on Ji`rah. He'll sleep for a while, I'd say."

He said, overseeing her; it was not that he did not trust her. If there was one person, he did believe it was Ki`arya. He was curious at the way she healed. There were no others to cast dispersions on her talents within the room. He also vaguely remembers how specialised her father's healing had been.

Ji`rah lay sleeping in twisted sheets tangled around his body.

The LZ`rqks were unusual. Their talent lay in their use of the 'third eye it was said that they could see beneath the skin and beneath the thoughts. That they travelled within the body of the one they healed.

Ki`arya sat on the side of Ji`rah's bed, Taelen pulled the desk chair over, straddling the chair and watched. He watched as she held her bandaged hands over the length of the wound. She stared blankly at the bandages; her own, he noticed, seemed to moisten as if the blood had started to flow again from her burns. He was alarmed to sense that his assumption was correct. Her eyelids closed halfway, and she had begun humming and smiling. She closed her eyes and uttered a phrase Taelen had never heard before in Sz`a`Th. Her bandaged hands had blood seeping from them.

Ji`rah woke suddenly. Not recognising her, he gripped her bandaged hands hard.

"Ji`rah NO!" cried Taelen moving sharply and crying out in pain from his back. "You bloody fool, it is Ki`arya…."

Ji`rah's eyes had glazed over as he had woken up. He had sensed he was under attack and was about to transform into the Wolf that he was. He heard Taelen and closed his eyes. His hand dropped to the bed as his breathing rested. A moment later, he opened them.

His own hands smeared in her blood from the

bandages.

"Shattas…" he said, watching the tears roll down her cheeks. "Ki`arya," he sat up without the pain he had felt and pulled her over to him.

"I'm so sorry, just so sorry."

Her tears fell, followed by pent-up sobs that cascaded from her.

"Hush, young one… I'm going to look at these fingers." She tried to pull away, but Ji`rah was stronger than her.

"Taelen, there is something not right with this." Ji`rah unravelled the bandages. He threw the sodden mess into the bin at the desk.

He swore again. There was no skin on Ki`arya's hands. It had been burned from Ki`arya's hands; their seeping bloody mess made him want to vomit.

"That's it!" he said, shaking his head. "You heal, but you heal the wrong way."

"No, you're wrong, Ji`rah. I just watched her heal your leg. If you removed the bandages, you'd find just a scar, nothing more."

"I know, but when she healed me, where were we."

"We were on the west wing ramparts. The rain was falling." Replied Ki`arya as she looked at her hands; she began the same process of healing that she had used on Ji`rah.

It was difficult for her to understand that she had to do it reversed to heal herself. Slowly, the skin recovered on her hands until the healing had finally finished after half an hour. She took a deep breath and smiled at what she had accomplished.

Ji`rah cut the bandages from his thigh; his wound had healed, swung himself out of bed and grabbed the trousers of the Death Watch that Taelen had brought to him from his own quarters.

"It seems we have found the problem. Now all that is being done is to heal the Lieutenant. That shouldn't be difficult." He pulled on the sleeves to the pale grey shirt and buttoned the shirt up.

Taelen shrugged, "Might as well try." He said gingerly, turning around so that Ki`arya could move across the bed to get to where he sat.

"I am unsure of this, Lieutenant. You, we share the same blood. I had never healed you, not even when we lived at the Keep."

"I had a paper cut once that I thought was serious, Ki."

Smiling at him, "You were eight winters old, and I think this is a tad more serious than that paper cut you complained endlessly over until I bandaged it."

Taelen swung his leg onto the other side of the chair and rested his head on the back of the chair.

"Heal in the same way you recently healed Ji`rah and the same word." Ji`rah pulled out a black blade from his boot and cut the bandages away. He just stood with the disgusting mess in his hands and placed it in the bin. Both he and Ki`arya were silent.

"Well, you two are just full of conversation."

"It's your back, Taelen; the skin is rotting."

"The visitor last night seems to have left his calling card to one of his own."

His Grandmothers voice came from the doorway. He did not bother to look at her; he sensed this had something to do with her after the comment of the Lord.

"Well, he did say to ask you about things in general," Ji`rah said, his voice low.

K`lton ran through the open door, missing his Grandmother's reaching arm and her stern voice after him.

He stopped, looked at Taelen's back, and held

Taelen's face, gently turning it to him.

His large green eyes held Taelen's, and he frowned slightly.

"I have seen this before, you have to call the Dragon, and he will heal it."

Taelen sighed and smiled at his adopted son.

"I can't call Dragons, K`lton. I don't know any." He smiled at the boy of twelve winters.

"I can watch me." The boy had opened the window and spread out his arms, hanging his head back. Ji`rah tilted his head, listening; K`lton's call was of an ancient primaeval animal; Ji'rah shivered inwardly.

"Can you hear that the boy he's calling something?" Ji`rah frowned as he listened to the silent howl of the boy.

"No, I can't hear anything, Ji`rah; you are Wolf; your hearing is more acute than mine."

"We have to stop him." His Grandmother went to get K`lton but was bared by Ji`rah.

"Not this time, Mistress, let the boy call. It may be all that is going to save your Grandson."

The wind came in squalls, blustering and loud. Then nothing. K'lton walked back into the room.

They all looked at the boy of twelve winters, who smiled at them and said to Ki`arya softly in a loud whisper.

"He said you are to heal him in the way of the elements, but…" he paused, frowning, "it must be how your father healed." He finished smiling.

"K`lton, I can't remember my father or his healing."

"I do," LH`Nejah replied with sadness in her voice. "Your father hummed a hauntingly beautiful tune, and as he did this, he called on the Mhyst and the elements all eight, but he reversed them. The tune went like this."

She began humming, and as if hypnotised, Ki'arya's

hands started drawing an invisible design over the festering mess that had blackened at the wound's edges. At times, Taelen flinched. Throughout the healing, K`lton held onto his father's shoulder, standing in front of him, his head resting on Taelen's bowed head. Ji`rah watched, amazed as white, purple and blue practicals of light fell from Ki`arya's fingertips onto the wound.

The Mhyst dissolved the rotting flesh, and new tissue appeared. She had taken over the humming and was now singing a haunting song in rune. Ki`arya then stopped and glanced at Mistress LH'Nejah. The older woman nodded as K`lton smiled and lifted his guardian's shoulders.

"I have to say thank you to the Dragon." He said in a loud whisper. He ran out onto the veranda and stood, arms outstretched, his head back. The wind returned stronger than before, and then rain poured down from the sky.

K`lton raced back inside, getting only slightly wet. His step had an exciting kick in it as he ran into the room and slid on the floor in his socks.

"I'm hungry. Can we eat breakfast now?" he said, his large green eyes dramatic.

Ji`rah touched the place on Taelen's back and was amazed that there was no scar, only new smooth skin. He handed Taelen his shirt and put on his tunic.

He rubbed his nose as Taelen dressed, both watching their Grandmother closely.

"If you knew how Ki`arya could heal, why didn't you let her know before this? Why didn't you let us all know?" His voice cut the air. "Which destiny did you sell?" Both stared at each other. The room's atmosphere had suddenly become very volatile.

Taelen watched as the hair stood on Ji`rah's head, forming a column. He had never seen this happen when

Ji`rah was in his human form.

"K`lton go down to the kitchen and sees what Cook is doing for breakfast. It should be pancakes and sweet spiced buns this morning."

Ki`arya had also seen the welling anger in the Sqh`xn Warrior she had come to like. K`lton looked at his father, who nodded for him to go. His footsteps ran down the corridor and jumped down the staircase to the Kitchen, two steps simultaneously. K`lton had to find Lord Za`qrn.

"Ji`rah, we can discuss this." His Grandmother said.

"To hell… we can." He snarled at her. "You… you let Ki`arya here suffer burns so horrible that there was no skin on those hands, nothing but pulp. A weeping bloody, messy pulps, who the hell! Do you think you are playing with your granddaughter's feelings? Which one of us have you sacrificed to him?" He growled low. "I am not your Grandson, not now, not ever do you understand me." He immediately folded down on himself and transformed into the black timber Wolf.

Lord Za`qrn stood at the door. He growled low and guttural at his nephew.

Ji`rah backed towards the veranda and ran, taking a flying leap over and landing down on all fours. He looked back at Taelen and Ki`arya and ran into the woods.

Taelen's Mhyst rose in him as he glared at his Grandmother.

"You, Mistress, have some explaining." The Mhyst rose again, and he raised his hand at her this time. The particles were similar to snow, but white, silver and blue hovered at his fingertips.

"Dismiss the Mhyst, Lieutenant." His Uncle said decisively. "I am ordering you, Warrior, to release the Mhyst you have called." Taelen's blue eyes seemed to shade over as his anger rose.

“Lieutenant Taelen Yassarn, I am ordering you to release your Mhyst now, or you will disobey a direct order and suffer the consequences. Stand Down Lieutenant” Lord Za`qrn watched as his nephew slowly defused his anger rising as a strong tide that would have killed them all if unleashed.

Taelen stood staring at his hands. He turned and picked up the ledgers and the silver necklace with the star of the Spellcasters J`nn. He looked at Ki`arya and realised how deeply Ji`rah’s feelings for her actually were.

“I will be in my Study, and I still will talk with you, Mistress.” His blue eyes glared at his Grandmother as he said coldly. “With my leave, Mistress Ki`arya, Lord Za`qrn,” Taelen nodded to them.

His footsteps were angry hard strides, and the door slammed to his study.

Lord Za`qrn took a deep breath. Then spoke to Mistress LH’Nejah.

“It is time you told them the extent of your dealing with Lord Ru`lun and that nasty piece called Lord Nul`YK. If you don’t, I suggest we just bury ourselves now to save Mah`sden the trouble of slitting our throats. I leave in twelve hours, Mistress, be warned, I will not leave unless you tell those two ‘puppies’ what you have done.”

“And if I choose not to.” She said curtly to him

He moved closer to her; his hand rested on her throat.” Then, Mistress, it will be I who slits this throat of yours.” He smiled sweetly. Then looked at Ki`arya and said.

“Ah, my lovely, sweet Ki`arya, nice to have you in the family. Remind me to talk to those two puppies once you are well.” He bowed dramatically and strode out of the room.

# CHAPTER 17

Lord Za`qrn knocked on the door; he could see his nephew's head bowed as he studied the ledgers on the desk. The quill in the young man's hand was placed in the crystal quill holder. Blue eyes glinted with the hint of purple that Lord Za`qrn had always puzzled over.

"May I?"

Taelen nodded his head for him to enter, closed the two ledgers, and slipped the necklace with the Spellcasters star into a narrow drawer to his left.

Lord Za`qrn noted the small movement and moved to the large window glancing outside at the snow now falling heavier.

"You leave soon, don't you?" asked Taelen, leaning back into the leather chair, creaking with his weight shift. Taelen watched the fire with its slow dance of death should he let it go out.

"Aye, I do. I'd like to take Ki`arya and some of the staff with me."

"M`ykn?" Taelen asked, glancing back at his Uncle.

"Ah, the Meade was exceptional, if not a touch young. But yes, I have asked him, of course."

"Of course," said Taelen, quietly rubbing his stubble, "why the staff and those two in particular?"

"The Coven is not safe, Taelen; there are cracks within the magic. These wards that weave like fabric are worn here. Lord Nul`YK does not make house calls. My dear 'puppy' he knows you now. Yes, you are Sahn`Frwh, and you sometimes provide him with those who travel his path within the 'shade' He knows more about you than you realise." He shrugged. "Besides, I lost too many Staff last time Mah`sden sent his men in."

“That is a lousy reason, Uncle, and you know it. What has happened to you to end your winter stay here? You hate travelling in snow, either as Wolf or a human. As much as it would be a blessing, this mantle is so heavy I carry.”

“The reason is your Grandmother. I have discussed her forthcoming discussion with you.” His eyes narrowed. “If the bloody ‘bitch’ lies.” dark eyes glazed slightly. “I will know, and I have told her I will slit her damn throat.” He smiled his full teeth smile. “Really, it is that simple. And the mantle, as you call it, is not fair. I acknowledge that”

“Have you asked Ki`arya? There are things to consider with her.”

“Really… I have noticed the missing leg Taelen. Yes, I have asked her. I need Ji`rah to return to help her feel comfortable with the notion. I think the girl assumes I live in some den in the ground. I am not that primitive, you know.”

Taelen suppressed a grin and bit his lip. “She is your niece; remember that, Uncle.”

Lord Za`qrn frowned at the comment as if thinking of something else.

“Yes, yes, of course, she’s family. One thing else, Taelen speaking of family, K`lton should not be left with her, your Grandmother, that is. He is with you or me, though I know whom he will choose. However, we are in dangerous times, and I would prefer the ‘pup’ with me. Can you see my point?”

Taelen knew Lord Za'qrn's intuition was acute, sometimes too sharp.

“I will tell my Ward he is to go with you; I will heed your unspoken warnings, Uncle.”

“Good, do not let your Grandmother know of this. Do you understand me when I say she has already compromised lives? See if you can get that hot head of my nephew back here to talk to Ki`arya."

He turned to leave. He narrowed his eyes at the young man before he was his blood, but he did not envy his nephew. The mantle of Dominion Lord was a burden that may end up crushing the young man.

"Taelen, the Mhyst will serve you, just use it for positive and not negative."

Taelen watched his Uncle leave without flourish or dramatics. The Lord's shoulders had sagged from the stress and weight of the family. His eyes scanned the particles of dust floating within a beam of pale morning light from the window. The dust particles drifted separately, never colliding with their dance partner of the atmosphere he breathed in like air.

His thoughts drifted to the Mhyst, and he wondered could the Mhyst travel separately contained by his own will. He had only ever seen it as a sphere. He smiled to himself and stood stretching. Sometimes the simplest things are just at the end of our perception. If he could separate his Mhyst particles, he could win his next conflict with his Lord Mah`sden.

The crack of wooden starves on others echoed in the early morning as Warriors drilled and honed a skill that would help keep them alive. Grunts and groans came partnered with the crack of the staves.

Amongst this came, the early morning peel of a bell hung a the highest point within the centre tower that stood as a silent pinnacle above the intersection of the four wings.

He heard the voices raised in a chant as Spellcasters paid homage to the deity they were asked to assist them this morning. Blue eyes opened as the familiar singing called the Spellcasters within him. He dressed quickly, hoping down the corridor, pulled his other boot on, and then fell into a run.

As he passed the kitchen, he detoured, grabbing a sweet bun and a cup of the bitter black coffee that any hotter would have burnt his tongue. He stood drinking down the bitter black coffee, felt his senses awaken as he ran back up the stairs, and took the next door on the left that led to a corridor with only a set of large oak doors with the pentagram design of the Spellcasters star carved into the wood.

He stopped inhaling the heady scent of incense as it wafted from under the door.

Breathing in the moment and the insense, he immediately felt a calm repose and entered the Chamber of Tongues.

The woman cleared her throat as she glanced from her ledger of chants with a query upon her features. She was in her fortieth winter. Spartan flecks of grey hinted that her hair would take its time in turning grey.

"Lieutenant…." Smiling only slightly as she looked at him quietly.

She said quietly. "It is prompt of you to attend the meditation, but you only half-dressed, Lieutenant." She said, trying not to smile as she raised her eyebrows with a silent question to the young Warrior.

Taelen looked from the woman to himself, checking his clothes. Of course, she was right, boots, trousers but no shirt, and he felt slightly embarrassed at his hasty dressing.

She inclined her head to the repository, which he sheepishly walked to, found a meditation shirt for Spellcasters, and returned, kneeling within the runic design of the pentacle on the floor.

The others that had responded to the meditation call surprised even him. Lieutenant M`hta was a Sz`a`Th and Sahn`Frwh; his mantle now includes confidant. Delph, the Sergeant at Arms, seemed as calm as the warm breath of breeze that came in the early weeks of summer.

The Coven's others were Corporal Den`ah and the Knights of the Death Watch Lieutenant Jarek and Kehan. Kehan nodded to him. Sergeant Kehan's blue eyes, like cornflowers set in his people's dark skin, were always startling. There were also the Spellcasters, Chian and Czhrn. He had presided over them the night of J`nn's attack by Brae.

An absent thought of J`nn, her features rippled through his mind and made him feel remorseful. She haunted his dreams and needs, needs that now had surfaced, needs he wondered if he would ever fore fill. Taelen closed his eyes, locking her away beneath his psyche.

The Spellcasters began with the sophomoric chanting. No power that Taelen knew was stronger except for the power of the Mhyst.

His lips began moving and the sound of his voice resonating through the star bell-shaped cathedral ceiling was powerful as he sang words that carried ancient melodies and part of his Lore.

The lore pulled every corner of his mind apart and then reassembled it to the point of perfect equilibrium. Darkness invaded slowly like rising water until neither light nor shade was within his mind. Then the voices stilled in one long note.

The flames that stayed eternally lit glowed green and blue and grew in their length within the pentacle star carved into the floor.

Then the voices fell silent.

Taelen lifted his eyes as the chant echoed within his mind. He stared at the dark grey rectangular banners that hung the length of the twelve-foot walls and moved slightly with the movement of the eternal flame. Their silver thread embossed the material with the symbol of the Pentacle star of the Spellcasters' belief, incorporating the region they lived.

Taelen stayed in his kneeled position within one of the pentacle points.

Distantly he heard the others leave, and their footsteps move across the stone floor seemed to him so far away. Within the points of the pentacle carved into the floor, the grooves were filled with silver ore. Taelen sensed all those who had come for the morning meditation had left. The carved doors closed in a whisper of air that flowed under the doors. He was alone within the Chamber of Tongues.

A flame in the centre of the Pentacle burned to blue, silver, and white. The silver inlay pentacle upon the floor shone, the angles of symmetry became startlingly clear to him at once, and the silver ore reflected upwards onto the walls and then the dome ceiling.

Taelen moved as if walking through his body that had breathed and eaten earlier and would bleed if cut by a blade. He turned to see himself kneeling; he knew he had moved to the spiritual plane where Spellcasters and Mhyst would extend themselves for healing.

His senses told him he was searching, but for what he thought. 'I am searching for myself; my knowledge lies in the book and words that flow from the black ink and quill of a Scribe.'

The air shimmered as it shifted as if sighing, but there was no physical movement.

Taelen moved to each point of the pentacle. His thoughts flowed and ebbed as an ocean tide. The Eight Books of the Mhyst floated before him upon the plain.

Taelen's thoughts fell to the centre of the Pentacle. He knew one person would sense this invasion into the Spellcasters pentacle.

Taelen no longer stood in his aura but within his body in the pentacle.

"So the bastard is alive." His Uncles demonic voice hissed as a black swirl of Mhyst appeared outside the pentacle. Taelen felt the hair that grew fine and down his back rise. No longer was the Mhyst, as he knew it. The Mhyst shade appeared; its odour of decay and death permeated his senses. It took all his willpower not to vomit. He repeatedly swallowed as his saliva glands worked, his breathing came fast, and his palms sweated as the bile whirlpool down in his stomach fought to rise up, his eyes pained as his head swam dizzily.

Taelen's Mhyst birthmark throbbed painfully as he stared at what had been Mhyst lore. The 'Third Reasoning' was now a reality. Taelen mentally warned the Coven.

"Very good…bastard, magnificent. Warn those Warriors; no one can enter the Chamber of Tongues now. There is none as strong as I alive, or are you the exception?"

Tilting his head slightly, Taelen watched the man he once called Father, now a sinister replica of poison. Lord Mah`sden's eyes, which had once been similar to his brothers' colour and Taelen's were now such a dark blue, seemed more black and watched him with no profundity, for he was his prey.

"Lost your speech, Bastard?" he began to move closer to Taelen. Taelen felt the fear rise within him. His heart leapt, pounding at his throat, as he pushed it back down. Lord Mah`sden stopped metres from him.

"Do I kill you, like I did that whore of a mother you had, or should I kill you like I did your father."

Taelen felt the Mhyst rising in him slowly. His eyes did not leave his Uncle's for even a moment.

"You think you are that good? Your ego has once

again tripped your vanity, dear Uncle. It seems you prefer easy kills to ones that make you break out into a bit of a sweat." His Mhyst rose higher, and he knew the birthmark now glowed white. "Or you could simply hand over the Seventh Book of Loss, and it shall be your loss."

His Uncle smiled as if it caused him great effort and pain as his dark eyes narrowed in thought.

"You mean 'Gain,' don't you Bastard." A red whip of energy cracked the air slicing Taelen across the left cheek; he felt the tingling of nerves and pain, then the warmth of his own blood trickled down his cheek, and red spots appeared on the shirt he wore.

"So should I slice you open like I did your Lieutenant?" He smiled slightly at the gruesome thought. "Foolish he was to think he could harm me."

Taelen raised his hands, flicking the black blades he had swiftly removed from their guards.

"Butter knives," laughed his Uncle, but even Taelen was surprised as he felt the Mhyst course through his fingertips and onto the blades. He cut the air with them, opening the flesh on Lord Mah'sden's cheek.

"There, Uncle, now we share the same look." His eyes widened as the blades then held themselves against his Uncles heart. "Now shall we be reasonable and hand me the Seventh Book of Loss."

"I see that you still can't listen to me" another arch of insidious red energy sliced into Taelen's thigh as intense hammering on the door began.

The air cracked and boomed as blow upon blow pounded from Uncle to Nephew.

Taelen's wound to the thigh was poisoned, and Mah`sden knew this with every blow he unleashed with the black Mhyst. Each contact meant the poison flowed deeper and deeper.

"You are a fool boy to think you could …." His words ended as Taelen let out a cry. Lord Mah`sden looked startled, if only for a moment, as he stood outside the pentacle.

"I call on First Lady LH'Nejah, Spellcaster of the thirteenth level…G`rnah… save me." He collapsed to the floor slowly, his head smacking the tiles splitting open an old scar on his eyebrow. Blood dripped into the silver ore, igniting a blue flame. The heavy large oak doors slowly opened, and the diminutive figure of the woman he had summoned strolled in.

She was dressed in a grey gown, silver embroidery surrounded the hemline in runes, her long black hair with the silver at her temples was loose and flowed around her as the air crackled in her atmosphere, but it was her eyes. They were blazing green and blue ethereal light.

Lord Mah`sden stepped back very slightly.

"I have little time for you, Mah`sden." She said as she kept him in her vision and noted where Taelen lay within the pentacle.

"Then witch," he said, "watch your grandson die." Black and red energy tentacles snaked to where Taelen lay in the blood from his thigh.

Instead, Lady LH`Nejah's magic blazed across the floor in purple flames separating Lord Mah'sden's magic from Taelen. Sparks ignited as the magic of the two individuals collided in a maelstrom of hate, anger, and deceit.

"So my mother–in–law, the whore arrives to save another bastard." Snarled Lord Mah`sden, his spittle hitting the floor hissing as it emitted a foul odour. The black smoke lingered in small lazy wisps.

"Beware the Chamber of Tongue's; the flaccid will never become strong here, my Lord."

Taelen looked across at his Grandmother between the shield of her magic of white and purple flames. He caught the look in her eye as she taunted her daughter's murderer with words and innuendos that he could only guess the truths behind their meanings.

"There is only one man in this room, and he lies wounded, but your wound is more evident to that privy with you." Her eyes darkened, and Taelen intuitively flattened himself down onto the floor.

Pure and tainted magic scorched a foot off the floor in all directions. The wave of iced air froze and ignited all things around him.

The explosion was deafening as both unleashed their magic simultaneously. The wall hangings only moments before Taelen had been admiring were now wall torches flaming high and higher, the flames licking at the ceiling pentacle dome of colour.

"You are so wrong, for it will be you who dies at my hands Lord Mah`sden, not my grandson's hands – but there is a long line up of those who would rather see your bones become brittle and dusty." Her hands swirled secretively; Taelen watched as she silently called upon the Earth Elementals and the power of the Shadows. Mistress LH`Nejah's hands were scrolling runes of containment in an invisible spell in a curse for the man before her.

"You are old and foolish; you have already broken Lore that has bound you to his Lore."

Lord Mah`sden rose to strike Taelen's form again when Mistress LH`Nejah's magic blazed across the floor and onto the Lord. Purple energy surged and dove deep within the man. The power crack blew the doors off their hinges and scorched the walls opposite outside in the stairwell.

The silence that followed was broken by Warrior's

boots clambering the stairwell; they had to climb over the splinted oak wood smouldering in their path.

The gasp of a child's anguish broke the older woman's composure.

"G`rnah!" cried K`lton. Then more softly, as he sat with Taelen's head in his lap, he rocked back and forth, tears flooding down his cheeks onto the stone floor beneath him.

"He should have called the 'Dragon'. He should have called the 'Dragon'." He said softly as he sobbed, burying his head into Taelen's neck.

LH`Nejah tried to console him; he pulled away sobbing frantically, dragging Taelen's inert body towards the centre of the pentacle when the pentacle shone green.

"Who calls… for help from the Nation of Drargon`H?" the voice, deep and rich with the accent brogue of the Drargon`H people, halted the boys' sobs.

A commanding voice that brought silence to those hovering near the boy, they stood silently waiting, and their hands-on blades where fingers twitched in brittle-edged anticipation of battle, and blood pulsed loudly in their ears.

The man stood within the green light of the Spellcasters Star. This man's appearance startled the Warriors. They now changed into a defensive stance, crouched low, and waited with blades drawn.

K'lton's eyes slowly studied the black boots that the man wore. Trousers of the darkest green, precisely tucked into the top of the boots below the knee, resembling the exact green of K`lton's eyes.

K`lton's eyes rested then on the insignia on the blade's pommel; its steel was the same dark green as the cloth of the trousers. He wore a simple white shirt with the same insignia on the left breast pocket.

The lad had stopped sobbing, eyes the same green colour as his own. He oversaw him.

Though his skin was darker than that of K`lton, some felt a connection between the boy and the Warrior before them. K`lton spoke slowly. Taelen was more than his Guardian, old enough to be an older brother, but he felt like a father.

"I…I…called for help, my Lord." He said warily. "My …" his eyes darted to Mistress LH`Nejah, who nodded at him to go on. "My father is dying, and I know only the 'Dragon Fire' can heal him."

He stared at the man before him, who would have been twenty winters older than Taelen.

"My Lady," Mistress LH`Nejah nodded at the recognition; his right hand moved to sit on the blade's pommel. No one moved. Everyone held their breath, and then he acknowledged LH`Nejah in a low bow down on his right knee, offering his sword to K`lton.

"Hold this young Warrior," he said, giving K`lton the magnificent blade. The man noted its weight-balanced comfortable in the boy's grip and. "Seems the blade is made for you, young Warrior." He smiled and nodded at K`lton.

Without standing from the bow, he now knelt at Taelen's side.

"May I?" he asked K`lton as he looked at Taelen's' wound without touching him.

"Aye, please." Said K`lton watching the dark-haired stranger's every move.

As he bent over and tore the trouser leg of Taelen's clothes, it was M`hta who saw the shadow of the tattoo of the Drargon`H Nation on the dark skin under the short dark hair of this Warrior of at least fifty winters.

"So this man you call father, does he have a name or a title that I might try and pull him out of the fog his mind is in?"

"He does, my Lord, but we do not know of you, understand we are wary of what may occur." M`hta stood now, his Sahn`Frwh sword beside him as he spoke levelly at the Lord before him, "We mean no insult to you."

An air of uneasiness seemed to invade the room they all stood in.

Without looking up at Lieutenant M`hta, the man glanced at K`lton and said.

"Place the blade's flat on the wound, my 'little dragon' and see the ancient fires of Drargon`H heal this man you call father."

He stood stroking K`lton's head of black hair and glanced at the Warrior that was M`hta.

"Lieutenant?" he said, raising his eyebrows, wrinkling his forehead, and exhaling slowly. "I am Lord Mi`an, a Knight of the First Fire of the Dragons. I am also Lord of Drargon`H."

An immediate response of sheathed blades and boots coming to attention came in one action, thumps to the chest as all saluted in the Sz`a`Th tradition.

"My Lord." Replied M`hta and bowed in the Sz`a`Th fashion. He stood and glanced sideways at Teh`c. Mistress LH'Nejah lifted the awkwardness when she spoke as if saying' another mess'.

"So this is what you look like now, not the pest that would place my braids in inkwells." Her eyes were filled with gratitude to the Drargon`H Lord.

His laughter was extended and brought instant relief to all those near.

"And you, my Lady, are still the centre of trouble, it seems." His eyes held warmth and relief as well. He glanced down at K`lton to see green flames dancing along the blade and along Taelen's skin.

"What is the Warrior's name?" he asked as he removed the blade from Taelen's thigh and resheathed it.

"His name is Taelen, my Lord," replied M`hta as he glanced from him to K`lton.

Lord Mi`an knelt, touched Taelen on the shoulder, and spoke his name softly.

Nobody was prepared for the cry from Taelen or the black ooze that he vomited; as the spittle touched the floor, it hissed, smoking.

Lord Mi`a held Taelen as he vomited till he could vomit no more.

"He needs to be chilled and quickly" he glanced swiftly at the Mistress and added, "This is Nul`YK black sorcery, my Lady; you had better do some fast-talking or lose one Lieutenant in four hours. I pray I am not wrong. Do you know of others working with Nul`YK?"

K`lton, hearing this screamed at the Lord of Drargon`H, "The Dragon Fire is supposed to heal, not kill", he sobbed, gulping lungful air.

The Lord looked down at K`lton, pointing at the boy with his dark finger.

"Dragons don't cry."

K`lton's eyes glared at him intensely. M'hta went and placed his hand on K`lton's shoulder. He felt the energy surging through the boy, but the boy shuddered and buried his head into M`hta's waist with no outlet to escape.

"The Lieutenant is my father; these Warriors and Mistress LH'Nejah are my family. You are not one to tell me what I can and can't do; who are you anyway?"

M`hta looked alarmed as he saw the eyes of the Lord go icy green.

"I take my leave, my Lord." He swiftly picked up K`lton, who sobbed into his shoulder; M'hta glared at Teh`c to follow him.

Outside the wall and within the thick stymies of the wing that was Taelen's room, all discussed and knew that Taelen would be brought there sooner than later.

M`hta moved around the study, packing ledgers, scrolls, quills and ink. He, in fact, packed all that was on Taelen's desk and the work he had begun since his arrival at the Coven. Teh`c noted an urgency about him but waited till M`hta had finished.

"Are you going to explain?" he asked when the urgent knocking interrupted his flow of words, and the door opened; Lord Za`qrn and four of his Warriors came in and left with the packed items.

"Time to go ', little dragon'" he said softly. K`lton looked up at his new Uncle; his hand slid into that of the Wolf Lord, and a small shudder from his sobbing shook his lip.

"And Taelen?" he asked, his large green eyes tired and worn from crying, looking up at Lord Za`qrn.

"The two Lieutenants here will bring him along shortly." He glanced back at M`hta as he grabbed M`hta's arm as Lord Za`qrn stopped at the door.

"You have your orders Lieutenant M`hta; times are critical. Be swift. We leave now while the wind blows easterly. Lieutenant, be swift. The snow comes early, which is not a good sign. May the gods protect us all?" He left with no dramatics but with a seriousness that made Teh`c swing M`hta around swiftly.

"Alright, what the hell is going on, M`hta, and don't just don't give me some long-winded waffle that is just elusive jargon…I am in no mood for Shattas?" His eyes drilled into the Warrior, who said nothing. "The Covens empty; there are so many damn wards and spells activated. I now know how it is to feel trapped."

"We are not trapped; only two ways are left open."

"OH, I think you've missed a few, like the

Drargon`H Lord just appeared through, not to mention the one that Mah`sden decided to visit though this place is like a sieve." His eyes narrowed. "What is going on." His voice was low and intense. "And where is Lord Za`qrn taking K`lton?"

M`hta looked sharply at his arm, held firmly by Teh`c. His strength was now sending pins and needles down his arm and hand.

"I would release me, Lieutenant; firstly, the orders are Taelen's, and secondly, that Warrior appeared. The Drargon`H Lord is K`lton's father. I will not go into the details about that now. Thirdly if both K`lton and Taelen are to stay alive, they must leave separately. K`lton at least has left." He sighed and rubbed his neck, trying to relieve the building tension.

Teh`c let go of the other Warriors' arm. He looked around the room; now bare of at least three winter's work of Taelen's deciphering of ledgers was gone to gods only knew where.

Mistress LH`Nejah came into the room as both Teh`c and M`hta turned to acknowledge her. She sat in the leather chair her grandson had sat in earlier in the day. An immense ebbing sadness seemed close to overwhelming her like an incoming tide, but somewhere she found strength and spoke to them both.

"Where is Lord Mi`an, Mistress?" asked M`hta, his eyes looking past her to the open door and emptiness of the corridor.

"The Lord has, on my request, left the Coven. He won't be returning." She said with difficulty that Teh`c thought strange but left his questions silent.

Looking at them both, she handed them a parchment each. Each parchment was sealed with the green wax of the Sz`a`Th and with Taelen's runic scroll.

"What is written within the parchments will vanish

when you have finished reading the words. I would read carefully when it is time; you will leave the way that has been opened for you."

Their hands did not tremble as they read the words of Taelen's flowing script. Their orders were simple and complete.

The Death Watch was their goal.

The parchments vanished, leaving them with empty hands and heaviness in their hearts.

"Mistress, what of you, can you not come with us?" asked Teh`c; she smiled sadly at him and raised her eyebrows in a thought of whimsy that flitted like a butterfly in the last moments of life.

"Oh dear boy, I would love to leave with both of you, but sadly my destiny was paid for in due. I must pay now for what little gain I have been offered. Be thankful for the small mercies in your lives, for you will never know what has been given before to save you from such grief and death."

She began to waver and fade, her own essence was being pulled to another place beyond the Veil of Spellcasters, and she had no resistance to them.

"Where are you going?" demanded Teh`c, strained by the sight of a fading Spellcaster he had come to like.

"I owe someone a life, Lieutenant. More than that, I owe the Dragon Lord a lifetime of thanks." Before either of them could decide how to stop her, she was gone leaving only the segmented star of silver on the desk before them. Teh`c picked up the silver pentacle and slid it into his pocket for the moment.

He looked around the room he had walked into many times over the last three winters, but Teh`c knew he would be back when his intuition would not let him know. He looked at M`hta, who seemed to have more onerous burdens than just what their orders were.

"I need to check something down in the archival vault," M`hta said, his mind sourcing ledgers of documents. Absently he glanced at Teh`c. "It would be wise if you came with me." He said, and they silently walked, lost in the void of thoughts.

The two flights of stone steps that led to the back entrance of the dungeons were steep, but the archival vault had been moved at the end of these steps. They were as empty as the rest of the Coven. It would be busy with students chasing knowledge for spells and lore on other days, but not now.

"So!" M`hta said as they stood centre where row upon row of leather-bound books stood silently on the shelves. Hundreds of maps lay sealed in airtight cylinders that showed the exact cartographies of each region.

"So what?" Teh`c said, glancing at the ledgers and maps. Desks and lamps sat neatly with ink bottles capped and quills with cloths unspotted by the ink lying systematically. Too neatly.

"We are in this together, Lieutenant, so I think we should place our prejudices somewhere for the moment."

M`hta referred to their homeland's hostility emanating from decades of war between their two regions and enslavement of M`hta's home by Teh`c's people.

He removed his tunic and left it wedged in the bars of what was now a library and not a cell. He pulled out the gold black fine-rimmed glasses he wore for reading and scribing. Cleaning the lenses, he sighed and slid them onto the bridge of his nose. Teh`c watched him, noting the subtle slide from Warrior to Scribe as if M`hta had just changed shirts.

"I agree with you, M`hta." He said, looking at the young man and his region that his land had been educated to hate.

“Come, we are both here to seek an answer.”

“Why?” Teh`c asked as he shoved his hands into his trouser pockets; books made him feel awkward; he was a Warrior, not a Scribe.

M`hta pulled a large ledger out by its spine, stiff and rigid. The young man’s fingers slid gently between the pages and lightly touched different information in the scrolling text he was quickly reading.

Then he moved to the pigeonholes where cylinder upon cylinder lay with different text at each end denoting the rolled encased region.

“Because…” He removed the wax seal and extracted the roll of parchment that was within the brass cylinder. Unrolling the large parchment, he searched the map coordinates listed and laid it on the closest desk weighing the corners down as they curled with the ledger and paperweights that were in boxes under the tables.

Both pulled up the stools and leaned on the worn pine table. M`hta opened the leather cover of the ledger; creaking leather and aged parchment hit M`hta.

Sneezing repeatedly, he pulled a handkerchief blowing his nose, his eyes watered, and he sniffed congested.

Teh`c frowned as M`hta then began coughing, and after moments of irritation, the allergic reaction subsided.

“Does this always give you so much pleasure? Teh`c asked, smiling as M`hta sniffed and blew his nose again. His eyes had become bloodshot and watered more.

“Sometimes, Teh`c, your questions are wisely left unanswered as this one shall be.” He turned the pages as he read page after page. Teh`c sat watching him; part of him envied such skills as this.

"Are you actually reading each word?" M`hta's green-gold and brown eyes looked up and over the rim of his glasses at the Warrior next to him.

"Teh`c, I was a Historical Scribe. I read in summaries." He said curtly, not wishing to elaborate.

Teh`c whispered, "How can you summarise without reading it first?"

"I have been reading this way since I was 'apprenticed' at five winters. I did this for thirteen hours a day for twelve winters. I think I know how to speed read." His voice was firm and with an edge that Teh`c did not fully understand why.

Teh`c shrugged off the rebuff and looked at the map. M`hta turned another page and started tapping the page excitedly.

"This is it!"

Teh`c looked up from the map he had begun to study. "What is it?"

"Why Taelen was placed in the snow to chill his body."

"It's not unusual; we do it in my homeland if we can. Encasing an injured person in the snow aids in some healing. As it slows down the body's functions and poison that has entered the body."

"Um… I choose to differ with you on that one, Lieutenant, and I was of the same thought initially. But not know." He spun the ledger around to show a very detailed drawing of the blood system. Teh`c frowned.

"This is the body with bone and muscle."

"Yes…yes, yes…but here." Pointing to the words scribed under the illustration. "Read this."

Teh`c smiled. "M`hta it is in Karanja script. I read Mhyst, rune and Ry`qzen script. I can't read this."

"Oh…" said M`hta, genuinely sorry. "I wasn't…I didn't mean…."

Teh`c patted him on the shoulder. "I know… now you tell me what it says."

"What Lord Mi`a said was true…."

"Well, that's a relief," replied Teh`c, but M`hta shook his head.

"No… Yes, it eases the pain, but if the spell is dark, which we can presume correctly that it was, it increases the poison."

"WHAT!" Teh`c voice was low, and the harsh whisper burned his throat.

"Taelen needs the opposite healing. They weren't to know; this is just a trap to kill Taelen."

"Thermal springs."

"I beg your pardon," frowned M`hta, still flicking through the pages and reading.

"Thermal springs," repeated Teh`c ", go get Taelen, and I'll meet you behind the Kitchen in the main bathrooms. Bring the four Warriors that were assigned to them and a perfect gag. We'll need it."

He took the ledger and the map and put them back.

"Ten minutes no longer." He said as M`hta left the room.

Teh`c looked at the other maps and realised he had no time and not the resources to take what he needed with him. Besides, such information in the charts would get his throat slit, which he was not keen on. He left as quickly as M`hta had and went to the large bathrooms the Warriors used.

No one saw Taelen removed from the packed snow; the night's dark shroud hid them well. They met as planned within the bathing room; their footsteps and movements accentuated by the acoustics there made them edgy.

Teh`c and M`hta stood aside as bewildered and curious the other four Warriors carried their quarry to a blank wall that held the design of the pentacle at chest height. Teh`c slid his hand into his trouser pocket. He held out the silver pentacle star of the Mistress LH'Nejah. While keeping Taelen alive was one thing escaping the Garrison and Coven was first of their orders. Keeping together was going to be impossible, and Teh`c knew this, for as soon as they hit the freshwater river below in the caverns, the current would take them to the coast and the ocean beyond, where the tidal rips were deadly. Orders were orders, but Teh`c wondered actually who or who ordered this; they could have quite easily gone with Lord Za`qrn. He shook his head to himself.

He looked at M`hta, who nodded. Teh`c's dark olive fingertips held the pentacle star and gently placed it into the carved edifice in the stone wall.

They held their breaths as moments dragged then a click sounded. Stone on stone slid noisily across each other as a door opened. Beyond lay nothing but pitch; winding down below were stone steps that only one had been privy to.

"In quickly, this has gone too easily for me." Urged Teh`c as he led the way in removing the silver pentacle before the last entered. He held the star.

"For all the god Mistress LH`Nejah, now is the time to guide, do not abandon us. We have Taelen with us."

"I hope she hears you," M`hta said with a note of sarcasm. In the darkness, all that could be heard was their breathing.

The pentacle shone pooling light around them. Below them immediately laid stone steps.

"Steps, be careful, run double time."

"I'll kill myself," said M`hta, who did not have a head for heights, especially in this darkness that clung to him like a frightened child.

"That is not an option," Commanded Teh`c, "Go, you take the pentacle; its light will guide you."

They could see the steps, cobwebs, and a chasm of darkness that made M`hta's heart leap.

"Just look at the steps and run. The others will do it two abreast with Taelen between them."

He looked over his shoulder. "Aye, and they're as sure-footed as mountain goats. You chose them for a reason."

"Go for the gods before discovery is upon us. Scribe!" he shoved M`hta down the steps with such force that the Knight was running; it took all his agility to master running down the steps and to forget the dark void beside him.

He also heard the running feet of the Teh`c behind him. M`hta glanced up from where his eyes were on the steps below him. Horrified as nothing but darkness came only meters away, he slowed warily, causing them all to bunch up dangerously behind him.

"JUMP M`HTA!" yelled Teh`c in his ear.

"Like hell, I will… are you a …" he never finished as Teh`c tackled him heavily. Both plummeted into the darkness. He heard Teh`c's words enter his mind.

"Don't even think of yelling if you want to live."

As it rushed past them, M'hta's heart was racing, his thoughts confused in the jump.

"Hold your breath, Scribe." More words entered his mind.

"NOW"

The impact of the warm water plunged his senses into a panic, raw and primaeval. M`hta felt the scream scorch in his ears. He felt Teh`c's arm push him up and up, his ribs screamed from Teh`c own grip, and his lungs felt any moment to explode when cold air cloaked his face as they both exploded to the surface.

Gasping and coughing, he felt Teh`c push him again through the slippery silkiness of the cold ocean's touch.

"I would swim, Scribe!" He said into M`hta's mind.

M`hta felt his exhaustion. He also sensed they were not at the end of whatever Teh`c had planned. Both were excellent swimmers, as were the others with them. Their training was extensive and lifesaving, sometimes to the extreme, as Warriors. Teh`c was the strongest of them all.

M`hta felt the sandy bottom with his boots as Teh`c pulled him by his arm; both gasped and wheezed. Teh`c fell on his back down onto the small beach, just concentrating on bringing life-giving air into his lungs that burned was more important than where they were. Somewhere distant, lightly pierced a portal into the darkness.

"Was that… all… necessary?" M`hta asked, gasping in the air as the pounding of his pulses within him slowly returned to normal.

Teh`c opened his eyes and pulled himself into a sitting position, his face masked in the darkness. Only his silhouette against the indirect light was visible to M`hta.

"Yes," he said, then looked towards the light as air burned fresh and cold into his lungs. "It has… all been… necessary."

"It…?"" M`hta asked.

M`hta was pulled to his feet abruptly; pain stabbed hotly in his shoulder region. Shaking off Teh`c hand, he asked, "Are you going to explain?"

"Back in the water, we have a long way to go." He said, ignoring the Scribes question

"Either you explain… Lieutenant or…"

"Or… what M`hta… You will climb back up those steps in the darkness without any knowledge of the footholds and then find the door. That's providing the door is still there."

M`hta looked up at what little rock he could see from the distant light.

He knew he had no choice, no choice at all. It seemed their orders, and the parchments had been different. He removed his tunic and shirt, tying it with great difficulty around his waist, following Teh`c's lead. Teh`c looked at M`hta with an apologetic repose.

"I will explain, but not here and not now, M`hta. I have my orders." He said, pulling the sleeves tighter around M`hta's waist.

"Is there any of the Mhyst up there in the Coven?"

M`hta glanced up as they waded into the dark, icy water and saw the smile form on Teh`c lips, his dimples accentuated in the half-light as he replied in a whisper.

"Maybe"

"Where are the others and Taelen?"

"Like me, they have their orders; we have split up M`hta. Our route cannot accommodate an ill man. We will meet up with them later."

M`hta was a strong swimmer, but his strength was not the same as Teh`c; the distance seemed leagues as they half floated with the now swift-flowing current. The water was considerably colder than the tepid water they had hours before plummeted into. M`hta noticed a definite change in the taste of the water. Saltwater had begun to change the taste of the fresh water.

The light had become considerably larger and a roar that M`hta had been silently praying not to be a waterfall.

"Be careful. There is a strong undertow here. If we are lucky, we will outswim the rip," all of which meant nothing to the Scribe.

M`hta felt the surge of the currents around him and

the panic deep in his heart. He was terrified of being pulled beneath the surface and drowning.

"M`HTA concentrate!" commanded Teh`c as he knew of the fears of M`hta.

"I will if you get out of my head." He snapped back. He did not see the smile or hear the chuckle from Teh`c as waves crashed around them and the luminous light of day blinded them.

They felt regionally disorientated, but only for a few seconds.

"M`hta swim, NOW", he called to his mind as waves crashed mercilessly down upon them. White foam and dark Black Ocean crashed down again and again. Then only a slight swell lifted them as he realised they had passed the waves that hit against the dark rocky opening under the water.

"Where are we?" asked M`hta again, annoyed at Teh`c's silence.

M`hta gasped, breathing in the taste of icy cold salt air and began coughing. He looked at Teh`c, whose own lips were tinged blue from the cold.

"NO talking… see that beach." Both were getting weary, keeping their heads above the water. As each swell raised them above the others, they glimpsed the land before them.

Teh`c pointed to a break in the inhospitable black jutting rocks of what was the ugliest coast that M`hta had the misfortune to sec. He realised his teeth were chattering uncontrollably from the freezing conditions.

"Ever 'body surfed' Scribe?" and smiled when he saw the blank look of response from M`hta. "You're about to learn," he said, grinning, "Just follow my lead."

He swam out with a firm stroke into the mounting swell that rose up behind them. M`hta was too cold to worry and followed Teh`c's every move. The black-green wall rose and held them with the icy clarity of the strength of the ocean. Teh`c swam out with it, and M`hta followed his eyes on Teh`c. M`hta followed as they let the wave propel them towards what Teh`c had innocently referred to as the beach.

As white foam from the waves and dark green tendrils of seaweed threatened to entangle their legs, he saw dull jutting blades of rock beneath the surface. He could not call out to Teh`c; suddenly, the upsurge of the next wave he had not seen lifted them high; M'hta saw the beach, its cold, white starkness of the sand on the coast.

He felt the crack of bone in his shoulder and the cold, wet fingers of the waves trying to pull him back into their grasp. M`hta's eyes jarred as his head hit the sand. At that moment, he knew his collarbone was broken. The wind was knocked out of him, and he lay still, the surf pounding and water filling his ears with each wave.

He lay waiting as his body recovered enough to breathe.

"TEH`C," he yelled, wincing at even such a simple movement that caused a current of hot, sharp needle pain in his shoulder. He twisted his head around to see if he could see him. He saw the still form of Teh`c twitch, but it was the dark red line that now stained the white sand and caused the ocean foam to turn red as it clawed at his legs with each wave like a savage dog.

M`hta cursed loudly and angrily as he manoeuvred himself to a kneeling position, eventually untied his tunic and shirt with freezing stiff fingers of one hand. The other hung uselessly. M`hta put the wet shirt on, which seemed to take a lifetime; his arm was painfully limp from the break in the shoulder. He then tied the tunic in such a way as to make a sling. He cursed the whole time angrily, swearing loudly that even Teh`c would have been impressed. M`hta somehow stood and moved to the side of Teh`c.

"Teh`c", he called, shaking the Warrior, who then vomited seawater down M`hta's hand. He was thankful for this incoming surf that washed vomit away.

"Teh`c…!" he again yelled above the pounding surf and free-spirited winter wind that made confetti of his words.

Eyes, amethyst and a dark autumn green, opened, blinking, and then he threw up again. Rolling onto his side and cursed, and moaned at his leg.

"Get up; we must get out of this weather and find shelter. Here put this tunic on."

Teh`c looked down to his thigh, seeing the stream of red running onto the sand and back to the surf. He pulled himself up and held his arm for the sleeve, watching his blood run from his thigh.

M`hta held the sodden tunic as Teh`c pushed his arms into the uncomfortable cold woollen weave material.

"They should be here…." His voice croaked with the strain of saltwater and the vomiting.

"Who should be here?" M`hta found a piece of driftwood. "This will do as a crutch until I can heal your leg."

Teh`c stood, and with awkward steps from both, they moved up the beach to the tall bushes.

"They should be here…" croaked Teh`c as sand was whipped onto their faces and unprotected skin stinging like thousands of ant stings.

"Use your mind to speak, or you will lose your voice," said M`hta, who was shivering. "We have to find shelter."

Teh`c lent heavily on the branch he was using as a

crutch, and his blood bandaging from M`hta was soaked. M`hta's shirt was soaked from slashes across his back that he tried to ignore. The black rocks he had seen beneath the surface of the waves had slashed them both as

"We have to head north," yelled Teh`c above the wind and the ocean. "There's a stone fisherman's cabin; it should be no more than an hour away. We were to meet other Sz`a`Th Warriors."

M`hta scowled at him. Teh`c shrugged; they could not stop where they were.

"Alright then, two to three hours in our present conditions." He added.

They shuffled in silence; M`hta found another branch for Teh`c, which he could then move forward and take the lead. M`hta's collarbone had broken through the skin; the break was worse than he had anticipated.

However, he said nothing, focussing on blocking the pain and looking for the cabin; Teh'c was positive existed. As the light became day, so was the need for water and shelter.

The trail they followed was rough and painful for them both; M'hta stopped exhausted and bloody after two hours. Branches whipped them, and tree roots caught their footing.

"I can't go any further." He said with pain clawing at his psyche. "You go on."

"You don't have to; the cabin is there." He said with a nod towards some stones.

M`hta looked up in Teh`c's direction.

Visible through the shrubs was a wall of stones. If nothing else, he could lie there until he could go further.

Grunting with the pure exertion of placing one foot in front of the other, he moved.

The overgrown bushes had hidden the walls of the

cabin. Above, rain began to fall heavier from the unforgiving blue-black clouds.

The door was closed but unlocked. Weak with blood loss and injuries, they staggered and dragged themselves into the cabin.

The cabin's first four rooms, one for eating and one for sleeping, had basic requirements; others lay off the hallway.

“It’s vacant for the winter storms.” Said Teh`c, who seemed to find his second wind. “Look, the pantry is full of preserves, pickles, cheese even….” He limped to the fireplace and lit the prepared kindling.

“I’m so glad for your stomach,” M`hta said with sarcasm brought on by fatigue and pain.

He gently undid his bindings and pushed one boot off and then the other with his foot. Removing his wet trousers, he pulled the chair over to the heat beginning to emit from the fire Teh`c had just lit.

He heard Teh`c limping back.

“Let me take the sling off and the shirt. Here are some trousers for us both.”

“Thanks” M`hta couldn’t move as the sling was removed. He heard Teh`c breath sucked in sharply through the Warrior's teeth.

“Did it ever pass in your thoughts to stop and say ‘this bloody hurts?’” asked Teh`c as he pulled a dark pouch from his sodden trousers.

“Let me heal that leg first,” M`hta said, knowing how much his injuries were.

“Let’s stop being a bloody martyr M`hta; anyone else would have fainted from the pain.” He fossicked the small black pouch in his hands, and looking up, he said.

“No… I can wait. I’m fixing this break.” Teh`c’s fingertips touched M`hta’s Mhyst marking, and he began to chant, sending M`hta into a trance. If anything, he was a skilled healer, and with the crystals that glowed at his breath, his healing was enhanced threefold.

He pushed the bone back into the shoulder, sending his crystals to knit the bone, then chanted as he healed the skin with the Mhyst.

Teh`c left M`hta still in the trance as he cut the now bloody rags of his shirt from his leg wound. Healing yourself was difficult, but Teh`c had learnt to combine crystal and Mhyst; only numbing the leg, he closed the twenty-five-centimetre gash, cleaned the wound with a damp cloth and dressed in the dry clothing he'd found.

He gently removed the trance from M`hta, who was grateful and relieved to see his shoulder free in its movement and with a good deal less pain than he had been enduring.

The fire warmed them both. Teh`c and M`hta ate what they found and dragged their exhausted bodies to the room with the bunks on each wall. Pulling soft wool quilts over themselves, sleep was instantaneous.

No dreams. They slept until hunger woke them. Teh`c was worse though his near-drowning and blood loss increased the fever that had settled in him.

M`hta could get no sense out of him; incoherent most of the time, he had, in the end, sedated him with herbal lore that he had learnt of in his days as a scribe.

He smiled, remembering how he used it to calm his allergy to ink and paper as he Cooked a dried fish broth for Teh`c. For two days, the fever raged within Teh`c as bad as the storm raged up and down the coastline.

As it was aptly named, the 'Q`rstn' Coast killed more Mariners than it had ever saved and curved the same way that the deadly blade 'Q`rstn was shaped along with the jutting black coral reef that lurked at different depths. It was a coastline that all avoided.

For that apparent reason, the land was harsh and

sparsely inhabited. Only very few lived there. The small fishing villages and coastal trading docks were all that occupied the coast.

The stone cabin was a seasonal fishing dwelling and served as a refuge for those who had the misfortune to fall into the icy waters.

M`hta sat reading a book he had found under a large flat stone that made the hearth. He had been tidying, and the sizeable flat hearthstone was uneven.

The book was strange. M`hta had deciphered the text, but it ran diagonally from bottom to top. The script was written in the flowing singsong language of the 'Saruh Headlands' people, mainly fishing and farming, which was the region just below Drargon`H.

The Saruh Headlands were a forgotten region because the land was as inhospitable as this coastline. He absently wondered how the book had come such a long way from its original home.

"I thought you had an allergy to books." Teh`c moved with stiff and bruised muscles but had not the black eye and gravel rash cheek that M`hta had suffered along with the broken collarbone when he crashed onto the beach.

M`hta looked over his matt black Warrior-rimmed glasses at Teh`c's bearded appearance. His friend looked wild and beast-like; he smiled at the thought of a rough mariner shipwrecked on the coast, for Teh`c's presence seemed to conjure up such a person now.

He poured himself a hot drink that was black and bitter but seemed to be what he needed. Teh`c glanced down at their boots and frowned at his friend. M`hta shrugged back at him.

"I found some oil, seal oil; I think it is. Our boots are back to being soft and not hard."

Teh`c stretched. "Let me guess, clothes washed and

mended, and dinner is ready, yes?" He asked with an arch of his left eyebrow.

"Sarcasm will get your head pounded in one day, Lieutenant."

Expecting a tirade of abuse but received nothing but a shrug from M`hta.

"That's probably true." He scratched his three days of growth. "I'd say you'd be interested in an explanation."

"More like what orders you were given as opposed to the ones I had about making our way directly to the Castle Dal`Qeit and the Death Watch."

"Ever wondered why they call it the Death Watch?" asked M`hta, not looking from the book.

"Aye, because it is said that Dal`Qeit was the last Imperial Sahn`Frwh Knight left standing, it was his watch; he called it the Death Watch. He was the last Warrior left alive at the end of the Four Hundred Winters War; it would be hard to be the last Warrior standing…looking over all those slain on both sides…the Death Watch, aptly named don't you think M`hta."

"Aye, Dal`Qeit was…is a hard man to emulate, I know I do not wish to be the last, and neither do you."

"Aye, what is life without those who make you smile."

M`hta closed the book and stood warming himself against the heat of the fire, thankful the storm outside was just that outside. The surf surging and pounding the beach made him shiver slightly.

"Changing the subject, Mistress LH`Nejah, felt distinctly that a trap had been set with the arrival of Lord Mi`an. Taelen's near-death with Mah`sden. That sword he gave K`lton and the comments about K`lton."

"How did the Drargon`H Lord Mi`an arrive?"

"Seems 'Dragons' have their own magic M`hta. Have you ever watched K`lton during a storm?"

M`hta's mind replayed the scene on the parapet of the West Wing during a fierce electrical storm. He had seen K`lton standing alone; his head was thrown back, arms flung out, hands splayed to the wind. The child seemed to command the natural forces of the storm. Dark black, blue clouds swirled thousands of leagues above the child uncannily. Lightning arced; this lightning was green, a dark grey-green connected with the boy's fingertips, forming a net with the forces of the storm elementals.

"Aye, I have." He looked back to the book in his hands and closed its hardcover." So the orders, are they the Mistress or yours?"

"Were to evacuate the Coven immediately and at all costs get Taelen to safety and hide K`lton."

"There were over three hundred people in the Coven Teh`c; where do you hide so many?"

"They travelled to places only Lady LH`Nejah knows of via the 'Dome'"

"That's impossible. She has been the only one to travel that Dome, and it was by Taelen; where's Taelen?"

"Seems the good Mistress has contacts that we mere Warriors do not. All I hope is that Taelen is alive and safe."

"And K`lton, where is the boy?"

"He was to go to with Lord Za`qrn; I just hope he did."

"Then who was to meet us? I thought it was those four Warriors and Taelen."

"Ah, an old friend of mine and yours was to have met us."

"How old," asked M`hta massaging his shoulder,

the deep ache that held the area seeming to drain his energy.

“Do you remember Lieutenant K`Lpn?” asked Teh`c stretching his muscles in his back. He felt as if he had been in a drunken brawl and had come out the worst.

M`hta rubbed his forehead. The man Teh`c spoke of was someone you could not forget. He was 6’3” with blazing blue eyes, hair as dark as coal and a physique that seemed to reel in women a league away. The handsome looks and other physical attributes seemed to leave women in a daze. In short, everyone loved him. He was a man’s man. He was the Warrior you would choose in any situation, a dependable and calculating one who could and would make the hard decision that no one else could. He would, in fact, give his life to save others if it came to that.

“How could I forget him?” M`hta answered.

“He is supposed to be here; that is concerning me.”

“More than likely, he’s in bed with a wench from the Tavern.”

”Or two, ménage….” Said Teh`c is ending his comment and frowning he asked. “The shoulder is giving you pain still?”

“Aye, I’m glad it is only my shoulder.” His face drained of colour from the pain.

“I’ll get you something for the pain; you know you can’t be a martyr forever.”

”First things first, Teh`c, what were your orders? You’ve avoided telling me the absolute truth.”

”My orders were to go to Storms Gate.” He said slowly, “We are to get to ‘Storms Gate’ without delay.”

“Well, we might as well empty our balls now because we are good as dead.”

Teh`c exploded into laughter; M'hta was known for his quiet and gentle ways. He was not of the drunk and womanising group that was an element within the Warriors. Rarely did he make such comments.

"You find 'Storms Gate' funny." He winced from the shoulder, groaned, and took a deep breath, bracing for the next spasm.

Teh`c composed himself, but he would never be able to hold the Scribe in the same frame of mind that he had. Pursing his lips and not winning at not grinning, his dimples more prominent than ever, he replied after M`hta said.

"What must we find?"

"Each book, as you know, as a Scribe, is a divine instrument of knowledge and power. A strong ward has secured each book by a runic spell, not to mention the single phrase that will free the seven books...."

"I'm listening, but I am beginning to have doubts about these books like Taelen," Said M`hta impatiently, more from the pain in his shoulder than the long-winded answers Teh`c gave.

"Well, you are not alone there. I have my doubts, too but will you just tell me."

"It seems we will only find what we are looking for at' Storms Gate'."

"Teh`c!" he snapped through gritted teeth. "Just bloody tell me." His forehead was misted with sweat. His complexion suddenly became pasty; dark black circles formed crescents under his eyes.

"Crystals." Replied Teh`c is, touching M`hta's forehead.

"You know what you can do with your bloody…crystals...and the …" spat M`hta uncharacteristically, cursing in words and slang that even Teh`c paused for a moment, wondering how he knew them.

Teh`c was no longer smiling but frowning with

concern at the change in M`hta he had never known.

Teh`c crouched down and gently touched M`hta's shoulder. The whimper from M`hta added with his eyes rolling back in pain.

"Do that again… and I will slice your balls open, Teh`c." He spat out at Teh`c as another wave of pain drove deep into his shoulder.

"How long has this been like this?" He said, ignoring M`hta's uncharacteristic comments about his anatomy.

M`hta opened his green, gold and brown eyes and then closed them tightly as the pain engulfed his senses again, drowning all thoughts in a darkening hellhole.

"From the bloody moment I crashed onto the accursed beach, how long do you think it's been?"

"My healing isn't compatible with yours, and I just don't understand why."

"Now you tell me, Shattas, it hurts, gods, it hurts." Groaned M`hta

"Maybe 'Blood Wars' go more profound than we realise, M`hta."

"So what you're saying is that instead of healing…."

"My healing is killing you." Their eyes met a silence of sincere regret and mateship that neither expected.

"I want you to go to bed. Concentrate on the Mhyst within you. I am going to go and find someone or anything that can help."

M`hta said nothing and watched the back of Teh`c leave, closing the door on the storm outside and the one that now took hold of M`hta.

# CHAPTER 18

**Meet me at the Pickled Sea Tavern.**

Wearing the clothes he had found in the cabin and the whole black three days old beard he still had, Teh`c looked the part of a coastal fisherman.

He had fished more than he had studied as a boy on the archipelago that he had lived in before his Mhyst calling.

He had no idea whether the people here were allegiant to the Sz`a`Th or Mah`sden; the lands were full of displaced people.

His walking for three hours along a road that had deteriorated with the inclement weather was mud, brown and creamy; it coated his black boots from shin to toe.

Teh`c was the colour of the mud. The rain washed the rest from him; his shirt clung to his skin like a poor second skin. Freezing to death was an option, he thought absently.

The dirt road took a sharp downward swing into a valley where he saw the village of KR`nh; smoke fought in the rain squalls as a dozen chimneys called to him that warmth was not far away.

Within the hour, Teh`c had negotiated two creeks swollen by the rain. He came to a Tavern at one end of the road in the village that showed no life at all.

The smell of roasting meats, ale, sweat, tobacco, and mud brought him to his senses.

The sign swinging noisily above his head from hooks read ‘The Pickled Sea’ in rune. He smiled at the apt name for the Tavern.

Opening the door, he saw in one-corner ten Warriors

in uniforms vaguely familiar. The other patrons seemed to be locals dressed similarly to him.

The Tavern Keeper was a woman with curly dark burgundy hair, olive skin similar to M`hta's, and slightly lighter skin. She eyed him cautiously as he walked up to the bar.

Teh`c noted the white blaze of runes from the corner of her eye to her temple, then on her left cheekbone, and a particular white rune. Her heritage was that of M`hta's; she was a Karanja. He wondered why a Karanja would be so far south.

Teh`c stood quietly at the bar; thankful no one paid him much heed except the Tavern Keeper, her eyes watched him and all the others in the Tavern. She handed him a towel, saying

"What is it you want?" she asked, eyeing him from the ground up; her eyes stopped at him, as she raised an eyebrow inquisitively at him. "Besides dry clothes." Her voice was only for him; nobody else could hear them above the din of the Tavern's patrons

"Mistress…" he glanced sideways at the Warriors. "I need a healer and information on a Warrior; he is 6'3", black hair, blue eyes, charismatic. Lieutenant K`lpn?"

She arched again an eyebrow, amused by him as she continued to wipe the bar top; its dark wood, stained from winters of liquor and dirty cloth, was firm under his elbows as he lent.  Tonight it did not need wiping. Her movements detracted from the Warrior before her and the ones drinking in the corner of the Tavern.

Her eyes held his "They are too drunk to worry about…and his eyes were blazing blue like lightning dying. Captured by Mariners of Mahsden on the quarter moon, three days are gone if he's lucky, he'll be at Kanaja Castle." She looked him up and down and tilted her head slightly. "A half-drowned…" her eyes travelled from his own down his body. She leant over the bar as her eyes moved down to his boots. He felt unnerved "…man, you have just described every Warrior from the humid north to the freezing south. Are you always so vague," she said, smiling and leant closer, so close her lips touched his ear, "who… is no fisherman and wears the boots of a Warrior of the Sz`a`Th." Her voice was a whisper that made him shiver.

She pulled back and poured him a small glass of red liquor. She crossed her arms and watched him steadily. Teh`c glanced down at his boots and cursed his stupidity.

He had changed everything but not his boots; his trousers were wet and long enough to hide them, yet this slightly built young woman immediately saw through his subterfuge.

"What type of Healer?" She asked. Her eyes mirrored M`hta's in their colouring, except hers reminded him of the change in the season from winter to spring. He thought a deeper green to light gold, just as the sun hits the top of the trees.

"Someone, who can heal my friend," he said, watching her and the others of 'The Pickled Sea', "only Karanja can heal their own."

"You have skills from the Islands to the east that uses crystals." Teh`c frowned at her as she smiled not for him but for those that may have been watching.

"Not it seems enough to heal him; blood wars may have changed the healing to killing."

He answered, drinking the spirits she offered. The fluid hit hard, burning like fire, igniting and astounding him. He did not cough. However, he instead placed the shot glass down steadily on the bar. His eyes smarted from the fumes that the alcohol emitted. His throat felt as if it had been torched.

"My friend is a Karanja, a Warrior of the Sz`a`Th, and so is the Warrior I have asked about." He caught the scent of her perfume, the sandalwood scent he would not forget easily and stared a second too long at the summer green eyes that watched his soul so personally; she stirred something deep within his psyche.

She lent it to him. Her lips touched his ear as she spoke. Teh`c breathed in her perfume. Her hands held his shoulders gently.

He wondered at the game she was playing; as he shook thoughts, he wished he was not contemplating with her, not at this moment anyway.

"I would not speak, that word in here if you wish to leave intact." She whispered, "With your organs still within you or your balls attached." She smiled sweetly at him.

"Seems my balls have a bit of a reputation today, and I don't understand why." He said with a wry grin. "Must have something to do with the Karanja sense of humour," his tone iced as he added, "do you think I play games, Mistress? If you do, I would think again." He whispered back in her ear, hissing through his teeth as she leaned back; his eyes flared angrily.

"Your Warrior was captured thirty-six hours ago; that is all I know of him; now, how far 'green eyes' is this friend of yours?" She asked flirtatiously, her nails trailing through his beard down around his chin and holding him.

"In this weather, three hours, and don't flirt with me," he snarled coldly. "Can I trust you?" His eyes sized her up. She was barely eighteen or nineteen winters, if that, the age that defies all males, he thought, and the dark burgundy hair was in a simple plait to her slim waist, curling corkscrews and wisps of her hair had escaped kissing the smooth skin around her neck.

She was of medium height for a Karanja woman. She came only to his chin. Beautiful gold earrings set in the shape of a star hung gently from her ears. She wore a gold ring with the same Spellcasters star upon her right hand with long fingers. Slowly she leant over the bar again, whispering in his ear, as Teh`c lent over, hunching his shoulders to hear her over the voices behind him.

"My question to you is can I trust you, and do I want to?" she asked cocking sharply one eyebrow. "And… if you want to leave this Tavern alive, Lieutenant. You will play this game with me because we are being watched closely by those Warriors you just passed, so heed me, Warrior, and play the part."

He realised she wore similar clothes to him; she was dressed in men's clothing, not women's, females did this to hide and blend, and he realised then she was in as much or more danger than he was.

"You have my honour, Mistress; my friend is important to me." He went to bow; she grabbed his arm, frowning.

"Are you a fool? Bow here, and you will lose those… precious balls?"

Her golden-green eyes glanced sideways. "Kiss me, and make it look like you wish to empty those balls of yours and make it good; those bastards aren't as stupid as they look; they seem to be interested in you now." As if she needed to explain her actions to him, she answered: "I do this to keep them all at arm's length. I pretend to have a Mariner who is my betrothed." She smiled at him so sweetly he could have knocked her head off. "You see, he's your height and colouring," her eyes travelled down to his groin, and she raised her

eyebrow teasingly. "I will have to add well hung in

the right places." Winking seductively.

"What!" He hissed at her angrily. Her provocative crassness was getting under

his skin.

"They are suspicious. The docks are just on the other side of the valley. I'll explain later. What's your name Warrior if you wish to stay alive here, or do you wish death for yourself and your friend - choose now?" she asked not too warmly.

"Teh`c," he said, shocked she knew he was a Warrior, though the webbing and his careless questions had sealed that well and truly. Before he could ask hers, she had leapt the bar. Teh`c followed her, moving his large hands, holding her at the waist and lifting her up to him; her feet touched nothing but air, as she firmly wrapped slender legs around his waist.

He was surprised by how light she was as his hands slid under the shirt. Around her slender waist and crossed over her back and around, holding her close, pressing her to him in an embrace that caught her off guard; the surprise in her eyes made his smile.

Not so tough after all, he thought to himself and wondered at what dangerous game she played. His fingertips were tempted to touch her body that pressed against him, and it felt inviting to say the least. He smiled a little laconically, thinking of her breasts' warmth against his wet clothes gave him. As he did, the dimples in his cheeks deepened; he felt her body harden beneath the cloth of her shirt and against his damp shirt and cold skin. She was scared, very scared. Teh`c inhaled her body scent through his teeth as his eyes rolled momentarily beneath his eyelids.

"I have wanted you so long..." damn, he did not know her name. She raised herself to his ear, whispering her name so softly it sent ripples through his body.

“I have wanted you, needed you, for so long, my sweet, sweet, D`mja”, he groaned as he buried his head into her neck, smelling her clean hair, its softness, the curve of her neck, her skin felt cool, he nuzzled her skin with his lips, biting her neck softly.

The urge to bed her there and then took him by surprise. So strong was his need for her. It had him curse himself. Teh`c blamed that on the tightness he now felt in his balls. His training quelled any desires immediately after the thought.

Her fingers laced his hair, holding it longer than it had been. She caught the wet hair in her fingers, twisting it firmly. Their faces were only centimetres apart; Teh'c kissed her nose softly, then her ears slowly, touching them lightly with his lips and tongue gently, caringly at the nape of her neck, nipping her with his teeth gently, slowly. Then his lips found her mouth softly and as intimate, as a lover would. His lips found hers. She tasted of mint, and if someone had asked him very inviting, his hunger surprised him, the heat at his crotch did not, and something told him he would not forget this woman in a hurry, if at all.

His mind traced the shape of her body against his, her warmth and his cold. He kissed her more profound than he intended to. The kiss was that of a man who had been away for too many months, without his heart's breath. His hunger throbbed through his body. His heart pounded loudly, and he was sure she could feel it beat against her skin. They stayed locked in an embrace for more moments than the patrons wished to disturb. That kiss was endless, sensual, and erotic, so much so that a few patrons coughed and looked elsewhere. For a moment, the Warrior in him was ignored as he continued in what seemed an endless embrace.

Reluctantly Teh`c was the one who broke the spell

and pulled away, she went to kiss him again, but he placed a single finger on her lips. Regaining composure was another thing his mind commanded; his body needed the touch of her flesh and the woman's scent. He inhaled as if he had free-dived onto the ocean floor of his island home, surfaced shuddering breath, and wanted to take her immediately on the bar to hell with the others. Gods, he thought Ji`rah would find that amusing and mention rolling in the snow. He mentally told himself not to think of Ji`rahs advice at moments like this. It worked, though. He turned off such intent, mentally shutting it down.

He just put it down to lust and laughed inwardly, trying to fathom this woman before him. Why did she have such an effect on him? Later he told himself he would think about it; besides, it had been too many moons since he had been with a woman.

"Later…" he said aloud huskily and lifted her onto the bar. "Lord, you move me in ways that are not for here and now, my Mistress. My heart and my body have missed you for far too long." He bent, resting his head on her lap.

"So you are the mystery Mariner she keeps herself for." A man's voice came from behind them amongst the sounds of the Tavern.

"If that is what she says, then it must be so." Replied Teh`c standing now without turning around to face the man who had spoken to him.

He heard her hiss angrily, a reply that would have made every Mariner in a thousand leagues twist in his watery grave.

Teh`c turned and faced her, his finger on her lips. He trailed his finger slowly down her neck to the collarbone and down the buttons of her shirt to her waist. And then to her hand and held her with his eyes. Teh`c spoke into her mind, which silenced her tongue.

‘I have bedded many a wench, but none with a gift of the language such as yours. Even whores speak better than you do! I am here to seek a Healer; I do not play games with the likes of a Karanja slut.’

She pulled him by the shoulders their noses touched. Her eyes narrowed.

“You do not know me, and how I speak keeps me alive. I will heal your friend. I stated that. Those Warriors are Mah`sden Warriors, you stupid bastard! Be thankful your beard hides who you are. And how I speak has kept me alive.”

A voice called to them, interrupting their thoughts.

“Hey D`mja, boyfriend causing problems?” asked one of Mah`sden Warriors. “D`mja is a wild one, Mariner. Take a lot of taming that one.”

The Tavern patrons laughed and continued conversations that no one heard.

“You are right there, Lieutenant”, he called back. “She’s grown wild in my absence, but that’s part of the fun. I like her feisty; I don‘t like my women to be like starfishes.”

Laughter and table banging came from the patrons, then eased as they returned to their drinking.

He saw her hand as it flew through the air; the crack of the slap across his face brought a deathly silence to the Tavern. He clenched his jaw and stood away from her, where she sat upon the bar. His fists closed and opened in anger, flexed bone and sinew.

Staring at her, his eyes boiled a brilliant dark green and then became as cold as the forest and the rain outside.

He spoke silently. ‘I said… I do not play games. Please do not test me, Mistress. My friend would rather die than feel your touch. We are Sahn`Frwh, and my friend better be alive.' He turned; his footsteps were that of a man who was not to be shamed. He stepped outside and into the rain.

The sign above his head creaked and swung in the massive storm that was buffeting the coast. It was all he heard as he slammed the door shut. Stepping into the mud, and began walking back the way he came down the centre of the muddy road.

She swore aloud as she knew her temper was fiery as the dark burgundy colour of her long curled hair. Cursing more herself and more for her stupidity and explosive temper, she jumped down from the bar she had been sitting on.

"If you want him as bad as I know you do, lassie, I'd go running. That type of man is a rare find." He shook his head. "You shouldn't have gone and slapped his face D`mja…that is something you shouldn't have done, lass, not here in the Tavern with others around, just shouldn't have gone and done it, lassie."

Lod`n was broad of chest and tall, but his heart was big, and he had more patience than he would have liked. His dark blue eyes were unexpected, with the snow blonde hair and beard. He shook his head at her as her eyes glared at him.

"Lod`n … shut up. I know…I know." She threw him the keys across the tavern to him, yelling above the loud voices, "Lockup…will you?"

"Aye… and one other thing D`mja…watch that temper, lassie, no man kisses a woman the way he just kissed you lass and not be genuine…some men are bastards, that lad is not one of them."

Lod`n stood at the open Tavern door watching D`mja run through the rain and slush, her booted feet splashing water from muddy puddles in the downpour.

"Teh`c!" she cried at the Warrior soaked back as his

steps stopped in the rain and mud.

He turned to face her as she ran. Teh`c was fed up and just looked at her with dark fury written all over his face. The rain teemed down, and he could not get any wetter or colder than he was. He just stood in the mud and waited for her.

“What is it?” he snapped back at her as the rain ran rivers down his hair. He grabbed her by the waist as she slipped in the mud and pulled her up. He was muddier now than he had been when he arrived.

“Lieutenant, I have a fiery temper, yes. I also have a sad gift of the language. I am sorry, but I am afraid you see what you get, not a ‘lady’. This attitude has kept me alive. Without it, I would be dead.” She said, “Take me to this friend of yours. I know that was all bravado in the Taven, but even though I like not to be spoken, we are equal, Mariner.”

“We are being watched.” He said as rain fell, greying the valley.

He ran his thumb across her lips and awkwardly felt mesmerised by their full shape and vibrant natural colour. Teh`c bent slowly, holding her golden-green eyes with his and tentatively kissing her lightly, pulling away twice; he then pulled her to him.

“You’re a strange man Lieutenant Teh`c.” she murmured, “I know nothing of you.”

”You know I am a Lieutenant, a Warrior of the Sz`a`Th; you know my name. I don’t think you need more.” He whispered as breath against breath, his tongue slid between her lips, finding hers and kissing her deeply. At some time, he heard the Tavern door close. He then slowly pulled away.

“It’s freezing,” she said. Her teeth chattered as her curly burgundy red hair hung heavily in corkscrews, water dripping massive drops from the ends.

"It will be so until I get you to my friend. Do you need anything?"

"No," she said, "But horses will make it quicker, come to the stables are across here, and Lod`n won't mind since he thinks were sweethearts and he is such an old romantic sod."

Teh`c glanced back at the 'Pickled Sea' Tavern, the pale lamplight reflecting yellow pools across the puddles in the darkness splashed rain dance across the puddles rhythmically.

He followed her into the dry stables. She threw him an oilskin cloak and put one on herself

"You're sure he won't mind."

"Only if they're not returned or paid for in full."

She said, mounting the horse with a person's ease at home with the animal. They rode out the back and skirted the village, climbing up and out of the valley and down onto the coastal road on which Teh`c had come in. The riding took them out of their way, but with her guidance, they were there half the time it took him to walk there.

They both entered, having tethered the horses within the barn attached to the cabin. The oilskins hung on the hooks outside to dry on the small veranda, and pools of water dripped onto the boards from them.

Inside, M`hta lay with the protection of the Mhyst; his eyes were bloody. Teh`c swore angrily at his stupidness as D`mja began to heal one of her own kind without questions or answers.

The young woman gently touched the white tattoo that was on M`hta's face; it ran from his temple to his cheekbone. This denoted his title of Scribe.

The white glow of the Karanja healing was intense. To the Karajan, it was a life force.

The rune on his cheek pulsed slowly. The light

seemed to dance across his skin erratically with no rule of thumb to speak of.

D`mja, though chilled to the bone, felt the warmth from M`hta. She consumed herself with him entirely. She sank deep beneath his subconscious, deep into his and his alone dreams and nightmares. Here she searched for a man, a stranger to her, yet one who had to survive as she had within the walls of a Castle with no hope for them to be free.

She spoke in Karanja, her voice calling him. She jumped, startled as a pale ghost-like figure stood within the darkness.

"Come, M`hta, Teh`c needs you." She pleaded with him in their language.

"I am tired, go; I do not know you, and I do not need your help." His voice was of a man who had chosen not to live.

She stepped back through the Veil and out into the world Teh`c was in.

"He won't come with me. He is dying Teh`c. But there is something else. What do you know about him?"

"That, he's a stubborn prick sometimes." Bemuse at the look she gave him.

Shaking his head, he answered, "Not much. He was a Historical Scribe of Ch`nel he is scared to death of heights…."

"You will have to strip him. Look for a mark hidden."

"He's dying, and you want me to strip him…." Teh`c shrugged his shoulders as he asked, "Can you tell me what type of mark I am looking for?" he removed the shirt and discarded it on the chair next to the bed.

"How long was he a Scribe?" She said, searching his torso for any mark at all.

"He told me he was apprenticed at five

winters…maybe four. I know he was very young."

It was her turn to curse; her fingers trembled as she smoothed chest hair to find a mark she knew too well.

"What are you looking for…I don't understand."

Tears had welled in her eyes as she lifted M`hta's arm up and rolled his arm over. There was a mark on the inside high on the upper part of his arm near his armpit. She made a small pain-filled sound. The red ink tattoo was the same as the blaze mark he wore on his cheekbone. This was in the soft part of the arm; she felt an eternal sadness engulf her.

"M`hta is left-handed, isn't he?" she asked, gently placing his arm down and pulling back up the covers.

"Aye, so aren't most Scribes?" replied Teh`c, unsure where she was going.

"M`hta was called in our language a 'J`rxqa' hard to pronounce, even harder to survive. In your language, he was enslaved; Karanja calls it, in your words forced indentured – there is no freedom. His parents were killed, as is the custom when the 'teachers' find one so gifted… and I use that term very loosely. The reason he is scared of heights is they would hold the children by the left hand out a window as punishment if they kept falling asleep while being taught over twelve hours a day." She took a deep breath.

"Only you can get him." She said, "He trusts only you."

"Stubborn bastard, tell him I can't go to 'Storms Gate' alone. He must come with me. He is the only one besides Taelen who can Scribe."

D`mja again entered M`hta's mind. Telling him what Teh`c had just said.

"Damn him; tell him I'll come to him." Teh`c snapped angrily.

"You can't get it…" she argued, her teeth chattering

from her cold, wet clothes.

"It will kill me …I know that. But if I'm quick?" said Teh`c hopefully.

They both entered again into M`hta's half-world. The wind became violent, hurling objects at Teh`c. He yelled at M`hta through the storm that raged in M`hta's subconscious.

"I can't go alone…M`hta, please, you must come." The darkness and the white path he walked were dangerously eroded by pain from M`hta's past.

Voices, not M`hta's, bellowed curses and abuse at Teh`c; he was picked up and hurled through the air, hitting a solid object winding him heavily; something lashed him across the chest.

M`hta screamed 'STOP'.

Teh`c fell to his knees. His chest wore a crimson mark where the flesh was curling back. Air stung deeply.

"M`hta come. The Pack is Pact" was all he said as pain buried deep in him.

Teh`c fell to the floor coughing. M`hta opened his eyes. He frowned slightly as if he was trying to recall something that had slipped quickly through his thoughts.

"I told you, you would catch a cold in that storm." He absently blinked his eyes as he looked at both of them with detachment.

Teh`c groaned as D`mja touched the slash on his chest.

"You get a bit tetchy when someone wants to save your damn life," Teh`c said, cursing as D`mja touched the torn skin again.

"For god's sake, woman, what are you doing? I don't need you adding to the pain I already have." He gasped and shivered with shock.

She glanced at him. "Lieutenant…just will you shut up for once …please."

M`hta sat up, surprised, and asked, “What woman?”

“This woman, sitting on the bed near me, who is attempting to heal me with pain, can you not see her.” Snapped Teh`c impatiently.

M`hta looked over to where he sat at the end of the bed. Teh`c half sat holding his chest.

“Who the hell did that to you?” Seeing the gash across Teh`c chest and the blood oozing onto his friend's fingers. He scrambled out of bed and knelt at his friend’s side.

“You did, M`hta!” he whispered as pain burned, sucking air from his lungs with the sharpness.

“By the Twin Moons of Dorsa, it hurts.” He held his chest tightly, trying to contain the pain and deaden the intensity of the surges.

“I can’t heal you,” D`mja said. M`hta looked at her with vagueness.

“Who are you?”

She glanced at him. “Can you heal him?”

“For my sake, take the fool's hand. No…no, the left one. M`hta put your right hand on the Mhyst.” M`hta was dazed, and his mind fogged. Confused, he did as he was asked and placed his hand on Teh`c’s chest where his Mhyst marking was.

Teh`c grabbed D`mja’s hand. “Don’t under any circumstances let him chant in Karanja…it has to be in the Mhyst.” She frowned, shaking her head, her eyes angry and confused.

“I don’t know Mhyst; I don't know what he is saying even if he does speak Mhyst.”

“Oh… by the gods, this hurts….” Teh`c swore as another tide of pain burned him.

“Repeat my words with M`hta…, and praying might help. I am not religious, but by god, I am questioning my sanity when I enlisted.” He said, seeing the still dazed look in his friend's eyes.

He closed his eyes, trying to control the pain. He then began the chant in the healing words of the Mhyst that crisscrossed between that Veil that separated the Sz`a`Th.

D`mja spoke hesitantly at first, but with Teh`c's patience, she followed without a stumble of words.

His arms stretched straight, his fists white and clenched Teh`c shut his eyes tight from the pain. Slowly M`hta remembered and began his Mhyst chanting along with Teh`c; slowly, the wound closed, and Teh`c relaxed, breathing little by little and sneezing.

"It's time you changed and went to bed. Nothing but rest will heal that cold," M`hta said.

He shook his head as Teh`c ignored D`mja's presence and striped, shaking uncontrollably; he slipped on the warm clothes given to him and curled up into a ball in the bed as he was covered up.

"He will sleep for a while now. I am sorry for his disrespect of you," M`hta said, picking up the wet clothes and closing the door.

"Believe me, Lieutenant, naked men do not impress me. I am afraid you look, all the same, seen one body. You've seen them all." Her smile warmed him. "All sized differently, men look much better dressed, you know." She added and then said, "I hope he does sleep, Lieutenant. You should too." She said quietly, taking the wet clothes. "He has a lot of respect for you, you know."

"Aye, I have for him, he is loyal, and his morals are high." M`hta smiled. "Well, maybe not his morals, I would have to admit. But yes, he's loyal, stubborn, determined, and as rough as they come in a fight."

D`mja laughed as she hung their wet clothes to dry near the fire.

"Yes, I can see that in him. But he is sensitive too."

"You haven't told me who you are or why you are here so far from home."

She sat in front of the fire, its warmth drying her hair.

"Karanja is part of Mah`sden Empire …it does not matter how I left or why I am so far south, and it never was home." Her shoulders rose as she shrugged; her eyes looked down away from him. "I run the Tavern at 'KR`nh', the village in the 'Vale of Storms'. Teh`c came into the Tavern looking for a Healer for you. I had to get him out of there before Mah`sden Warriors became suspicious of a very wet Mariner."

"How drunk were they?"

"Why"

"Teh`c is no Mariner; he just isn't one for the life of a Mariner, fishing yes,  yes, and ships definitely not."

"Well, they believed me." She said, hugging her knees. She hoped they did at least, and she took Teh`c's advice and prayed to the gods above.

"You both must have been very persuasive in convincing them."

D`mja smiled as he handed her a hot spiced tea.

"You could say that." She sipped the tea, letting the steam warm her face.

M`hta stared at her. The Karanja tattoo opened emotions he thought he had buried long ago.

"Why are you staring?"

"I'm… I have not seen someone from Karanja since I was a boy. Seeing you just re-woke  old memories, just memories, I apologise if I made you feel uncomfortable."

D`mja eyed him. Also, it had been only moons since her flight from the war, but M`hta confused her.

"What did you do?"

M`hta looked at her confused, then realised what

she was asking him.

"OH… you mean in Karanja."

"Yes."

"I was the Historical Scribe of Ch`nel. Surrounded by books and inks since four or five winters, I suppose, hard to judge, or maybe my mind has chosen to erase those thoughts." He touched the tattoo on his face. "But this tells you that anyway." He said, watching her and picking up the closed book he had been reading.

"Only that you were a Scribe." D`mja smiled and said without thinking as she recalled what she had heard about the young Scribe. Her eyes shone as she added, "Sneezing in rapid succession with each turn of the page."

He closed the book. "How do you know that?" smiling at her remark.

"Oh, I think I heard about you somewhere in the Markets of Kali."

"I never went to the markets, have you forgotten? Those employed within the palace are there for life, never seeing the outside. I always wondered about the truth of the translations I did. The world outside my living rooms seemed so foreign."

'Lieutenant, I understand because…."

"You're not a slave; I…was a slave." He said quietly, staring at the closed book in his hands. He managed to bury old thoughts and prejudices that always seemed there.

"What did you do?" he asked.

"I thought my rune would tell you that, Lieutenant." She said quietly.

"I know what the rune depicts, Mistress. It means you are a 'pleasure for the King'."

"Teh`c said you were polite, and I am grateful. The term used in the Warrior's quarters was 'Kings Slut'."

She said coldly, the pain evident in her voice and the way she hugged her knees close and began rocking herself slightly.

M`hta knew of the King's taste. He also knew that the Cooks had ways of saving the girls.

"It seems we both have lives that managed to get us here for good or bad. How old were you?" and wished he had not asked the stupid question.

"Sorry, no tact, and I am sorry." He lowered his eyes to the floor, mentally wishing he had kept his damn mouth shut.

"Cook managed to delay the inevitable until I was 10."

"T`Mon…?" He thought of the old Cook, who was a wonderfully generous man.

"Aye, T`Mon…he's dead now. He died getting me out of the palace when the Warriors attacked us. You want to know something…."

"If you want me to know…." He said, watching her, hoping her wounds would one day heal and she, like him, could live freely without the ghosts that still haunted even him.

"He said one day he saw you being held out the window. He said you deliberately would do that to save the other children."

"Aye, I used to…."He chewed his nail and began to think of the Warriors from the Tavern. "Do you know if you were followed here, it's just Teh`c, and I have a place we must get to at all costs."

"Storms Gate…?" She said quietly, "He told me when I was trying to heal you."

"Promise me something." He said to her. "Promise me you will love someone with all your being; give yourself that small indulgence. Love is the only thing we have that's free."

She smiled and said nothing as the rain fell more substantial and more onerous. She looked up from the fire and said.

"They will go to the Docks on the other side of the valley. There they will ask about Teh`c. Then they will go from cabin to cabin if they know Mah'sden wants him. Are you wanted?"

"Me, yes, I am wanted by Lord Mah`sden, but, Teh`c no, I doubt it, if only because he is a Sz`a`Th Warrior, that would be all."

"Have you a love, Lieutenant, besides books."

"No," he said; he smiled slightly ", one other promise; you must make it to the 'Death Watch' and tell them I sent you."

She shuddered at the name and looked up at him. She was confused as to why he would want her there and afraid because she did not know how to get to the Death Watch.

"You are Sahn`Frwh?"

"Aye, we are Sahn`Frwh Mistress, not the monsters you have imagined us to be. It just keeps us alive. Get to the 'Death Watch' and give them this from me."

He pulled the black dagger from his boot and one from Teh`c's.

"When you get there, give the Guards these. They will know they belong to us." M`hta sighed. She looked so vulnerable. "Pack what food you can and warm clothes, travel as a man. I will scribe a short note in Sz`a`Th for you now. Come on, then move my Mistress quickly, and if there is someone you need to travel with, who you owe a life to, take them as well."

He could not shake the feeling that the wrong Warriors would soon discover them. He needed to make sure others would know of their fate.

"But this will leave you short two blades,

Lieutenant."

"Aye, and that is something I will have to live with, but it will give you two chances." He smiled. "Now pack, and take the horses. We will go on foot."

He helped her pack, and she left in the rain with the evening light for cover. He prayed he would see her again, not for his sake but for Teh`c's sake and for the boy in him who saved others once like her a long time ago.

# CHAPTER 19

M`hta needed to escape the memories the young woman had opened doors to in his mind. Memories he needed to shut firmly away and forget again.

Dawn was a washed-out palette of greys. The rain continued to fall relentlessly outside, which meant that the creeks Teh`c had crossed last night were impassable. Both had woken early, and M'hta walked down to the beach; Teh'c said he would follow soon.

The ocean's blackness was in moody contrast to the brooding white breakers that punched into the beach and echoed up and down the coast in a grumbling din softened by the wind that still gusted in squalls.

M`hta's moodiness had taken him down to the beach. He sat heavily, angrier with himself, he hung his head to meditate, but it was the sounds of shouts and metal on metal.

He turned to see two Warriors coming out of the green-grey thick scrub that hugged the coastline. Their blades were already drawn. He knew it was pointless to run or even begin to pull on the one dagger he had left. To add to his dilemma, he smelt the taint of their Mhyst on the wind.

"Stand, slowly. Hands up, Warrior, and open them so I can see no weapons and no magic." Over the sound of the breakers came the voice from in front of him.

M`hta swallowed as he stood, hands out. His ears ached to hear the following command. His hands cruelly yanked hard behind him, stung the tight leather thong cut the skin. He was searched thoroughly. Someone pushed him to his knees and grabbed his short hair pulling it backward sharply; his face was to the pale light of dawn.

"He's Karanja." One of them said low. A blade came up and pointed millimetres from his cheekbone tracing a fine line at the white tattoo.

"One blade, and I found these." M`hta's eyes watered in the icy wind. He knew that his quills had been found.

The wind cut in and chilled him just as cold as the steel blade glinted in the pale light.

He felt another nick. The skin through his shirt at his heart stung with the blade's sharp point now pressing intently at his heart.

M`hta swallowed again and pulled himself, mentally aware.

Four Warriors were around him. Past them, he saw nothing to indicate whether Teh`c had managed to escape.

His head suddenly wrenched backwards as the tattoo on his face, and his hairline was scrupulously checked for any tattoo or mark. He knew that one of them had noticed the Red Crescent.

"Your Sahn`Frwh and a Scribe?" the Warrior demanded above the sound of the surf.

Again, his head was wrenched hard by the Warrior holding him. He stared at the Warrior, glancing at his shoulder rank.

"I am both." He said through clenched teeth.

"What type of Scribe?"

"I was the Imperial Royal Scribe to the King of Karanja and the Royal house of Ch`nel." He heard the intake of breath as one muttered something about finding gold.

"And now, what are you, Warrior?"

His shirt was sliced open at his heart; he did not close his eyes for them. He needed them to see the fear that was curling in a wave at the edge of his sanity.

"You are Sz`a`Th then, a Knight of the Death Watch."

Someone whispered 'Sahn`Frwh, ' unnerving the others as the wind took the whisper away.

The Captain spoke for the first time; he seemed to be the only command rank amongst the small marauding party.

"Bring him with us. He can keep the dog company."

"Hey… Scribe ready for a bit of heavy reading?" M`hta just looked at him, resolving his fate but wary; the red-headed Warrior's breath made him want to vomit; discoloured teeth and food bits caught reeked on the Warrior's breath.

"Smile, Scribe. Had you not been so talented, your intestines would have been breakfast for the gulls and your carcass a meal for the sharks."

The Captain looked at M`hta as they yanked him suddenly to his feet.

"What rank within the Mhyst?" He asked more as interest than an interrogation.

"Does it matter?" M`hta replied as the wind billowed the slashed shirt that caught the rain, beginning to fall heavier. His blood smeared down his shirt in a pale red watercolour of life.

"He's a Lieutenant." M`hta's resolve now froze within his mind. He wondered how Corporal Den'ah came into this group of Mah`sden Warriors. Why still would he give M`hta's rank away?

"Then we can leave; seems it's been our lucky day, lads, luckier than theirs", Captain sneered.

M`hta was pushed, kicked and dragged back to the cabin. There he was ordered to stand.

"Seems you and your friend picked a good place to swim ashore."

M`hta felt a cold wave of fear wash over him. He

mentally tried to seek out Teh`c, and to D`mja, it was his last thought as he felt Den`ah Mhyst shroud his mind as someone struck him hard. The Corporal's voice was the last thing he heard in his mind, ‘be on guard, Lieutenant’.

The iced cold saltwater hit his face, gasping suddenly and hungrily for air. It stung his heart as the cold silk sensation splashed across his skin; he shook his head and wished the gods that he had not. The thick massive ache in his head made him vomit violently. Another bucket of iced salt water splashed, stinging his face, eyes, and wounds.

The wind raced across his wet skin, rippling goosebumps, causing him to shiver. He heard the strain of canvas above him. Light upon his eyes, lids glowed a rusty orange-red. Slowly he squinted. His senses slowly acknowledged the movement of a ship on the ocean beneath him. The creak and groan of timbers on a full sea woke him. The sky above was grey-blue black; the ship was trying to outrun a storm.

He looked around him. The ship was triple masted, the ship's sails the colour of grey near blue. No marking of their alliance was of note on the ship.

The Mariners were mainly bearded with their uniform he did not recognise, nor their language. All the ships Mariners were armed with a weapon that turned his stomach. Each wore the three-pronged ‘Su`tah blade, the blade shredded skin like a wheat slasher in autumn.

A thick piece of leather tied M`hta to the central mast; the leather was attached to his feet. His hands were tied but had a twenty-five-centimetre leather thong so he could at least move with the ship's roll.

Two Mariners stood guard on him, their hands held tightly to the hilt of the ‘Su`tah`. He closed his eyes but opened them when he heard a voice near him. Both guards were discussing prisoners.

He saw Den`ah come towards him, walking deliberately slow. He looked at him, then concentrated on the horizon for his gut's sake, heaving with each massive wave the ship rode.

Den`ah crouched down with food and drink. His amethyst green eyes stared at M`hta.

"He won't let you die." M`hta spoke Karanja, but in the dialect that told he was enslaved, Den`ah wasn't; he was just a 'Master of Tongues'.

"Just the same, Lieutenant; he won't let me die either. Linguists have always used it in a time of war."

M`hta's eyes swung around. The repulsion Den`ah saw there took his heartbeat away; he shook his head slowly at the Lieutenant.

"Is that look for me or what you will do to me, Lieutenant?"

"So, where does your alliance lay, Corporal?" He snapped as the wind again filled the sails above them.

The Corporal knelt on one knee; his uniform was of the Sz`a`Th, but he was of the Mhyst Shadows; very few were chosen for that wing of the Sz`a`Th, and the cost of the soul was always high.

"I am Sz`a`Th, Lieutenant, just as you are, and just like you, I was given orders! They are my concern, not yours." His anger was controlled as he spoke. "Unlike you, I am to keep any Sz`a`Th Warrior I have found alive, no matter the cost to me…sound familiar?" He tilted his head sharply at M`hta to get his message across to him and handed him the plate and a hot, bitter drink.

"The drink removes the seasickness you feel; I advise you to drink it now." He said, handing the metal cup to M`hta's bound hands.

He studied the Corporal, knelt on one knee before him, then took the cup and drank it all. There was no taste, which surprised him.

"Give the herbs a few minutes to work, then eat." His eyes swung up to a man on the upper deck. "Others are down in the hold."

"Sz`a`Th?" asked M`hta, trying to control his stomach, ears roared, and rapid breathing. He knew it was not the herbs, but his mind made him feel very sick.

His face tingled, and he wished he was on land and not on this ship by all the gods.

"You might say that." The Corporal replied, watching now as the herbs worked on M`hta's seasickness.

M`hta lay back in a cold sweat as the roaring stopped in his ears, and his stomach now felt hungry, but his mind could not focus on that task at the moment. Only M`hta could convince himself that he now felt well.

"Mind over matter," Corporal Den`ah said and smiled. "My advice is, do not watch the waves but focus on the immediate, such as me. Put the ocean in the background. It is but seascape, Lieutenant, just as the earth is landscape."

"Aye… easy to say, Corporal, a lot harder to do in practice." Den`ah smiled for the first time and patted M`hta's knee.

M`hta knew of his healing and how Captain JA`rvis and Corporal Aq`ten had, through their joint healing, brought both Sqn`xn and Ten`qrn Wolf Nation dark green eyes now had two slashes, one of yellow and one of white diagonally through his iris. He wondered how high the cost of this War would be to them all.

"Den`ah"

"Aye, Lieutenant?" he answered as he healed a deep cut on M`hta's chest with the Mhyst.

"Thank you for saving who you save – one favour I

sent a young woman to travel to the ‘Death Watch’ before Teh`c and I were captured, her name is D`mja, here is her appearance, just touch my third eye” the image the last time he saw D`mja dressed and on the horse looking over her back. He saw the white tear rune.

“Aye – done deal, Lieutenant. I will see if she gets there for Lieutenant Teh`c. It is Lieutenant by my word, but right now, the Captain’s First, I`Chq, their term for First Mate, will speak to you.” He stood up as a man came toward them.

“The Corporal tells me you are responsible for those men below. Is this correct?” The Mariner was of average height, possibly 6’ 2.”

M`hta rose to his feet, more out of respect for the rank than the worry of a swift kick. He was aching and sore more from the beatings of his last encounter.

“Aye,” he said, his eyes held the Sub-Lieutenants. He, in turn, studied M`hta.

“You are a Lieutenant of many talents, it seems.” He said and handed him his quill box. “Seems, so are the Warriors below.” His dark grey eyes reminded M`hta of ink diluted to match sketches done in the lead. The Mariners' short blond hair and beard were neatly trimmed. As the wind blew M`hta’s dark hair across his eyes, he caught a hint of something he did not quite understand in the Mariner's features.

“It seems, I am your prisoner, and so are the Warriors below….”He fleetingly looked at Corporal Den`ah and remembered his orders, and Den'ah said. “It also seems you are to have access to our Talents.”

“Why is that, Lieutenant?”

“I would rather live.” He felt dirty; his clothes were part Warrior and part fisherman from the cabin. Caked with mud still and crusted with salt.

“You may think twice, Lieutenant, when taken

before the Warrior Brae."

M`hta narrowed his eyes at the Officer before him.

"If I regret it, it will be mine alone." He said, "I have had the misfortune to meet Brae."

"Brae is something we all regret." The Mariner said quietly, more to himself than to M`hta. "Your men will be brought above deck soon, Lieutenant."

He turned to walk away but looked over his shoulder, gave a slight salute, and nodded as he continued to the upper deck and the Captain's counsel.

When the other prisoners were brought above, he was sickened by their appearance. They, in turn, we're relieved to see M`hta. He shuddered as Taelen was laid on the deck along with Teh`c.

Den`ah returned to remove their bindings when the Bosun came up to M`hta. Tall, dark-skinned man with sincere kindness in his character.

"Lieutenant," he said as those brought to the deck coughed with the fresh sea air hitting their lungs. "Captains orders, clean clothes, and they are to wash." He opened a box he had carried on his broad shoulders and placed it on the deck.

"You are to be armed as well." He flipped the lid open. M`hta stared at the weapons. There were only two kinds, the Sahn`Frwh sword and the Su`tah blade.

"Why give us these weapons?"

The Bosun's broad chest inflated as he sighed, "The Captain will explain, Lieutenant, in good time. Also, the Captain gave me this blade to give personally to you."

M`hta was handed a blade curved like those of the Karanja used. Curved and black as night with no shine, it was the weapon of choice for those who served the King of Karanja. The King was dead; it seemed though assassins never go out of favour with those who deal in death.

At the hilt of the black-handed matt black blade were the three blue-black stones forming the triangular star of Karanja. Not many knew the meaning of the 'three lives of freedom' or the common name of Nh`s

His eyes flew to the Captain, and M`hta raised his lips, kissing the flat, curved blade. The Captain nodded to him and went about his duties.

The saltwater and soap were as cold and coarse but welcome. Hair and beards were trimmed. M`hta healed their septic wounds, and they dressed in a uniform of the enemy. But enemy to whom he wondered. Taelen was still recovering; black circles pooled under his eyes.

The Bosun returned with more food, fresh food and a fish chowder that even M`hta wondered at the recipe.

"Lieutenant, the Captain wishes to speak to you." M`hta looked at the five men he was now responsible for. "Their safety is assured." The Bosun replied without M`hta asking.

"One thing, Lieutenant, what ails the one with the eyes of the sky?"

"He made the error of battling Mah`sden alone." He glanced at Taelen, who should have been at the Death Watch instead of the deck of the three mastered clippers. "I'm afraid Mah`sden poison will kill him."

Bosun smiled and said with a grin that was as brilliant as dawn on the ocean crests.

"Maybe not... I will see what can be done." The Bosun watched others dress the young Warrior they were discussing.

"You can." He added, "But he is of the Mhyst, Spellcaster and Scribe; how you heal Bosun depends on how those three entities accept you as the healer."

"Aye, Lieutenant, I'm well aware of that. As I said, the Captain wishes to speak to you."

M`hta climbed the ladder to the top deck, saluting

both the Captain and I`Chq returned his salute in their own custom.

M`hta held the curved blade out to the Captain returning the weapon.

"Keep it, Lieutenant; you may need it before this is all over. "

M`hta felt a flicker of recognition in the dark-skinned Captain. Something familiar twigged at his conscious. He glanced down at the curved blade in his hand. A memory faded with time, and all the winters that had past came curling into view. He looked at his childhood friend.

"It seems, Captain; I have not changed so much." He said quietly within the voice of the winds that filled the sails above and before them.

The Captain grinned broadly.

"Actually, I didn't recognise you; it was something you carried when they brought you aboard. And a beard hides a multitude of sins like tattoos and scars."

"I'm sorry," he said, "I don't recall very much, only that I was hit from behind after my capture."

"M`hta..." The Captain said, pronouncing his name in the Karanja way where the 'ht' was enunciated as 'c'. "I have never known any Scribe to carry his ink and nibs in his boot, for that matter, in the way a Warrior carries his blades. Only you…" His eyes, the colour of the black pearls of KR`Nh, noted his facial tattoo.

"You said one day you would be a Knight…I still see the Scribe." He replied, smiling at M`hta.

"You were always the Mariner Jo`sha…it has been a long time," M`hta said as he watched the Bosun lift Taelen onto his shoulders and carried him to another part of the ship. "Are we prisoners, and if we are, who are we prisoners to?"

Both men eyed him. M`hta again looked down on

the deck from which he had come. Only two of the Warriors that had left with Taelen were with them; the other two Warriors were dead. Teh`c and the other Warrior, who was Sahn`Frwh, watched him closely.

They were all Death Watch, all Sahn`Frwh trained. Someone had been doing a search and cull; it seemed to M`hta.

"Our loyalties lie with freedom; for that reason, they have gone underground. For us, the fight above is no different to what 'was' no one wants to go back to the days when …."

"We were enslaved." M`hta's eyes rose to him cold and hard. "I was a slave…you were not."

Jo`sha would not react to M`hta's emotional pain; he too had suffered, especially after M`hta had killed the Warrior and escaped when they were boys of twelve winters old.

"Now is not the time for the past. We are all Warriors of a war that will last winters and decades. How we stay alive is up to us."

"How did you come across, Sz`a`Th Warriors like us?" he asked the Captain.

Jo`sha s eyes did not meet M`hta's. They could not.

"I buy cargo M`hta, human cargo, and when it is Sz`a`Th, I will pay the highest price." M`hta lunged at him, the blade at the Captain's throat; his second in command was taken off balance.

M`hta could hear footsteps coming up to the ladder. His eyes blinked as he held the blade just from the Captain's jugular vein.

"M`hta put the blade away." Teh`c voice was low and firm.

"This is personal, Teh`c." His jaw was firm, as wind-tufted hair, black and straight, stood stiffly with the salt in the ocean air.

"So is this M`hta! I am not asking you, M`hta. I am ordering you to put the bloody blade down. I do not give a damn. How personal your grievance is with the Captain. This ship and its crew are not what we fight. You know I know that, and they bloody know that, so pull your … head in." Teh`c was furious with M`hta, and it was not the first time.

The Captain looked past M`hta and his white anger towards Teh`c's broiling displeasure.

M`hta heard Teh`c unsheathe his blade and felt the cold steel held at his own throat.

"Your orders were to release the Captain and your blade." He then spoke in Sahn`Frwh to M`hta, who slowly released the Captain. The Captain's fist slammed into M`hta's face knocking him down and out cold.

"Lieutenant Teh`c, I believe I owe you my life."

"Not, Captain, M`hta has his reasons for doing what he does, like all of us. Sometimes he just doesn't think as a Warrior should." Sheathed M'hta's blade and slung the fallen Warrior over his shoulder. "My apologies, Captain, to you and your crew. It won't happen again." He then smiled. "Not to you anyway, more likely me." He began taking him down the ladder to the deck when the Captain hailed him.

"Place the 'hot head' in my Cabin, Lieutenant; there are things I need to discuss before we are in our last port of call. You seem to be the man of the reason for the moment."

"Aye, Captain, your command", Answered Teh`c as he continued down the ladder and through a hatch directed by one crew.

He returned to find the Captain alone on the Bridge of the clipper. Teh`c stood at ease, waiting for the Captain to speak.

The ocean had become quite rough, the clouds

darker and treacherous. Teh`c noted the weather and wished the gods they were on land, not on the heaving waters that looked black in the light.

"Do not fret, Lieutenant; we will outrun the storm by two hours at the most, enough to dock and batten down everything necessary.

"There is one question, Captain, why are you wearing Lord Mah`sden colours," asked Teh`c.

The Captain turned to face him; his smile was of necessity and a hint of a rogue.

"Very observant Lieutenant, the Lord's uniforms, yes, but there is no colour to denote our allegiance. We are obedient on land to him – to a point, but out here, we are our own master, and I will slit anyone's throat that chooses to differ."

Teh`c did not reply but stood silently gauging the fall of the deck to which stance would save his backside from timber splinters should he fall.

"Our next and last port of call is Karanja." His voice had an edge of reluctance.

"That port has been closed to all shipping for the past decade, which I am sure you are aware of, Lieutenant, as you are of the Archipelagos to the southeast, are you not?"

"Aye, I am Captain, but I left them as a boy, and I choose not … sea roads but the earth roads for my travel." Teh`c watched the horizon appear and vanish with each massive white-crested wave that dwarfed the ship with each wave.

Jo`sha smiled then his features took on a more serious note.

"M`hta's freedom came at a cost, Captain; I do not think he is in any hurry to return to the land that enslaved him."

"I know the cost of M`hta's freedom, Lieutenant."

A massive dark blue wall of water rose beside them and then crashed onto the deck. “It is time we went below.” He yelled above the roar of the elements. Quickly then went below deck to his cabin.

“We will outrun the storm, Lieutenant.” He said as he removed his tunic and then his shirt. As he went to grasp another dry shirt, the lamp caught a scar that took Teh`c’s breath away.

The Captain slid the shirt over his head and pulled out a chart. “You read maps, and I presume, Lieutenant?” He unrolled the parchment and unceremoniously jabbed thumbtacks into his chart table, holding the chart firmly as the ship lurched and groaned in the weather.

The Captain’s finger jabbed at a place only Teh`c had heard of but never been to.

“This Lieutenant is Karanja, and that is where the First of the Seven Books is.”

Teh`c head reeled, “That you are mistaken, Captain, the Dominion Lord has the first book.”

The Captain shook his head, “Sorry I choose to differ; that hot head over in my bunk found it when he was a Scribe. We were hiding from one of the many beatings we endured as children. M`hta dragged me out on a ledge and through a window. We must have been eight or nine winters old,” he shook his head again at the memory. “The room is round, and the walls are covered in ancient bookshelves and ledgers. I know the book is in that room.”

”Why are you so sure of this when I have seen books that are said to be of the seven we search for?”

His eyes leapt to another time. He saw two young boys racing through the female quarters with a guard running after them.

The woman had distracted the guard, but they still

had to hide. Jo`sha could feel the rush of blood and his pulse and heartbeat pounding loudly. M`hta had dragged him onto a stone ledge from the Princess's room. The height did not bother him as much as it did, M`hta.

The round tower had only one door locked for whatever reason. The book Jo`sha sensed along with M`hta as they fell in through the long window had been on the floor where a shelf had broken tumbling ledgers of all shapes and sizes.

He recalled picking it up and getting a heat-tingling sensation through his fingertips. He hurriedly gave the book to M`hta, who had frozen it in his hands. The ledger had glowed softly. Fearing detection from the glow of the book M`hta had climbed up on Jo`sha's shoulders and jammed the book firmly in a loose timber skylight that rattled with the wind.

His eyes focused on Teh`c's green eyes.

"Because I just do know, now tell me the Dominion Lord is young, is he not?"

"Why do you ask me?" replied Teh`c staring at M`hta's sleeping form on the Captain's bunk.

"Because you are Sz`a`Th Lieutenant, and Sahn`Frwh just as the Dominion Lord is. A woman has tricked the Dominion Lord. That is all I am saying, and I have already said too much."

"Why did you find us, Captain? I remember the cells we were in when you came down to buy your human cargo. We had been beaten, tortured…."

"You were all alive; that was a dangerous thing, Lieutenant. You are all Sahn`Frwh. The most feared and revered Sz`a`Th Warriors of all the lands that is what I buy, and that is what I release."

"And now we dress like traitors." He said in a hushed tone.

"You dress as Lord Mah`sden's, 'The Shadows of

Sahn`Frwh' I am afraid the Red Crescent you all wear was somewhat noticeable."

"I have heard of the Black Crescents wear M`lak's over their faces but a red S`ahrn Turban. Just as we do with the black S`ahrn Turban," He said, glancing at his childhood friend asleep.

"Aye… just as you wear a Black S`ahrn Turban. You will wear the M`lak when we dock, as it cannot be removed except on orders of Lord Mah`sden. So, in short, it hides the identity of the Black Sahn`Frwh, and in this case, the Red Crescents."

The Captain pulled out another chart; this was an architectural map of the Castle.

"You need to study this; it is something I do not need, as I am of the Castle."

He said, handing Teh`c the map. He went to leave when Teh`c` asked.

"The scar on your back, Captain…?" Teh`c asked as he watched the Captain, the man took only a second to answer, but he fought to control his memory in that second.

"The scar is the price paid for M`hta's freedom, Lieutenant." He answered without hesitation.

He glanced at Teh`c and added, "I had the skin shaved from my back over a month; each time it scabbed, they would shave it deeper with the Th`rokz blade. I think your people use one similar when they fillet fish. You could say they filleted my back. If you come across a Captain called Zn`tih, shaft him with the Sahn`Frwh blade for me." He grabbed another tunic and left.

Teh`c was as seasoned as they come, but he could never get used to the acts of torture used on others. He felt suddenly cold because he remembered M`hta had said once that he had escaped at fourteen winters. He closed his eyes and took a deep breath, then opened them. Unrolling the Castle chart, he pinned it in the same fashion as the Captain had the sea chart. The lamp over the desk swung severely, so much so that the strobing of the light had managed to make Teh`c ill. He instead went above deck.

He clung to a railing as mountainous seas tossed the ship like a cork. The cold icy air in his face and the saltwater crashing down on him eased his nausea.

He did not know how long he stood there until someone touched him on the shoulder.

"Come up on the upper deck, Lieutenant." The first mate yelled; Teh'c nodded and followed; the journey up the laddered steps was arduous and dangerous. He slipped more times than he cared to admit. He lost his footing in the mountainous seas and walls of water that plummeted down on them from vertigos heights.

On the upper deck and hanging on more securely than on the lower deck, Teh`c understood why some loved the sea more than those who loved the land. The seas and were magnificent in all of the elements before Teh`c lay a seascape that could not and would never compare with the earth.

The ocean seemed to breathe with each explosion of waves. The colours of blues, greens, and greys etched by white and black moved like an unknown entity. The ocean was a lover who could caress, undulate, and explode emotions more vividly and complexly than those orgasmic thrusts felt on land between a woman's thighs.

Teh`c smiled now, knowing why the sea was a mistress and master to many and a rival to anyone on land. There was no contest; the ocean and seas would win every time, for she unconditionally accepted the Mariners and their survival skills. Mariners came in all genders; he mused some of the best Mariners from his homeland were females; they had an innate sense of the and winds, and he learned a lot from those female Mariners. Once at sea, always at sea, they would tease him, but they needed the freedom of the ocean to be themselves.

"Great, isn't it," Jo`sha yelled at him as the wind tore words into fragmented stutters. All Teh`c could do was nod and laugh. He saw glimpses of land and pale light showing calm waters on the horizon.

"That is our last port of call," Jo`sha yelled again, his fragmented sentences broken and tossed like confetti.

Teh`c, after an hour, went below as they were closer to Karanja and was concerned at how M`hta would take the news. He also had to find Taelen.

M`hta stood looking at the dark grey uniform in his hands and 'M`lak' worn over the face of Sahn`Frwh Warriors in battle.

"What caused you to leave the Castle A`qrn in Karanja, M`hta?" Demanded Teh`c, the others glanced up from sitting playing cards. Teh`c began to strip out of his wet clothes and into the uniform of the Black Crescent Warrior.

"What…? I left for reasons no concern for you to know," he said, shrugging and sliding the blades into his boots.

"Well, I need to know the damn reason because that's where we will retrieve a book."

M`hta froze; the pure dread and fear that crossed his eyes slowly dissipated as he fought to control the emotions he wanted going.

"I… killed a Warrior." He said quietly as he gave Teh`c a towel to dry his skin.

"So what is the problem, who and how," Teh`c asked as he dried his dark hair and body; throwing the towel on the chair, he began pulling on the trousers and boots. “M`hta, I need to know.”

“I was…teaching the Princess to scribe one evening.” His voice was quiet.

“That was allowed?” he asked, pulling on the dark grey shirt and the tunic jacket.

“Aye…”

“You didn’t kill the Princess?” said Teh`c smiling, then grimaced at the look M`hta gave him. “Just trying to hurry the story along, M`hta.” He said, sliding blades into his boots. Two long slender blades slid into the leather sheaths by his hips. He bound the wrist guards firmly and slipped two more daggers on because this was one shit fight he wouldn’t lose.

“Don’t be so daft; I was a bloody slave, not the King's Assassin.”

Teh`c raised his eyebrows at that point in the conversation. “From what I know, I choose to differ, M`hta.”

“I killed him with the ‘Su`tah’ from throat to pelvis…opened him up like a pig.”

Teh`c threw on the dark cloak that came to his shins. “I just hope he deserved to die, M`hta.”

”Aye, he did…” he said quietly.

“Who was he… the Warrior, I mean.”?

“The King's son….”

Teh`c cursed crudely and angrily. “You don’t muck around, do you, M`hta?”

“And now we are going back to hell,” M`hta said quietly to himself, but the others heard the fear in his voice. “I am B`atr.” He said, using the slave slang for a dead man.

“Not if my blade is at your back, Lieutenant.” Teh`c said.” You do not just disembowel a man for no reason. The reason must have been worth it.”

"The life was worth it, Teh`c" He threw on the cloak.

“It seems the Captain thinks so.”

M`hta smiled quietly for the first time. “Aye, he would.”

Was all he said and refused to elaborate at all; Teh'c knew little of M`hta but enough to see that he was not going to push it further, well, not right now.

“There’s one other thing I must tell you before the Clipper docks. Lieutenant Brae is evidently in residence, and J`nn is in the prick's company.”

He growled; he caught the look in Taelen’s eyes.

“Lieutenant, guard your emotions well, just as the Dominion Lord would; remember it is his orders we follow. For it is, her, we need to take with us when we get the first book, not your corpse or hers.”

M`hta climbed the steps to the outer deck and lent on the rails facing the ship; moments passed, Teh`c held against the ocean's railings.

‘By the way…the Karanja woman, from the Tavern ‘The Pickled Sea’.” M`hta spoke quietly.

“Aye…what about her?” asked Teh`c cleaning his nails with a narrow blade as he stared at the ocean.

“I sent her to the Death Watch.”

“You what!…what the hell for?… she’ll be dead before she can breathe, M`hta...what did you go and do that for?” He returned the fine blade into its wrist sheath.

M`hta laughed more to himself and his past, a silent ironic joke.

“Slaves have a common thread. Save a life, owe a life. She saved our lives; I owe her two lives like you say the pact is pack?” He smiled, adding, “I believe she is just as strong and swift as any of our female Warriors…slaves have a reason to live when freedom opens slightly. They take it and run, and run. Never underestimate any gender who knows the cost of death, life, enslavement, and torture.?

Teh`c's heart raced a little as he thought of those golden-green eyes of spring and that wild burgundy hair corkscrewing down in drenched ringlets.

"I am curious; what did the rune on her face mean?"

"She didn't tell you?" asked M`hta, his voice hinting at the pain he had no wish to share.

Teh`c turned to him as M`hta concentrated on something above in the rigging.

"M`hta, what did the rune mean? I'd like to know."

"You will soon find out, and when you do, tell me if your heart still beats the same."

Teh`c glanced at his friend and then looked up at the ship rigging; nothing was out of place.

# CHAPTER 20

J`nn tried to press herself into the bed's mattress; fear dried her throat, already hoarse from screaming. She could not shake the memories or fear of the man now her master.

Rain lashed the sizeable six-foot length of the windows that led to a vast veranda. She sensed the massive storm approaching, and something had also arrived with the elements. There was no point in staying in bed tonight. She needed to get out. The rooms she was in and had been since Master L`unh's disappearance six moons ago were close to the walls of the Castle that led down to the harbour.

J`nn climbed out of the large mahogany canopy's bed. Its four posts were significant as a Warriors' thigh. She went to the wardrobe and took out a gown; its white pureness made her shudder. Instead, she fossicked into the depths, found her grey shift of the Spellcasters, and slipped it on.

Then with her dark grey cloak, she pulled the cowl over her head, slipped on her soft black boots, and left the room.

The Guards nodded at her as she hurried past them; they had become accustomed to her leaving her room for long walks in all weather. They had also become aware of the beatings she had suffered since arriving at the Castle.

J`nn ran down the steps and onto the uneven flagstones, careful not to slip now wet with rain.

The streets were unusually busy with people dressed in black robes, brilliant white masks, and red tears on their cheeks. Confused, she then remembered it was the

Mourning of the Moon; the month was Ok`t`br. She had forgotten entirely. Her time as the prisoner had moons swimming into the other. Time had lingered for her but, in essence, had moved on.

Jostled from one side of the street to the other, she quickly headed down to the piers and oak wharves.

Rain tumbled upon the flagstones as lamplight fell onto the pools and puddles. J`nn stood under the yellow light of a wharf lamp, watching a three-mastered clipper dock. She also knew the ship she had seen, the Captain, and the cargo he had dealt in.

Her feet began to move towards the ships docking port. She seemed drawn to the vessel for reasons beyond her reasoning, particularly those coming ashore. The weather was gusting worse than when she had left her rooms. The wharf area could be dangerous, but for J`nn, it was a sanctuary much safer than her room in the Castle.

She stood a solitary figure on the pier as Mariners and Warriors secured the ship and battened down anything loose. Warriors and crew moved down the gangway to the wharf area, loaded with boxes and cargo.

The Spellcaster watched a Warrior walk slowly down the gangway; his moves were of someone unfamiliar with ships or the destination. The M`lak hid his face. She sensed he was a Sahn`Frwh Warrior, yet he wore the uniform of a Black Crescent; others she sensed familiar to her contradicted the uniform. This confused all she felt. Her senses screamed; unsure, she moved back to the lamp.

The Captain came down in his usual swagger; he had watched her walk down the crowded street from the Mourning of the Moon festival. He knew the woman as the Spellcaster brought back by Brae; some said he had taken the young woman as his own. If that was the case, the Captain and others were of the same thought.

That no one envied her, they all knew she was a prisoner of Lord Mah`sden, and Lieutenant Brae just happened to be the one who was her keeper.

A gust of wind swung her cloak open and tugged the cowl off her head, revealing the Spellcasters gown. Her pale brown hair flew free, caught by the wind. Pale strands shimmered in the lamplight as the wind fanned her hair around her like a shawl of pale brown. The young woman's eyes seemed so huge to the Captain and sad in their pale grey tone.

He bowed, acknowledging her; she, in turn, returned with the curtsy of the Spellcasters' tradition of a half curtsy.

"Mistress, you are out late on such a night of Mourning the Moon, and with the storm approaching, tis dangerous night to be about, Mistress."

"It is peaceful down here, Captain, and I feel…" she stopped as the Sahn`Frwh Warriors disembarked from the ship. The same Warrior she noticed now looked at her, but a Lieutenant restrained him. Something pulled at her mind and her emotions. Why were these men familiar to her? "Captain, I did not know of more Sahn`Frwh coming to the Castle? Does the Lieutenant know of this?"

"I am sure the Lieutenant is well aware of this increase in manning, Mistress. Did he not deploy the last Sahn`Frwh to the mountains?"

"Yes, he did…." She said, confiding in him as she watched the approaching Lieutenant.

One of the Sahn`Frwh marched over and saluted his M`lak had not been across his face. The Warrior stood in the shadow away from the pool of lamplight that the Captain and the young woman stood in.

"Captain, there is a problem." The Captain looked

past Teh`c's shoulder to the Warriors.

"He is one of your Warriors, Lieutenant Teh`c. You deal with him."

J`nn's hand shot to her mouth to stifle a scream; the Captain placed his arm around her. Her sudden distress caught him unawares. He could feel her tremble as he held her. She was slimly built beneath her gowns as he held her.

"Mistress…?" The cowl that had flown back upon her head slipped entirely off as she fell against the Captain.

"These Warriors are Sz`a`Th Captain, Teh`c…I know the Lieutenant?" she whispered against his chest. "Do you deal in sacrifices now as well as enslaving others?"

She saw Teh`c's face as he secured the M`lak across his features.

"Lieutenant Teh`c?" she whispered. As the Captain placed his cloak around her, he replaced her cowl hood back on her head.

"Mistress J`nn…he was right. It was you." He turned to the Captain and said: "We need to talk; Jo`'sha, things have just complicated themselves more than you can realise."

"Then we talk here and now before Lieutenant Brae realises she's not in his bed."

"I am never in his bed, Captain." Her voice was low and hard. He squeezed her shoulder and said

"That's what we all hope for, lass; we all hope." He kissed the top of her head and gave her a small heartfelt hug.

"Lieutenant, the problem is, I realise your Warrior recognises Mistress J`nn. She is a Spellcasters from the Coven that you were all attached to."

The Warrior that had been watching J`nn from a

distance preoccupied her. He broke rank and stood in the shadows watching her. As J`nn moved away from the Captain and the Lieutenant talking, she walked towards him, her heart thumping hard, just as hard as she now found it to breathe.

J`nn stood in front of the Sahn`Frwh Warrior. His black-gloved hand touched the bruises on her face. The scar on her forehead had not been there before, and his fingers trembled as he gently stroked the bruised and scarred flesh.

"Bruisers, J`nn, have replaced mud," he said, "Seems we're always destined to be standing in the rain."

Her voice was soft, barely audible, as she took his black-gloved hand in hers.

"Lieutenant", she breathed, too scared to say his name.

Taelen held her close against his chest; he lifted the M`lak partly away from his face, and his lips kissed her softly; unlike the other kiss in the forest that seemed to burn her lips, this one stirred something deep within her emotions, lighting a heat in her body she had never felt before.

Her hand lifted to the beard he now wore, dark and thick across his features, accentuating the colour of his eyes. Softly she stroked the beard feeling his body warmth beneath.

"Oh my Spellcaster, I thought…I thought I'd lost you forever." His voice thickened with emotion; the heat burned deep within his soul.

He sensed her smile as she pulled away, and the M`lak swung down over his face once more. Her arms held his back, feeling his lungs fill as he breathed; she inhaled his scent wanting not to move, just to keep this moment eternally.

No one saw them in the darkness of the night storm.

Only the fractured illumination of lightning left them as two shadows in the night.

His arms enveloped her holding her just as tightly as she did him, she had lost weight, and something felt fragile in her. Then Taelen bent down and whispered in her ear three words. She, in turn, breathed them back to him.

Those stolen moments gave more to Mistress J`nn and Taelen than a lifetime together. Reluctantly he stepped back into the ranks, and J`nn moved back to the Captain and Lieutenant, who were still talking in the rain and the pale yellow lamplight.

"I must return, Captain. Would your Warriors escort me back to the Castle? The crowds are getting noisy with midnight coming on. I need to return to my room and ward the door so Brae cannot enter."

"Mistress, I think Lady LH`Nejah would like you to have this." Said Teh`c as he held in his hand the silver pentacle. J`nn's eyes watered with tears. Tears dropped heavily onto her gown.

It took all of Taelen's willpower and training not to go to her.

"It's time you escorted Mistress J`nn to her quarters." He turned then to Teh`c. "You have your orders, my friend. May the gods protect us all?"

Teh`c said to himself in a whisper, 'we'll need more than the fucking Gods on this mission.' The other Warriors gave the Lieutenant a look was one of – then we die with our Sahn`Frwh swords flying. We die free. Even J`nn felt the surge of energy from this male and female Warriors group.

Now she understood why Warriors had such a camaraderie, closer than family; one had told her, trying to explain that he and his female Warrior were not involved.

The female Warrior was a Green Crescent. Rarest of all. Her allegiance was first to the Green, then to the Sz`a`Th.

Corporal Xan`eiq, at 5’8”, with her hundred-moonlight wide smile and quick retort, made J1nn laugh at times. Eyes as black as the sands of the Tal`iz Coast. Her hair was wild in red tints of golden sunsets. She was forever putting wayward and flyaway strips of hair behind her ears.

Corporal Xan`eiq replied bluntly, attempting to explain, ‘ Corporal Piz`Eqh, Gods no Mistress. Intimate never. Yes, his green eyes are enticing, yes, he’s tall and a body the other Warriors train for but never get.’ her laugh rippled like water running over river stones. ‘and that black hair he has short and the way he trims his beard. She smiled ‘but oh gods no, Mistress.’

He is all I am; we eat, sleep, shit, fart, laugh, get drunk, get quiet, cry together – love the bastard to death. What Warrior’s like Piz`Eqh and I have um, it's like an unspeakable love, utter respect without the complications of sex’, she saw in the female's Warriors face.

And Piz` that even in death they would not part as they were called to duty he turned and said ‘ die for each other we would…love her to death…she drives me crazy and, we can yell and tell each other to fuck off, but be there for each other in a heartbeat when needed.’ J`nn hoped both were safe; the Sz`a`Th were scattered, proving a problem for them and a bonus for Mahs`den.

The Captain knew only a few would return to his ship. He looked seaward at the lightning and prayed they left after the storm's death, not in its climax.

With three Warriors on either side of her masquerading as Black Crescent Sahn`Frwh, she felt safe for the first time since her capture.

The streets were awash with people in black gowns with white masks, and bright red tears painted on the white face masks honouring the deaths of past ancestors and friends.

The rain did not hinder the festival. Cymbals and drums, along with whistles, played loud and in a staccato rhythm could be heard everywhere. White masks swam seemingly formless in the dark, for no lamps were lit this night.

As a tight group, they walked at a comfortable pace, more for J`nn, than for the long stride of Warriors that towered over her in height. Their long and elaborate Sahn`Frwh swords arched over her.

They had made their way up to the Castle walls and the first gate by midnight.

The moaning accustomed to the festival hit fever pitch as voices raised in grief sang their own tears and regrets as the gate opened.

The sizeable ornate steel gate closed, and the lock clicked louder than the hinges that screeched on bare metal and not grease.

They held their breaths, for the castle was staffed by the Dark Sz`a`Th Warriors of Mah`sden. Black Crescents were, it seemed, elsewhere.

"About time those others were replaced." A Sergeant of the Guard stood impassively as Teh`c's Warriors halted. His left hand was a tin mug of hot tea, undoubtedly spiced with alcohol to ward off the cold weather.

"Where are my Warriors to be billeted, Sergeant?" Teh`c watched all in the courtyard closely. The anonymity of the M`lak was a godsend.

"Sergeant, can these men escort me to my room," J`nn asked the Sergeant as rain fell like diamonds in the yellow light inking out into the night.

The Sergeant smiled as J`nn's un-cowled head slipped between two of the Warriors.

"What have you been doing, lass? You looked drowned."

"Down on the wharves, Sergeant D`run, fresh air, just had to get out for a moment."

The Sergeant of the Guard walked down the steps into the rain to talk to her.

"He's not here, J`nn; seems he was ordered elsewhere, but we both know that can change." He held her slight shoulder, and she flinched. Frowning and without thinking, he said.

"Another beating, lassie…?" he asked, "Come to show me what the bastard did this time…I swear I will kill him…."

She shook her head. The Sergeant slightly undid the lacing at the back of the gown and turned her back to the light of the Guardhouse that flooded the immediate area.

Those guarding her saw the markings, and all slowly went cold and clenched their swords firmly.

Dark red welts swelled and became purple to outline the weapon of use. The T`tyn' was a wood switch from the willow with runic rises on the wood. J`nn's shoulders wore those runes. To have used ancient weapons as the T`tyn Spellcasters individually to control them with the runes was forbidden under all Lore; evidently, someone had not read the rules they all thought

"It seems the prick will stop at nothing to plant his seed in you, Mistress." He said with contempt for the Warrior called Brae.

He loosely secured the stays at the back of the gown and held her chin with the stub of a finger with two missing joints.

"We'll talk later, lass; these Warriors need rest." He called Teh`c. "Aye, take the Mistress to her rooms; you are billeted in the same wing as she is."

Teh`c looked at the Sergeant closely, then to the Spellcaster. He smiled and realised in his way that the Sergeant was trying to protect the young woman as much as he could. Such a dangerous game meant that more of the Warriors that were first thought of was not with the allegiance of Lord Mah`sden.

The Captain on the Clipper had thought this was so. The next couple of days would take a lot of work, not the one-night stand they had initially hoped for. The longer they stayed in the Castle, the more chance Lieutenant Brae recognising them.

"Aye, Sergeant, anything else we should be aware of."

"Aye, lad, I think there is. After taking the Mistress back to her wing and out of this bloody rain, I need to talk to you." He stood back under the awning of the steps, his uniform already wet.

Teh`c` said nothing and saluted. They passed through three more gates, entering through the kitchen. M`hta had become slightly distracted as Teh`c talked to the Cook. The Bosun suggested they stop to source more information even though M`hta knew the Castle well. Hidden behind the M`lak, he could and was noting staff he remembered from all those winters before when he was the Imperial Royal Scribe. M`hta said nothing and stood passively as he just watched.

Much later, they climbed the six flights of stairs in close formation. J`nn unseen as she walked within the tight pack of the Warriors.

The corridors that held the colourful works of the many artisans were now empty cold corridors of despair.

Their footsteps echoed loudly the march of Sahn`Frwh its sharp click of the boots hard heal on the floor was difficult to master. Once mastered, though, it brought fear to all those who heard it in a march. The effect of their boots on the marble floors was chilling. No carpets softened the sounds. The pale glow of lamps reflected sharp, twisted shadows that jutted severely on the highly polished marble floors.

Taelen had looked down quickly to see the mailed face of the Black Crescent Warrior, unrecognisable by the dark grey uniform on the mirrored surface. He had never seen rock so highly polished before.

They halted sharply and precisely with Teh`c's sharp command. Moving away from J`nn to rooms they had been allotted, they also walked around the wing in silence, noting the layout, windows, doors, sounds and how far a sound would travel in such an acoustic area.

Taelen stood alone in the dark corridor outside J`nn's room; he had not spoken to her since they had entered the Castle, and now all his being needed to talk to her,

J`nn stood at her door half ajar. She removed the cloak she had worn and turned, not knowing what to do. She looked at the man dressed as a Black Sahn`Frwh Warrior. The chain mail veil of the M`lak hiding his features also hid the emotions that were swirling through his psyche.

"I need you to be safe, Mistress. I need you to go to the Clipper and leave with the Captain."

"And if I asked you the same thing, your reply would be different, Lieutenant" Her voice, a whisper, sent shivers through his soul as they stared at each other.

"I have my orders, Mistress; all I know is I could not live without you in my life."

"And I could not live without you in mine." She said and stepped into the corridor and to him where he stood. "Remove the glove on your left hand," she said as she removed hers quickly and then held her hand up to him with fingers splayed.

Taelen gripped the leather fingers of his glove in his teeth and pulled the glove off, splaying his fingers opposite hers. His hand shadowed hers, enveloping the slender palm and long fingers in the darkness of the corridor.

"You said three words to me on the docks that I thought I would never hear in my lifetime." Her large grey eyes seemed like two ethereal full moons staring at him.

"You told me, Lieutenant, that once I was of the 'Kh`irz', yes, there are those who say we are part of the prophecy if we live long enough to fulfil the prophecy".

She closed her eyes and touched his fingertips with her own. The energy between them is connected. In Taelen's mind, he saw the Seven Books of the Sz`a`Th, the ones he had were mirrors of the ones he needed. His mind seemed to vibrate; he felt like they were one person, not two. He realized then that the seven books were guides only. What they searched for was, in fact, the lives of seven people. Was he the first book or the last?

As she opened her eyes, she said those three words he had spoken to her, and the intensity of the energy at that moment took his breath away. He struggled and gasped rigidly for air to breathe. He staggered and choked; then, she released him as he took gulping amounts of air and bent over to breathe easier.

"Are you trying to kill me, Mistress J`nn?" he said breathlessly.

"No, Lieutenant, I was just ridding your body of your taint; now you know me, and I know you. It seems we still have a lot to learn." She lifted up his mail, covered his face and smiled.

"If I ever need you and you need me, just open your

palm as you did, like this…." She opened her hand and repeated those three words; her handprint appeared before him. "Then you will know where I am and what must be done, and I, in turn, will know your Lieutenant."

She blew the air softly, and the handprint slowly vanished the same way the wind blows across the sand, with no trail, only ripples.

"It seems we share the same fate and destiny, but… I must go to my room before Brae sees you and me together. I will be safe." She kissed his lips softly as he tried to regain his breath and closed the door behind her.

Teh`c went to the room where he had been billeted, simply furnished with a large bed, chest of drawers, and a chair. No drapes, but then he doubted the chance of sleeping in. He hung his cloak and tunic on the brass hook shaped like a dragon's head. He did not remove any of the blades he carried; kneeling at the large fireplace, he lit the kindling and then the two oil lamps.

Later he heard Taelen's footsteps and M`hta's enter his room. Both had disrobed as far as he had and, by their own choice, had, like him, kept the M`lak and S`ahrn on.

As Sahn`Frwh, they had their dialect in speech, especially the Red Crescents, which for the moment, suited them. Walls had ears, and Teh`c no doubt felt that this wing, in particular, had the most prominent ears of all. M`hta had mentioned the secreted narrow hallways behind walls that staff used when necessary.

"I am going back to the Sergeant; I suggest we keep things as normal as possible to make our appearance here to be". Teh`c looked at his clock on the wall. "Two hours at the most that will make it 3 a.m.; you have your orders." He stood from his kneeling position; he wanted to say a lot but could not and turned. His footsteps echoed the entire length of the wing.

He passed a Lieutenant on the stairwell who greeted him. Briefly, Teh`c prayed that those on the floor above kept their M`lak's and S`ahrn.

Teh`c had to find a Lieutenant that only the Sergeant would know of. He prayed the man was still alive and not gutted in some forest or alleyway.

He found the Sergeant, his baldhead down his right-hand busy writing reports in the Guardroom that he had stopped at on the way into the Castle.

Teh`c entered, and the Sahn`Frwh boots are clicking on the polished stone had the Sergeant's shoulders rise in a sigh. He put down the quill with a sigh and leaned back into the chair.

"You are prompt, Lieutenant, which is good. It will keep you alive if you are lucky."

The Sergeant pushed the chair away from the desk and stood stretching his worn body. He leaned over and grabbed his tin mug.

"Come, I need another black tea, and this is not a place to talk about orders."

Teh`c said nothing and followed the Sergeant to the galley and up a steep flight of stone steps to an empty rook above the gates and the Castle. The door slammed loudly behind them. As if to explain the noise, the Sergeant said.

"To let all know I am here and not be disturbed." He took out a pipe, lit the tobacco, and glanced at Teh`c.

"Don't worry, Lieutenant. I will more than likely die of the blade than of this weed. I will keep this short in length if possible, for there are too many ears for Mah`sden and Brae than I like. Lieutenant Sasson has passed you in the stairwell just now. He will take one of your men with him to the P`rna. What they do is not my concern; it is if they harm those people. I know they won't. They must get them out before a Raven takes flight, and that's fast."

He paused and took a swig of the tea he had made moments before. "Brae is away for at least two nights, but that can change just as quickly as the wind. The moment he returns is when the Castle falls."

"Why tell me this, Sergeant? For all you know, I could be one of these Black Crescent Warriors."

"Aye, if you are, let me finish smoking this pipe before you spill my guts over the rook."

He smiled, scratching at the growth now on his face.

"Lieutenant, I have been many things in my life. And I have worn this uniform and others for as long as you have breathed the air. I know my loyalties; I have seen more blood spilled on this earth in the name of peace to last too many lifetimes. How I have stayed alive, I put down to being good with a blade and knowing when not to draw the bloody thing out."

He tapped his pipe and relit the tobacco, taking a large lung full of the smoke; slowly, he exhaled and relaxed.

"Captain Jo`sha is a good man; many think he provides the slave trade. They are wrong, of course. Still, you and I both know that is a lie but a thin lie. That is the danger of the game we play."

He smoked his pipe quietly, watching the lightning above them vein brilliantly across the early morning sky. "We have two days to evacuate the Castle without letting that privy to Lord Mah`sden realize that something is in the wind."

"This will be a long war, Sergeant. The seven books are not something easily found," Teh`c said quietly.

The Sergeant smiled as he removed the pipe from his mouth. "The art of research is to look for what is not obvious; is that not true?" He asked as he tapped the pipe on the sole of his boot again. "Some describe the obvious some describe the subliminal thought of the title."

"I am a Warrior Sergeant, not a Scribe or Philosopher."

"Aye, when you look at me, it tells you that I deal in the blade. That is obvious; that is what the eye sees when it sees the uniform. The first book describes a person, as some of them do; the second book is the confusing one."

"Who are you?" Teh`c asked, watching the aged and worn Sergeant smoke his pipe in a very early morning drizzle.

"Ah! Lieutenant, I could ask you the same thing. I am a Sergeant of the Guard to the Royal House of Ch`nel. I have worn many uniforms, and I am no consequence. The second book is not here; the first is. It is the second book at 'Deaths Gate', and only you and Taelen can get the book."

"I choose to differ' Sergeant, I have my orders, and two of us must go, and it is not the one you called Taelen," replied Teh`c suspiciously.

"No…the destiny of the other is not to be shared with you, Lieutenant. His is with the darkness of night." He stood brushing the white grey tobacco ash from his grey trousers and drinking the now cold tea. He screwed his nose at the taste.

"How do you know this?" Teh`c stared at him through the M`lak as the Sergeant stood on tired bones.

"Teh`c you must believe and old man, and keep the Spellcasters J`nn alive, she is linked in the same chains of destiny that Taelen is, just as you are and M`hta, Ji`rah, NK`Las who you have not met, there are others to be found, T'tamu, two more will enter the star, Heart Guards, to he, who is the Dominion Lord. Have faith we are the Nations of Man, but we need the Nations of Myth to win this battle."

He passed his hand across Teh`c's M`lak. Standing before the young Lieutenant stood Master L`unh with a cheeky grin.

"Surprised!" he raised his eyebrows and returned to the form of the Sergeant. "By your silence and slack jaw, I'd say you were a touch, taken back. Do you think I would let Mistress J`nn die?"

"But your head…."

"Aye, that was a tad tricky, son. Not something I do not wish to do again. I got sick after that." He looked at Teh`c and smiled, saying, "Close the jaw, Lieutenant, now let's get down to business. I doubt young M`hta remembers where he shoved the book, but Sasson does…" his voice went low, and so did Teh`c's

"How long will Brae be away?" asked Teh`c as he looked out over the town in its darkness, no lamps were lit, and it would not be until dawn, and the 'Mourning of the Moon' was ended.

Master L`unh looked at him through the green eyes that he and the Lieutenant shared. "It will be two days at the most; he has grown stronger, Teh`c, which concerns me. He has not touched Mistress J`nn yet."

"Oh…" he glanced at the Master Spellcasters and saw the glint of mischievousness in his eyes. "What have you done, Sergeant?"

"Oh, just a little spell…have you heard of the 'heat of lust' by chance."

Teh`c frowned but then smiled. "You mean it exists?"

"Aye, lad, and it worked so well on Brae. He just has to touch Mistress J`nn, and his skin blisters…evidently, he has problems peeing now." Eyes widened mischievously at Teh`c.

Teh`c burst out laughing. "You mean he got that close."

”Aye, lad, he’s a tad persistent. I'm told the scabs that hurt the most, his groans are heard from the showers daily.” He said, chuckling. “Anyway, we had better go back down, or they will think I have fallen asleep. You’re not to tell anyone I am alive.”

“Aye, Sergeant, hate to have the ‘lust spell’ on me.”

The Sergeant sucked in the air through his teeth and grimaced. “Oh, neither would I, lad, neither would I.”

He glanced around and spoke in mind speak. Teh`c’s Achepligo’s language took the Lieutenant a moment to understand a language he had not spoken in too many winters.’ down behind the central kitchen in the vegetable larder behind the potatoes…get Lieutenant K`Lpn on board that ship or a horse. He’s worse for wear – cancel the ship – my orders. I will do a bit of spell-breaking. You go straight to K`lpn and know the other Sz`a`Th and affiliated regions. He’s to get every Warrior out that’s been captured – I am good at illusions; they go the Death Watch. My orders Teh`c, there are enough horses, and the trees have been told to protect through the forest. I don’t need them to be heroes; there will be enough heroes, alive and dead, when the Castle goes up; they need to be out in two hours. I have put in specific wards for their safety. Safe footfalls, Teh`c.’

The door slammed behind them, heralding the Sergeant's return to the Guardroom below.

# CHAPTER 21

M`hta's green, gold, and brown eyes smarted as lightning blitzed and thunder exploded above him. He stood at the window and inadvertently ducked with reaction to the storm, making Sasson chuckle genuinely.

"Pleased you still find me amusing," M`hta said, smiling at his friend.

"Ready to go look for a book?" he asked as he produced a blue bottle from his trouser leg.

"If that is what I think it is…."

"We're not going to drink it, you fool. Hell, I don't want a bloody hangover." He sprinkled it liberally over their uniforms, then gargled and spat out the rest of the alcohol.

They were laughing when Teh`c came back into the room. He could smell the fumes from the one hundred percent proof liquor.

M`hta went to explain, but Teh`c shook his head, smiling.

'You took your time,' said M`hta silently, and Teh`c filled them in. It was one thing to fight in a War but another to be covert, knowing that time was not on your side.

"One thing I do know about you, M`hta, is that you don't drink these. It's the strongest I have seen you drink was watered down lager, and you spat that out and then drank tea, for god's sake" he sniffed the bottle and took a swig sucking in air and coughing.

"So you two are off whoring in the early dawn?"

Sassoon laughed. His dark grey eyes crinkled, and it was not hard to laugh with his humour.

"Can't think of a better way to spend what is left of

the night when we have been at sea for eight moons fighting."

"You have a point there. Be back here when you can."

Both swaggered out if they were blind drunk. Teh'c hoped they kept their balance and did not trip down the five flights of stairs to the quarters they sought.

A change of the Guards stopped them for the 0400 hours duty shift. Staggering and trying to hold each other up, they reeked of alcohol.

"Lieutenant, I do not know you," a Captain came up to M`hta, who breathed on him and stifled the laugh he felt was coming.

With his voice slurred and his words tripping, he replied.

"Thass oright Captain, I don't know uze effer." He said, beginning to slide down the wall slowly. He saw the group of guards trying not to laugh behind the Captain's back.

The Captain looked at Sasson, whose own breath was equal to M`hta's in alcohol content.

"Werz off tha Clipper…." Sasson saluted sloppily and hiccupped at the same time. "Captain Jo`sha will vouch for uz." He slurred, pulling M`hta back up by his epaulettes.

"Let me guess, you're both off to the Prn`a for some relief."

"Yez suh…"Sasson smiled as if the promise of the P`rna was a prize worth having.

"I thiingk …I'm gonna throwz up…" muttered M`hta with a sad look on his own face.

"Get away with the both of you…." the Captain said, then added, "throwing up might be all you too can get up tonight," he said sarcastically and shook his head.

"Ayz Captainz…" Teh`c was frowning sadly at the

thought of his penis being flaccid.

They waited until the guards had passed, all smirking as M`hta and Sasson tried to look sober.

They collided with the female Cook who M`hta knew from the Kitchen as they turned the last corner. Since his hasty departure from the Castle at fourteen winters. Five winters was a long time.

"Mistress M`rly, our apologies," he said, forgetting the accent he had acquired while being in the Sz`a`Th. Sasson hit him across the shoulders, groaning loudly.

She knelt to pick up the tray and spilled cups from her hands.

Her blue-grey eyes widened at his voice and the phrase of the wording he used. He had crouched down to assist with the cups as Sasson shook his head. As her hand touched his skin, a deep scar ran the entire length of his hand to his wrist and forearm; Sasson looked at Mistress M`rly, putting his finger to her lips, shaking his head; they both stopped for a moment as the realization hit her.

Her voice croaked with emotion as she tried to form the name, his name.

"M`hta…is that you?" She asked as she stared at the impenetrable M`lak across his face. "You are Sahn`Frwh." She stood slowly.

"You still wear lavender perfume, Mistress."

Sasson was edgy and pulled both of them to their feet, managing not to topple the cups that somehow had not been broken in the collision.

"Look, this is nice and chummy, but it isn't the place for a bloody reunion."

He looked at the door next to them and opened it to see the bare arse of a Warrior and the long legs of a young woman in a position he told himself was unattainable even with his vivid imagination.

"Whoops…sorry," he said and looked at the other doors. "Quickly, Mistress, we have to talk. For God's sake, find us a not busy room."

The Cook wanted to laugh. Instead, she guided them to a room at the other end of the wing.

Closing the doors, she turned and placed the tray on a small table against the wall. Her hands smoothed down the long apron she wore over the dark blue dress.

"I really do not need to know why you two are here, obvious yes, in character no, unless you have changed so much."

"It is a complicated and long involved saga, Mistress; boys grow up," he grins.

"Sasson, I am well aware of a man's needs."

M`hta unhooked one side of the M`lak, letting it fall, "Mistress we…I must get to the tower next to the Princess's room."

"Well, you wouldn't have got too far the way you were going, M`hta. Even Black Crescents must remove the M`lak here. The tattoo would have given you away immediately as a Royal Scribe." She twisted the corner of her apron as she watched them both.

"Who has survived of the Royal family?" Asked Sasson, pacing the bare stone floor. His hands ran through his hair as he walked.

"Only the Princess is alive." She said reluctantly, "It is a battle to keep her from Mah`sden and his Lieutenant."

"Could I move more freely as a Scribe?" M`hta's mind was dancing between avenues of thought and the castle floor plans in haste that scared him.

"Of course, you could, nobody would have a second thought, but should you be found as a slave, you would be skinned alive. Both you and Sasson can go to the P`rna."

"Well, there is, then, one thing, Mistress, the message from Captain Jo`sha's, Bosun. When the Castle falls, you are to go to the wharf." M`hta said to her.

Frowning, she shook her head. Her hands had now rung the apron into a tight ball of twisted cloth. She let fall with disbelief at their request.

"When the Castle falls, do you two realize what you're saying."

"Aye, Mistress, we are both well aware of what we have just said."

Both kissed her on the cheeks and went to the door before she could say any more.

Both went in different directions, and she smiled. Something had not changed. They were using childhood tactics of disappearance. Sighing, she picked up the tray and walked through the door, closing it in a single movement. Standing there in the semi-darkness of dark dawn that was only hours away, she realized that maybe she might become free for the first time in her slave life. Her footsteps were purposeful, smiling. She went down the steps quicker than she had for a long time.

Sasson ran and slid on the floor, deliberately taking the hallway to the P`rna. He became a drunk, quickly passing more Warriors. Smiling and holding the wall as he staggered slightly.

M`hta slowly touched the rune design on the wall before him. He had gone down a different hallway than the one Sasson had gone. His fingertips danced across the runes as if he was playing a keyboard. His heart raced as it had when he was a young boy. The click sounded soft, and then the wall parted just wide enough for him to slip through and into darkness.

M`hta was hit with a sudden wave of childhood emotions spiralling around him. He closed his eyes and pictured Mistress M`rly, her hand on his heart saying to him, 'M`hta listen, you can do this. It is only darkness. No one can touch you …' her voice trailed in his mind as his breathing became normal.

His hand recoiled from the cold wall as old scents and textures brought more memories. He shook his head only to have the door behind him open, and Sasson, not knowing what it was, fell over in the darkness. Blades were drawn, and curses were exchanged as they sat in the dark.

"Brae's back, Sh!" Both fell silent as muffled footsteps were heard on the other side of the thick stonewall.

"That does stuff things around," M`hta said when it was evident those searching for someone named Sasson had left.

"What sent them after you?"

"I walked into the wrong room."

"Again…!" M`hta smiled in the darkness. "Come on, this isn't getting the damn book, is it?"

They sheathed their blades and moved on; rats scurried out of their way. M`hta slowed down here somewhere. His hands ran across the stone for a series of carved runes.

"Here, I have found the runes. Now, remember we're rather drunk and hell-bent on a night of debauchery."

"Since you put it like that …can you sense anyone out there, M`hta," he asked.

"No, there are no Warriors, only those of the P`rna."

"Then follow me."

Sasson's fingers found the runes engraved edges in the darkness, and his fingers pressed them in the sequence that they both knew so well. The soft click opened the door. They stepped into a corridor lightly lit with pale crystals at knee height along the length of the hallway. This part of the P`rna was actually two corridors from the one Sasson had escaped from.

"Sh…" he half laughed as he placed an arm around M`hta's shoulders.

"Shush yourself," hushed M`hta in the drunkest tones he could find.

They staggered, and half fell, making crude comments as they went to the first door that they knew was the rooms that belonged to the heated pools and massages that were part of the P`rna.

"Do you knock or just fall in?" Asked Sasson laughing totally. They lunged towards the door as it opened.

"Sh." they both hushed each other trying to widen their eye as they held each other up.

"I might have known it was you, Lieutenant Sasson." A very young woman would have been sixteen winters if that "I could hear you right down the hall and probably the whole castle."

"Oh, Sarni… it's not all bad… "He said, standing his hand on his heart, looking as innocent as he could." I brought a friend … He's shy!" he smiled a smile that tore down her façade, and she smiled at them both.

"I'm not," replied M`hta standing just as straight. They both laughed as she sniffed their clothes.

She screwed her nose up and began to remove their tunics and shirts. M`hta grabbed her wrists as she went to remove his shirt. Sasson pulled her close to him.

"Now you're starting a bit early." Startled, she stepped back.

"I am only teasing you, Sarni," Sasson earned a sharp slap on his chest from her for his troubles.

"I was removing your uniforms for laundry, Lieutenant. You both smell as if you have been bathing in alcohol. M`hta released her wrists. The M`lak must be removed, though."

M`hta removed the M`lak, his heart beating loudly in his ears for fear of recognition that he may receive. He held the M`lak out for her.

"No, just been drinking this." Sasson swung the bladder of alcohol up, nearly knocking M`hta's head off in the process.

Sarni quickly relieved him of the wine bladder, sniffed the contents, and shook her head at him.

"This came from the blue bottle; I think you two can come with me. I'll just empty this." She took a sniff that made her cough.

"It's a wonder you two are still alive, Sasson."

He reached for her, grabbing her around the waist and sliding his hand up her back.

"I'm still after you." He said, feigning disappointment as she slapped his hands away.

"Sasson, where have you been hiding?" She asked as she led them to the rooms set aside.

Sasson hiccupped, "Secret… Sh. Come, Sarni, be a good girl and come to bed with me."

"Sasson, you know I am not of age yet." M`hta raised his eyebrows as he looked at her carefully. She had the body of a woman. He smiled as his eyes took in the rise of her breasts cresting from the beautiful muslin lace low neckline. The cleavage and lift of the soft skin made him think. His eyes wandered down to the waist he caught glimpses of as the light shift clung to as she walked in front of them. He sighed and said.

"I need a shower." And hiccupped, then added, "I think I will throw up."

"Lord… Sasson, not only do you get him drunk, but the poor Lieutenant will end the whole night with his head in a bucket. Nice friend, you are to have."

"Maybe not, missy," he said, "if you'll come with

me instead of Sasson."

"You've been in the forests too long."

Sasson laughed. His friend smiled at him from behind the young woman who opened a door and turned to him. M`hta quickly returned to the drunk he was portraying.

"In here, Lieutenant, remove those trousers, and someone will come and sober; you up."

"Does that mean no, my Princess?" Said M`hta, the realization of what he had said made him feign vomiting, and he ran half-slipped; through the door and fell into the spa pool.

Sasson went to swagger after him.

"He'll drown in there with all that water."

"Sasson, he nearly did in that alcohol you two have poured down your throats. Lord, you smell like the floor of a Tavern, Sasson."

"Oh… you still love me then." She laughed at him and smiled as she opened another door. "If you go, Sasson, I`zel will tend to your ego and body. Just don't chaff anything this time." She blew him a kiss and quickly ducked out of the doorway as he went to grab her again.

Her footsteps went back to the spa where she had seen the Sahn`Frwh Lieutenant plunged into the tepid waters. M`hta sat with his bareback to the door. He had a black towel around his waist. Resting his head in his hands, he did not look around to see who had entered the spa room. His clothes were on the floor in a heap where he had left them. He had removed the blades and his quills and placed them on the other towel.

"So you can swim; you have many hidden talents, Lieutenant." The sound of her voice from behind him made him shiver.

M`hta's back had thick jiggered scars from his last

encounter with Brae. Deep and purple, the warm water had reddened them. Two scars were deep and angry. He had not turned at her voice and now listened to her footsteps and watched her as she picked up the wet trousers. M`hta looked down at his feet as she came towards him.

"Lieutenant, do you need a woman or …something a bit different."

M`hta smiled and looked at her. He shook his head. She was different from what he remembered, but she had been much younger.

"You're not like the others and Sasson. He will have his fill of girls and more."

"Sasson is all bravado, Mistress; I know him better than he does himself, behind those dark grey eyes and long dark eyelashes, that dark hair…he's good…, I can be like him but not now. I prefer a dry uniform and something to kill my head."

She smiled. "No doubt you do. Come, I'll show you a room, it's quiet, and you can sleep there. M`hta picked up his blades and other belongings and followed her.

The clothes she carried dripped a dark wet trail along the stone corridor.

M`hta walked behind with the black towel around his waist and feet, and the rest of him was now feeling the cold. With teeth chattering, he was grateful when she stopped and opened a door.

"You will be left alone in here, Lieutenant. I will go get a dry uniform for you." She turned and closed the door. M`hta did not have to look around the room. He knew the place well. He dropped his belongings onto the large bed and squatted down, lighting a fire he hoped would bring immediate warmth, but he knew it would not.

He was standing lighting a lamp when the young woman returned with what she had promised and a drink.

"Your dry uniform, hope it fits. I had to judge from all the others hanging up." She shrugged as M`hta took the uniform, grateful for warm clothing at last, and turned, dressing and ignoring her. He had too much on his mind to worry about what was proper in M`rly's eyes and what was a necessity in his. He smiled as he thought she would always see him as a boy of fourteen winters and into as much mischief as he could.

"Why are you smiling? I've seen naked men before. Believing me, most if not all look better clothed."

He raised his eyebrows, laughed, and pulled his trousers on.

"I would not tell Mistress M`rly that if I were you."

"Lieutenant, may I ask why you wear the mark of a Royal Scribe and Sahn`Frwh?" M`hta looked at her through his fringe as he pulled his boots on.

"You can be both as a Warrior; the two do not conflict."

"Where do you come from, Lieutenant? I have not seen you here before?"

"Why? where I am from is no consequence. I shall be gone soon."

"You just reminded me of someone I knew when I was little. I don't remember the Scribes name."

"Then he mustn't have been remarkable." Said M`hta drinking the hot tea she had brought him. "If he had been important to you, you would have remembered his name." He looked at her, smiled, and continued eating.

"Why are you not married off as is the custom of Karanja?" she ignored his question and instead asked one of her own, watching his reaction.

“Why did you call me Princess back there?”

“Maybe you reminded me of someone I once knew, but I remember her name. That is the difference; she also asked too many questions.” She blushed deeply as he then looked around the room. All the beautiful artwork he remembered was gone, but the bedroom still was regal.

“This room is far too rich for a Lieutenant. Why did you put me here.”

”It was once a Princess’s room…M`rly suggested I should. She seems to like you a lot,” she stopped as she too looked around the room.” Do you like books, Lieutenant?” She asked, changing tack.

“Why books, Princess?” She smiled when he called her that.

“When I was little, the Royal Scribe told me books were written to tell us stories of what life was, is, and could be.” She replied, memorising M`hta’s exact phrase all those winters ago. She was smiling at the memory.

“Wisdom comes with knowledge.”

”That is what he would say. He was wise….”

“Old?”

She laughed. “Come, I shall show you some books, and to me, he was old, but when I think about him, he was probably the same age as I am now.”

“Yes, show me your books.”

“This way, Lieutenant…what is your name? Mine is Sarni.”

“I think it is better to call me just by my rank. It is easier to remember rank than a name. He said, “Now, you say I am interested in these books. Where are they”?

“I trust you, Lieutenant.” Her eyes were a deep ocean green colour. “I don’t know why, but I feel safe with you for some reason.”

“Well, tell M`rly that when you see her. I am sure

she will ask for some very intimate questions."

He followed her down roughly hewn steps, the lamp shone a yellow gold, and they were in the narrow back corridors used by servant's slaves and others.

She turned abruptly. He followed; he knew the exact path she was taking, he could have walked it with his eyes shut, but he said nothing and followed diligently.

"I hope you aren't afraid of heights." She said, sliding sideways. The ledge was narrower than even he remembered.

As a boy, it was this way and others he had escaped if M`hta slipped, he would be wedged firmly and die.

They followed the narrow ledge to the screen side and climbed into a small window.

The girl then said, "I have to go back."

"Why? Because M`rly said to?" asked M`hta as he stood in the round room.

She smiled at the Lieutenant standing in a room that once hid young boys from the beatings of their masters.

"Actually, she did. She said something strange. That whatever happens. I'll never forget you, Lieutenant." Her head came to his shoulder as M`hta lent down.

"Maybe you never have Princess." He kissed her on her cheek lightly as he always had.

"You're a strange man, Lieutenant." She then stepped back onto the ledge, leaving him with the lamp.

"You know your way back if you feel inclined." He said after her, he heard a faint 'I know. Then he was left alone in a room that had given protection all those winters ago.

Books were all around the wall; he knew them by heart. M`hta sat down on the worn rug, aged and dirty. The small room seemed the only place in the Castle that had been left untouched by Mah`sden.

M`hta lay down, staring up at the white dome of the

room. He remembered one night working late when a storm had picked up his papers. He had placed the only chair on the table and climbed up, wedging the sky window shut.

The dark-framed sky window had an awkward angle to it. M`hta again stood on the table. He pulled the object he had wedged firmly into place nearly a decade before. Dust coated the ledger thickly on a grey carpet. Yet the tingling sensation of runes beneath his fingertips sang to his senses.

He found some tarred paper, began wrapping it firmly, and then left, extinguishing the lamp.

Back in the room, he had been given, he stripped to his shorts and climbed into the bed. He checked his blades and lay back into the pillows.

“Who's here?” came a small frightened voice.

“Me…Sarni, what are you doing in my bed?” he asked. He could hear her sniffing as she wiped tears beneath the bedsheets and blankets.

“He has come back tonight; he wants me….”Her voice broke with emotion.

“Who wants you?”

“Lieutenant Brae.” Her voice was only a whisper, and he had to listen hard to understand what she had said.

M`hta spat out his disgust at the man returning so early. He heard the footsteps and was glad one lamp was on and the fire. He smiled. The scene was set.

“He’s coming,” she whispered.

“Seems we're about to have company, Princess; well, let’s put an act on, shall we? You’ve seen the girls and were cheeky with Sasson, flirting with him.” M`hta listened to doors opening and voices raised in abuse at being disturbed by it seemed a Sergeant and his two Warriors.

"Yes." Her voice was but a whisper.

"Get the clothes off quick." M`hta slid his shorts off and threw them on the floor; he grabbed her clothes and discarded them quickly.

"Why do we have to do this?" She asked as M`hta pulled her to him. He gently laid his body over hers to protect her from those who were about to burst into the room.

"So the damn prick doesn't torture you, Princess. Now swing those slender legs outside these damn sheets and around my backside."

She giggled and squirmed as she felt his skin against her own.

"What's so damn funny?"

"You've got a hairy backside." He heard the door open; he had no time to think and held her; his lips instinctively found hers. He knew by her response that her eyes were wide open and shocked by this move. He pressed harder, kissing her with want he would kick himself later for.

The door flung open with the Sergeant at arms bellowing.

"Where's the Princess."

M`hta pulled away; his eyes swung at the Sergeant who had picked up their clothes and his M`lak.

"What the .... Put the clothes down, Sergeant, and get the hell out of my room," M`hta lent across her face grasping the blades he'd placed on the small wooden tabled beside the bed and deftly threw the black edge of the Su`tah. The blade slashed the Sergeant's hand and pinned the uniform tunic to the wall behind him.

"As I said, leave the uniform alone and get the hell... out... of my room."

"Your Sahn`Frwh." He said, staring at the sword standing near the bed.

"Your quick Sergeant, now get the hell… out of here. Alternatively, that sword will be shafting you. I haven't spent the last six moons gutting the bloody Dormas and Drargon`H." M`hta climbed out of bed naked. He pulled the Sergeant close,

"If you want to be next, I don't mind messing the floor, do you?" His eyes wide glared into the stunned Sergeants. M`hta turned and climbed back into the bed, pulling the sheets over him.

"As I said, I have orders to find the Princess."

"Good go and find the bitch; I'm with my Princess tonight just like everyone else in the P`rna."

"Which ship did you come in on, Lieutenant?" The Sergeant pulled out a piece of parchment.

"Captain Jo`sha's bloody Clipper…Leave off, princess." He heard her giggle, climb around his back, and draw on his back with her nails.

"Hell Sergeant, I came ashore with Lieutenant Sasson. He's whoring somewhere now. Do you mind?"

"One other question, Lieutenant."

"Aye," grumbled M`hta trying to swat her hands away from his chest. His thoughts cursed women in general.

"There was a light in a tower. Did you see anything"?

He looked at the Sergeant to say, 'what the hell do you think I've been looking at all night?'

The Sergeant wrapped his bleeding finger in his notes and left.

M`hta lay on his side with his arms around her naked body, holding her close. Her silence now was driving him mad. "Let me guess, too hairy," the door opened again.

"Hells sake… Sergeant, what is it this time?"

"Sasson verified you, Lieutenant, my apologies."

"Aye, now get the hell! Out of my room and lock the door!"

The door closed, and he heard the lock click three times. M`hta lay back onto the pillows, exhausted. He was numb, but his damn body was not as it responded to Sarni's body in his arms. He wanted to bed her. He cursed angrily and threw the sheet off his body.

"Your safe now," he swung his legs out of bed and pulled his clothes on. He handed back her clothes. He took a deep breath and picked up the bound ledger, the runes giving his fingertips pins and needles. "Believe me, Princess, I do this to save my own balls; M'rly will have a vice grip on them knowing we were in bed and naked."

"Where are you going?"

"Places, Princess. They will not be back. Get your arse out of here now and flee the Castle. There is a lot of shattas about to happen to quote a friend of mine. I'd like to know at least you will live." Before he left, he freed the tunic pinned to the wall by the Su`tah blade. He went closing the door behind him.

Finding Sasson was not hard, for the Lieutenant always left his shirt hanging on the door outside a room. M`hta had never asked why and now was not the time or the place.

The room was warm, and he could see the tangled limbs amongst scrunched bedding. Pillows strewn on the floor over clothes lay exhausted and twisted.

"Sasson, wake up." He thumped his friend hard, knowing how heavily he slept, picking up clothes and handing them to Sasson as he untangled his legs from the woman he was with.

"Sasson…"

"I hear you, for hell's sake."

"Then hurry. I found what I was looking for."

“So I heard,” he replied, pulling trousers and boots with haste, putting on his tunic, and as he left, the room blew the woman a kiss. Stopping for seconds, he grabbed his shirt and tied it around his waist.

“What?”

“You got a bit?”

“No, but I felt like it. Come on. All hell is about to break loose, and we don’t want to be here when it does.”

They ran the darkened corridors; no one stopped the two Black Crescents or questioned their urgency. Both ran with the long Sahn`Frwh sword angled across their chests.

They found all in order back on the wing where they had been billeted. The Sergeant at Arms and Teh`c looked relieved when they both stopped running.

“You have the book?” asked Teh`c as Taelen came out from his room to stand with them.

“Aye, and who are you, Sergeant?”

“You would have difficulty believing us if we told you, just let’s say an old friend.”

M`hta handed the ledger to Taelen, but Teh`c stopped him as the Sergeant said to them.

"The Dominion Lord cannot touch the First Book. Read the title if you would, Lieutenant M`hta.”

"I know the title reads merely ‘Scribe, Spellcasters, and Mhyst’ I don’t understand why I can read it and no one else can.”

“Because Lieutenant, you are the Scribe just as he is. You don’t recall your parents, do you? For your mother was the Mhyst and your father, the Spellcaster.”

He then turned to Teh`c and said: “It is time to leave Teh`c, Brae is back in the Castle, and this needs to be elsewhere.”

He waved his hand across their faces as he became Master L` unh once more. “It is time we left, the others will come with me, and you and Taelen are to get as many out of the Castle as you can."

The other Warriors joined Mistress J`nn and the aged Master L`unh as he cast a spell of removal. Teh`c stood with them as the air became cold and foggy in the hallway where they had all stood. As M`hta and Taelen watched them fade, they heard footsteps behind them.

They both turned around at once with their Sahn`Frwh swords across them defensively.

"M`hta, I wish to talk to you and now." M`rly was not going to take no for an answer as she glared at him and Sasson.

"Now is not a good time." Replied M`hta. "Besides, I know what you're going to say anyway."

"You, of all people, should know your place." She looked at him as he removed the M`lak. Her anger had made her step over that invisible line between slave and non-slave.

"Oh, I know… my place, Mistress, believe me, I bloody do. For your information, no one touched her. As far as I know, her maidenhead is still intact, but I didn't get down there to see with my own eyes or feel with my fingers."

Her hand flew through the air slapping him hard, and she instantly regretted it. M`hta replaced the M`lak. His anger surprised Taelen, who had never seen the Lieutenant lose his temper.

"I have seen younger girls than her tortured by Warriors and left to bleed to death, the Princess will be a virgin till that happens, and it didn't happen."

"Now I suggest you go ring the bell in the Northern Bell Tower; we are

Sahn`Frwh Knights of the Red Crescent and Mhyst and tonight we war. Do one thing, for me, Mistress, use the secret passages? Bosun wants you alive, not shredded. The Sergeant at the Second Gate will meet with you. Now go."

He pressed the 'Su`tah' blade into her hand, "Use it, M`rly" He turned on his heel; their running could be heard loudly down the empty marble corridor.

She turned to look at the walls near her and picked up one of the oil lamps.

Pressing her fingertips on the rune markings, she heard the coded click of stone, then the door was opening, she stepped into the opening and darkness as shouts, and the clash of blades could be heard.

The thud of a body made her heart jump to her mouth. She lifted her skirts and ran through the pitch of the narrow corridor. The Cook scared more rats than she really wanted to think about. M`rly knew the passages clearer than her own mind. She tentatively felt for the blade, and her skin tingled. Her feet ran faster and faster and then up steps two at a time. She wished she had worn trousers; she slowly climbed as muscles burned like hot knives had been driven into them.

The door to the northern Bell Tower was stiff to open; she pushed with her shoulder and squeezed through.

She pushed the soft candle wax that had softened around the large candle that showed the tower light into her ear canals and reached up to the thick rope and pulled with all her weight

The vibration of the large bell could be felt rumbling as it connected with the enormous hammer. Breathing heavily, she tugged and pulled up and down, up and down. Useing her weight to her advantage and wishing she was more substantial.

As M`rly pulled the tolling bell down hard on the rope, she knew it would be heard from the mountains and far out to sea.

Torches exploded the hidden caches of explosives that had long ago been set, as booby traps should the Castle ever be taken over by another force.

Karanja exploded into oranges, reds, and whites. Fires were exploding, and rooms became infernos, corridors, and buildings as far as the eye could see. The chain reaction had been set into place, and a domino of fires exploded.

A city empty of occupants except those who had chosen to stay fought on the side of the Sz`a`Th.

M`rly tolled the bell for an hour. She hurled it over the stone window ledge with another thick rope, its height of thirty feet stuck in her throat.

"Holy Mother," she whimpered as a Warrior burst through the door M`rly hand held the Su`tah blade. 'Forgive me, 'she whispered to the stunned Warrior as the blade sliced his neck open; the light died in his blue eyes as he fell his head fell awkwardly back half severed. She sobbed as she stripped him and herself, changing into his clothes. She was thankful for her tallness and the Warrior's slimness for once.

'Holy Goddess,' she repeated as she ran down the steps placing the Warriors the M`lak on. Half sobbing, she dived into an alcove to meet another of Lord Mah`sden Warriors again. She slashed with the Su`tah blade; he ran as he fell; blood poured from the neck as it lay twisted and half detached from the body like a broken doll.

M`rly ran like a Warrior, for she'd never been one for a sashay of the hip, her height and slimness never gave her that gift, but it gave her speed. She found the 'Sergeant at Arms of the Second Gate.

"Hell, M`rly, you look like you've been butchering in a slaughterhouse."

She caught a sob with her bloody hand against her

mouth, tasting the saltiness of blood and vomiting.

"Sorry, lass, I have a big mouth, haven't I." He said, gripping her shoulder, "Come, Mistress. I'll have you at my back anytime."

M`rly swung around as a Warrior lunged; she caught him with the blade across the throat. She went to her knees and vomited again as the Sergeant hoisted her up to her feet.

"Good Girl, let's get out of here."

The building exploded around them as they ran. The wave of red heat and flame pushed them with furious intent. The glow of the light behind them showed the way out, silhouetting their running figures against the hot orange and red flames and destruction.

"Sweet… mother of the Oracle." Hissed the Sergeant; the inferno they were escaping had now cut them off. Fireballs erupted, ripping through walls metres thick.

"Into the river M`rly…jump." He said, grabbing her hand as they both jumped off the rampart. Another explosion erupted on the other side of the bridge that would have brought them to the fourth gate; the gust of orange inferno wind pushed them further out into the water.

# CHAPTER 22

"So the Dominion Lord has sent his confidant to finish me off?" Brae said as he gripped the pommel of the Su`tah blade buried deep in his right thigh.

M`hta lay still where he had fallen from one of the explosions. He had thrown the Su`tah blade as Brae had struck him profoundly at the base of his skull. M`hta lay with eyes that saw nothing.

Groaning as he wrenched the blade from his thigh, he went to lunge the short sword deep into the still form of a Red Crescent Warrior.

"Not this time, Lieutenant." Taelen's voice made him frown and gave M`hta hope.

Brae looked up as a Warrior of the Red Crescent stepped out of the smoke and flames. The hall behind him erupted into an orange, white blaze.

"You were saved once… why because he felt the need." He said, "Since that day, you have butchered, tortured, and maimed more Warriors, women, and children than I care to think." He walked around Brae, stalking the Warrior so that M`hta was closer to him. "Yet you said once you would help destroy Lord Mah`sden, well I am here, and I am waiting, and I have all the time in the world right now."

His eyes burned from the smoke as they both coughed in the heat and ash that was increasingly everywhere.

"You owe me the last book, number seven." He said and picked up Brae, hoisted him high, and dropped him out of the window. "Hope you can swim, prick." He yelled as he watched the Warrior fall into the river below.

Another explosion ripped the side of the Castle, knocking Taelen to the ground. Timbers from the ceiling fell around him as he chokingly went to M`hta's side and carried him on his shoulder, looking for a way out.

"M`hta, you make it hard to save you. There is no way out that I can see." He said

"Go to behind the third stone column, and there you will find the rune script with the rune sign of defence and water. Push hard and then step through and hang on."

Taelen had no choice in the matter timbers crashed around them as he made his way over to the stone column that M`hta had mentioned. He found the runes, pressed, and punched them, but they did not move.

"You're sure you have the correct runes, M`hta. There is one for Gateway." M`hta had fallen unconscious as Taelen pushed at the rune for Gateway. The column shifted as he stepped into the darkness. He realized there were no steps. The massive void of darkness was of polished marble, and they slid.

"M`hta…wake up…" M`hta's eyes flicked open, slowly focusing on Taelen.

They travelled entirely straight for where he did not know, and he had trouble holding on to M`hta, who had landed before him.

With no lights to show their descent, Taelen used his inner sight to see where and what they were on.

There was nothing to see. The polished marble was a tunnel, and they were the sole occupants.

Taelen's senses could detect a lot of water and not still water. He gripped tightly onto M`hta as they hit a wall of icy saltwater.

Taelen's world became blurs of greens, blacks, and the sparks of nerve endings. Gripping onto M`hta, the burning pressure on his lungs felt like they were about to explode. Instead, his head erupted out of the water and into the air. Kicking to stay above the depths below them, Taelen lay back, pulling M`hta with him, and kicked.

The water stank, and he knew they were now somewhere in the sewers. How they arrived there, he had no idea. Dead rats and human excrement flowed with them, and blood was snaking down the drains.

His boots hit the bottom of the tunnel they were in, and standing on the slippery rock was difficult as he held onto M`hta, still a dead weight in his arms. Hauling M`hta onto the narrow surface of the ledge meant they were outside the Castle walls was even more difficult.

Taelen looked at the light above them through a barred grate where the drains emptied refuse and cascading filthy water; he could hear voices. Rain poured through the grate, and stormwater blinded him, coughing and spitting. He tried to hear whose voices, for he knew they were near the docks. Slowly Taelen smiled, recognising those voices he knew quite well.

"TEH`C…TEH`C…!"He yelled and could hear the searching steps of the Sz`a`Th Warrior above them in the street.

"Where?" Teh`c yelled his reply, calling others to aide him from the surface above Taelen. Taelen hoped this would not take long. His smell of the sewers would last him a long time.

"HERE! LOOK DOWN INTO THE GRATE…HURRY." He called as the lamplight poured down on him and M`hta's unconscious form. The Warrior below struggled to hold the other in the flooded chamber of the sewer.

Blades suddenly appeared above levering the grate, and water poured down into the flooding drain from the rains above, making the work even worse. The current was sweeping and dragging. Taelen fought for footholds and gripped the sharp-sided stymies for advantage as he struggled with M`hta to keep them both anchored while those above worked to free them.

Pulling from up above was not working. Teh`c looked through the grate and flooding waters at his friend struggling to keep hold. Their eyes met as a wave of water submerged both Taelen and M`hta. The metal had rusted.

"WE GET THEM OUT NOW, OR THEY ARE DEAD WARRIORS!" Yelled Teh`c to those around him, scrapping furiously at the rusted and fused grate in the ground.

The ship's crew then tied a rope to the winch on board the Clipper and wound it until the grate, at last, broke free.

First, M`hta was hauled out of the sewer, then Taelen; M'hta had again fallen unconscious while Taelen was physically spent. His body had no more strength, and he let the willing hands of the crew carry him.

"Get them on board. We leave immediately." Captain Jo`sha's orders from the top deck were in a voice; no one cared to argue. His words told them how imperative it was to leave with their heads still attached to their bodies.

Had they stayed, that physical connection would have been severed and shafted on their swords to remind others that Lord Mah`sden was superior. This time he was not.

Taelen and M`hta's clothes were stripped from them; they were quickly washed down with buckets of seawater and then helped onboard the Clipper. Jo`sha's Clipper sailed through the heads that opened onto the southern ocean of C`non and into the gale winds that screamed around the southern tip of land they were now leaving. One man watched as the Castle A`qrn of Karanja burned.

He turned to his friend, whose eyes stared blankly in the wind and wondered if his friend would ever see him again. His heart asked if the loss of his friend's sight had been worth it and how many more would suffer for the Seven Books.

Weeks later, the same Warrior sat next to a fire that glowed in the pale grey-white of winter dusk. He sat crossed-legged on the cold white sand. Limestone cliffs rose behind him in a vertical wall of eroded coastline's jaggedness and silence, trapped forever by severe weather. Toasting the thick bread, he drank tea's tan bitter hot drink. White sand beneath him was bloody cold, but it was winter.

Jutting white rock marked the small cove, semi-protected from the beatings of an angry, relentless winter ocean.

The torn coastline of the island married well with the icy capped steel blue, the black ocean that held the small island in a tenacious clawed grip of unrequited love.

He sniffed, wiping his nose on the handkerchief, and pulled the cloak around him to keep some of his body warmth from the chilling gale that pierced his ears with crisp sharpness, and his eyes watered from the icy slice of the bladed wind.

He sighed, straightening his shoulders. His spine made clicking sounds as bone and disk aligned once more. He watched the rowboat from the ship anchored after negotiating the unrelenting surf toss. Their oars upright, the tiller fought the current and swell. Warriors leapt into the white foaming surf, simultaneously hauling the boat. The wooden hull grating across the cold, coarse sandy beach stopped, and all that could be heard above the wind and surf was the seagulls surfing the wind and calling each other.

The Captain stood legs apart, his hands in his fur-lined Mariner's jacket for warmth that evaded him in this most southern region of the  did not keep him warm just now.

They had lost much that night Karajan burned, Mistress J`nn and Master L`unh had not been found, along with half his crew. The deaths and the ones who were reported missing pulled at their consciousnesses. Many blamed themselves for not holding onto others in the chaos of the fire and explosions.

Guilt, chewed away at their souls. The first thing they were taught as Sz`a`Th or Sahn`Frwh was ‘no one was left behind dead or alive all were brought home. He took a deep icy breath and exhaled slowly as the gale escaped with the warmth of his body.

He noted that his friend’s eyes had become darker, he thought, and his black beard had grown thicker when he had been on the isolated island. The young man’s dark hair had also silvered at the temples.

“Taelen,” he said, “We are ready if you are.”

The Captain's orders and requests were always short and straightforward as always. He thought as he looked at Jo`sha standing just beyond the reach of the waves.

He drank the last of the tea that had gone cold and stood in one motion. He threw the mug on the fire. The pottery popped from the sudden exposure to heat, the halves falling apart like a heart irreparably broken. He dusted the sand from his trousers and covered the fire with graded movements from his boots. Too soon, the fire was extinguished. His heart felt as cold as the wind that now held him.

The young man ran his thumb down the length of his bearded chin and looked over his shoulder to the hill, jutting out to form a cliff some twenty feet behind him.

Stark white of the limestone cliffs, pockmarked by erosion caused by the iced winds and heavy seas that dominated the seasons held one he could not bring back.

A rock chiselled into a thirteen-pointed pentacle stood solitary in its monument.

"Aye," his voice croaked. He blinked through eyes pained from burden and grief and sighed, wiping his nose again and sniffing. The ache of guilt unwarranted hurt Taelen deeply.

"Aye, Captain…let's go."

The Captain turned to a cage where a white-crested sea hawk sat passively waiting and watching. Dark eyes blinked back at the Captain.

"Guard, Lieutenant M`hta's soul, my pretty one. Guard all he has till we return." The hawk blinked, then climbed onto the Captain's leather-protected forearm, later rising into the solid southerly gale. Higher up to the cliff, then down onto the Spellcasters Stone.

As they launched the rowboat through the surf to the ship anchored out in the deepwater of the small cove, a lone figure stood dark upon the grey-green slope near a thick forest of tea trees covering nearly the entire tiny island.

All except the west coast of the small island, where the coast and inland were protected by the thick pines of the N`an Island Pines, which were named after the island it's self

The seahawk again took to the air, spiralling down into the medium-height timbers, alighting upon another's leather-clad forearm. The man was dressed in thick firs, the snow would be soon, and winter always came early to the southern .

"So, 'my eyes, tell me, have they left safely." He could see that in his mind's eye. His own eyes had paled from green to dark pale jade. The great Karanja fire of last winter had seen to that, or had it been Lieutenant Brae's final act of revenge?

"Go, my sweet, go and see our island home." The hawk flew alighted as a white timber Wolf came to his side.

'Are you worn, Lieutenant?' came Wolf's thoughts into his mind.

"No, S`hael, tired only of not seeing beauty. I see but with the eyes of a blind Scribe." He replied as the cold icy wind made him shiver under the winter fleece of his jacket.

'Remember what Lord Taelen said,' nuzzled the Wolf into his palm. The cold, wet nose made him smile. Her pale golden brown eyes looked at the Warrior standing beside her, who could no longer see.

"Aye, I know. But my friend does not see with the eyes of a blind man; he cannot understand how I feel."

'No, but his searches for the books as one Lieutenant.' Thought the Wolf to his mind, M`hta exhaled, sensing his breath's misting in the wind. His thoughts were of the first book, the dark near, black polished leather of the book's hardcover but more of the carved runes on the book, which were filled with the purest silver ore. He absently wondered who the artisan had been. His mind's eye told him all he needed to know. The eyes of an Elf looked up at him from long ago, 'welcome,' they said. He wondered what he was being welcomed to.

The Wolf was quiet as they walked along a sandy path through the thick Tea Tree forest to the cabin where they would wait for the arrival of the Second Book.

M`hta's eyes were healing, his sight was not as it had been, and it was different as if more intense, auras and vibrations could be seen around individuals, and his sight became as precise as Eagle and Wolf combined.

For someone who did not have a head for either heights, nor the night vision of Wolfs. The Elf and Wolf Nation's gift of M`hta's sight meant the day was night. In many ways, this would aid him in the times to come.

M`hta sensed that there was the eighth book. He could feel it so strongly, but who would believe him? He wondered when now many were doubting that the books were salvation.

He could not believe that M`hta, the enslaved person, was the first book. It was so difficult to understand that his life had already been planned before conception, and he also wondered who was behind it all and the ultimate gain. It was not peace.

**The End**

**Coming Soon -**
**Second Book of the**
**Sz`a`Th Chronicles**
**E`rth, A`r, W`tr, and F`r**

# Bibliography

Mhyst

Mhyst activates at 16 winters upon females' upper left high breast and pectoral muscle on males. Giving the ability to heal wounds and illness, but Mhyst Lore restricts this to injuries that can be sewn and bandaged. The design is of particles of Grey, white, silver, mauve to purple and in Taelen, pure white. Nation of Wolves has similar Mhyst all Sz`a`Th Warriors and those whose lineage includes Sz`a`Th who may not be aware they have the Mhyst symbol of Mhyst in Ogham and rune, elements magic and may consist of their own region's beliefs. Looks like a tattoo until activated

Regions

H'dn E`rth:

Below the surface of the earth is the sanctuary of the roots of trees. Have built a labyrinth of regions, disused and forgotten covens.

Trolls live peacefully in their Hd`m E`rth regions, alongside the Dark Elves and Dwarves who mine some areas most keep out of each other's regions.

Op`n E`rth

Regions of extensive mainland and islands, archipelagos,

an alliance with the Sz`a`Th, Elf Nation, Drargon`H, Wolf Nation, and its many regional Packs, Ravens, Dwarves, and Trolls really can't be bothered as long as they have blue glow lights; hence an issue arises.

Veil

A pathway unseen by most, only a few know how to travel the Veil that links one region/dimension to another. All regions have Veil Walkers, most Trackers, Assassins, and black racketeering.

There is more than one Veil. One can only use the Veil by knowing what essence trail of another has been left like neon tracers in the darkness is the Veil.

Imperial Houses of Regions

Imperial House of G`sharell (Dormas Region)
Mother Mistress Iz`sen Jy'atis's brother is S`Ellen
Aligns the Dormas with Lord Mah`sden
Imperial Sz`a`Th

K`lton becomes Ward of the Mhyst-Sz`a`Th and adopted son to Taelen at twelve winters old

Dragonhead birthmark at the nape of the neck in the hairline

Deep green eyes and olive skin

Dark hair and cowlick at the left side of the forehead

Knight of the First Fires of Dragons – comes of age, and all Sz`a`Th are tattooed with K`olton's birthmark of the Dragonhead.

DRARGON`H Nation

Lord Mi`an, dark skin, green eyes, fifty winters when killed. K`olton's father.

Imperial House of Sz`a`Th
Castle Zsr`n`Th

Tar`eiz depository of Knowledge and history Book 3 re another world? Another side of the Veil

Elemental Lords

Lord M`orus Elemental Lord of E`rth

Lord Lod`n Elemental Lord of W`tr

Large boned man loves working as a Blacksmith and Tavern owner

SPELLCASTERS

Spellcasters' ten-point Silver Star, segmented for the different levels of magic

Thirteen-segmented stars of the three added segments are colours purple, white and blue of the Mhyst, i.e. the third degree is the immortality of the human soul, the emblem of mortality of life and death. They are called 'Kh`irz' ancient orders of secular Monks.

J`nn Sah`ski; -

Pale grey eyes; long pale brown hair;

Sixteen winters old

Talkative and lively assaulted by Lieutenant Brae

Spellcaster and Sz`a`Th she is very gifted direct lineage of the thirteen-segmented star and is Kh`irz but unaware of how strong a talent she has been empowered with till she holds the 'Book of Shadows

Kh`irz extends to Ravens, a nation of Warriors who have the gift of change from that of person to Raven.

IL`ya -

Spellcaster known to Lord Yassarn

Elf, long black hair with grey streaks she wears in a single plait down her back

Deep earth brown eyes

Mistress LH`nejah; -

Spellcaster of the 13th level.

58 winters old

Taelen's maternal Grandmother

Long black hair with stark silver at the temples to the knees

Spellcaster, Dream Caster and of the Sqh`xn Nation of Wolves

Veil walker moves between magic and reality.

Blue-green eyes that blaze ethereally when angry.

Master L`unh - 90 winters old

Senior Spellcaster has shapeshifter tendencies and can fool even the wisest and most talented

Healer Maikim -

Elderly woman with the healing powers of the four elements

Pal`thic

Mistress Yhy`h; -

Eyes Oyster grey

Hair Brown and wavy

Calming mental powers of persuasion and having a dark purple runic design of a tear on the right cheek that runs from the corner of the eye appears at 12 winters.

Teacher, Spellcaster, Scribe

Elf descendant

The black cloak had the same silver and dark grey embroider that denoted the rune Guild of Scribes on the back of the riding cloak. On her black gown, she wore as well as the dark grey panel that was their apron. Black gloves with Guild insignia in silver on the front of the gloves

The forests of SH`runa is her home region

LZ`rqk Guild

Sz`a`Th Soul Healer – Ki`arya

The lyrics of the song Ki`arya sings in her father's people's language are the soul healers. She sings and heals what the Mhyst can't heal. Her voice is ethereal in its pitch as she sings.

Taelen's cousin, this fact is unknown until the end of Book 1

SQH`XN NATION OF WOLVES

Lord Za`qrn

Lord of the Wolf Nation

Bald with dark skin

Eyes dark brown blood-red slash across the eyes

Fluent in all languages.

6'5" tall, very fit but loves good red wine and lager and mead

Forty-seven winters old and flirtatious, eloquent and outrageous and deals in the black market at the drop of a heartbeat, he has lost track of his known dalliances of both sexes and puppies from these. He has an eye for the ladies and for the men, which more than often causes him the grief of the heart, not the soul

Captain JA`rvis; -

Silver hair, Master Healer

Eyes palest blue with silver fleck diagonally

30 winters

Grandson of LH`nejah, cousin to Taelen

Transforms to a large silver-coated timber wolf

Nephew of Lord Za`qrn, half-brother to Ji`rah

Lieutenant Ji`rah

Eyes whitish-blue with a slash of Green diagonally

through each iris

Coal Black beard

Dark olive skin

2nd Lieutenant of the Sqh`xn

Cheeky with attitude, short fuse

Nephew of Lord Za`qrn

Prince of the Sqh`xn Wolves

Red Crescent Sahn`Frwh Warrior

Sergeant Ry`arma Chronicle 1

Silver Crescent Sahn`Frwh Warrior was taken from the Lake City of Cran`dk in the winter past when Mah`sden's poison infiltrated The Sz`a`Th by dark magic.

Earth's brown eyes slashed, startling with startling gold. Sister to Ji`rah

Honey brown wavy hair to her waist-worn in the intricate braid of the Sqh`xn Nation.

5'10" slim athletic build.

Corporal Sar`tq

Deep brown, dark eyes white slash through his Black iris hair, dark skin white tattoo of rune down the left side of his guild's neck.

Sahn`Frwh 6'2", 20 winters old

Extensively trained in all weapons

X`qwet Pack desert region

H`ta had blazing red hair cut short with a design that showed the tattoo of her pack on her skull Corporal H`ta Imperial Archer, 5'10, not as large as the male wolves of her nation, and she belonged to one of the desert regions pack of X`qwet. Independent, blunt, forceful, bravado excellent Warrior is cheeky as she hides her hurt from wolf massacre deep down.

Her eyes were brown with a gold flash through the

iris X`qwet were known for being tall and a larger build

Corporal Kurr`etun

Taelen's first wife was deceased 15 winters, murdered by her father.

Lieutenant Ji`rah's sister's yellow-green eyes

Gifted in Archery.

Syn`a Wolf Pack

Lieutenant Den`eq

Brown eyes sprinkled green, and her Mhyst birthright glows with runes symbols. Her straight Black hair was in a long plait to her waist, and she wore the Red Crescent along with an intricate tattoo in black ink on her hand that ran from her left jaw down her neck along her whole arm in a sleeve of symbols in meaning the Warrior knew there the deep meaning of Clans and Guilds.

Ten`qrn Wolf Pack

Corporal Aq`ten – Ten`qrn Pack. South Region wetlands fine tattoo left temple white of the Greenman three lines three dots at the end of each mark backward slash, centre slash, forward slash. Left wrist mark of a paw branded onto her light olive skin.

Tracker of the 9th degree.

Black hair with two white blazes common in the Ten`qrn Pack is braided in a braid only known to her Wolf pack; she has black, brown eyes with an iridescent lime green slash.

Survived the battle of Zira`taq Village in the Qlee`han wetlands. Few survived the attack. Zira`taq means flames on water.

Tah`n Wolf Pack

Tah`n Wolf the Tah. The saying easier to train a Tah`n Wolf could be taken in many ways as an insult, compliment, endearment, and most mercurial of the Wolf Packs. A Tah`n Wolf was not one colour but brindle and myriad in between. If ordered to do something, the reply would be nah yeah…nah done, leaving one perplexed as to whether the command would happen. Tah`n Pack was straightforward. Going rank meant nothing, rules, maybe.

CREATURES

Drakk`or, take the body of the one it kills; if it injures, it sends the victim insane with illness and fever. Death is the only humane end to a person now taken over by a Drakk`or.

DARK SZ`A`TH Warrior's

Lord Mah`sden
Dark Blue eyes, blonde hair
Captain Yassarn's brother.
Brutally cruel becomes poisoned by Necromancer Lord Nul`YK

Lieutenant Brae 1Wounded at the Taayra'Ge Keep battle and taken by Lord Mah`sden as a Prisoner of War, he succumbs to the poison, but part of him exists
6'3" well muscle,
Arrogant, brutal, cruel, lost.

Necromancer Lord Nul`YK

SZ`A`TH WARRIORS: including Knights of the Death Watch

Captain Tou`hia Yassarn:

(Taelen's father)

Blue, amethyst eyes and fair hair

His first wife, K`iaz, dies in childbirth, actually poisoned by Mah`sden, his brother.

Mhyst birthmark is purple to blue to white. He is the only one that can decipher the Seven Books but tells no one.

Taelen Yassarn;

widowed young married to Archer Kurr'etun Sxq`rn Warrior

Mhyst Lord/ Dominions Lord

Rank- Lieutenant

Imperial Scribe hides his identity.

A thin blue stripe of Scout on his trousers, regardless of rank, the mustering of Scout remains

Sahn`Frwh is a Knight of the Death Watch

Wolf Nation's allegiance through marriage and blood.

Spellcaster latent knowledge (not good at magic, bit haphazard)

Amethyst blue eyes with purple flecks and olive skin with black hair

He encompassed all the nations, hence 'Dominion Lord, ' and was born at A`hres, a monastery for monks.

While doing his apprenticeship at the Taayra`Ge Keep, he deciphers the Imperial House of Ar`rz and the 300 winter war with the Trolls

SERGEANT Anston - Chronicle 1

Taayra`Ge Keep, the Widower, loses his arm below

the elbow. His prosthetic has a few unique attachments. Sergeant at the Keep trains the Warriors in all the swords and blades, including the broad axe. Taelen was saved as a six-winter old boy and saved him again at sixteen winters old.

Sahn`Frwh of the Taray'Ge Keep escapes following Captain Yassarn's orders with two grooms.

Corporal Sar`tq

Main Guard, at the Gates of the Death Watch. 6'2"

Deep brown, dark eyes slashed with white

Wolf Pack classed secret when asked he says

His layback attitude he may be of the Tah`n Wolf Pact though is not brindle fur, as a Scout, no one has actually seen him in Wolf form

T`Aogh

Imperial Archer and Blades man

Earth brown eyes and fair skin

30 Winters old but youthful

Corporal X`ysta

Coal black, brown eyes, Sahn`Frwh, 18 winters,

Sergeant Rior`dan

Imperial Sz`a`Th Scribe worked with Taelen at the Tarraya`Ge Keep

Captain T'nyson

Captain of Taayra'Ge Keep Garrison

Sahn`Frwh red crescent

A`Dn

Crossbow Archer and Blades man, 22 winters old, 5'8" wounded at the Taray'Ge Keep attack survives. Female Red Crescent Sahn`Frwh. Dark brown eyes with silver flash, dark olive skin wears white tattoo over her left hand from her region

D` Ron

Swords, Broad axe and Cross bolt, 5'10" dark brown eyes with a neon blue flash she is 23 winters, wounded at the Taayra'Ge Keep attack

Corporal Ez`rhn

Dark lashes shadowed the green pastel iris that resembled pale jade. Sahn`Frwh Warrior 6'2" dark skin. Black thick hair and beard. Laconic grin, handsome, easy going, Knowledgeable on all regions, Master of all weapons 21 winters old

Trained Cartographer

Corporal Den`ah -

Dark Green eyes

Due to soul torture becomes part of Wolf Sqh`xn Nation and now has Dream Casting abilities

Master of Tongues

Mhyst Shadows - Veil Walker

Qlee`han wetlands of the southern region landmass.

Lieutenant Teh`c -

Sahn`Frwh Red Crescent

Also called a 'Heart Guard' by the Elf Nation 'Shadow Knight.'

He uses the Islander crystal lore of healing and his people's Lin'eh dialect when healing.

Dai`h, which meant he was not full Sz`a`Th he is Dai`h mixed blood.

Olive skin and dimples in his cheeks, about 6'3" black hair and beard.

Green eyes, speak Lin`eh, the language of the Thes`q Archipelago

The Archipelago of the Thes`q means 'where the sunsets and the moon rises with a single kiss.'

His rank is the fine red line down his trouser leg

Swordsman, a Healer, speaks six languages, including that of the mammals of the oceans.

Corporal Tad`c -

Wounded from the Taayra`Ge Keep

Expert in the small Taayra`Ge Keep Crossbow, a classic Swordsman and deadly with the short blade.

Pale smoke-grey eyes, brown sandy hair beard

Corporal A`Dn -

Wounded from the Taayra`Ge Keep

Swordsman, Crossbow, Double Broadaxe

Dark blue eyes, black hair beard

Sergeant Dek`hlan

Green Eye's widowed wife and child are dead,

Sergeant of the Arches and Night Guard

Corporal-Lieutenant M`hta (x slave- J`rxqa of Karanja)

6'3"

Almond-shaped eyes, green gold and brown

Hair Black

Left-handed

Historical Scribe of Ch`nel

'White rune' on his cheekbone resembles a stab of lightning from his eye to his temple

He is called the 'Blind Scribe'. His sight is damaged from an explosion when the Karanja Castle falls. Red ink tattoo on upper inside of arm rune sign of bolt of lightning meaning enslaved person.

Captain S`en Rq`arnh
Blonde hair and pale blue eyes widowed
Brother-in-law to Corporal Saoirse
Speaks the language of C`rieq
Sahn`Frwh Red Crescent

The slim grey line down the leg of his Sz`a`Th trousers denote the rank of Captain, Widower.

Captain at the City of Guilds and Cran`dk Garrison then evacuates to the Death Watch.

Sergeant T`Aogh
Eyes rich earth brown
Skin fair and freckled
6' well built.

WO1st Class Js`yah
Eyes lightning blue
6'2" well built

Corporal Del`qt

Tall and solid, brilliant tactician, and Qkt`ilht his artist skills involve the elementals

Lieutenant K`Lpn 6'3" Blazing blue eyes, black hair and a way with women, charismatic.

Corporal Saoirse
Silver grey eyes
Psychic
6'4"

Born in the D`rakkn Mountains and a member of the Death Watch

Lieutenant Dan`e

Red Crescent Sahn`Frwh Warrior

relocated to the Death Watch from the Southern Region Coven

Brown eyes sprinkled green has a blaze of gold diagonally through the iris of Zyn`a Pack Wolf, and her Mhyst birthright was glowing with symbols of runes

Healer

Hair straight and long, she wears it in a plait to her waist.

chin to sleeve tattoo denoting clans and guilds in runes

Raven works in a network of spies for the Nations of Myth.

Sergeant Bae`da

Black brown eyes Sahn`Frwh Silver Crescent 6’ 2” best mates with Tar`iqa

Sergeant Tar`iqa

palest of blue looking nearly white, Sahn`Frwh Silver Crescent

5’8” short haircut with tattoo in runes on her head

SAHN`FRWH KNIGHTS OF THE DEATHWATCH:

Red eclipse moon quarter tattoo at left eye creases on temple Heart Guards to Taelen

Lieutenant Taelen

Lieutenant Ji`rah

Lieutenant M`hta

Lieutenant Teh`c

All who are stationed at the Death Watch are Red Crescents. All are Sahn`Frwh of all nations of O`pn E`rth

Silver Crescents
Corporal KH'Din
Tracker, Assassin,
Sahn`Frwh Warrior Silver Crescent of the Death Watch, Veil Walker
These Warriors fall under the Ogdoadic Knights; their missions are unknown to others

Green Crescents
PA`Lin: Blonde hair, pale blue, mauve eyes, tanned skin, Ah`niqtar particular martial arts. Best Horseman the Sz`a`Th have.

Corporal Saoirse pronounced Seer`sha
silver grey eyes
Sisters- Danann 4 winter old
Sha`HR was adopted out at 12 winters. 18 winters red arrowhead on wrist denotes Kings property
Ar`lin 8 winter old
Siofra- married to a Mariner, lives southernmost island D`un
Corporal KH`Din- Sahn`Frwh Warrior Silver Crescent of the Death Watch, Veil Walker.
Specialist - Assassin, swords, cross-bolt, daggers, swords.
Corporal Bo`dan, brother to Saoirse and sisters, is killed and dies just as KH`Dn gets to him.

Lieutenant Jarek:
Sahn`Frwh Warrior, Knights of the Death Watch
pale milky green eyes
Fair-skinned and blonde like those who lived east in the lands where ice and snow lay ten winter moons.

Lieutenant Ln`sahr:
Sahn`Frwh Warrior, Knights of the Death Watch
Dark brown hair, violet eyes, dark brown skin

Sergeant Ez`rhn Cartographer
Green pastels jade eyes
Dark skin
Dark hair
Strikingly handsome

Corpora Js`yah
Dark skin and dark eyes contrasting startling with cornflower blue eyes – Chronicle 1
eyes lightning blue promotion to Sergeant

Corporal Del`qt- Qkt`ilht artist of the four elements and a large lad

Corporal Xan`eiq
Green Crescent, Sahn`Frwh of all her allegiance, was first to the Green, then to the Sz`a`Th;. 5'8" with her hundred-moonlight wide smile and quick retort made her laugh at times, eyes as black as the sands of the Tal`iz Coast. Her hair was wild in red tints of golden sunsets. Her best mate calls her by her nickname 'Brindle' due to her hair colour

Corporal Piz`Eqh,
Red Crescent, Sahn`Frwh6'4", fine black hair and beard, athletic build. He is gay, but his best mate is Corporal Xan`eiq. They would die saving each other, closer than family. He keeps the idiots away from her, and she keeps the females and checks out if his new partner is good enough for her best mate.

Lieutenant K`lpn

6'3" blazing blue eyes with thick black coal-black hair and beard and handsome, he's a man's man, supposed to meet Teh`c and M`hta at Sahru Headlands but is captured instead by Mariners working for Mah`sden

D`mja

Bar person of the Pickled Sea Tavern in the village of KR`nh, translated to Sz`a`Th means, Vale of Storms

Dark thick burgundy hair in think long curled natural ringlets to her waist

Golden green eyes are like Autumn leaves in the sunlight.

She does not tolerate idiots and can hold her own in a Tavern of Warriors and Mariners

She is of Karanja white tattoo tiny teardrop left temple increase of eye. Eighteen winters old 5'9" slim trim figure. Wary of males, trust no one.

Regions

Tal`iz Coast has black sand on the coast with black limestone rock cliffs. The only white is the surf thundering down onto the black sand

Saruh Headlands

Village of KR`nh – Pickled Sea Tavern

KR`nh noted for the black sea pearls of the A`outh regions of the west coast

GA`ryn forest

Teluna`HD River

Plains of De`hcct above

Dormas Region

WARS

Imperial House of Ar`rz was again destroyed in the 700 Winter Wars in the 3rd Troll Wars. This is why Sz`a`Th can exist here. There are not even ruins of the Ar`rz anywhere.

400 Winter War with Rh`varnh and Sz`a`Th

Troll Wars, no one is sure, but they chose pretty blue light starves for peace.

E`boda Plains 6 Winter War – first known use of the Mhyst for healing. Commander of the Taayra'Ge Keep was a young Warrior at that War

MARINERS

Captain F`isq

Captain - Jo`sha

Dark skin eyes resembling the black pearls of KR`Nh rescue Sahn`Frwh Warriors and Sz`a`Th from the slave markets and then transport them to which ports are safe.

COLLOQUIAL SLANG

The Dq`tng but spoken fast is Dq`tng is a curse that is secretly spoken by 1 Warrior, from each nation of Myth and Man of O`pn and H`dn E`rth

Elves of O`pn E`rth

Corporal- Lieutenant NK`las – Elf-

Deep forest green angular eyes, dark brown hair. A white scar across the left side of his forehead cuts through his eyebrow. Protects Taelen when he can.

www.ingramcontent.com/pod-product-compliance
Lightning Source LLC
Chambersburg PA
CBHW011736010726
47496CB00010B/2966
* 9 7 8 1 7 8 6 9 5 8 1 1 2 *